BELLE CATHERINE

JULIETTE BENZONI

BELLE CATHERINE

Translated by
JOCASTA GOODWIN

UNABRIDGED

PAN BOOKS LTD : LONDON
By arrangement with
WILLIAM HEINEMANN LTD
LONDON

First published in UK 1966 by William Heinemann Ltd.
This edition published 1968 by Pan Books Ltd.,
33 Tothill Street, London, S.W.1.

330 02057 9

Published in France by Editions de Trévise as
La Belle Catherine

Printed in Great Britain by
Cox & Wyman Ltd., London, Reading and Fakenham

CHAPTER ONE

The Awakening

Catherine half opened her eyes. A ray of sunlight filtered through her lowered lids, and she hastily shut them again and snuggled deeper into her coverlet with a little sigh of satisfaction. She was warm and comfortable and she could sleep a little longer yet. Before dropping off again, she reached out automatically to touch Arnaud's body which lay sleeping beside her. There was nothing there. She opened her eyes and sat up.

The boat was still tied up where Arnaud had hidden it when the first dawn light came stealing across the sky. It was buried in a clump of willows, up a narrow creek shaded by willows and alders. The painter was twisted round the greyish trunk of an old gnarled tree: a perfect hiding-place, invisible both from the river and the countryside around. Catherine could see the water glittering in the sunlight through the tall green spears of the reeds. But Arnaud was not with her. . . .

Catherine was not particularly anxious. After the night's exertions and the short sleep, which was all they had had, Montsalvy had probably felt the need to stretch his legs. Gradually Catherine's mind cleared and she began to remember all that had happened. Under this sunny sky it was hard to believe in death, danger and war. And yet, it was only yesterday . . . yesterday, May 31st, 1431, that Joan of Arc had paid for her devotion to king and country with her life. Only yesterday that the executioner of Rouen had ordered them to be thrown into the river, sewn into a leather sack, and they had seen death's grinning face thrust close before good Jean Son, the master-mason, had rescued them and given them this boat to take them to Louviers, where they could rejoin the French forces.

It seemed a fitting sequel to an unusually tumultuous existence that she should find herself here, tucked away in the heart of enemy occupied territory. Search her memory as she might, Catherine was hard put to it to think of a single peaceful interlude in her life since, at the age of thirteen, she had been forced to flee Paris during the Caboche riots and seek refuge with her Uncle Mathieu. In a kingdom torn by war there could be no peaceful interludes, not even for the subjects of the mighty Duke of Burgundy. And then there had been that deplorable marriage to Philippe the Good's Lord Treasurer, a marriage contrived by the Duke so that he might the more easily make her his mistress. Catherine always felt a pang of regret when she thought of her husband, Garin de Brazey, whose terrible infirmity Philippe had so coolly exploited. For him she had been the torture of Tantalus incarnate, and, if his sufferings had finally unhinged him and led him to crime and murder, who could blame him? The culprit in this sad tale was destiny herself and the fierce passion which bound her to Arnaud de Montsalvy, captain of Charles VII and enemy of Philippe of Burgundy, since the moment their eyes first met. So much had conspired to keep them apart: war, honour, even the blood which ran in their veins . . . but it was all right now: the road to happiness lay fair and open before them. . . .

As she sat up, Catherine noticed her dress and petticoat hanging over the side of the boat. Then she realized that she was quite naked but for the coverlet over her, and she could not help laughing. Then she blushed, remembering what had happened after they found their hiding-place among the reeds.

It seemed incredible that, after the previous day's ordeals and rowing throughout most of the night, Arnaud should have wanted anything but sleep. But no sooner was the boat made fast than he took Catherine in his arms and pulled her down into the bottom of the boat.

'I've been dreaming of this moment ever since they first threw us together in that sack,' he said, half serious, half mocking, '. . . and before then, too.'

'Well, whose fault is that? I wouldn't have objected if you had condescended to treat me like a proper wife when we were sleeping in Nicole Son's attic. Anyway . . .'

But she had never finished her sentence, because he started to kiss her. They had not spoken again after that, oblivious to everything but the rediscovery of their love in all its former strength and passion. Only now there was no hate or mistrust between them; nothing but a great love which finally dared declare itself. When Catherine at length fell asleep with her head pillowed on Arnaud's shoulder, she was overcome by a deep and delicious lassitude. She had never in her dreams imagined a more glorious moment – the reality had far exceeded her dearest hopes.

The sun shone softly down through the alders. Catherine

could not resist having a quick dip before dressing again. The water was cool and she shivered at first, but then her blood began to run swift and warm and she abandoned herself happily to the sparkling water.

Suddenly Catherine was struck by the absolute stillness around her. There wasn't a sound to be heard other than the gentle murmur of the water. The countryside was plunged in silence; no birds singing, or dogs barking or bells ringing. She slipped into her chemise, lacing up the bodice with hands which were beginning to tremble. Then she called out:

'Arnaud! ... Arnaud, where are you?'

There was no answer. Catherine froze, listening anxiously for the sound of a footstep beyond the trees ... but none came. Only the flutter of a bird in a near-by tree which made her jump. A cold shudder ran along her spine as she wrung out her wet hair and twisted it up on top of her head. Where could Arnaud be?

Catherine left her hiding-place among the trees and pushed through some bushes till she found herself in a field, or what must have been a field before the tide of war crushed and up-rooted the grass. But, towards the east, smoke ascended peace-fully from a cottage chimney. ... In the distance, she could just make out the bell-tower and massive piles of the Pont-de-l'Arche under which they had passed during the night. Else-where the countryside was strangely desolate despite the spring weather, strangely empty and deserted. ... There was nobody to be seen anywhere. ...

Catherine's mind was working feverishly and the idea came to her that Arnaud might possibly have gone to that remote little farmhouse in search of food, although Jean Son had pro-vided them with almost everything they could require, or in-formation about the dangers of travelling through that part of the country. She decided to go there herself since she could not see anyone coming away from it.

She went back to the boat and took the little bag of gold which Jean Son had given them, apologizing for not having returned Catherine her jewels, and hid it in her bodice.

'I thought it would be safer not to give you such things to carry. Brother Etienne Charlot will give them to Queen Yolande for you at the first available opportunity.' This was wisdom itself and Catherine had thanked the good mason for his thoughtfulness. She knew that the jewels would be safe while they remained in his keeping.

Before setting off, Catherine suddenly realized that she was
starving, and took with her a piece of bread and cheese. The
cottage was not far and, if Arnaud were to return meanwhile,
he would doubtless do as she had and wait a while. As she
walked along, Catherine devoured her little meal. She was confident of finding Arnaud at the farm. Perhaps the sight of the
smoking chimney had put him in mind of a bowl of hot soup.
He would probably have had to wait by the hearth till the
meal was ready. . . .

But when she came near enough to see the entrance to the
house clearly, she was surprised to see the door swinging from a
broken hinge. Here, too, there was utter silence. Seized by
sudden premonition, Catherine hurried on. She crept up to the
house and looked in. What she saw from the threshold made her
cry out in horror and sent her reeling back against the wall, her
heart beating wildly. There were two corpses in the house: a
man's and a woman's.

The man's legs had been tied to a plank and were thrust deep
into the fire where they had been all but consumed. It was that
which had caused the pretty plume of smoke rising from the
cottage chimney. His face was twisted in terrible agony. A
large bloodstain on his chest showed that he must have been
stabbed at the end. The woman was more horrible still. She was
stretched out on a rude wooden table, quite naked, arms and
legs tied to the four table legs which stood in a slowly coagu-
lating pool of blood. She must have been raped many times
before being eviscerated. The entrails protruded through a
gaping wound in her stomach. . . .

Appalled and revolted, Catherine staggered out of the house
where she leant against the cottage wall and vomited up all
that she had just eaten . . . then she was overcome by panic.
Stumbling over the uneven ground, she began to run wildly in
the direction of the river calling for Arnaud at the top of her
voice. . . . She flung herself into the boat and huddled in the
bottom like a frightened child, trembling lest the monsters who
had murdered the unfortunate peasants should suddenly appear.
After a while she grew calmer. The unbroken silence quieted
her frantically beating heart. Soon she was able to give her
attention to the problem now facing her: where could Arnaud
have got to?

It never crossed her mind that he might have abandoned her.
Even if he had wanted to be rid of her, he would never have
done so here in this war-torn countryside. He would have waited

till she reached safety. Besides, the night they had just spent together made that impossible. Arnaud loved her, Catherine was certain of that. ... She thought he might possibly have stumbled upon the brigands at the farm and been set upon like the unfortunate couple there. But there had been only two corpses. ... Perhaps he had managed to escape and had avoided returning to the river in case he gave away Catherine's whereabouts. ... But all these questions remained unanswered. ...

Catherine stayed huddled in the bottom of the boat for a long time, undecided as to what she should do, hoping against hope that he would return. But hours passed and the silence was unbroken save for the flight of a bird or a jumping fish. She was too frightened to move....

At last, however, as the sun began to set and the air grew chill, she roused herself. She could not wait there any longer. It had been foolish enough to waste so much time in that place, but Catherine had not wanted to leave the one spot where she might hope to find Arnaud again soon. Now it struck her that her one chance of rejoining him was, in fact, to go to Louviers. La Hire, if he were still there, and she had no reason to suppose the contrary, would surely be able to tell her what had become of Arnaud. After all, La Hire, after Xaintrailles, was Arnaud's closest and most loyal friend and brother-in-arms. The three captains had fought together for so long against the English that one of those indissoluble bonds, woven of dangers and triumphs shared, had grown up between them. La Hire was much the oldest of the three, but this was no bar to their friendship. And since La Hire commanded Louviers, that would surely be the place to which Arnaud would go in the event of danger.

Galvanized by this thought, Catherine sat up. She ate a large piece of bread and the rest of the cheese and immediately felt better. Then she drank a little river water, and, her spirits quite restored, she decided to set out at once. She would be better protected at night against chance encounters, and it was still light enough to see the way. Arnaud had pointed out Louviers to her that morning and he had said that it was only two and a half leagues away. She took the bag of gold and as much food as she could carry. Then she wrapped herself in the mantle with which Jean Son had provided her and left the boat. She followed the river for a while and then, as it seemed to be curving away towards the west, she headed south. She stepped out boldly across the fields, moving at a good pace, and made a wide detour to avoid passing near the cottage whose chimney had now stopped smoking. She forced herself not to think of Arnaud. She had far too much need of all her courage and strength to give way to the distress which his disappearance had awakened in her.

Several hours later, exhausted but hopeful, she came in sight of Louviers. It was too early to seek entry and she lay down on a tussock to wait, rolling her mantle more tightly around herself, and slept till she was wakened by the song of a skylark.

As she approached the town gate, Catherine glanced at the banner flapping from the highest tower and heaved a sigh of relief. The great flag bore the device of a black oriflamme crossed by a silver vine and the soldiers on guard were not wearing the green tunics of the English army. La Hire still held the town, then. ... Catherine snatched up her skirt and raced through the dark archway into the town, bumping into a man-at-arms who shrugged and grinned, but did not trouble to intercept her. She ran like a deer down the narrow street which twisted along between two rows of gabled houses. At the far end, on the left, stood the ancient House of the Knights Templar where the town commander was quartered. Catherine was so excited that she cannoned past the soldiers on guard who were too astonished to put up their weapons.

'Hey! ... You there. ... Stop, woman! ... Do you hear? Come here!'

But Catherine took no notice. She burst into the courtyard just as La Hire clumped heavily across to where a stable lad was watering his horse. The captain seemed to be in a bad humour. As he walked he flexed his knees as though to reassure himself that the joints of his greaves were working properly. Catherine leaped towards him with a joyful cry and such force that she almost knocked him over. He lost his temper and gave her a cuff which sent her flying.

'Curse the hussy! Are you mad, wench? Here, you lot, get rid of this peasant for me!'

But Catherine was sitting on the ground laughing with relief at having found the irascible captain again.

'You have a rude way of greeting your friends, Messire de Vignolles. Or don't you recognize me?'

At the sound of her voice, he turned towards her, a look of stupefaction on his scarred face.

'You? Here alive? And Joan ... and Montsalvy?'

He rushed across, snatched her up and shook her, like a plum

tree in August, torn between joy and anger. Anger was his
normal state of mind: twenty-four hours out of twenty-four,
La Hire spluttered with rage, cursed and fulminated with fury
and exasperation. His voice boomed above the cannon's roar
and set the battlements aquake. He was storm and hurricane,
a brute natural force in its purest state, but to those whom he
loved, La Hire showed a child's nature. He was foaming at the
mouth now, because Catherine did not answer his questions
fast enough. But she had suddenly gone as limp as a puppet in
his arms. Two words the captain had uttered had had this
effect: 'and Montsalvy?' So he too had no idea of Arnaud's
whereabouts ... A wave of anguish swept over her. La Hire
roared at her, quite beside himself:

'Good God. ... Can't you speak? Can't you see I'm half mad
with anxiety?'

But her heart was breaking. With a cry of agony she flung
herself against his mailed shoulder and sobbed so bitterly that
he stood dumbfounded. La Hire had no idea what to do with
this weeping woman. His men stood around watching, some of
them concealing their smiles with difficulty. La Hire comforting
a woman was a novel twist of events.

Deciding to continue the interview in greater privacy, La
Hire put one arm round her and led her away towards his lodgings. But before they crossed the threshold, he turned and called
over one shoulder:

'Hey, Ferrant! Get you to the Bernardine Convent and tell
the porteress to send along the woman called Sara to me. ...'

A sergeant stepped out from the squad of men drawn up
near the gate and disappeared through the gateway. Meanwhile,
La Hire closed the massive, iron-studded door and made Catherine take a seat on a bench covered with cushions.

'I shall have a meal brought to you,' he said with unaccustomed gentleness. 'Methinks you have need of it. But, for the
love of God, speak! What has happened? Here they are saying
that Joan was condemned to life imprisonment, that ...'

Catherine took hold of herself with an effort. She wiped her
eyes and murmured, not looking at La Hire:

'Joan is dead! The English burned her at the stake the day
before yesterday and her ashes were thrown into the Seine ...
and then ... then Arnaud and I were thrown in too, sewn into a
leather sack.'

La Hire's ruddy face paled below his cropped, grey thatch of
hair.

'Burnt! ... Like a witch! The dogs! And Arnaud at the bottom of the river ...!'

'No, not *that*! As you see, I am here before you now.'

Catherine recounted the last days of their stay in Rouen: their attempt to rescue Joan, their arrest and imprisonment, and finally their sentence, from which the courage of Jean Son had saved them at the eleventh hour. She spoke of their flight by night, how she had awakened only to find that Arnaud had inexplicably vanished.

'I found no trace of him anywhere, not even in that ravaged farm. It was as if he had vanished into thin air.'

'A Montsalvy does not vanish like a puff of smoke,' La Hire growled. 'If he were dead, you would have found his body ... anyway, he's not dead! I feel it ...' he finished up, striking his chest with a huge mailed fist, ' ... here!'

'How so?' Catherine asked, a little sharply. 'I would not have believed you so sensitive, messire.'

'Arnaud is my brother-in-arms,' the captain replied, somewhat grandly. 'If he were no longer breathing, something would have told me. The same with Xaintrailles. Montsalvy is alive. I'll swear to it.'

'Are you trying to tell me that he simply got up and left me? Quite callously? Of his own free will?'

La Hire's patience was strained to breaking-point. His face flushed and he became his old, violent self again.

'Are you out of your mind? Who says he abandoned you? He is a knight and a gentleman, you silly goose! He would never leave a defenceless woman in enemy territory. Something has happened to him! Just what, I'm about to find out! As for you, don't stand there like a ninny....'

A cold, nonchalant voice interrupted the captain's angry outburst.

'You seem to forget that you are addressing a lady, Messire de Vignolles. Such language!'

There was something odd about the newcomer. It was not so much the extravagance of his attire, though that was striking enough in this austere and soldierly setting, as his face itself. A short, blue-black beard framed a face whose features were finely formed and waxen pale, a face which would have been handsome, but for the cruel curve of the sensual lips and the cold gleam of his black eyes. His stare was unblinking and it made Catherine uneasy. She had recognized him at once: it was Gilles de Rais, Marshal of France since the King's consecration, the man who had tried to climb into her bedroom window one night in Orleans, and whom Arnaud had fought. She nodded curtly in reply to a bow so sweeping that it left his gold-embroidered violet silk sleeves trailing in the dust.

'Messire de Vignolles has every excuse,' she said gently. 'I don't look much of a lady in this rig! More like a peasant or refugee!'

Gilles de Rais's arrival seemed to have dissipated La Hire's anger.

'I'm afraid I forgot myself,' he stammered. 'You must forgive me, Dame Catherine. I didn't mean to upset you, but, you see, I love Montsalvy as if he were my own son!'

'In that case,' Catherine cried passionately, 'you must help me rescue him. Send someone to find him, or help him, if necessary.'

'What has happened to the valiant Montsalvy?' Gilles de Rais inquired casually, not taking his disturbing gaze off Catherine for a moment.

La Hire was obliged to inform the noble lord of the tragedy of Rouen and of Arnaud's disappearance. He repeated Catherine's story of Joan's trial and the death sentence for witchcraft passed by the Church tribunal headed by Cauchon, secretly in league with the Earl of Warwick and the Bishop of Winchester, and, finally, of her death at the stake. He spoke with bad grace, because there was no love lost between the two men. La Hire was much older than Gilles de Rais and he felt a deep aversion to the extravagant Angevin. He instinctively mistrusted this cousin of the devious La Trémoille, whose inexplicable inertia had surely played its part in allowing Joan's death. The captain put the blame for the King's indifference on the wicked advice and jealousy of Charles de la Trémoille, and in this assumption he was correct.

'So Joan is dead,' Gilles de Rais muttered gloomily. 'She whom we worshipped as an angel turns out to have been a mere girl like any other. They burnt her as a witch, and a witch is doubtless what she was! What if God Himself should punish us for having hearkened to a mad shepherd girl?'

Catherine looked at him in astonishment as his expression changed to one of credulous fear, identical to the look she had seen on Philippe's face when she had pleaded with him to set Joan free: fear of damnation, the ancient terror of Satan and his handmaiden, the witch. In an instant, noble lord and fearless warrior had been supplanted by the less edifying spectacle of a man in the grip of a primitive terror which harked back to the dawn of time, a horror of the unknown, born of the dark soil of the black, Druidic forests, and bloodthirsty, heathen gods.

La Hire stood listening with bulging eyes as Gilles de Rais spoke. Before Catherine could intervene, he burst out in a fury:

'A witch? Joan? You wouldn't get anyone to believe that, Messire Gilles, except that damned scoundrel, La Trémoille! Are you so little of a Christian that the verdict of one corrupt bishop, hand in glove with the enemy, is enough to change your allegiance?'

'The leaders of the Church cannot all be wrong,' de Rais answered in a neutral voice.

'That's your view! Allow me to give you one piece of advice, Sir Marshal – never, *never* repeat what you have just said! Because I swear, as my name is La Hire, that I will ram your words down your insolent throat if you do! With the help of this!'

He made as if to withdraw his sword from its scabbard and Catherine saw that the Sire de Rais's eyes were bloodshot with sudden anger.

She had always mistrusted him and now she found herself positively hating him. She was disgusted by his remarks about Joan, and by the ease with which he had sided with the Church tribunal. How could Gilles de Rais so easily forget the brotherhood-in-arms, and the mighty exploits he had shared under the Maid's dauntless leadership? A trembling hand flew to the dagger at his belt and his nostrils whitened with rage. She heard him grind his teeth.

'Is that a challenge? I demand satisfaction!'

Slowly, without taking his eyes off him, La Hire sheathed his sword again and shrugged his broad shoulders.

'No, it was a warning which you are welcome to pass on to your fine cousin, who has ever desired to be rid of the Maid. But to me, and many others like me, messire . . . she comes from God! It has pleased Him to take her to Himself again . . . as He once took his Son, long ago, on another gibbet. Lord Jesus came to save mankind . . . and mankind knew Him not . . . just as some now refuse to recognize the Maid. But I . . . *I* believe in her!'

The commander's weatherbeaten countenance glowed with a strange ardour, and his eyes seemed to scan the distance, as if he hoped for the dazzling gleam of a suit of white armour. But it was for one second only. The next moment La Hire struck the table with his fist.

'And I forbid anyone to say a word against her!'

Before Gilles de Rais could reply, the door was thrown open so forcefully that the walls shook. Sara, dishevelled, half-crying, half-laughing, shot into the room like a cannonball and seized Catherine in her arms.

'My darling ... my darling! Can it be you? Have you really come back to me?'

The gipsy woman's eyes shone like stars and great tears streamed down her brown cheeks as she crushed Catherine to her, cradling her against her massive bosom and covering her face with kisses, stopping only to take another look and re-assure herself that it really *was* Catherine! Catherine wept, too, quite overcome by the emotions of the moment. It was impossible to make out a single word of what the two women were saying. La Hire soon lost patience. His stentorian voice rang out, making them both jump.

'Enough of this foolery! You'll have plenty of time for that later. ... Go back to your convent with your maid, Dame Catherine. I've got other things to do.'

Catherine detached herself from Sara's embrace, her eyes shining with new hope.

'You mean, you're going to look for Arnaud?'

'Of course. Tell me exactly where that farm you mentioned is ... and then pray God that I find a clue of some sort. If I don't then it'll be those others who'll need praying for, the ones who cross my path afterwards!'

Catherine explained as best she could, straining her memory for every tiny detail which might help the captain. When she had finished, he thanked her briefly, donning his visor and gloves, and strode into the courtyard as gaily as if his heavy steel armour had been a mere silken tunic. He made as much noise in motion as a cathedral bell-tower. Catherine heard him bellow:

'Into the saddle, all of you!'

A trumpet sounded and a few seconds later the domed ceiling echoed to the thunder of a company of men in full armour clattering away towards the city gate.

When it was quiet, Gilles de Rais, who had remained quite motionless, went up to Catherine and bowed.

'Allow me to escort you to the convent, fair lady.'

She shook her head without looking at him and slipped her arm through Sara's.

'Many thanks, seigneur, but I prefer to go alone with Sara. We have a lot to talk about.'

The evening came, but still La Hire did not return, and Catherine kept an anguished vigil from the convent tower, straining her eyes while the light remained for any cloud of dust which might be a troop of horsemen.

'They won't return tonight,' Sara told her when they heard the creaking of the massive town gates being closed for the night. 'You ought to go to bed now. You are so weary. . . .'

Catherine stared at her like a sleepwalker.

'I am weary, but I could never sleep, so what is the point?'

'What's the point?' Sara exclaimed. 'Why, to get some rest, of course! You know that if Monseigneur returns tonight, you will hear the horn calling for the gates to be opened. And he would send for you at once, in any case. I will keep watch for you. Go to sleep for a while . . . just to please me. . . .'

With one last glance at the ravaged countryside whose scars were fast vanishing under the sombre cloak of darkness, Catherine allowed herself to be led away to the cell in which she had slept before that wild trip to Rouen.

Sara undressed her, put her to bed and tucked her in like a baby. She folded Catherine's clothes up carefully and placed her white coif on the wooden dummy designed for this purpose. Then she grumbled:

'The Seigneur de Rais came to inquire after you just before evening prayers. Mother Marie-Béatrice informed me of his visit, and I told him you were asleep. The Holy Abbess couldn't lie to him, but I had no such scruples. I don't like that man's looks!'

'You did quite right!'

Sara dropped a kiss on Catherine's forehead and stole out of the room, closing the door behind her. Catherine was left alone in the narrow cell whose walls were streaked with flickering shadows from a fluttering candle flame. Little by little, the needs of her exhausted body took the upper hand of her anxiety and sorrow and at last, just as the nuns were leaving their hard beds to hear Matins in the chapel, Catherine fell asleep.

But her slumber was not peaceful. Deep in her unconscious, she relived all the hours of joy and terror of the last few days. A vision of the filthy hole where she had been imprisoned spun before her, lit up, suddenly, by the leaping flames of a human bonfire. Then she saw the leather sack gaping before her, and black figures trying to force her into it. But this time she was alone. Arnaud's shape appeared for a fleeting second, only to vanish again into the shadows despite her entreaties and desperate attempts to reach him and hold him fast. The executioner's hands closed upon her and she called out after the figure which inexorably vanished. But her hands were bound and an irresistible force dragged her towards the open sack which grew and grew till it was like a dripping tunnel swallowing her up. She wanted to cry out, but her voice was only a feeble whisper and her body was paralysed with fear. She felt herself dropping into a great chasm and suddenly, with a cry, she awoke and found herself dripping with sweat. Sara was standing over her with a candle and shaking her by the shoulder.

'You must have had a nightmare. . . . I heard you cry out. . . .'

'Yes. . . . Oh, Sarah, it was horrible. I . . .'

'No, don't say anything! You'll only frighten yourself all over again. Now you're to go to sleep, and I'll stay here by you. Your nightmare won't return.'

'It will until I find Arnaud again,' Catherine said, half sobbing. 'Till then, it will never leave me. . . .'

The rest of the night passed peacefully enough. Day dawned and still there was no sign of La Hire and his men. Catherine was consumed with impatience. As the hours passed, her confidence ebbed.

'If they had found Arnaud, they would have been back by now.'

'You can't be certain,' Sara said soothingly. 'The expedition may have ventured farther afield than expected.'

But despite Sara's comforting words, it was impossible to drag Catherine away from the bell-tower. She might easily have stayed there all night if, towards dusk, a cloud of dust had not appeared along the westward road. Soon she could see the gleam of armour as the setting sun touched the swirls of dust. As the black pennant carrying the silver vine came into sight, Catherine raced down the steep, winding stairway.

'They're here! They have returned!' she cried, heedless of the sanctity of the spot. She shot like a cannonball past the astounded Mother Superior, thrust open the door and ran out into the square with Sara at her heels and then down the street leading to the city gate, her skirt gathered up in both hands to run faster. She reached the gate towers just as La Hire's charger crossed the drawbridge, and all but fell beneath the horse's hooves.

'Well, have you found him?'

The captain fought to stop his horse from trampling on her, swearing brutally. Under his raised visor, his drawn face was grey with dust, each line and wrinkle etched in black.

'No,' he said curtly. 'We haven't.'

Then he saw Catherine falter, white to the lips, and was ashamed of his brutality. He jumped from his saddle and reached her side just in time to catch her before she fell to the ground in a faint.

'Now, you aren't going to collapse in my arms for the second time? I haven't found him, but I know that he is alive. That's something, isn't it? Now, come along. We can't talk about it here in front of all these people.'

Alive! The word revived Catherine quicker than a couple of slaps. She gazed at La Hire with shining eyes and allowed herself to be escorted towards the Templars' house. They were followed by the rest of the men-at-arms, filthy and weary, and they all passed beneath the blackened porch and filed into the courtyard. It wasn't till the soldiers dismounted that Catherine noticed that they had a prisoner with them.

Till then he had been hidden from sight in the throng of horses and riders, but he was a huge man, one of those blond Normans built like a battering ram, a visible link with his old Viking forebears. His hands, which were tied to Sergeant Ferrant's pommel, were broad and powerful, powdered with golden hairs, but one sensed that they were deft, intelligent hands. He wore a tattered linen tunic which barely covered a torso and shoulders like a bull's, surmounted by a brick-red face whose features, apart from piercing grey eyes, were rather indeterminate. Those eyes, guarded by bristling brows, reminded one irresistibly of a clear spring set in tangled undergrowth.

The captive did not seem especially concerned about his situation. The gaze which he allowed to dwell on his surroundings was calm and alert, inquisitive rather than anxious. When it reached Catherine, it kindled with a sudden spark of interest.

'Who is this?' she asked as the men-at-arms took the prisoner into the main hall.

'How could I know?' La Hire said, shrugging. 'We found him unconscious in the cellar of that famous farm of yours. He had a cask of brandy under one arm. Some English looter, no doubt! Since we returned to Normandy, the Godons have been having a

great deal of trouble exacting their toll from the peasants and
they tend to take their payment where they can.'

The man's voice rang out so powerfully that the low-beamed
ceiling echoed like a cathedral vault.

'I am no Englishman, but a good Norman and a loyal subject
of King Charles.'

'Humph!' La Hire snorted. 'Well, you speak our language,
and that's something. What is your name?'

'Gauthier! Gauthier, the woodcutter, but they call me
Gauthier Strongitharm.'

'Why is that?'

The forester laughed shortly.

'Because, when I have my stout staff in one hand, I'm a
dangerous man to fall foul of. I do not wish to boast, Sir Captain, but I have the strength of ten.'

'Explain how you came to be in that house, and who knocked
you out.'

'I knocked myself out! Now that I know you are one of the
King's captains, I shall tell you all I know. ... Before, I thought
you might be a brigand and thought it best to keep silent.'

La Hire shrugged and grimaced. He had, in fact, been a bit of
a brigand at times, when the war slackened off. It was hard to
turn one's hand to anything else when one was trained to fight.
La Hire's moods were of no interest to Catherine, however,
who was seething with impatience. She spoke to the prisoner
herself.

'What were you doing in that house? Do you know what
happened there?'

'Yes,' the man said sombrely. He cast a sharp look at Catherine and went on: 'Magloire and Guillemette, the poor wretches
who lived there, were my cousins. I sometimes stayed with
them when food was scarce in the forest. They were kind,
helpful people and no poor soul ever sought their help in vain.
I was there, asleep, the other morning when a man arrived. He
was poorly dressed, but he looked like a nobleman. You could
tell it a mile off. He gave Guillemette a gold piece and asked
her if she had any milk. The English money struck Guillemette
as strange. She started questioning him, but the traveller refused to talk. He merely said that he came from a different
part of the country, that he had been working in Rouen and
was on his way home. There was something about him which
inspired confidence, and yet that unconscious arrogance of his
was unexpected. However, Guillemette allowed herself to be

convinced. Gold is such a precious commodity! She was just off to the cowshed to get the milk when the others arrived ... swine; ravening, murderous wolves! They hadn't heard them coming while they were talking.'

La Hire grabbed the man by his doublet and shook him in a fury. 'Who were they? Did you know them?'

But for all his strength, La Hire was no match for the prisoner, even with his hands tied. With a swift movement of his shoulders, Gauthier Strongitharm shook him off.

' 'Course I knew them! I saw their banner. It was that Richard Venables, the English butcher, a crueller jackal than even Satan, his master. He has his lair in the chalk caves of Orival and the old ruin of Robert, the Devil. Oh, it was not a pretty sight! ... poor Guillemette ... poor Magloire!'

'And you mean to say you stood by watching and did nothing to help?'

'Now, look,' the other burst out angrily, his eyes flashing. 'Don't provoke me too far! Venables has four fewer men now than a short while ago thanks to my unaided efforts. But there were ten more of them who came after me ... they half knocked me out and tied me up ... and I shammed dead. It seemed the best thing to do, since I was powerless to help. I'm good at that ... but you cannot imagine what I suffered! I was trussed up like a sausage and my eyes were too swollen to see out of, but I heard it all. It was terrible! Oh, but the man with the gold piece fair laid about him, too! He picked up a bench and knocked them flying like skittles, but they got him in the end. He finished up beside me trussed like a goose and out like a light, with a huge great lump on his forehead turning black and blue. Lucky for him ... didn't hear them scream ... poor little Guillemette and Magloire ... I thought I'd go off my head, and I thanked God when they fell silent and I knew they were dead. . . .'

He paused, and made as if to try and wipe the sweat which was pouring down his face. Wordlessly, Catherine approached and mopped his brow with a corner of her veil. The poor man gazed at her with a look of infinite gratitude.

'Thank you, fair lady!'

'Please,' Catherine interrupted hurriedly, 'please go on. What became of Messire de Montsalvy, the one you call the man of the gold piece.'

'Ah, didn't I say he must have been a gentleman!' the man cried triumphantly. 'Venables knew it too. When it was all

over, I heard him telling two of his men to fetch him along
so they could put in a claim for ransom.'

'How came it that they left you alone, then?' said La Hire
slyly. 'A sturdy fellow like you is worth a little money, too.'

'I've already told you – they thought I was dead. As they
left, they threw a lighted bundle of hay under the table, thinking that the whole place would go up in flames, and me with
it, but the moment their backs were turned, I put the fire out
... and then I ran away.'

'Ran away? But why?' Catherine exclaimed.

He turned towards her once again, and tears shone in his
eyes.

'Try and understand, madame! I loved them both, and to
see them like that ... it was more than I could bear. I just
ran and ran till I reached my wood, with my hands over my
ears, because I still seemed to hear their screams of agony. All
day long I lay under a tree weeping and trembling ... but
then, I felt ashamed. I went back, because there was something
still to be done. Poor wretches! They deserved a corner of
hallowed ground after such a martyrdom. So I wrapped them
round as best I could and carried them over my shoulder to the
village graveyard where I buried them both.'

'... and then you went back to see if Venables's brigands
had not left anything behind?' La Hire asked sarcastically.

Strongitharm turned a face to him so swollen with rage
that it was almost purple.

'A King's captain should know one or two things about
life! I went back, yes, but only because I knew that Magloire had hidden a barrel of *eau-de-vie* and I wanted to drink
myself stupid, do you hear? Drink myself under the table so
I wouldn't hear Guillemette's screams any more ... and that's
how I came to lay myself out against a beam.'

A silence fell. La Hire paced up and down the low-
ceilinged chamber, hands clasped behind his back. Meanwhile,
Catherine took a closer look at the strange woodcutter. She
could not help feeling a spontaneous sympathy towards anyone
who could tell her something of Arnaud. Then, suddenly, La
Hire stopped in front of Gauthier.

'You are sure you have told me everything ... and that it's
the truth? Your tale has a hollow ring to it. I have a good mind
to put you to the torture.'

The woodcutter shrugged his massive shoulders and burst
out laughing.

'If that would amuse you, messire, don't let me stand in
your way! But let me tell you, the man has not yet been born
who could persuade Gauthier Strongitharm to speak anything
but the truth!'

It did not do to trifle with La Hire. The captain flushed and
shouted:

'Accursed knave, we shall see if you mock me so saucily
at the rope's end. Hang him!'

'No!'

Catherine had put herself in front of the prisoner and flung
out her arms as if to protect him. More quietly, she repeated:

'No, messire. ... That would be an unnecessary cruelty. I
believe what he says. This man is no liar. Anyway, why should
he be lying? He has done nothing to deserve such a sentence
and he could be useful to us! Didn't you say a moment ago
that he was worth his weight in gold?'

'I don't like people who mock me!'

'He wasn't mocking you. I beg you, Messire La Hire, in the
name of your friendship for Arnaud, do not kill this man.
Give him to me ... I implore you.'

Not even La Hire could refuse Catherine anything when
she asked for it like that. He looked at her sharply and then
more angrily at the prisoner and, at last, he shrugged and
strode out of the room, calling out as he went:

'Do what you will, and much good may it do you! He is all
yours.'

A few moments later, the gigantic woodcutter, freed from
his bonds, knelt humbly before Catherine.

'Lady, I owe you my life. Do with me what you will ... but
allow me to serve you. The fairest lady may have need of a
faithful dog.'

That night Catherine slept well enough. She was less anxious
for Arnaud, knowing that his life was not in actual danger so
long as the brigand could hope to get anything for it. And then,
the next morning, La Hire would be off with more men to
smoke the fox out of his lair and free his prisoner. And to
whom could she look more confidently for the rescue of
Arnaud?

Before retiring for the night, Catherine entrusted Gauthier to
the convent gardener, a move which drew some acid comments
from Sara.

'What are we supposed to do with that great brute?' the

good woman grumbled. 'He's too tall for a page, too smelly for a valet, too uncouth to serve a lady of quality and, when all's said and done, much too large!'

'But he will make an excellent bodyguard, and I have a feeling we shall need one. As for being a savage ... that's the very first time I've heard you use that word as an insult, Sara. Have you renounced your own origins, then?'

'I don't deny my own origins, but I fail to see why I should dance for joy because we have this great dragon treading on our heels from now on.'

'A man like that can be useful in these times,' Catherine said in such a decided tone of voice that Sara did not pursue the point.

The night that followed was peaceful, but shortly after dawn the next morning, the little town was shaken by an unusual commotion. Noise, hoof-beats, men's cries, startled the sleeping echoes around the peaceful convent buildings as the long file of white-robed nuns left the chapel for the refectory.

Catherine and Sara, both veiled and carrying Missals, followed close behind the Mother Superior. Catherine had never found it so difficult to give her attention to the Mass. From the Gospel onwards, as the first sounds reached them from the town outside, her mind kept straying towards the outside world and she needed every ounce of self-control to stop herself rushing out to see what was happening. Her head was buzzing with ideas and she could not help wondering whether La Hire had decided to make a nocturnal expedition against Venables. ... Perhaps this noise was the sound of his men returning, ... And what if they had Arnaud with them? ... The *Ite, Missa est* had come as a happy release for her and she left the chapel with a sigh of relief, though she wished the long procession could have moved a little quicker. Could the nuns be so detached from the world that nothing outside the convent walls interested them at all? But, just then, Mother Marie-Béatrice stopped her measured pace and seemed to listen. The convent was like an island of calm in a sea of noise and excitement. Now they could make out cries of 'To the ramparts! ... To arms!'

The Abbess turned towards the porteress.

'Go to the lodge, Mother Agnes, and see what the meaning of all this commotion may be. I think an attack must be brewing up. ...'

The nun bowed and ran to the other end of the garden, but

she was intercepted before she could get to the lodge. Another
nun ran headlong into her as she sped across the formal garden
along paths bordered by clipped hedges and herbs. She was red
with excitement and her coif had slipped to the side of her
head.

'Messire de Vignolles is here, Mother,' she burst out, dropping
a quick curtsey. 'He says the Englishman is coming and wishes
to speak to Madame de Brazey with all haste.'

Mother Marie-Béatrice frowned. She disliked these incursions
of rough soldierly men into her peaceful convent, bringing an
atmosphere of feverish excitement with them, ill-suited to a
place of meditation.

Catherine was about to rush to see her visitor, but the Mother
Superior took her by the arm and drew her aside.

'Cannot Messire de Vignolles leave us to pray in peace, at
least on a Sunday?' she asked crossly. 'This is a convent and
not the great hall of some feudal keep. It seems to me . . .'

She got no further. A quick, metal-shod footstep rang along
the cloister and La Hire's mighty voice boomed out while nuns
scurried away in every direction with startled screams. The
captain marched straight up to the Mother Superior, whose
face was scarlet with annoyance between the white folds of
her wimple.

'Mother, I have no time for arguments or niceties of behaviour. The enemy draws near. If you didn't hear the citizens
of this town running to man the walls, you must either be hard
of hearing or the convent walls are uncommonly thick. I must
speak to the Dame de Brazey forthwith. Would you inform
her at once and have her maidservant pack her bags immediately. She must be out of this town within a quarter of an
hour. I shall wait.'

Mother Marie-Béatrice would doubtless have argued the
point, but at this moment Catherine stepped between them,
unable to contain herself a moment longer.

'Here I am, messire! There is no need to shout so loudly.
And be sure of one thing . . . I do not leave this town till Arnaud
has been found and rescued!'

'In that case, madame,' said La Hire, who was beginning to
lose his temper, 'the chances are that you will never see him
again, and that you will lose your own life into the bargain.
Now, listen to me, because I have no time to lose. I must defend
this town and I can't stand around bandying words for hours on
end. I recognized the banner of the leader of the force which

is marching on the town. It belongs to John Fitz-Allen Mal-travers, Earl of Arundel, a brave and formidable soldier, and I do not say that without reason. I have few men, whereas he seems to have many, and, if you climb to the ramparts, you will see a cloud of black smoke on the horizon. Pont-de-l'Arche is in flames. Perhaps we should evacuate Louviers and leave it to the mercy of the conquerors. . . .'

'How can you say that?' Catherine cried, seizing the Abbess by the arm. 'You can't leave the city undefended! What will happen to the inhabitants and the nuns?'

'The fortunes of war, my child,' the Abbess said gently. 'We, the brides of Christ, have nothing to fear from the English, who are Christians like ourselves. The submission of the town may be the best protection for the inhabitants. The English are short of money and provisions. They cannot afford to reduce us all to ashes!'

'What about Pont-de-l'Arche, then?'

'Enough argument!' La Hire interrupted impatiently. 'You must leave now, Dame Catherine, because I can no longer answer for your safety and your presence would only be an extra worry for me. . . . I am a soldier, not a lady-in-waiting.'

Catherine was shaken with despair and anger.

'Really? A soldier? And yet you would send me out on the highways? And where am I supposed to go, may I ask? And what about Arnaud, in Venables's power? Have you forgotten him?'

'I haven't forgotten. I have just deprived myself of some twenty men on his behalf – a sizeable number to lose when the enemy approaches. The Maréchal de Rais will be helped by the fact that a large contingent of English will be stationed about the walls of this town. As for you, your place is with Queen Yolande. The Queen now resides at the Château de Champtocé, which belongs to Messire de Rais, where she is con-ducting highly important negotiations with the Duke of Brit-tany. You shall rejoin her at Anjou. It is there that de Rais will take de Montsalvy when he has rescued him from Venables either by the sword or with gold.'

Catherine heard him out without interrupting this time, but her face lengthened as he spoke. At last she shook her head.

'I'm sorry, but I'm staying here! I don't trust Messire de Rais.'

La Hire's patience was at an end. A trumpet call from with-out the walls was the last straw. He began to shout.

'Nor do I! But he is on our side, he has no reason to betray us and furthermore, he would not dare! Besides, neither of us has any choice! This is war, madame, and if Montsalvy were here, he would be the first to remind you of that and send you to safety.'

'To safety? On the highways?' Catherine asked bitterly.

'You have a stout bodyguard: that unkempt young lout whom you rescued from the gibbet. We shall equip him with a stout staff since that is the weapon he knows best. Go and rejoin Arnaud at Champtocé. I command you!'

'That's an order?'

La Hire paused for a second, then added peremptorily:

'Yes. It's an order. You must be out of the city within a quarter of an hour, by river. Or else . . .'

'Or else?'

'Or else you will leave tomorrow, with all the other extra mouths. We have only got enough food for twenty-four hours.'

He bowed, took a step backward into the shadowy cloister and was gone. Catherine was swept by sudden panic. She felt as though the knight had thrown her, naked and defenceless, to the wolves. But this was only a fleeting impression. She was too used to dangers and fear to argue further. She was already busily planning her escape. Champtocé? How could she be sure of finding the way to the château where the Queen was staying? She was afraid of nothing once she was with Yolande. There she could wait in relative peace for the return of the man she loved. Only a few more days apart! After that, it would all be easy again. Of course she would pay this small extra price for the happiness which lay ahead! After all, it had cost her so dear already! A little more or less could not make much difference. Monseigneur Jésus and Madame the Virgin Mary would surely watch over the road and guide her safely to the haven which the Queen of the Four Kingdoms represented for her.

She straightened up. Her voice ran out, clear and firm, just as La Hire reached the lodge.

'I will obey you, Messire de Vignolles. I shall be ready to leave the town in a moment. And Heaven forbid that you should ever have to regret sending me away from here.'

'I am not sending you away,' La Hire protested somewhat wearily from the doorway. 'I am sending you to safety, which would be impossible once you fell into English hands. And I shall have nothing to regret. God be with you, Dame Catherine!'

CHAPTER TWO

The Viking

An hour later a small boat was slipping along in the shadow of the walls of Louviers. Aboard it were Catherine, Sara and their gigantic companion, whose presence was soon to prove providential. The long oak pole which propelled their boat seemed to weigh no heavier than a hazel twig in his hands. He stood at the stern and plunged the pole into the water, sending the boat gliding swiftly forwards with a mighty push. Soon the city walls vanished from sight behind the trees. The heat was suffocating by the time they passed under the small bridge over the river.

'I would love to swim,' Catherine murmured, trailing one hand in the warm water.

'A marvellous idea!' Sara exclaimed sarcastically. 'The English would merely have to scoop you out dripping wet when they arrived.'

'They won't come here,' Gauthier said positively, 'because of the swamps. They might get swallowed up.'

Sara did not deign to reply, but Catherine smiled at him. She began to congratulate herself on having rescued this man. Gauthier was one of those rare individuals whom nothing astonishes, who adapt to anything and are not prodigal with words or gestures. Earlier, when they had gone to fetch him from the gardener's cottage, he had not uttered a word. He had merely reached out for the heavy axe which one of the men-at-arms handed him and, after testing its edge on his thumb, had pushed it into his belt.

'I am ready,' was all he said.

At Catherine's suggestion, the gardener had replaced his worn and tattered clothing with something more suitable: a short black fustian tunic and long brown tights which made up the garb of a well-to-do peasant. The shoes had proved more difficult. They had had to improvise a pair from some sandals belonging to one of the Franciscan Friars from the monastery next door. Gauthier had put them on with a grimace of disgust and taken them off again the moment they set foot in the boat.

One thing had struck Catherine. Before leaving the convent, she had slipped into the chapel for a moment's prayer. Sara went with her, but Gauthier refused. When she looked surprised he explained:

'I am not a Christian,' he said curtly, apparently indifferent to the scandalized expressions of the various onlookers.

'But you told me the other night,' Catherine said later, 'that you buried your friends in Holy Ground.'

'True. They had the right. They were believers: they had been baptized. Not me.'

'Later on, I shall see that you receive instruction,' was all that Catherine said, but now, as the boat slipped along over the calm water, she thought of all this and watched the tall Norman under lowered lashes. Gauthier inspired conflicting feelings in her. She liked him, but was also a bit afraid of him, not so much on account of his prodigious strength as because of that strangely clear, penetrating glance of his. He seemed oblivious to everything just now, and yet she was sure that he was straining his ears towards the town and its gradually waning sounds. The cries and commotion of the burgesses and poorer folk barring their shutters, running to the ramparts to patch up ancient breaches in the defence, piling up firewood and faggots, collecting pitch and stones or fetching weapons and armour down from the attics to use in defence of their city, then the chanting of the Franciscans invoking a last blessing before the fight, and, above it all, the mighty voice of La Hire himself – all this was slowly giving way to the peaceful murmur of the water lapping against the sides of the boat, the rustle of a rabbit speeding away through the long grass or the call of a blackbird from a near-by branch. Catherine felt herself slowly surrendering to the peaceful atmosphere of this beautiful spring day. The river, which was broad at this point, flowed between banks thick-clustered with willows, wild apple trees, cherries and sapling oaks. It gave out a pleasant, fresh scent of young growing things and rising sap. Had it not been for the fact that each thrust of the boat was taking her farther and farther away from the man she loved, and whose plight was causing her such anxiety, Catherine might have found peace and delight in the silent gliding along beneath green branches through which scraps of indigo sky could be seen.

La Hire had explained to Catherine and her escort the route which they must take. It was simple to follow, but hazardous,

because much of the land they would be crossing was held
by the English. They were to go up-river as far as Chartres. The
great cathedral city, where pilgrims still flocked, despite, or
perhaps because of, the war, was the safest point from which
to set off across the ravaged, famine-stricken countryside which
lay between Chartres and free Orleans. That would be the
hardest and most dangerous stage of their journey. From there
on, they would take the watery highway of the Loire river as
far as Champtocé itself. The Loire! What memories of hopes
and sorrows that name conjured up for Catherine! Once before, that long ribbon of water had led her to Arnaud, through
tears and suffering, and now she was about to place herself
under its protection again. Catherine had no great wish to be
the guest of the sinister Seigneur de Rais, but it was impossible
to think of anything dishonest or dangerous happening anywhere near Queen Yolande. They must press on, as fast as
they could go. This was to be the last trial – the very last!
Afterwards she and Arnaud would never be separated again.
She would be his wife ... his *wife*! The word made her feel
quite faint with joy. ...

This thought warmed her heart, and life suddenly seemed
bright again. She smiled at the verdant banks, at Sara, who
stared at her in amazement, and finally at Gauthier.

'What a lovely day,' she exclaimed, almost gaily.

But the tall Norman did not smile. He was frowning at
something on the far horizon.

'Praise not the day till it is done,' he murmured, 'nor the
sword till it has struck, nor the ...'

'Why did you stop?' Catherine asked. 'What were you going
to say? "the woman"?'

'You guessed right, madame. But I don't think you would be
amused by the rest of that old Danish proverb. Anyway, this
is not the moment for talk.'

Catherine turned in the direction he was pointing and stifled
a scream. A moment later, they heard screams down the river.
Some women appeared from nowhere running with all their
might. They were washerwomen who had been hidden till
then among the reeds and tall grass, and who appeared to
be fleeing from an unseen enemy. Their blue gowns were caught
up in their belts, revealing bare legs, still rosy from standing in
the cool river water, beating dirty clothes on the stones, and
their hair had become loosened in their flight and was slipping
down over their shoulders.

'Why are they running like that?' Catherine asked.

No one answered. Four soldiers in green tunics had appeared and were now racing after them down a forest path. With a mighty push, Gauthier guided the boat deep into the reeds along the river-bank.

'The English!' he breathed, and pushed Catherine down in the boat with one hand. 'Hide yourself! . . . You, too,' he whispered sharply to Sara who had pretended not to hear. 'You aren't old enough to be out of danger yet!'

He said no more. Sara grumbled a little, but crouched down obediently beside Catherine. Instead of joining them, the Norman stepped over the side of the boat as silently as an otter. When Sara looked up, she saw him standing, waist deep in the water, one hand on his hip.

'Where are you off to?'

'To see if I can help those women. They're Normans like me.'

'Oho!' the gipsy replied. 'And I suppose you think the two of us are going to stay here in this water-rat's nest? You may swim, but I shall follow at a safe distance.'

She stood up, picked up the pole and pushed the boat out with one powerful stroke. Gauthier did not argue the point. He was swimming downstream towards a little creek from which cries and oaths could be heard. The giant swam like a fish. His huge body sliced through the water as swiftly and surely as an otter's, and Sara had some difficulty keeping up. Kneeling in the bow, Catherine craned her neck forward to see what was happening. She knew what an English tunic looked like now, after her time in Rouen, and she was not afraid, but she was dying to see what her strange bodyguard would do next.

Soon the creek came into sight, a loop of dark green water shaded by tall pines whose black branches rose stiffly into the sky above the river. Once again, Sara hid the boat by pushing it into a clump of reeds where they could watch without being seen. The Englishmen were there, their backs to the stream; four men intent on raping two girls whose screams filled the air. One of them lay on her back, shrieking with terror under a huge, red-headed archer who held her down with one hand over her face while he stripped off her clothes with the other. The three others were busy tying her companion's hands to two pine trees, laughing so uproariously the while that they almost drowned the noise of their victim's screams.

Catherine saw Gauthier reach the bank and raise himself cautiously and silently out of the water. His hand went to his

axe and seized it and, at the same time, a strange cry broke
from him. The axe whistled through the air and struck the
red-headed archer squarely between the shoulder-blades. The
man's roar of pain and Gauthier's cry made the other three
turn round, but by now Gauthier had scrambled up the bank
and stood ready for them, dagger in hand. The two women
could see the angry red faces of the three soldiers from where
they were hidden. They had drawn their swords and were
advancing slowly upon their assailant, quite confident of their
ability to deal with him. As he stood there with his back to the
river, he was like a wild boar facing his hunters. Then, suddenly, they met head on. The three soldiers leapt at Gauthier,
brandishing their swords and Sara immediately snatched up
the pole.

'If they overpower him, we'll escape as fast as we can,' she
hissed.

'There's not much likelihood of that,' Catherine said impatiently. 'Keep quiet! Look!'

As she spoke, the giant shook off his attackers as easily and
effortlessly as a bullock shaking off flies. He got the better of
one by snatching him up in his arms and stabbing him in one
swift movement, then he flung him like a projectile at the legs
of the other two men and sent them both sprawling. Gauthier
moved like lightning. He flung himself upon one of the fallen
men and the dagger flashed again. He straightened up to deal
with the one survivor, but the latter had taken to his heels and
was running off across the fields as fast as his legs would carry
him.

There were three corpses at his feet. The huge, red-headed
archer was in his death agony. A large, red stain spread slowly
over his green tunic. But the girl beneath him had stopped
screaming. His dying hands clutching at her throat had
strangled her. The other girl was alive. She stood waiting quietly
for someone to come and untie her. Catherine gathered she
was saying something, but she could not make out what it was.
Gauthier stooped and cut her bonds and she stepped free. Her
dress had been so badly ripped that it hung in tatters about
her hips. Her only covering was her long, corn-coloured hair
which streamed down over her shoulders and full breasts. She
seemed quite unconcerned about her nakedness. Catherine
watched, amazed, as she came towards her deliverer and wound
her arms about him, standing on tiptoe to reach his lips with
her own.

'Oh!' Sara exclaimed, horror-struck. 'That's too much!'

'Why?' Catherine asked. 'Everyone gives thanks in their own way!'

'Certainly, but just look at them ... look at that girl, she's throwing herself at him.'

It was true, and Catherine found herself frowning involuntarily. The blonde girl was beautiful; her rosy body had the fullness and purity of line of a marble statue and, as the man's hands reached for her hips, Catherine had a lump in her throat. But she had misread the gesture. The giant was simply pushing the girl away. Then he dropped a quick kiss on the tip of her nose, strode back to the river and dived in. Catherine saw the girl call out to him and fling out her arms to hold him, but her arms fell back to her sides, then she shrugged and soon vanished from sight among the trees.

'Let's go!' Sara exclaimed, and pushed the boat out. A few seconds later, Gauthier hoisted himself back on board, streaming wet and panting. He flashed a smile at Catherine which displayed his strong white teeth.

'There! That's over. Now we can set off again.'

But Sara's tongue was itching. She could not restrain herself a moment longer.

'Bravo!' she said sarcastically. 'But why did you not accept the nice present you were offered?'

The man was still looking at Catherine and it was to her that he spoke, though she had not said anything.

'So as not to keep you waiting.'

'Otherwise ...?' she asked.

'Well, otherwise ... I would have accepted. Why not? One must accept what life offers when it comes along.'

'Oh, marvellous!' Sara cried, outraged. 'And I suppose those four corpses wouldn't have bothered you?'

This time Gauthier Strongitharm deigned to speak to her. He fixed the gipsy woman with a grave, piercing glance.

'Love is the brother of death. In these harassed times those are the two things which matter.'

He took up the pole and the boat was soon gliding forward again beneath the green tracery of the trees. They continued in silence for a while. The two women, huddled together in the prow of the boat, seemed lost in their private thoughts, but there was still something Catherine wanted to know. She turned round.

'A little while ago ... when the English attacked you, you

called out something, it sounded like a name!'

'It was. The Norsemen, who sailed southwards to these lands in their swan-necked boats, and whose blood runs in my veins, always gave this cry in battle.'

'But you are not a knight, nor even a soldier!' the girl said with a touch of unconscious hauteur which was not lost on the former woodcutter.

'Does that make my blood less pure? Not all the sons of old kings live in castles, and I know of more than one nobleman whose ancestors groaned under the Vikings' whip-lash. I am descended from a great chieftain called Bjorn-Ironsides,' he said, striking his chest which reverberated like a drum. 'And I have the right to call upon Odin in the hour of battle!'

'Odin?'

'The God of War! I told you I wasn't a Christian.'

And, as if to make it clear that he had no wish to say any more, the great Norman started to hum. Catherine turned away, glancing at Sara. Neither of them spoke, but this time she read neither anger nor indignation in her friend's dark eyes; only surprise and a sort of admiration.

A kingfisher flashed past them towards the water. The boat travelled onwards in peace.

At sunset Gauthier started hunting about for a place to spend the night. The day's excitement had exhausted both women and even he was beginning to feel a little weary. At length he found a little beach near a ruined mill half swamped by greenery.

'We shall be safe there,' he said.

It seemed so natural that he should take charge that they did not speak. It was soon clear, however, that Sara's temper had darkened like the day itself. During the last hour or so of the journey, she had been sitting motionless in the prow, staring in front of her without speaking. When they stepped ashore and Gauthier went to make a rapid survey of the site, Catherine commented on this.

'What's the matter? Why are you like this?'

'I feel uneasy,' Sara said. 'And now night has fallen, I am afraid.'

'But why? What are you afraid of? Surely we have nothing to fear with a man like Gauthier to look after us.'

Sara shook herself nervously and came to sit next to Catherine, her arms clasping her knees.

'But it's *him* I'm afraid of!'

T—B

Catherine gave a start and looked at her friend in astonishment.

'You must be mad!'

'Do you really think so?' Sara said with controlled violence. 'What do you know about this man and his past? Only what he has told you, which you seem to believe as if it were Holy Writ. But what if it were not true? A man would say a lot of things to save his own skin. Suppose he murdered those wretched peasants after all?'

'I don't believe it!' Catherine exclaimed angrily.

'Hush, please. He might come back and it would be silly to annoy him. We aren't rich, but the little gold we have and our few possessions would be a fortune to a man like that. We are as helpless as lambs led to the slaughter. He can take advantage of the darkness to rob or kill us ... or worse still!'

'Worse?' Catherine echoed, round-eyed. 'I don't see what could befall us worse than death.'

'Not to me, perhaps ... but you ... You don't know how that great brute looks at you when you can't see him. I've seen him and I didn't find the sight reassuring. I've never seen such a look of naked, insolent desire.'

Catherine felt herself blushing, perhaps because she felt a little guilty. She had, in fact, encountered a few of these glances herself, but she had refused to take them seriously. Pride rebelled at the thought that a simple rustic like Gauthier might look upon her as a mere woman. The anger in her voice when she answered was directed at herself rather than her companion.

'And what of it? I can look after myself, Sara. I'm no longer a child.'

'There are times when I wonder.'

Sara had the last word. The sound of heavy footsteps near by silenced both women. Gauthier was returning. He did not appear to notice their air of restraint and went and stretched himself out on the ground a little way off.

'All quiet!' he remarked. 'But I shall keep watch part of the night all the same. And you, black woman, I shall wake you two or three hours before dawn to take over the watch. ...'

The 'black woman' almost had a fit, but Catherine felt a dangerous desire to laugh. After all, it was not so long ago that Sara had been known as 'Black Sara' by the tattered court of the King of the Beggars. Gauthier had hit on the truth.

They ate a little bread and cheese which the nuns had given

them, and then the two women lay down on the sand, wrapped
in their cloaks, while Gauthier took up his position on a large
stone near by. Catherine could just see him from where she lay,
silhouetted against the dark blue sky like a brooding lion. He
was quite still, but she felt a tremor pass over her body. Re-
calling the savage passage-at-arms she had seen that afternoon,
she told herself that Sara could be right after all – this man,
with his fighting skill and superhuman strength, might prove
dangerous. But then her fears subsided. The Norman was crooning to himself as he sat. She couldn't understand a word, but
there was something wild and noble about his song.

So absorbed was she in this strange melody, that the harsh
cry of a night bird near by did not break the spell. Slowly,
sleep was weighting her eyelids and she lost consciousness,
joining Sara who was already snoring happily beside her. The
night passed uneventfully. . . .

The next morning, as they were about to set off again,
Catherine went up to Gauthier while Sara bathed her face in
the river a little way off.

'I heard you singing last night, but I didn't understand a
word.'

'That was the old Norse tongue which you would not understand. The song was known as the Saga of Harold the Brave.'

'What did it mean? What was it about?'

Gauthier turned away to loosen the boat's painter from the
tree where he had made it fast and said, not looking at her:

'It says: "I am born of a high country, where the thunder
booms; my vessels strike terror into the enemy's hearts; I have
heard their ribs crack on the peaks of hidden reefs far beyond
the last habitation of man; I have ploughed great furrows in the
sea . . . and yet, a daughter of Russia scorns me." '

When he had finished, Catherine did not reply. Instead, she
wrapped her cloak more closely round herself and went and
sat in the bottom of the boat, cheeks aflame. Decidedly she
would have to keep a closer watch on Gauthier!

One evening, four days later, as the sun sank to rest in a
splendour of liquid gold, the towers of Chartres soared before
them, black and arrowy, into the blue. Here the Eure ran, blue
and silver, between banks overflowing with vegetation, running
like bands of green fur across the ochre velvet of the great sun-
scorched plain. Their great watery highway had dwindled to
a path and their voyage by river was perforce coming to an

end; fortunately the journey had not been very arduous. The two women had barely had to lift a finger and there had been food enough for all. Strongitharm's terrible axe was equally accomplished at bringing down game and he knew the life of woods and fields like few others.

Below the brown walls of the old city of Carnutes the Eure divided up into several channels, one of which ran beneath the walls, through a heavily barred archway, to power the mills and tanneries, while another filled the wide moat around the city. Gauthier beached their boat on a small bank of brown earth at the foot of one of the massive towers which guarded the Drouaise gate.

'I'll try to sell it, or exchange it for a mule,' he said, as the two women climbed ashore. Catherine looked up, shading her eyes with one hand against the fierce sunlight, to where the slate pepper-pot towers stood outlined against the hard blue sky, and a gilded carving of the Virgin and Child hung fixed to the wall just above the drawbridge of blackened oak. Higher still, there fluttered a banner with the rampant leopard device of the English Army. She indicated the banner with a nod to Gauthier.

'What are we to do? The town is English, but we must eat ... and rest awhile, and find horses. We may not look very impressive, but I wish we had safe-conducts.'

The tall Norman was not listening. There was a frown on his face as he studied the wall carefully, and his expression darkened. Catherine began to feel frightened. She had learnt to respect the judgement, as well as the strength, skill and quick-wittedness of this strange youth whom she had taken under her wing, though she still kept a watchful eye on him.

'What is it?' she asked in a low voice.

'Nothing, apparently. But this strange silence, these deserted walls, these unguarded gates. One might suppose the town abandoned. And look there!'

He pointed towards the top of the hill where the great square keep of the old Count's castle crouched like a huge mastiff alongside the twin towers of the cathedral. A black pennant flapped at the end of its staff high above the stone battlements.

'Someone has died,' said Sara, who had just come up. 'Someone important.'

Gauthier did not answer. He was already striding towards the drawbridge. The two women followed. They crossed the bridge and found themselves looking up the old rue Porte

Drouaise with its uneven cobblestones, painted shop-signs and
wooden houses which looked as if they were kneeling under the
weight of their great brown roofs. ... It was all empty ... a
sinister, desolate emptiness.

The three travellers went on more slowly. The deserted
street was unnerving and they found themselves walking
almost on tiptoe. All the doors were closed, the shutters barred
and there was no sign of life. Even the two inns appeared to
have been abandoned. Halfway up the hill, near a well whose
mossy cover glowed green under its wrought-iron canopy, they
saw something else: two great, nail-studded doors, barricaded
by stout planks nailed down on either side. The sight of these
two doors made Sara and Gauthier turn pale, while Catherine
stared at them uncomprehendingly.

Suddenly the silence was broken. Somewhere up that hill,
sanctified by ten centuries of pilgrimage, arose the sound of
deep, sonorous voices intoning a religious chant. They seemed
to come from a procession of monks, because the sound was
moving. It was Catherine who first recognized it.

'The *Dies Irae* . . .' she said in a strangled voice.

'Let's go on,' Gauthier exclaimed through clenched teeth.
'We must find out what is happening!'

A little farther up, the road curved, marked by the sign of a
spur-maker: three stirrups and an iron rowel. From here, it
was possible to see as far as the Bishop's palace in front of
which something very strange was happening. Several soldiers
in metal cuirasses and helmets, armed with long iron pikes,
were piling fuel on a pyre from which arose a column of acrid
smoke. They wore cloth masks over the bottom halves of their
faces. Close by, apparently supervising their work, stood an
extraordinary-looking person dressed entirely in leather and
wearing a long pointed beak like a bird's on his head.

The man with the bird's beak, who was in fact simply a
doctor, held a hazel wand in one hand and a cloth bag in the
other. From time to time he took handfuls of some greenish
powder out of the bag and threw them into the flames. The
smoke from this powder had a pungent, spicy perfume in
strange contrast to the appalling stench coming from the pyre
itself, where a heap of corpses, piled on top of each other,
were being slowly consumed. More corpses lay about the place,
awaiting their turn. Still more were being carried up by
prisoners in chains, wearing masks like the soldiers. Every now
and then they threw another body into the flames. The pyre

had only just been set alight, it seemed, and it emitted thick, suffocating clouds of black smoke.

The spectacle before them made the hair of all three watchers stand on end. Now they understood why the town was deserted, the walls unmanned and the gates unguarded, and why a black banner floated above the palace which used to belong to the Counts of Chartres: the worst of all calamities had befallen the city of God. Black Death stalked the streets. Chartres was stricken by the plague!

From a near-by guest-house, which appeared to have been transformed into a hospice for the sick, a new chain gang had emerged, dragging bodies, swollen and blackened by the disease, at the end of hooks.

This sight destroyed the last remnants of Catherine's courage. It turned her stomach, but galvanized her legs to such an extent that she turned tail and ran – with a cry of fear – towards the Drouaise gate, blind and deaf to everything but panic fear of the place where this dreadful scourge lay waiting. All she wanted was to escape! Escape, escape, find the green grass and fresh air again, and sun which was not blackened by smoke! Behind her, Sara and Gauthier followed with all the speed they could muster, stumbling on the uneven paving-stones.

But the shaft of sunlight which had shone through the ancient stone arch only a little while earlier had now been sealed off. In its stead appeared the rough-hewn planks of the drawbridge, now raised. Catherine's wild race was cut short by the implacable grille of the portcullis, where she clung, weeping and breathless.

'The gate!' she sobbed. 'They have closed the gate!'

Hearing her cries, a soldier emerged from the guard-room and tried to pull her away from the bars.

'Forbidden to leave. Governor's orders. No one! Orders of the Bishop, too, Sire Jean de Festigny.'

He spoke clumsily, fumbling for the words, hampered by his English accent, but Catherine went on clinging to the portcullis, scraping her hands on the rough wood.

'I must get out! I must get out, I tell you! I don't want to stay here . . . not here!'

'No help for it,' the soldier explained patiently. 'Governor's orders: anyone trying to get out is to be hanged.'

Gauthier and Sara had reached Catherine by now. The gipsy gently loosened Catherine's hysterical grip and folded her in her arms. The giant seemed to be meditating as he stood there stroking a chin now ornamented by a thick, reddish thatch, a chin which had not seen a razor since he left the convent gardener's cottage.

'What shall we do?' asked Sara.

'Try and find a way out,' he said, shrugging his massive shoulders. 'I haven't much desire to stay here till the Black Death makes me into a stinking corpse. How about you?'

'Need you ask?' Sara spat out scathingly. 'But how are we to get out?'

'We shall have to think hard,' Gauthier said, shifting the bundle containing their possessions into a more comfortable position on his shoulder. Sara carried a smaller bundle which held a few clean clothes. Such gold as they possessed was stitched into a pocket sewn to the inside of Catherine's petticoat. The giant put out a hand to help Catherine along.

'Come. And don't cry any more, Dame Catherine. I'll find you a hole through the walls somewhere in this town. For the moment we must eat, because we won't last long without food, and then get a bit of rest. And I shall reconnoitre the ramparts meanwhile.'

Catherine let herself be led along. They went back up the steep hill now almost hidden by smoke and fumes till they reached the doctor again, still pursuing his lugubrious task. As they drew near, he shook his fist at them angrily.

'Get out of here! What are you doing in the street? Go indoors!'

'Where?' Gauthier asked. 'We don't belong here. We have only just come into the city for a bite to eat and now we find the gates are closed and no one is allowed to leave.'

The monk-doctor's voice reached them from under his thick leather mask, somewhat milder, but still irritable.

'Well, you can't stay here. I'll show you a place to go. . . . This is the far end of the Notre-Dame Cloister. That door leads to the Canon's dwelling,' he said, pointing to a stone arch across the narrow street. 'Farther on, on the right, you will see a long building with stone pillars along the front and a tall slate roof. That is the Loens.'

'The Grange aux Dîmes?' Gauthier interrupted.

'You must be a Norman, my friend. That word came from the sea with the long-boats.'

'I am a Norman,' Gauthier affirmed proudly. 'I still speak the old tongue.'

'Very well. Go to the tithe barn . . . the town poor who are

no longer able to go and scratch their pittance from the surrounding countryside or take refuge in the rich households
barricaded against the Black Death, have gathered there and the
monks of St Peter are supplying them with food. Not much, alas,
because supplies are running low and the barn is empty. But
tell Father Jerome, who is in charge of the provisions, that
Brother Thomas sent you. When you have eaten, go to the
cathedral to add your prayers to those who beseech Our Lord
day and night to avert this terrible scourge from us.'

Silently the three companions followed his directions.
Catherine felt light-headed, her body strangely feeble and her
will-power non-existent. This town was like a trap which had
suddenly snapped shut and imprisoned her. She dragged herself slowly onwards, leaning on Sara's arm.

'You'll feel better when you have eaten,' Gauthier said
gruffly. 'I've noticed that it pays to eat in times of crisis – it
restores the spirits.'

They had no difficulty in finding the tithe barn, which was
full of people. A wretched grey rabble milled about the white
robes of a tall thin monk who was distributing bread. A torch's
flickering light played over his tonsured head and parchment-
coloured features. Gauthier pushed through to him leaving the
two women near the door.

'Brother Thomas sent us to you,' he said. 'There are three of
us. We were passing through when they closed the gates. We
are hungry.'

The monk took three pieces of black bread from a basket and
gave them to him.

'Here, eat this.' Then he picked up a great pitcher and filled
a jug with water and handed it to him. 'Drink.' Then he turned
back to the crowd. The three refugees sat on the ground to eat.
Catherine devoured her piece of bread and took a long swallow
of the water and felt better. Her strength was returning, bringing life back into every part of her strong, healthy body. Sara
was already nodding off beside her. She had eaten too fast, like
a ravening animal, and now she was overcome with drowsiness.
As for Gauthier, seated next to a ragged, emaciated figure in
faded red, he was eating methodically . . . slowly, like a man for
whom every mouthful counts. From time to time he spoke
briefly to his neighbour.

From where she sat, Catherine could hear every word. The
Norman seemed to fascinate the man in red who was staring
at him with undisguised admiration. At first, Gauthier had

replied indifferently to the man's questions, but then the man
had said:

'I have never seen you around here. Where are you from? I
come from Chazey, a village near here.'

At this, Gauthier's nonchalance had vanished. He looked at
his companion sharply.

'Chazey? Near Saint Aubin-des-Bois?'

'You know it?'

'Not personally, but back in Normandy I knew a girl once. She
came from your parts. The English had seized her when they
sacked the village because she was pretty. After that, she stayed
with them like the rest of the camp followers, but she was
terribly frightened, so frightened that finally she went a little
mad. She wanted to return home, it had become an obsession
with her ... one night she tried to escape. She hoped to flee
to the woods, but an archer shot at her. I found her at dawn,
lying at the foot of a great oak with an arrow in her shoulder.
Of course, I took her back to my hut and did what I could,
but it was too late. She died in my arms the next night ... she
was called Colombe! ... Poor little thing! During all that day,
while she lay dying, for as long as the light lasted, she spoke
about Chazey. ... "A handful of houses beneath a great dome
of sky," she said. "And nothing for miles about but a great
endless plain." '

'There's nothing left now but the plain and the sky,' the
other man said bitterly. 'And a few blackened walls. The English burned the hamlet down because the people wanted to
stay faithful to King Charles and believed that Joan of Arc was
a saint. My parents died in the fire, but I know that one day
the village will rise again from the ashes and I shall return
there.'

Catherine had been listening with growing interest. She had
been full of speculations about Gauthier's past, ever since they
had left Louviers. The little incident he had just recounted
raised a corner of the veil which covered this strange man and
confirmed her liking for him. There was, she sensed, something
fine and generous about him. He had proved it by rushing to the
assistance of the washer-women, and now she found it easy
to imagine him caring for the dying girl, sweetening her last
moments on earth. Sara might say what she liked: the man was
undoubtedly strange. But that did not prevent him from being
appealing.

The sun's heat was becoming oppressive now, towards

mid-day. In spite of the heavy vaulted roof overhead, the heat under the arches of the old building was stifling. All these milling bodies raised a fine cloud of dust which looked golden in the sunshine, but made one choke, and there was a stink of dirt, sweat and ordure. But the fear which bound these people together was stronger than disgust or discomfort. Each felt that, outside this asylum, where God's ministers tended them, death itself lay in ambush, lurking in those little alleys ablaze with sunshine.

Catherine feared the plague, too, but she soon found the smell of overheated humanity intolerable. She was suffocating. When the monks appeared to be leaving, having distributed all their food, she rose to her feet. Gauthier's watchful eye fell upon her just as she was about to cross the threshold. She smiled at him.

'I can't breathe here,' she said. 'I'm just going out for a little air.'

He seemed reassured and resumed his conversation with the tall thin man. Sara was sound asleep, occasionally brushing off a fly which had settled on her nose.

Outside, the heat fell about her like a cloak, more stifling even than it had been in the tithe barn. It fell like lead from a blazing sky, but at least there was a little air to breathe and it did not smell so bad.

Catherine took a few steps along the street, taking good care to remain in the shadow of the gables and overhanging eaves. She sat down on a mounting block outside the door of a draper's shop and took several long, deep gasps of air. The projecting gable shaded her from the incandescent sky. She might have dozed, with her back against the sun-warmed stone, if something had not caught her eye. A little way off, at the corner of the road, a man was making discreet attempts to catch her eye.

She sat up and looked about her. The man was still beckoning. He stood at the corner of the street, at the foot of a statue of the Virgin. Catherine pointed questioningly at herself. The man nodded vigorously. She rose to her feet, curious to know what he might want, and went over to him. He was a little, ugly fellow, filthy beyond belief. His arms and legs were black with layers of dust and grime and they protruded from shapeless, tattered garments. He gave a twisted grin as she approached.

'Do you want to see me?' she asked. 'What is it?'

The man's grin broadened.

'I heard what you said to Brother Thomas earlier on. I know you want to get out of the city. I think I can help you.'

'It's dangerous. Why should you take the risk?'

'You might be able to spare a poor wretch a little money. I haven't seen so much as a silver groat for two years now.'

'In that case wait a moment. I'll go and tell my friends. . . .'

The man took her arm.

'No. It's taking too much of a chance. I'll show you what to do and then you can come back and get your friends. You'd do better to wait till nightfall, anyway.'

Catherine hesitated. She did not like the idea of leaving Gauthier and Sara, but, on the other hand, the man was quite right. Too many people would attract attention. And certainly, if there were a chance to escape, it would be madness to let it slip by. With a backward glance she said:

'Is it far?'

'No. Close by. The ramparts are near here. Come!'

He took her hand in his grimy paw and pulled her along. She was in such a hurry to continue on her journey that she followed. He turned down a tiny alley just wide enough to let him pass. It appeared to be a cul-de-sac, tailing off amid a jumble of huts and hovels behind which rose the tall, grey northern wall of the city. Catherine's guide went up to the hovels, but when he stooped to pass under a low doorway, she suddenly paused instinctively. He looked at her through narrowed eyes and once again flashed her his curious grin.

'If the hole were in the middle of the road,' he snorted, 'the soldiers would have filled it in a long while ago! Come . . . this is the way. . . .'

Catherine assumed that it must be some cellar with a tunnel under the walls which took one out into the fields. She made up her mind, bent down and followed him into a sort of aperture, too dark and slippery to deserve the name of passage. It seemed to plunge down into the earth, but at the far end she could just make out a door of rough-hewn planks. The man pushed the door open and pulled her after him with a sudden violence. As the door banged shut behind him, he cried out triumphantly:

'I kept my promise, lads! Just see what I've brought you.'

Catherine had no sooner glanced round the place into which she had stumbled than sudden panic overtook her. In this cave, dimly lit by a single grating, there were some twenty ragged

men, lying on the ground or propped against the wall. As she
looked about in terror, she heard growls of satisfaction and
coarse laughter, and saw the faces of human wolves raised towards her, their eyes burning like hot coals. Anger at having
fallen into a trap momentarily surmounted her fear. She turned
to her guide.

'What's this? Where have you brought me?'

The man sniggered. He still held her arm – with surprising
strength for so puny a man.

'I've brought you to some fine fellows who haven't laid hands
on a woman for far too long! They took us out of prison to
burn the corpses, and they've given us this cave to rest in during
the heat of the day. There is bread and wine, but no women!
The only ones we could have had are sick or dead or in hiding.'

An ogre of a man with a scarred face and one leg shorter than
the other came limping up while the rest gathered round.

'She is beautiful,' he croaked in an ugly, nasal voice. 'But
where did you find her, La Fouine? You know the punishment
for taking a townswoman?'

'Yes, indeed, but she isn't from the town. She had only just
arrived when the governor ordered the gates to be shut. That's
when I first spotted her a while back near the fire. And then I
kept an eye on her at the tithe barn. Tell me now, isn't she a
fine woman?'

'A dainty fit for a king!' the ogre agreed. 'You have earned
your pound of flesh, La Fouine. . . .'

Catherine tried to dodge away when the man's filthy hand
pinched her chin, but there were two other ruffians behind her
barring the way. In a flash she understood: she had fallen into
the clutches of the chain gang, the terrifying men she had seen
earlier on dragging corpses about at the end of long hooks. Her
legs trembled under her. The hungry circle seemed to be closing
in. All she could hear was the hurried breathing of these men,
their faces alight with dreadful lust under the layers of filth.

The ogre's hand caressed her cheek as her arms were pinioned
to her sides by invisible hands. He came so close that she received his foul breath full in the face. She trembled with rage,
shame and loathing as he calmly unfastened her bodice and
unlaced her dress. The other ruffians watched, with wide eyes
and bated breath, like assistants at some strange rite. But when
her round shoulders and breasts came into view and her satiny
skin gleamed in the dimly lit cave, the sight was like a signal.
They all leapt on her at once. Catherine shuddered with re-

vulsion as a forest of hands snatched and tore at the rest of her clothing and clutched at her body. They were falling over each other to get close enough to touch her. Then the ogre's voice croaked out:

'One at a time! There's plenty for everyone. But I'm the chief; I go first. Hold her down!'

In a twinkling Catherine found herself stretched out on the ground on a bed of mouldy straw, held down by the wrists and ankles. Terror struck her dumb for a moment, but then the life flowed back into her and she found her voice again. Writhing and twisting in the grip of these hands which pinned her to the ground, she cried out:

'You haven't the right. . . . Let me go! Help!'

A hand clamped down roughly over her mouth. She bit it. The man cursed and struck her so hard that she almost lost consciousness. But before he could cover her mouth, she screamed at the top of her voice. Then the hand clamped down again. She felt herself suffocating under it and hoped desperately that she would lose her senses. She writhed with horror as the man's hands roamed over her body amid the coarse comments of the other men. Hot tears rolled down her cheeks. The idea of being raped by these monsters filled her with horror. But then, all of a sudden, something like a thunderbolt seemed to strike the room. The greedy circle was broken as if by magic and the place was full of confused figures running this way and that. There were cries of pain and fear, and something like the mutter of thunder overhead. A voice boomed out:

'Filthy swine! I'll make you sorry you ever tried to lay a finger on her!'

After such a shock, the sight of Gauthier hardly surprised her. He fell upon the men like a ton of rock, wreaking terrible havoc where he struck. His huge fists hammered out, knocking teeth out here, smashing a face in there, sending a body flying against a wall. Lying on the floor, as helpless as a newborn child, Catherine watched him and thought he looked like a reaper in a field of corn.

Also, she was vaguely aware of a tall, reddish figure near the door who methodically seized the Norman's victims, one after another, and flung them through it. Soon, there was no one left but the lame man. He tried to spring at the Norman's face to gouge out his eyes. The giant lifted one leg. His foot let fly like a catapult and struck the man in the face with such force that Catherine heard bones cracking. The man slumped in a corner, his face unrecognizable. He was dead.

Catherine saw that the cave was empty and she was alone save for Gauthier. She was suddenly aware of her nakedness and began looking around for her clothes. She spied them in a corner and was about to get up when the Norman knelt beside her. He was panting like a smith's bellows, and not solely from his recent exertions. His pale eyes were devouring her body so hungrily that she suddenly felt afraid again. Her defender was looking at her now the same way those human animals had done before they had been put to flight. ... She held out a shaking hand as if to push him away, but he did not move a muscle. He hardly seemed alive, kneeling there so still, and he looked altogether so formidable that Catherine's heart sank. Sara's warnings came back to her and she cursed herself for a fool. She did not know much about this man, and here she was, in his power. In a moment he would give way to the desire in his face, and there was nothing she could do to stop him.

She was too weary to struggle any more. With a little moan, she slipped back on the floor and waited for the inevitable. Then a timid, hesitant, strangely gentle hand despite its calluses, touching her hip, reawakened her fighting instincts. In a voice she hardly recognized as her own, she moaned:

'No! Please, Gauthier! No. ...'

Instantly, the hand was withdrawn. The Norman shuddered from head to foot. He turned and looked at her with eyes to which a normal expression was gradually returning. She saw a flash of disappointment but almost at once, he bent and took her bare feet in his hands and kissed them humbly.

'Forgive me,' he murmured.

The next moment he stood up, completely himself again.

'I will get you your clothes, Dame Catherine,' he said in the most natural voice in the world. 'And then I'll wait outside till you are ready.'

He brought her things and left without looking back. At the door, he was joined by the tall figure in red.

'Come, we'll leave her to dress.'

Catherine was soon ready. Outside, she joined the two men and recognized the other as Gauthier's companion at the tithe barn. Their looks embarrassed her.

'I need some water,' she murmured. 'I feel so dirty.'

The man in red replied with a burst of laughter. It was a slightly foolish laugh, but not disagreeable.

'You will soon have water to your heart's content, fair lady. And what has just happened could happen to any pretty woman in these fine times of ours. The main thing is that we arrived in time.'

'How did you know where I was?'

'Thanks to him entirely,' Gauthier explained. 'When you vanished, he started to get suspicious. It seems something of the sort happened to a shepherd girl a week or so ago ...'

'I thought I recognized La Fouine,' the other interrupted. 'I don't trust him farther than I can see him. Those convicts do much as they please these days. And then we heard you scream.'

Gauthier's companion did not seem unduly perturbed by what had happened. He was absent-mindedly chewing a straw as they went along.

'What are we going to do?' Catherine asked.

'Wake Sara,' Gauthier replied. 'And then the two of you can go and wait in the cathedral till nightfall.'

'And you?'

'Well, firstly, I have no business in a church and secondly, I intend to go and look around with Anselme L'Argotier here to see if we can find a way out of this accursed place.'

'Oh?' Catherine said meekly. 'I suppose *he* knows a way out, too? Or says he does!'

Anselme did not seem offended by her tone of voice. He smiled at her and bowed as gracefully as a page.

'Yes,' he said sweetly. 'But I happen to be telling the truth.'

Catherine's later recollections of that afternoon in the cathedral were hazy like the dreams one has just before waking. The emotional shock she had just suffered seemed to have left her more than ususally aware of the striking contrast between the pathetic, greyish human flock huddled at the foot of the great rood-screen and the triumphant miracle of the tall windows whose blues and crimsons were jewelled by the afternoon sun. They had come in their hundreds to beseech God's mercy for their threatened city. Some had sought refuge from the scourge by camping in the holy place itself, as they had done in the times of the great pilgrimages. This was possible because, unlike other churches, there were no tombs here. Dedicated to the glorious Assumption of the Virgin Mary and protected from death, this building was never to be soiled by the dead.

After the horrors of the convicts' cave, Catherine found a solace in the contemplation of such beauty. She prayed for a

while before finding a seat in a corner where she could await
the coming of night. She prayed that she might soon find
Arnaud again. From the crypt, where the sick were crowded
about the miraculous well, came groans and complaints. In
spite of this, Catherine managed to snatch some sleep. She
dreamt that she was alone, in a deserted, sunlit street. The road
glowed like red-hot iron, but she hurried down it regardless,
because, in the far distance, she could make out the figure of
Arnaud. He wore his black armour and walked with a slow,
regular pace. Catherine ran and ran to catch up with him, but
the road seemed to stretch on for ever and the distant figure
grew smaller and smaller. Catherine tried to cry out, but her
voice stuck in her throat. . . .

She woke with a start and found that it was dark outside, but
that hundreds of tapers had been lit in front of the high altar,
making a pool of golden light. Up there in the choir, rich and
sonorous voices chanted the Miserere, the crowd making the
responses. Sara, who was praying beside her, glanced at her.
Then she saw something beyond her head and her eyes gleamed.
She stood up.

'Come,' she said. 'They are waiting for us. . . .'

Outside, Catherine and Sara found Gauthier and Anselme
L'Argotier waiting for them. The blue sky of earlier on was
heavy with massing clouds presaging a storm. Outside the
cathedral walls, the heat was stifling, and to it was joined the
reek of smoke from the pyres. Everywhere people were burning
herbs and even perfumes as a protection against infection. The
town smelt of incense and death, and the silence of the grave
enveloped it like a winding sheet. Catherine was too awed to
speak. She whispered instead:

'Where are we going?'

'To the tanneries,' Gauthier replied. 'Our only hope is to get
through the grid across the river. Anselme and I have made
sure that it is not guarded.'

The little band left the white shadow of the cathedral and
plunged into the labyrinth of old streets. Sometimes as they
passed a closed door, they caught a murmured prayer or
muffled sob.

Before long they had reached the foot of the hill near the
river where the tanneries and fulling sheds stood. Anselme
walked in front, one ear cocked for possible dangers. He stopped
close by a little bridge and pointed to a narrow gate in the
city walls a short way off. It was carefully barred and bolted.

'The Tire-Veau postern gate,' he whispered. 'The grid is just below.'

Below the postern gate they could see where a stream passed through a grid before joining the moat outside.

'We shall have to enter the water,' Gauthier said. 'I shall prise a bar out so that we can get through. Luckily there are no guards here. The walls are much too high at this point.'

Anselme took a long object from his pocket and handed it to him.

'Here is the file. Good luck, and may God go with you!'

'Aren't you coming with us?' Catherine asked in astonishment.

She sensed rather than saw the odd fellow's smile.

'No, fair lady, much as I would like to. I have things to attend to here.'

'And . . . the plague?'

'Bah! The plague will pass and I have every hope of finding myself among the survivors.'

A deep bow and he was off, loping with long, silent strides up the steep-pitched street. Gauthier was in the water and Catherine heard the grating of the file against the bar. Fortunately, the sound of a little waterfall near by covered the noise he was making. Even so, Catherine could not repress a shiver. Those iron bars looked enormous and Gauthier was working in difficult conditions, clinging to the grid because of the depth of the water; but he set to with a sort of cold fury.

Catherine had not mentioned her afternoon's adventures to Sara. She felt strangely embarrassed by what had happened, and nothing on earth would have induced her to confess what had passed between Gauthier and herself. Sara would have made a scene and told her that it served her right for trusting him. Catherine, however, found some comfort in the incident, because it confirmed her suspicion that the Norman was in love with her, and proved the extent of her power over him. The scene in the cave must remain a secret between them both. She would never mention it to a soul! Possibly because – for a moment – she had been tempted to surrender to the fiery passion she sensed in him.

An hour later, panting and soaked through, Gauthier crawled out on to the bank again. One bar had been cut through and bent back to leave a small space. He glanced round the little quay and then at the two women.

'Can you swim?'

They nodded, though it was years since either of them had tried. In such heat, the thought of a dip was not disagreeable. Making a quick decision, Catherine took off her dress.

'What are you doing?' Sara whispered in shocked tones. 'Surely you aren't going . . .'

'To strip? Yes, I am. I'm going to tie my clothes in a bundle and carry them on my head. It's the only way to save them from getting wet.'

'Yes . . . but that *man*?' Sara added with an anxious look at Gauthier who had slipped into the river again. Catherine shrugged.

'He has better things to do than look at me! You'd be well advised to do the same.'

'Me? I'd rather die . . .'

And Sara descended into the water with great dignity, fully dressed. The next moment Catherine followed her. She had made her clothes into a large bundle fastened round by the bodice strings of her dress. The cool water felt delicious. She stretched in it luxuriously and let it carry her to the grid where Gauthier was waiting. Her slender body slipped through the aperture without difficulty, gleaming pale and graceful in the clear water. Perhaps that was why Gauthier closed his eyes as she went past. He did not open them again till a slight rustling of the reeds on the far side told him that Catherine had found herself a refuge against inquiring eyes.

CHAPTER THREE

Bluebeard's Castle

A week later, a little before sunset, Catherine, Sara and Gauthier came in sight of the Château de Champtocé and paused for a moment. The most powerful fortress in Anjou was worth a second look. There were eleven stout towers, each of which carried a long golden banner with a black cross and *fleur-de-lis*. Granite walls were reflected in the green waters of a lake, and beyond stretched the dark green pelt of a distant forest. A little farther off, grouped round the foot of the castle mound, the usual russet and blue roofs of a village were clustered. But Catherine had a strange feeling that they were cowering away rather than clustering round for protection. Champtocé village seemed to look to the tall spire of the church as if to shelter from the crushing weight of the fortified château. From those black, silent towers which stood out against the deep blue sky, a deep sadness emanated as well as a vague atmosphere of menace. She was taken by a sudden longing to escape. And Sara too, with the sharpened senses that came with her nomadic background, seemed to feel the same disagreeable influence.

'Let's go away from here,' she whispered, as if she feared the sound of her own voice.

'No,' Catherine said, gently, but firmly. 'It is here that I am to find Arnaud again. It is here I must stay.'

'You can see that Queen Yolande isn't there. Her standard would be flying from the battlements – I can't see a single royal banner,' Sara protested.

'I see some *fleur-de-lis*, though,' said Gauthier.

Catherine nodded.

'When King Charles created Messire de Rais a Marshal of France, he gave him permission to use a border of *fleur-de-lis* round his own family arms. The other banners must be those of his grandfather, Craon. Whether or not the Queen is there, I am afraid we must go there ourselves.'

She turned her mule's head towards the great barbican which guarded the main gate of the fortress, and the other two were reluctantly obliged to follow. These mules, together with most

of the luggage carried by the baggage mule, were a gift from
Maître Jacques Boucher, the rich burgess of Orleans, with whom
Joan of Arc had once lodged and who had taken Catherine in.
He and his family treated the young woman with a true and
abiding affection.

By the time Catherine and her companions reached Orleans,
after an exhausting journey across the ravaged and desolate
plain of Beauce, they were so worn out that they were on the
point of collapsing by the wayside. Gauthier had somehow summoned up reserves of that herculean strength and carried Catherine who could not walk another inch. Sara dragged herself
along as best she might, holding on to the giant's belt. The
Bouchers had welcomed them with that rare and lavish hospitality which rich folk of old prided themselves on. Dame Mathilde, the burgess's mother, and his wife, Marguerite, were
delighted to see Catherine again, but Mathilde had not been
able to resist saying:

'My dear Countess, I have never known a great lady lead
such an extraordinary existence! Are you really so passionately fond of travelling the highways?'

'Quite simply, I am in love,' Catherine smiled, not appearing
to notice the way Gauthier's face suddenly froze.

The three wayfarers stayed two days with these hospitable
folk. The evenings were passed in endless talk of Joan of Arc.
Catherine described her trial and martyrdom and the halo of
glory which had encircled the dying girl, blood-red close to the
pyre itself, but golden with sunlight as it rose to Heaven. And
all who heard, masters and servants, clustering around the
hearth, wept freely, to hear of so much suffering. Then, for the
tall Norman's benefit, the people of Orleans had told of the
marvels of their deliverance, the days of battle, the cowardice
of the English and the splendour of the Maid clad in her silver
armour. The giant forester listened closely, eyes wide with
wonder at this tale of blood, love and glory in which his savage
spirit found echoes of the old Nordic sagas, tales in which
warrior maids galloped away into the clouds with the souls of
dead warriors fastened to their sea-coloured pommels.

But, when Catherine said that she wished to go to Champtocé, they all fell silent. Later, when the servants had retired to
bed, Dame Mathilde turned to Catherine with a look of concern.

'You mustn't *think* of going there, my dear! The place has a
bad reputation and the Baron de Rais is an unsuitable man for a

rich and beautiful woman to consort with. His old robber father, they say, is worse still. Do you know that, after forcing little Catherine de Thouars to elope with him and marry him so he could get his hands on her vast fortune, he then abducted his mother in-law, Béatrice de Montjean, and forced her – under threat of being sewn up in a sack and thrown into the Loire – to yield him her two fortresses of Tiffauges and Pouzauges.'

'But the Queen has gone there!'

'Only under duress! These people would not hesitate to stop her cortège and maltreat her followers. Believe me, my dear, they fear neither God nor the Devil. Self-interest and pleasure are the only motives they know....'

Catherine smiled sweetly at her old friend. She threw her arms around her neck and kissed her.

'I am no longer a little girl, Dame Mathilde, and I am not at all rich. My whole fortune at the moment consists of a little bag of écus sewn into my petticoat. My jewels are at Rouen, in the care of Jean Son, until Brother Étienne finds a way of bringing them to me. I would not be a very interesting prize for these two piratical gentlemen ... besides, I have faith in Monseigneur de Rais's word. He has sworn to seize Arnaud de Montsalvy from Richard Venables and I am sure he will.'

Jacques Boucher sighed, an anxious frown creasing his brow.

'But he is cousin to La Trémoille who completely controls our lord the King, if what they say is true.'

'Yes, but he is above all a King's captain,' Catherine persisted. 'and I have no choice but to go there if I am to rejoin Messire de Montsalvy.'

Nothing, the Bouchers realized, would stop Catherine going to stay with the sinister Messire de Rais. They did not pursue the matter, but when the time came to leave, Dame Mathilde slipped a fine gold medal stamped with a figure of her patron saint about Catherine's neck, and pressed a tiny enamelled reliquary containing a minute fragment of St James's bones into her hand.

Catherine had had to repress a smile on seeing this. It brought back a whole host of memories: Barnaby's hut in the Grand Cour des Miracles in Paris, the Cockleshell Man himself with his great nose and long legs and fingers in the glow of the log fire. How often she had watched him, with round, admiring eyes, putting hundreds of little fragments into just such little boxes as this! She could almost hear the sly voice of Hachefer, King of the Beggars, chaffing him:

'With all these years you've been putting him in little boxes,
he must have been the size of King Charlemagne's elephant,
this St James of yours. . . .'

Perhaps this very reliquary had come from Barnaby's indus-
trious hands, in which case its value as a relic was suspect,
but this made it all the dearer to Catherine. Those few ounces
of copper, gilded and enamelled, were a link with those far-
off times. It was like a friendly hand extended from the grave
across all those vanished years. . . . Holding the box tightly
in her hand, she kissed Dame Mathilde with tears in her eyes.

Catherine thought of all this as she rode towards the stately
but forbidding castle. Instinctively, her hand in its pale suède
glove felt for the tiny bump under her bodice which marked
Barnaby's reliquary and held it for an instant as if summoning
the courage she needed. She was just about to turn her mule
under the barbican when a little troop of soldiers emerged,
their long pikes and leather-shod feet trailing in the dust. They
dragged a ragged man along with them. His hands were tied
behind his back and his eyes blinked in the setting sun. Another
man in black, with an ink-bottle attached to his belt and a
heavy hood over his sweating face, brought up the rear, a roll
of parchment in his hand.

The soldiers took the road which skirted the lake and soon
vanished below the overhanging branches. The two women
crossed themselves hurriedly, suddenly realizing that the prisoner
must be on his way to execution. Catherine shivered. As he
passed her, the wretched man's eyes had met hers with a look
of inhuman agony and suffering.

'Not even a monk to speed him on his way!' Sara muttered.
'Who are these miscreants we are venturing among?'

Catherine's hand clasped her reliquary again and she was
strongly tempted to turn tail and run. It might be better to
take lodgings in the village inn and wait till Gilles de Rais
returned. But then she bethought herself that any news which
reached the château would never find its way to her. And then
it occurred to her that Gilles de Rais almost certainly had not
yet returned, and it was unworthy of her to be afraid of an
old man. Finally, what if Arnaud were to send word to her
there telling her where they were to meet?

Just then, the watchman's horn sounded overhead and a
rough voice called out:

'What do you want, strangers, and what brings you to this
castle?'

Before Catherine could answer, Gauthier cupped his hands round his mouth and shouted back:

'The very noble and puissant lady' – the time-honoured formula made Catherine smile inwardly, since her puissance was now only a memory – 'Catherine de Brazey, here at the invitation of Monseigneur de Rais, demands to be admitted. Go tell your master and be quick about it. We are not accustomed to be kept waiting.'

Sara was amazed by his arrogance and gave him a startled glance. Really, this man was a mine of surprises! Where had he suddenly found the manner and address of an authentic herald? His arrogance had not been wasted. The soldier's helmet vanished from the battlements. While he went for his orders, no doubt running as fast as his legs would carry him, the little band of travellers crossed the barbican and the approach bridge reflected in the green waters where reeds and watercresses grew. Before them towered up a massive drawbridge made of huge planks criss-crossed by immense iron bolts. The walls rose high and sheer overhead, so high that the rough-hewn stones of which they were built were lost from view in the shadow of the overhang. Below the crenellations, long black streaks testified to old attacks and fierce defences. Champtocé was like one of those soldiers who have grown old in their armour and prefer to die on their feet, sustained to the last by their pride and belief in their own invulnerability.

A trumpet blared from one of the highest towers. The sun had gone down by now and a flight of ravens flew, croaking, across the pale green sky. With solemn, even ominous, slowness, the great drawbridge sank down before them. . . .

Catherine was impressed by the astounding luxury of the great hall at Champtocé, although she had been familiar with the splendours of Bruges and Dijon, and the treasures amassed at Bourges and at the château at Mehun-sur-Yevre where King Charles maintained his court. A fortune's worth of massive gold plate studded with precious gems was displayed on dressers and chests about the room together with statuettes in brilliant enamels and a magnificent chess board of gold and green crystal which stood waiting for use on a table between two blue velvet-covered stools. And the dais reserved for the lords of the manor sparkled and gleamed as richly as a bishop's cope with its hangings of cloth-of-gold and forest of red tapers.

As she went in, Catherine's first impression of this brilliant

décor of red, blue and gold was almost oppressive. It reminded
her of the dazzling costumes sported by fat Georges de la
Trémoille who never felt he was properly dressed unless he
dripped with gold. In this blaze of colour and riches, her eyes
were too dazzled at first to discern two much less ostentatious
forms: those of an old gentleman in black and a young woman
dressed in grey. A moment later, the former rose from his
chair and came forward to greet her.

'Greetings, noble lady! I am Jean de Craon and I am in
charge of this place during the absence of my grandson, Gilles
de Rais. It is several days now since a messenger arrived to warn
us of your approach. We were quite anxious about you.'

'The journey was an arduous one and took longer than I had
foreseen. But I thank you for your concern for me, sir.'

As she spoke, her eyes strayed to the young woman and it
was towards her that Jean de Craon now turned.

'This is my granddaughter, whose name is Catherine, like
yours. She comes of the noble house of Thouars and she is
Gilles's wife.'

The two young women curtseyed formally, observing each
other covertly under modestly lowered lids. The Dame de Rais
must have been about twenty-six or -seven and would have
been pretty if her soft brown eyes had not had a perpetually
harassed expression. She was tall and supple, but almost skinny,
and her face had the faded colouring of an old pastel drawing.
Her small head, with is pale blonde plaits coiled over each ear,
was poised on a long graceful neck. Except for a certain aristo-
cratic air, she strongly resembled Catherine's sister, Loyse, who
was now a nun in the convent of Tart in Burgundy, though Loyse
had never had that look of gentle, timid resignation. Although
the Dame de Rais was much the taller of the two she inspired
Catherine with a strange feeling of strength and confidence,
and a deep desire to protect this melancholy young woman.

The young woman's soft voice broke in on her thoughts. She
saw that Catherine de Rais was smiling at her and she smiled
back warmly. She liked the look of her far more than the old
man who stood watching them. The latter's appearance lived
up to his reputation as an old brigand. He was tall, straight and
lean as an old tree in winter and his most striking features were
stern black eyes and a large hooked nose which dominated his
thin face. He was clean-shaven and there was a sarcastic twist
to his thin lips, while the expression of his eyes, shaded by
bushy grey eyebrows, was inscrutable. Catherine did not need

to remind herself of what Dame Mathilde and Brother Thomas had said about him to realize that with Jean de Craon, it was wise to be on one's guard.

She heard the young châtelaine offering to show her to her room.

'Very well, very well, my child,' Croan approved. Then he turned to Catherine. 'My wife is out hunting, a sport in which my stiff leg prohibits me from indulging.'

Before leaving the room, Catherine asked the question which was burning on her lips.

'Monseigneur Gilles gave me to understand that I would find Queen Yolande here. I am one of her ladies-in-waiting. Is she no longer here?'

It seemed to her that the young woman blushed and looked away. It was the old man who answered.

'The Queen left here several days ago. Her negotiations with the Duke of Brittany were successful and she is now at Amboise preparing for her youngest daughter's marriage with the Duke's heir.'

'In that case,' said Catherine, 'I shall not need to impose on your hospitality for more than one night. I shall leave tomorrow to join her.'

The old man's eyes flashed briefly, but his dry lips parted in something like a smile.

'Such haste! Your presence here would be such a delight to my granddaughter while her husband is away. Will you not do us the honour of remaining for a few days longer?'

Catherine hesitated. It was hard to refuse without seeming rude and she had no wish to offend the Maréchal de Rais, so long as Arnaud's safety depended on him. She curtseyed.

'I thank you for your kind welcome and for your invitation, seigneur. I should be delighted to stay here a few days longer.'

On leaving the brilliant room, Catherine had the impression of diving into a dark tunnel. The handsome stairs which led to the floor above were painted with frescoes representing scenes from Exodus and lit by clusters of torches held by bronze claws. Her eyes were beginning to weary of so much richness. The pale grey velvet train the Dame de Rais was wearing fanned out behind her as she climbed the worn stone stairs. Presumably out of shyness, she did not utter a word. She climbed the stairs slowly, holding up her skirts with both hands and Catherine, feeling suddenly awkward, did not like to break the silence. They reached a sort of gallery down which the châtelaine turned and then she opened a low door almost hidden by its massive carved frame. She stood back for Catherine to enter.

'This is your room,' she said. 'Your maid is already waiting for you.'

The soft glow of red candles in a wrought-iron candelabrum spilled out through the doorway into the gallery, but, before going into the room, Catherine stopped and looked her hostess full in the face.

'Forgive my curiosity, Dame Catherine,' she said softly, 'but why are you so sad? You are young, beautiful, rich, noble and your husband is attractive and famous. . . .'

The Dame de Rais suddenly raised her transparent lids and looked at her guest.

'My husband?' she echoed dully. 'Are you so sure I *have* a husband, Madame de Brazey? I trust you will rest till supper time. The meal begins in one hour.'

Catherine entered the room without saying more, while her hostess closed the door gently and vanished. She took a few steps forward and looked around. It was a fine room entirely hung with tapestry scenes. There were two windows with leaded panes. In one corner, there was a fireplace decorated with painted coats of arms and hunting trophies. The furniture consisted of an immense bed hung with green velvet, a high-backed chair, a tall carved oak cupboard, two stools covered with green velvet cushions and a brass-studded coffer. There was a little door in the wall near the head of the bed, which suddenly opened and Sara's powerful figure appeared. She was still wearing her travelling mantle and her face, beneath the tan which no amount of beauty milks had ever succeeded in removing, was as white as her cap.

'Are we staying here?' she asked before Catherine could open her mouth. I have heard that the Queen is at Amboise.'

'Yes, I know,' Catherine replied, undoing the strings of her voluminous blue coat. 'I wanted to set off again tomorrow, but our host insisted that we should stay a few days longer. It would have been rude to refuse.'

'A few days?' Sara asked suspiciously. 'How many?'

'I don't know exactly how many – four or five, perhaps. Not more than a week in any case.'

Sara's face darkened at the news. She shook her head.

'It would be better to leave at once. I don't like this place. Funny things happen here.'

'Your imagination is running away with you,' Catherine

sighed. She was sitting on one of the stools, unplaiting her hair. 'You would do better to help me get rid of some of this dust.'

She had barely finished speaking when the door of the room burst open and Gauthier rushed in. He was ashen-pale and the disorder of his clothing indicated that he had just been in some sort of a brawl. Before either of the women could speak, he cried out:

'We must go, Dame Catherine! We must escape at once! This château isn't a place of refuge for you, it's a prison!'

Catherine went white. She stood up and gently pushed Sara away.

'What do you mean? Are you out of your mind?'

'I wish I were,' the giant said bitterly. 'Unfortunately, there can be no mistake about it. I dare say you were welcomed with every courtesy, but the soldiers had no such scruples towards me. When I asked the way to the stables, an armed sergeant took the reins from me and said that I need not bother about that, because these mules all belonged to the lord of the manor now. Naturally, I protested. Then the sergeant shrugged and said, "You're a simple fellow if you think your mistress will be able to leave here without Messire Gilles's permission. We've all been given our orders concerning her, and my advice to you is to make yourself scarce as possible if you don't want to get into trouble." Then I'm afraid I flew into a rage. I seized the man by the throat! Some soldiers came up and rescued him and I managed to give them the slip, but . . .'

Just then a veritable company of men-at-arms poured into the room. In spite of his great strength, Gauthier was soon overcome, the more promptly since there were three longbows pointing at him and further resistance would simply have meant a fusilade of arrows in his body. Catherine lost her temper. She went straight up to the commanding officer, eyes flashing, and ordered him to release her servant at once.

'And leave the room! How *dare* you?'

'Sorry, noble lady,' the officer said, raising one hand awkwardly to his cap. 'Your servant struck a sergeant. He must now come before the castle tribunal to be tried and I have orders to take him to the dungeons now.'

'He did *right* to strike him! 'Od's blood! You have a strange idea of hospitality here! What! You seize my mules, you are insolent to my servant and yet you expect him to do nothing! Release him, I tell you!'

'I am sorry, madame, but I have my orders. This man must be locked up.... I am simply obeying my orders.'

'And I suppose your orders were to arrest my servants?' Catherine said bitterly. 'Why not lock me up too, then? Why don't they put me in prison? It doesn't look as if I shall be allowed to leave of my own free will.'

'You must ask the Sire de Craon that, madame. ...'

The officer bowed stiffly, ordered his men to take the prisoner away and went out. Gauthier turned back at the threshold.

'Don't worry about me, Dame Catherine. Forget about me and take my advice – flee from here while you still can!'

Catherine and Sara watched, rooted to the spot, as they took him away. The door closed. Catherine's eyes, which had gone almost black with rage, sought Sara's.

'And that is the man you were telling me to be wary of!' she exclaimed bitterly. 'Should I still be suspicious of him now?'

'I grant you that he behaved like a loyal servant – for some sentimental reason or other,' Sara conceded. 'But what are you going to do now?'

'I am going to find out what this is all about,' Catherine cried. 'And let me tell you, I don't intend to let another minute go by without getting to the bottom of it.'

She began feverishly trying to re-plait her hair, but rage made her clumsy and she could not do it properly.

'Let me do it!' Sara broke in, taking her mass of hair in her hands. 'I will do your hair and then you must change your dress. Better to appear as dignified as possible – not like a dancing girl!'

But Catherine refused to smile. She sat down, very straight, while Sara rearranged her hair and brushed away the dust of the road; Sara could see Catherine's slender fingers twisting and untwisting in her lap.

'I must be calm!' she kept repeating to herself. 'I *must* be calm!'

When the trumpets sounded for the evening meal, Catherine was ready. Sara had dressed her in a velvet gown with a headdress of two lace horns. She looked very beautiful and more than a little forbidding. She slipped from Sara's hands like someone trying to escape and marched towards the door with such resolution that Sara could not repress a smile.

'You look like a little fighting cock,' she remarked.

'You're lucky to be able to make jokes at a moment like this,' Catherine said crossly.

Catherine's arrival in the great hall where supper had been laid out interrupted the voluble and passionate account which a tall, thin, grey-haired woman was giving to Jean de Craon and Catherine de Rais, with a wealth of histrionic gestures. She had a hooked nose which closely resembled the old man's and wore a gown of russet satin lined with gold and she was imitating the flight of a falcon when she caught sight of Catherine.

'How do you do, my dear!' she cried amiably. 'Glad to see you've arrived safely.'

After which, she plunged once more into the description of the day's hunting during which she had brought down two herons and six hares. She finished at last:

'All of which is another way of saying that I'm dying of hunger. Let's go to the table!'

'One moment,' Catherine interrupted coldly. 'Before going to the table, I would like to know where I am to sit – with my hosts or with my gaolers?'

The intrepid huntress, who was none other than Anne de Sillé, Catherine de Rais's grandmother, whom old Craon had married a year after Gilles's wedding, gazed at the young woman with astonishment not unmixed with admiration.

'By the womb of my mother!' she exclaimed.

But old Craon's brows were knitted and his lower lip stuck forward in an ominous grimace.

'Gaolers? What gave you that idea?' he demanded.

His tone was harsh and his expression far from reassuring, but Catherine was too angry to be alarmed. She stared at him icily.

'The simple fact that, barely an hour after my arrival, I saw my squire seized before my eyes, in defiance of all the laws of hospitality.'

'The man struck a sergeant of the guard. It seems to me that that is a sufficiently discourteous action to deserve some punishment.'

'And I would have dealt it to him myself, if his behaviour had not been provoked by some mighty strange words! He was forbidden to see to the stabling of our mules on the pretext that these were now your property and that, in any case, I should not be needing them in future since my stay here was to be much longer than I realized. Any loyal servant would have taken offence at remarks like these, messire, and, if you ask me, your sergeant only got what he deserved. . . .'

Jean de Craon shrugged.

'Men-at-arms are not always very intelligent,' he said crossly. 'You shouldn't attach too much importance to what they say.'

'In that case, there's a perfectly simple way for you to prove your good faith, messire. Release my squire and have my mules saddled. I will make all the apologies you think fit ... and I and my servants will depart this evening.'

'No!'

The word cracked like a whiplash in the strained silence which had followed Catherine's last words. She was conscious of the other two women waiting with bated breath, looking anxiously first at her and then at the old man. She felt a tightening of her throat from sheer shock. She swallowed hard, but did not flinch. She even managed a scornful smile.

'You have a passing strange idea of what is meant by hospitality, messire! Am I then a prisoner?'

Limping slightly, Jean de Craon walked slowly towards her, a very upright figure in her black dress, standing on the threshold. When he next spoke, his voice was much gentler.

'Now, please understand me, Dame Catherine – since the time has come to speak plainly. This château belongs to my grandson. He is the master of all who live within its walls ... myself included. His wish here is law. I have received orders from him concerning you: you are not to leave the castle under any pretext whatsoever before his return. ... No! Don't ask me why, I don't know! All I do know is that Gilles expects to find you here on his return from the war and I shall not disappoint him. Rest assured, however, that your wait will not be long. The fighting north of Paris is too fierce to continue till winter without one side calling for a truce. The English need a breathing space even more than we do. Gilles will soon be back. And ... isn't he bringing someone with him particularly dear to your heart?'

Catherine felt a hot rush of blood to her face. Her anger at Gauthier's imprisonment had momentarily put Arnaud out of her mind, and she felt as though she had committed an act of sacrilege. The thought of the man she loved calmed her a little. It was true that Arnaud was to meet her there, and the thought of seeing him again, hearing his voice once more, filled her heart to overflowing. If she left the château now it would be all the longer before she saw Arnaud again.

Unknown to her, Jean de Craon was able to follow her thoughts clearly enough by simple observation of her face.

When she looked up at him again, he was holding out his hand
for her to lean on with an air of old-world courtesy.

'So, you see, you must be patient and sensible. Now, will you
join us at the table?'

But she did not place her hand on his.

'Very well,' she said finally. 'I will stay, but at least you must
release Gauthier for me.'

Craon's refusal was none the less firm for being polite.

'I cannot, Dame Catherine! The laws of the château are ex-
plicit on this point. Anyone who strikes an officer of the watch
automatically stands trial ... a fair trial, I assure you! When
Gilles is here, he holds court once a week and he alone can
judge a case involving one of our soldiers. All I can promise
you is that Gauthier will not be ill-treated, that he will be given
enough to eat and imprisoned in a decent cell. He will not have
long to wait, either.'

And this, Catherine realized, was his last word on the subject.
She was temporarily out-manoeuvred and she decided to accept
the appearance of defeat gracefully, but she was raging inwardly as she picked up her long velvet gown in both hands
and passed, tall and proud, before Craon, who slowly let his
proffered hand fall back to his side.

Squires came forward bearing basins of clear water and white
cloth napkins. The diners took their seats in silence down one
side of the long table and the ritual ablutions began. Then the
chaplain, who had just joined them, mumbled a short grace,
after which the first dishes made their appearance. Anne de
Craon literally fell upon her food with the raging hunger which
one gets from a day in the open air, but, from time to time,
she gave Catherine a sideways glance which was not unsympathetic. She seemed to approve of people who spoke their minds.
Catherine, however, hardly ate a thing. She sat very upright in
her chair, rolling a piece of bread absent-mindedly between her
fingers while she fought hard against a feeling of mounting despair. Her thoughts kept returning to Arnaud: his strength and
matchless courage; Arnaud the best blade in France along with
Constable Richemont; Arnaud ... his intractable character, his
flashing smile and impossible pride ... but his wild kisses too,
and gentle hands and the soft words of love he spoke so well.
Once he was there, he would know how to protect and look
after her. It would take more than these walls, however strong,
to keep her there once Arnaud was beside her. Who would dare
oppose the will of a Montsalvy?

Anne de Craon was yawning and stretching quite unrestrainedly.

'Eh, well, I'm off to bed! I'm going boar-hunting in the morning. Barthélemy has picked up the spoor of a male boar the other side of the Rosne.'

The old lady dipped her hands in the gold basin a page held out to her and wiped them on a red towel. Then, without another glance in the direction of her unwilling guest, she took her husband's arm and went across to the door. Her granddaughter followed and Catherine brought up the gear, but, just as they were leaving the well-lighted area round the dining table, Catherine suddenly felt a hand touch hers and slip a tightly folded scrap of paper into it. Her heart leapt exultantly and she closed her hand about the note. On the threshold, there was a formal exchange of bows, curtseys and good-nights. Then, one by one, the various parties to this strange meal set off for their rooms preceded by torchbearers.

No sooner had she closed her bedroom door behind her than Catherine rushed to read her note by the light of the candles. It was short and unsigned, but that did not matter to Catherine.

'Come tomorrow to the chapel at nine o'clock in the morning. You are in danger. Burn this note.'

A cold sweat ran down Catherine's neck. She felt a sharp sense of menace and suddenly everything around her seemed charged with hostility. She looked round nervously and gave a jump of terror. In the flickering candlelight, the figures in the tapestries seemed to have come alive. The walls swarmed with soldiers brandishing sabres and massacring infants in swaddling clothes. Here and there women knelt with pleading, outstretched arms. One of them staggered back from a sabre blow, bleeding from a gash in the throat. There was blood everywhere, and lips parted in screams which Catherine almost seemed to hear. The whole tapestry was alive!

Sara, who had drowsed off sitting on a stool near the bed, suddenly woke and gave a cry of alarm when she saw how pale Catherine had become. Her lips were trembling and her body was stiff with shock. She gave a smothered exclamation.

'Lord! What's the matter with you?'

Catherine shuddered. Her eyes came back to Sara. She handed her the note.

'Here, read this,' she said dully. 'You were right. We should never have come here. I'm afraid we have stumbled into a hideous wasps' nest.'

The gipsy read the note carefully, spelling out each word to herself. Then she handed it back to Catherine.

'Well, we may find it easier to get out than you think. It appears that we have someone here who wants to help. Who is it?'

'The Dame de Rais. She is shy, silent and apparently terrified out of her wits, but it is hard to tell what she is thinking. If only I knew what it was she was afraid of . . .'

A timid voice which appeared to come from the chimney sent them both whirling round.

'She is afraid of her husband, like all of us here. She is afraid of Monseigneur Gilles.'

A very young girl, dressed like a servant, appeared from the darkness cast by the heavy stone overmantel. She was slender and her thick blonde hair threatened to burst out of the little cap crammed down over it. Catherine saw that her eyes were filled with tears. Suddenly, without any warning, the little maidservant fell at her feet and clasped her round the knees.

'Forgive me, madame . . . but I'm so afraid! I've been afraid for such a long time now! I hid here to beg you to take me away with you. You are going to go, aren't you? You're not going to stay in this accursed place?'

'I would like to leave,' Catherine said, trying to free herself from the girl's clinging hands. 'But I fear that I am a prisoner here. Come, get up and try and compose yourself. What are you so afraid of? Monseigneur Gilles is not here now.'

'Not now, but he's coming back. You don't know what sort of man this Bluebeard is! He's a monster!'

'Bluebeard?' Sara exclaimed. 'What a funny name!'

'It suits him well,' said the girl, who was still kneeling. 'Most of us who work on his lands call him Bluebeard when the soldiers are out of earshot. He is harsh, cruel and treacherous. . . . He takes what he wants without a care for the suffering he causes.'

Gently, but firmly, Catherine lifted the maidservant to her feet and sat her down on a chest. She sat down beside her.

'What is your name? How did you get here?'

'My name is Guillemette, madame, and I come from Vill-moisen, a big village not far from here. Monseigneur Gilles's men brought us here last year, me and two girls from the village. They said we were to serve the Dame de Rais, but I soon found out that it was really her husband we were to serve. He

T—C

came back to the château for a few days. Jeanette and Denise, my two friends, died soon after our arrival.'

'Died? Of what?' Catherine asked, instinctively dropping her voice.

'Monseigneur and his men amused themselves with them. Jeanette was found in a hayloft ... strangled, and the washer-women found Denise at the foot of one of the towers one morning. Her back was broken.'

'What about you? How did you escape?'

Guillemette gave a tremulous smile and then began to cry.

'They thought I was too thin ... and then the master had to leave before he could find time for me, but he has promised to see me when he returns. So you see, you must take me! I beg you, madame! If I stay here I shall die too, and I want to go home so badly! If you escape, let me go with you. You are my only hope!'

'But I'm not even sure whether I shall be able to escape myself, my poor child. I'm as much a prisoner as you are. . . .'

'I know. All the same, there is a chance for you ... in that little note you've got there!'

Catherine stood up and took a few paces across the room, folding and unfolding the scrap of paper in her fingers. Her face was shadowed by anxiety, but nevertheless somewhere deep inside her a new hope was stirring. The Dame de Rais was bound to know all the ins and outs of this château and any secret entrances or exits. . . . There were certain to be cellars, underground passages. She came back to Guillemette and placed a hand on her shoulder.

'Listen,' she said gently, 'I promise to take you with me if I find a way of escape. Come here tomorrow about midday. I'll tell you then if anything has been arranged ... but you mustn't let your hopes run away with you, you know.'

The girl's face had brightened magically, and her eyes shone with renewed hope. She smiled radiantly at Catherine, then stooped swiftly and kissed her hand.

'Thank you! Oh, thank you, most gracious lady! I shall bless your name and remember you in my prayers till my dying day! I will follow you about like a faithful dog ... if that is what you want.'

'All I want for the present,' Catherine interrupted with a kindly smile, 'is for you to calm down and hurry away from here! They might come looking for you!'

She had barely finished speaking when Guillemette sped from

the room, swift as a bird freed from the cage, dropping a hasty curtsey on the threshold. Sara and Catherine stood gazing at each other in silence for a moment. Then Catherine slowly crossed the room and burned the Dame de Rais's note in the flame of one of the candles. Sara shrugged.

'What are you going to do about that frightened girl?'

'How should I know? I have given her a little hope, and calmed her down a little. Tomorrow I may be able to answer your question. Now, come and help me undress. We might as well try to get some sleep.'

Catherine undressed silently, absorbed in her thoughts – as was Sara herself. The silver comb swept through Catherine's long golden tresses again and again, wielded by the gipsy's loving hands. Sara loved attending to Catherine's hair, and her gestures were gentle and almost ceremonious. She was passionately proud of this crown of living gold, much more so than its owner, who often found these hairdressing sessions tediously long.

'The Lady of the Golden Fleece . . .' Sara murmured. 'Your hair gets more beautiful all the time! I'm sure Monseigneur Philippe would agree with me, for one.'

'I don't wish to hear that name again,' Catherine said briskly. 'The Duke of Burgundy is simply the Duke of Burgundy to me now, and therefore an enemy. And I don't want that Golden Fleece title he's so proud of!'

Just then a terrible cry echoed through the castle, a long-drawn-out howl of agony. The two women stared at each other, white to the lips.

'What's that?' Catherine whispered hoarsely. 'Go and see. . . .'

Sara seized a candle, ran to the door and out into the corridor. Voices could be heard outside, calls, shouted orders and the clank of armoured feet running heavily. Catherine stood with a beating heart, listening. A few minutes later Sara returned. She was ashen-white and seemed scarcely able to stand. Catherine saw her lean against the door jamb and stumble as if about to fall. Her lips moved, but no sound emerged.

Catherine ran and slipped an arm round her waist, leading her to a stool. Then she went and filled a cup at a pitcher which stood near by. Sara's teeth were chattering and her eyes seemed twice their normal size. Deep greenish lines had appeared at the corners of her mouth. She took a few sips of water and shivered. . . .

'My God!' Catherine whispered. 'You frightened me! What

did you see? What has happened? That cry . . .'

'Guillemette . . .' Sara faltered. 'They have picked her up in the courtyard. Her body was smashed to pieces!'

The bronze cup slipped from Catherine's hands and rolled into the hearth.

A certain bustle and stir in the castle woke Catherine from the heavy slumber which had overtaken her towards dawn. She had lain there for hours on end, with Sara beside her.

The noise in the courtyard was growing louder. Catherine leapt to her feet at the foot of the bed, climbing over Sara's recumbent form. She ran barefoot to the window which looked out onto the great courtyard. She pulled open the solid wooden shutters, blinking in the bright sunlight, then pushed open a little leaded window and leant out. Horsemen, packhorses and mules and a swarm of servants thronged about an immense litter in which an imposing wet nurse in a red dress, white bonnet and apron was just settling herself with a little girl of about eighteen months in her arms. A few moments later, Catherine de Rais emerged at the top of the stone flight of steps. She wore the same long grey gown with a matching cape. A light veil shaded her face, but her eyes were red-rimmed and she looked drawn and tired.

Without a glance at the castle windows, she took her place in the litter and a footman lifted up the steps and closed the door. The procession started off and Catherine watched in dismay as it passed under the low archway which led into the outer courtyard and vanished from sight. A moment later there were only three servants left there, sweeping the flagstones.

Catherine slowly shut the window. She saw that Sara was awake and lay watching her from the bed, propped up on one elbow.

'What's the matter? What was that?' she asked, stifling a yawn.

Catherine slumped down on the bed.

'That was my last hope departing! The Dame de Rais has just left the castle with all her goods and chattels. But certainly not willingly!'

CHAPTER FOUR

The Sky Grows Dark

Harvest time came round and Catherine was still seeking a means of escaping from Champtocé before Gilles de Rais returned. But, as time went on, her hopes of succeeding grew fainter and fainter and she began to resign herself to the inevitable confrontation.

Not one messenger had crossed the drawbridge since her arrival and she knew nothing of the events in the outside world. Had Gilles managed to rescue Arnaud de Montsalvy from Richard Venables, or was the captain still a captive of the English? Sara maintained that, if the fighting was still in progress, it was unlikely that Arnaud would rejoin Catherine till a truce was declared. However much he might love her, the love of battle and his sense of duty were too powerful for him not to have insisted on resuming his rightful place among Charles VII's captains.

'At all events, when Messire de Rais returns, you will know how things stand,' she said, hoping to calm Catherine's fears which grew as time passed, especially after an incident which occurred at the end of July, on the Sunday when they were celebrating the Feast of the Sheaves.

On that day, which marked the end of the harvest, the peasants, according to tradition, walked in procession to the château to make an offering of the Javelo – the last wheatsheaf decorated with flowers and ribbons – to the châtelaine. Catherine de Rais was still at Pouzauges, so it was the intrepid Anne de Sille who received the beflowered swathe and provided the customary banquet in the castle courtyard. She had invited Catherine to preside over the repast with her.

'You need a little amusement,' she said. 'Since my noble lord will not allow you the pleasures of the hunt, at least avail yourself of such as may be found within the castle walls.'

Anne de Sille was not unsympathetic beneath her rather masculine manner. Nothing in the world would have induced her to disobey her noble lord. The idea of entertaining her guest would not have struck her had it not been for Catherine's pale cheeks, and the large violet shadows under her eyes. She was much too fond of her own gallops in the open air and in all weathers not to feel pity for a young woman cooped up in a fortress. When she was not too weary from her hunting to lift so much as a finger, she did her best to alleviate her reluctant guest's boredom.

'I am in no mood for rejoicing, madame,' said Catherine. But the châtelaine would hear no excuses.

'Zounds, my dear, you really must take a hold on yourself! You won't spend the rest of your life in this old keep. I don't know what Gilles wants from you, but I do know that he is much too self-absorbed to concentrate on any woman for long ... however beautiful! Now, come and see our country folk sing, dance and make merry. They sing as tunefully as peacocks, but they dance with great energy and drink like fish.'

In some respects, the elderly huntress reminded Catherine of her old friend, Ermengarde de Châteauvilain: the same unflagging energy, intransigent manner, overflowing physical health and appetite for life. Perhaps that was why she accepted her invitation to the feast, to which she went accompanied by Sara. Also, perhaps, because since the sinister death of Guillemette, the little servant girl, nothing unusual had disturbed the even tenor of life at Champtocé. But no sooner had she entered the huge courtyard where long tables stood covered with white cloths and wild flowers, and whole pigs and sheep roasted over bonfires, when she suddenly clutched at Sara's arm for support. It might have been the pungent smell of the roasting meats, or the inevitable stench of the near-by stables, pigsties and cowsheds, but she felt all at once as if the world was wheeling round her and the ground slipping away beneath her feet. A wave of sickness washed over her. She went white, then green. ... Sara cried out:

'What's wrong, Catherine? She's sick! Help!'

Anne de Craon and her ladies-in-waiting were beside them in a moment. The old lady passed an arm round Catherine's waist and barked a stream of orders to her women.

'Here, lay her down – look, this bank will do. Dame Alienor, go and fetch me some water and you, Marie, run to the château. Tell them to bring a litter. Run! Run, you lazy wench!'

The two ladies sped away like arrows to carry out her orders. Anne bent over and studied Catherine's waxen face. Then she flashed a haughty look at Sara.

'Why didn't you tell me she was pregnant?'

'Pregnant?' Sara echoed, flabbergasted. 'But how ...'

Catherine herself had had few doubts on that score since the night she and Arnaud had spent on the boat after their escape from Rouen.

'You don't see who the father can be, is that it?' Anne said, laughing. 'I imagine your mistress must have her own theories about that. Don't look at me all round-eyed! Look, here's Alienor returning – there's no need to let her get wind of this; she's the worst chatterbox in the province. In fact, that's why I keep her,' the old lady added with a chuckle. 'She amuses me!'

Catherine slowly revived under the cold compresses which Anne de Craon laid on her forehead. She blushed and then went pale. At first, she felt a sort of terror. It was alarming to find herself physically weakened just when she most needed her strength and all her wits about her. But the feeling soon passed and a surge of joy swept over her as it dawned upon her that the child she was carrying was Arnaud's too. *Arnaud's* son! It must be a son – handsome and brave as his father . . . and probably as intractable, too. The thought made her smile. So that passionate impulse which had thrown them together in the little boat, that first moment of real freedom and unclouded happiness, was going to have a flesh and blood sequel! Nothing more wonderful could have happened, nothing which would bind her closer to the man she loved! A baby! For a second, her thoughts returned to the child she had lost, the little Philippe who had died, far from her side in Ermengarde's arms. Remorse had tormented her for a long time after his death. She had reproached herself instead of leaving Ermengarde to supply all the love in his life while she amused herself at Court. She had often wondered how she could have spent so long away from him. Perhaps it was because she had not really loved his father. . . . The royal blood of France had flowed in little Philippe's veins. It had all been too grand and imposing for her and she realized that now, for her the child had always been, first and foremost, the Duke of Burgundy's son.

But the one who was now on his way, who already burgeoned within her, would be truly flesh of her flesh, her love incarnate. Something which the little Moorish doctor, Abou-al-Khayr, had said to her a long time ago, when she was carrying Philippe, came into her mind:

'Now that you are following the child's star, any other way would be darkness and night.'

'How pleased Arnaud will be when he knows. . . .' Catherine murmured to herself, radiant with joy.

'Assuming that we get a chance to tell him,' Sara grumbled.

But Catherine refused to allow anything to tarnish her present happiness. All that day and night, while viols and tambourines struck up a sprightly measure for the dancing feet of the good people of Champtocé, Catherine nursed her dream under the watchful eyes of a Sara grown suddenly silent and protective.

During the whole of August, Catherine was so sick she thought she would die a hundred times over. She was attacked by fits of giddiness and nausea. Her stomach could not stand any form of food and what little strength she could muster was drained by painful attacks of vomiting. The scorching heat which dried up the wells, set the dry hayricks alight and even penetrated the thick walls of Champtocé was the severest test of all. All day a burning sun shone in a blue, cloudless sky. The wells had shrunk so much that sweet water became worth its weight in gold. Even the Loire itself began to dry up, exposing its sandy bed here and there like the weft of a piece of frayed cloth. But Catherine never complained. She bore her distress stoically simply because it was Arnaud's child who caused it. Her only fear was that things might go wrong and the child be lost.

She lay in bed all day long, covered only by a light sheet, with the wooden shutters almost closed. Sara would keep her company and sometimes the Dame de Craon too, now that the great heat had put a stop to her hunting. She consoled herself, however, by spending interminable hours telling Catherine of her exploits of former years.

The only person never to cross the threshold was Jean de Craon. Each morning he punctiliously sent along a page for news of his prisoner's health, but he kept as close a watch on her as ever for all that. From what the châtelaine told her, Catherine had a pretty clear picture of the old nobleman's character. It could be expressed in a few words – a blind, passionate love for his grandson. For Jean de Craon, Gilles represented the flower of his race, his god, the being for whose greater power and glory he was ready to commit any crime.

'Gilles was only a child,' Anne said, 'when my husband started encouraging him to kill, pillage and burn his own villages so that he might know the extent of his power. He had great chests of gold dragged before him so that he could tell him that it was all his, that gold was the sovereign good, the key to all happiness.'

'It isn't difficult to guess what the Maréchal is really like,' said Catherine. 'I imagine he loves only himself.'

'That's quite true and I have often deplored it, especially when he ran off with Catherine, my granddaughter. I knew she was bound to be unhappy. That is why I consented to marry my lord. . . . While I'm alive, I can protect Catherine.'

'But doesn't it ever occur to you to question your husband's decisions?'

'No. He's my husband and that is all there is to it. He is the master and I must obey him.'

The word sounded strange on the lips of this arrogant woman, but Catherine was too weak to feel surprised for long. What she missed most was not having a chance to see Gauthier again. She knew that he was kept locked up in the east tower and that he accepted his imprisonment patiently, even philosophically. His cell was clean and reasonably healthy and, above all, cooler than the rest of the castle. He was fed well enough and he was well aware that his fate was in some way bound up with a mysterious bargain between Catherine and Gilles de Rais. All he asked was the right to sell his life dearly if it were ever demanded of him. At the moment, the only thing bothering him was his enforced inactivity. His jailers visited his cell every morning to make certain that he had not started trying to demolish the château stone by stone. This visit was paid by a squad of no fewer than ten men, such was the respect the giant's strength inspired. This ceremony always struck the prisoner as irresistibly funny and he generally accompanied it by roars of laughter. Certainly, Gauthier was in no way agitated about his own fate, but the thought of Catherine's plight did distress him. It was Anne de Craon who had passed all this on to Catherine.

At the beginning of September, when the heat-wave suddenly passed, all Catherine's sickness vanished as suddenly as it had come. She could eat freely, and gradually but surely her strength returned. The morning when the first rains came, she felt strong enough to get out of bed, dress and go to her mirror. It reflected a tiny, wasted face in which huge eyes looked back at her, more strikingly than ever.

'There's nothing left of you but eyes!' Sara grumbled as she laced up Catherine's gown. 'You need to put on a little weight in the face . . . and elsewhere, otherwise this baby is going to be as thin as a rail. No one would ever guess you were pregnant. Your waist is no bigger than a girl's.'

'Don't worry, that won't last! I feel a bit weak still, but how refreshing this rain is!'

The beneficent rain which followed the crushing summer heat soon proved itself just as obstinate. For days and days, a watery curtain was drawn across the countryside, swelling the streams, turning the parched fields green again and the dusty highways into rivers of mud. The day the watchman blew his horn to announce the return of Gilles de Rais to his ancestral home was a day of torrential rain.

At the sound of the horn, Catherine's heart leapt in her breast. Despite the late hour and the lashing rain, she wrapped herself in a thick cloak and climbed up on to the battlements. No one paid the slightest attention to her. Soldiers dragged their armour to and fro, servants ran about with festive clothes, while valets rushed up and down with their arms full of candles knocking people down in the corridors. No one bothered about Catherine, who was allowed to go where she liked within the castle walls.

The wind flapped the banner on the watchtower, catching Catherine's cloak as she stepped out of the narrow winding staircase. Apart from the watchman leaning over the battlements, she was alone.

'Are they still far off?' Catherine asked.

The man at-arms started, because he had not heard her approach. The rain streamed off his helmet. He sketched a salute with a dripping, mailed hand and then pointed towards the river.

'See for yourself, madame! The first banners are appearing along the river.'

Catherine leant over to look. The advance guard was just coming into sight along the road which followed the winding course of the stream. At first, she could only see indistinct shadows among the trees and the rising river mist, but then she caught sight of the banners which hung, heavy with rain, and the dull gleam of armour and, farther off, the wave-like motion of men on horses. A fanfare of trumpets momentarily drowned the drumming of the rain on the slate tiles and the splashing of the great puddles of water. Straining forward at her post, Catherine tried desperately to make out a suit of black armour, or a sparrow-hawk on a helmet, Arnaud's armour and device. ... But night was coming down fast and, as if to sharpen her agitation, a raven croaked overhead like a herald of doom.

'Dame!' the soldier warned. 'Take care. You might fall.'

She reassured him with a smile, but did not move. Her cloak cracked about her like a wet sail. Soon there was the thunder of horses' hooves, the fanfares grew louder and the men more distinct. Catherine had the impression that the exhausted soldiers were making one last effort so that they might make a worthy entry. Chests seemed to swell and stooping backs straightened proudly.

'There is Monseigneur Gilles,' the watchman cried behind her. 'Look, Lady, his violet trappings stand out clearly now. He is riding Nutcracker, his big black war-horse.'

The man's voice vibrated with pride. At that instant, the drawbridge fell with a crash and a great crowd of servants and soldiers rushed out with torches and cries of joy to meet the new arrivals. The inner courtyard was like a great well of fire, glowing flames triumphing over darkness and rain. The watchman had finally taken up a position next to Catherine, his eyes gleaming with excitement.

'Ah! There will be good times now that Monseigneur Gilles is back! He may be hard, but he is generous, and *he* likes the good life!'

In the tone with which he said *'he'* there was a wealth of implied resentment against old Craon, but Catherine was not paying any attention. She went on peering into the darkness. The raindrops dripped into her eyes where they shone like tears.

'You have good eyesight,' she said. 'Can you tell me the names of those surrounding your master? Can you recognize them?'

'Surely,' the watchman answered proudly. 'I see Messire Gilles de Sille, Monseigneur's cousin, and the Sire de Martigne. There is our master's brother, René de la Suze and Messire de Bricqueville...'

'You don't see a seigneur in black armour with a sparrow-hawk crest on his helmet?'

The man stared at the company for a long time and shook his head.

'No, Lady ... I can't see anyone like that. They're close enough now for you to see them clearly.'

She found she could see Gilles de Rais quite plainly now. He rode at the head of his party, an arrogant figure with his nodding plume of violet feathers. Behind him came a group of nobles who could be clearly seen now in the lurid light of a hundred torches. The happy shouts which reached them, coupled with the scent of wet earth, found no echo in Catherine's heart. She leant heavily against the stone wall, suddenly drained of strength. Arnaud was not with these men. ...

She knew now that, up to the very last moment, she had been hoping and expecting to see him again with his mocking smile, the way he had of narrowing his eyes when he looked at her and, above all, to fling herself into the haven of his arms. ... The watchman stared at her, alarmed by her pallor.

'Dame,' he murmured, 'the rain is pouring down again and you are wet through. You are trembling, too. You should go in now.'

He held out a hesitant hand to her and, with the other, took down a torch to light her down the stairs. She gave him an uncertain look and a wan smile and stood up.

'Thank you. You are right, I shall go in. Anyway ... I have nothing more to do here.'

She tottered slightly as the gale caught at her and the watchman had to help her as far as the stairs. The happy cries seemed to have penetrated every nook and cranny of the huge castle and, in Catherine, they aroused as much anger as sorrow. She was not going to stay a moment longer under the same roof as this man who had tricked her so shamefully. She should order him to release Gauthier and open the gates for her so that she could leave this accursed castle at long last. Even if it meant returning to Normandy and attacking Richard Venables with her own two hands, or even crossing to England, she would do it if it would help get Arnaud back. ... As her anger increased, her step grew firmer and her courage and determination returned. She almost ran down the last few steps.

When she returned to her room, Catherine found Sara in conversation with an unknown page whose damp clothing proclaimed him a new arrival. On seeing Catherine, he made her a bow a little too brisk to look respectful.

'I am Poitou, monseigneur's page. He sends me to say that he wishes to see you at once, madame.'

Catherine frowned. This boy, who must have been around fourteen years old, was strikingly beautiful: dark, with fine features and a well-built body which was both powerful and graceful. But he appeared all too aware of his attractions and his insolent manner displeased her. She passed before him and held out her cloak to Sara without looking at him.

'I don't know where you were brought up, my boy, but I
would have thought that, in view of the Maréchal's high rank,
his followers would have been more courteous. At King
Charles's Court, and at Philippe of Burgundy's, pages were boys
from good families.'

The boy's smooth cheeks crimsoned and anger flashed in his
black eyes. He was clearly unused to being treated like this.
Then Catherine turned her violet eyes upon him. She saw him
clench his fists, but then, very slowly, he bent one knee.

'Monseigneur Gilles,' he began again in a muffled voice, 'sends
me to ask Dame Catherine de Brazey to have the kindness to
pay him a visit before the great banquet which is to take place
tonight.'

Catherine looked at the kneeling boy for a moment. She
smiled briefly, then said curtly:

'That's better! Thank you. But I'm afraid there is no question of my going to see your master ... or of my attending the
banquet. Go and tell Gilles de Rais that the Dame de Brazey
awaits an explanation of his behaviour.'

This time, Poitou stared at her with undisguised amazement.

'Go and tell him ...?' he began.

'Yes!' Catherine interrupted. 'And at once! I shall await your
master here. It is high time he learnt whom he has to deal with,
I think.'

The page rose and left without a word. Catherine turned to
meet Sara's glance.

'You have made yourself an enemy,' the gipsy remarked.
'That boy is stiff with pride. He must be the master's favourite.'

'What do I care? I don't see why I should ingratiate myself
with anyone here any more. Gilles de Rais has broken his word.
Arnaud isn't with him.'

'In that case, you are right, and he owes you an explanation.
But do you think he'll come?'

'Yes,' said Catherine. 'I do.'

A quarter of an hour later, Sara opened the door to Gilles de
Rais. He had somehow found time to change his clothes. He
now wore a long, dark blue velvet robe whose sleeves and hem
trailed upon the ground. The signs of the zodiac, embroidered
in gold, silver and red, decorated this garment and gave the
swarthy nobleman the air of a wizard. A huge ruby flashed
red fire from the index finger of his left hand. He looked both
splendid and majestic, but Catherine was in no mood to be
impressed. She sat, very upright, in the only high-backed chair

in the room, leaving her visitor nothing but a stool to sit on, and she had dressed herself in black velvet with a deliberately severe effect. A transparent black veil added to the melancholy effect of her appearance without hiding the gleam of her blonde crown of hair. Sara stood behind with her hands folded over her stomach in the discreet pose of the well-trained servant.

Gilles de Rais greeted her, seeming a little surprised at her haughty bearing, and his smile gleamed in the blue-black darkness of his beard.

'You sent for me, fair Catherine? Here I am, at your command.'

Ignoring both greeting and compliment, Catherine went straight to the point.

'Where is Arnaud de Montsalvy?'

'A strange welcome! What, not even a smile, my dear? Or a kind word? Why this fierce expression to greet one of your most devoted slaves?'

'First answer my question, seigneur. The greetings can wait. How is it you have returned without the man you promised to rescue and restore to me?'

'I have rescued Arnaud de Montsalvy. He is no longer in Richard Venables's hands.'

Catherine felt a surge of relief. Heaven be praised! He was no longer in English hands! But this was quickly followed by a new anxiety.

'Where is he, then?'

'In a safe place. . . . May I sit down? The long ride in the rain has quite exhausted me.'

He pulled out one of the stools near Catherine's chair and sat down upon it, carefully adjusting the heavy folds of his velvet gown. He seemed quite at ease and the smile lingered on his face like a mask, but his deep-set black eyes were cold and watchful.

'What do you call a safe place? With my lord the King?'

Gilles de Rais shook his head and his smile deepened, gaining a slightly ironic edge to it which was not lost on Catherine.

'I call a safe place the château of Sully-sur-Loire whence I had the honour of escorting him and where he now is.'

For all her efforts, Catherine could not conceal her surprise.

'At La Trémoille's? But why? What is he doing there?'

Gilles de Rais stretched out his long legs and held his hands out to the fire. They were exceedingly white hands, of an

almost feminine delicacy. He must take great care of them. ...
He sighed. When he spoke again his voice was very gentle.

'What is he doing there? I really don't know. ... What state
prisoners usually do, I imagine!'

The word struck her like a blow. She sprang to her feet,
gripping the arms of her chair with both hands. She was scarlet
to the roots of her hair and her eyes flashed fire. She felt a
furious desire to kill this nonchalant man who had only been
toying with her these last ten minutes like a cat with a mouse.

'State prisoner? The King's most loyal captain? What is this
nonsense and what sort of fool do you take me for? Enough of
this rubbish, messire. Let us speak plainly, for you appear to
be mocking me. You gave me your word and I believed you,
in spite of the way I have been treated in this house. You know
very well that you were not supposed to take Arnaud to Sully,
but here! *Here!*'

With a sigh expressive of great boredom, Gilles stood up,
thus enabling him to look down on Catherine from his full
height.

'Things have changed since Louviers, my dear. It appears that
you are completely ignorant of recent events ... as, indeed, I
was at Louviers. The days of hollow dreams, illusions and
will-o'-the-wisps are over and the days of sensible folk have
arrived. My cousin, La Trémoille, has the King's ear these days
and he has decided ... shall we say, to tidy away ... anyone
who shows too marked a desire to interfere with his policies
and return to the misty visions of that wretched girl who was
burned by order of Holy Church. It is time that power was
exercised by someone born to the part and not some half-witted
shepherd girl!'

Catherine lost her temper.

'Which merely means that your cousin is "tidying up" so
that he can sit back and grow fatter at his ease, that the poor
King is more under his thumb than ever and that that bloated
ruffian is attacking all Joan's faithful followers ... that
"wretched girl" whom you served on your knees only a year
ago, Messire Maréchal.'

In spite of her anger, Catherine's mind was working fast and
she was watching her adversary. She saw him go pale when
she mentioned La Trémoille's name and concluded that she had
touched him on a sore spot. In her concentration on her love,
she had hardly given a thought to politics and the possible
repercussions of Joan's death on the Court and King. Georges

de la Trémoille and his clique had been fighting against God's emissary for so long now.

Joan embarrassed these greedy nobles whose one idea was to enrich themselves at no matter what cost or whose expense. They had always slyly fought against Joan's influence and had not lifted a finger to save her from the English, and now that she was dead, these unscrupulous people had regained their power over the weak-minded Charles VII. In the wily hands of La Trémoille, the King was but a toy. The fat chamberlain knew his master's weaknesses too well: give him women and amusements galore and one could do with him what one liked. . . .

But Gilles did not reply. His black eyes observed her. She said dryly:

'I should like to know what accusations La Trémoille was able to bring against Arnaud, the very soul of honour and loyalty.'

'Ah, what a fine thing love is – and how I envy Montsalvy for having made such a conquest! Love is blind! Your lover violated the law, my dear, when he entered Rouen without the King's permission, our Lord the King having judged it wiser to abandon the celebrated Maid to her fate. Trying to rescue her was an act of disobedience against the King.'

'I also tried to help in the rescue.'

'And you too are guilty of a crime, dear Catherine. You have been entrusted to my care as Arnaud de Montsalvy is entrusted to my cousin's. You are forbidden to leave this place under penalty of being thrown into a dark dungeon in some dismal fortress somewhere,' the Maréchal explained with silky charm.

Only Catherine's pride prevented her from faltering at this blow. She motioned Sara's hand away and smiled at him with a look of withering contempt.

'Well, well, and to think I took you for a gentleman and thought one could trust the word of a Marshal of France! And you're *nothing*: La Trémoille's lackey, ready to sell his friends to the highest bidder, but you forget that there are others who know the truth about Arnaud and me. La Hire . . .'

'La Hire is a prisoner at Louviers which the English have retaken and your friend, Xaintrailles, has also been taken prisoner. And don't talk to me about the Constable Richemont! He has been banished from Court under pain of death. As for Queen Yolande, his Majesty's meddlesome mother-in-law, she has been given to understand that her properties in Provence demand her attention. She must be at Tarascon by now. ... That's a long way away – Tarascon!'

This time Catherine remained speechless. She felt dizzy before the abyss which Gilles, with calculated cruelty, was opening under her feet. Now she grasped the full subtlety and extent of La Trémoille's machinations. He had steered his craft cleverly, encouraging the King to banish his most loyal supporters and the country's surest bulwarks against the English: the Constable Richemont and Queen Yolande, his wife's mother. And the wretched Charles VII, forgetful of services rendered, his towns reconquered, the consecration at Rheims, had slipped back – joyfully enough, no doubt – into the snare of a facile existence and dubious pleasures.

'So all the blood which was spilt means nothing,' she said sorrowfully. 'The real King of France is La Trémoille and you do not scorn to serve him – you who have the rank of prince!'

'La Trémoille is my cousin, fair lady, and a treaty, signed by both of us, unites me to him for better or worse. But the worst does not seem imminent.'

'In that case, you ought to hand me over to him, too, as you did with Arnaud. We were together at Rouen. We should share the same punishment, since you seem to think we deserve one. Take me to Sully. . . .'

Gilles de Rais burst out laughing, so fiercely and abruptly that Catherine could not help thinking that if wolves ever laughed, they would laugh like that.

'I serve my cousin, but I protect my own interests, my dear. Maybe later . . . I will take you to Sully, but not till I have got what I want from you.'

'What do you want?'

'Two priceless objects for a man passionately addicted to beauty, like myself: you, first of all . . . and then a certain black diamond which has made you almost as celebrated as your admirable hair. . . .'

So that was the object of these tortuous exercises! Was that what Gilles de Rais wanted? Hatred and disgust took possession of her soul. She laughed in his face.

'Are you mad? I wouldn't dream of giving you either of those things, Monsieur le Maréchal. I no longer have the diamond and my body is no longer my own: I am expecting a child. . . .'

De Rais's face darkened with disappointment. He stepped up

to her and took her wrist, then stood back to examine her figure, her slightly thickened waist.

'True, i' faith!' he exclaimed in a shaking voice, but he managed to pull himself together with an effort, and smiled again.

'Ah, well . . . I don't mind waiting, for the woman as well as for the diamond! I know you no longer have this matchless stone with you, but it still belongs to you, as soon as you are able to contact a certain messenger . . . this monk who seems to have such easy access to the city of Rouen. Isn't that so?'

Heavens, he knew everything! Catherine was in his power, as helpless as a new-fledged chicken, but her own position troubled her less than Arnaud's handed over, defenceless, to his worst enemy. What would happen to him in La Trémoille's château, encircled by the Loire? Feeling suddenly drained of strength, she sank back in her chair, struggling against an attack of faintness. All at once she longed to die, to stop battling against such enormous odds. No sooner had she overcome one obstacle, than she perceived a larger one behind it. Doubtless it would continue like this till the end of time, till her strength gave out. . . .

'What is the use?' she said to herself, unaware that she was speaking her thoughts aloud. 'It's all hopeless. I expect Arnaud is already dead. . . .'

'If it rested with La Trémoille alone,' Gilles replied casually, 'that would doubtless be the case, but our dear Arnaud is so attractive . . . and my fair cousin Catherine has always shown a marked weakness for him. Do not fear, my dear, the Dame de la Trémoille is watching over him as tenderly . . . perhaps even more tenderly, than you yourself would be capable of! You know that she has always been attracted to him!'

This last jibe and all it implied was too much for Catherine. With a cry of pain, she collapsed into Sara's arms and began to sob uncontrollably, pierced to the quick. The sight of her sufferings dispersed Sara's caution to the winds.

'Now go, monseigneur!' she said roughly. 'You have done enough harm already.'

He shrugged and started towards the door. Then he turned and addressed Sara:

'Harm? Come now, it all depends how you look at things. Catherine has no reason to leave this house where she will always be treated as she deserves . . . like a queen! I don't see what's so tragic about that. You should tell her, my girl, that a clever woman has a lot to gain from running with the wolves. My cousin is all-powerful . . . and so am I!'

'Really?'

Sara let Catherine go and stood up. Her face was ashen-pale and her dark eyes fixed and dilated. She flung out an arm and walked towards the Maréchal with the shuffling steps of a sleep-walker . . . he frowned and moved back . . . Catherine realized that Sara was in the grip of one of those strange moments of second sight when the secrets of the future were revealed to her, and stopped weeping and held her breath. Sara's voice rose eerily:

'Your power is founded on dust and ashes, Gilles de Rais. . . . There is blood around you, pools of blood . . . and you are drowning and choking in it . . . I hear cries of pain; mouths crying out for vengeance; outstretched hands imploring justice. And justice will come . . . in time! I see a great town by the sea . . . a great crowd . . . a triple gibbet! I hear the sound of bells and prayers. . . . You will be hanged, Gilles de Rais, and your body devoured by the flames!'

The prophetic voice fell silent. The Seigneur de Rais gave a cry of terror and fled. . . .

All night long, the château resounded to the sounds of feasting and merrymaking. In the great hall, Gilles and his family and captains ate and drank while the soldiery and the women servants amused themselves riotously below stairs, in the kitchens and guardrooms. Cries, laughter and drinking songs penetrated even the massive stone walls of Champtocé, rose from the courtyards up the staircases and as far as the room where Catherine was racking her brains to think of a way to escape from her prison.

'Why didn't I listen to you?' she kept repeating to Sara. 'Why did I venture into this wasps' nest? I should have gone straight to Bourges and tried to see the Queen.'

'You didn't know how carefully the trap had been laid. How could you? Besides, the first armed guard would have arrested you and flung you into a dungeon.'

'It couldn't have been worse than this château! I'm well and truly trapped! Even my body has grown heavy and imprisons me. What am I to do? How am I to get out of here?'

'Calm yourself,' Sara murmured, caressing her hair gently. 'Calm yourself, I beg you. God will send you help, I'm certain of it. You must wait and pray . . . and watch for a favourable opportunity. The first thing is to escape. Then ...'

'... Then rush off and help Arnaud and ...'

'You mean, go to Sully? And risk falling into La Trémoille's
hands for the sole pleasure of finishing up in the same dungeon
as Arnaud? I should think not! First look for a place where
you will be safe, and then find someone who will champion you
and present your case to the King ... even if it means going all
the way to Provence to ask Madame Yolande to plead your
cause. Try and rest, my pretty; the mind works more clearly
when the spirit is tranquil. I am here beside you; I will look
after you, and between us we shall find a way out. ...'

Lulled by her old friend's voice, Catherine gradually calmed
down and took courage, but, towards dawn, a mailed fist
crashed on the door. Catherine saw her room invaded by
soldiers, like a scene in a bad dream. She cried out, but before
she could even protest, Sara had been snatched away from her
and dragged into the corridor....

'Monseigneur Gilles has ordered me to arrest the witch,' the
sergeant cried before the heavy oak door swung shut behind
him. And then Catherine realized that she was alone, forsaken
by everyone and even by Heaven itself. Desperate sobs shook
her body as she fell back among the pillows. ...

CHAPTER FIVE

The Ways of the Lord

Catherine's mood of despair did not last long; indeed, she would never have given way to it had the events of that night not brought her to the very limits of her courage and endurance. The fighting spirit was too strong in her. Before long, she was ready to pitch herself head first into the fray again. A wild anger seized her, warming her weary muscles, sending the blood racing back to her heart, working on her like a restorative. She leapt from the bed and made a rapid toilette, throwing water over her face to reduce the puffiness from her weeping, but she put a lot of time into doing her hair, brushing and brushing it till it gleamed and her features slowly returned to normal. Catherine had always known that her beauty was her strongest weapon and, if she wished to win this new battle, she must not present herself with a victim's ravaged face. Instinct told her that weakness was a disadvantage with a man like Gilles de Rais!

After she had dressed her hair, she felt better. She put on a little perfume and a brown velvet dress lined with white satin and edged with a narrow band of white ermine. She decided against any of the traditional and slightly cumbersome head-dresses then in fashion and threw a floating white veil over her hair instead. She found some gloves, picked up her Missal and went to the chapel where the castle chaplain was in the habit of saying early Mass for the servants. In her weakness and loneliness she needed the solace of religion.

There, too, the after-effects of the banquet and merrymaking were plain to see. Apart from the chaplain and a small acolyte, the little chapel was empty and Catherine felt as though she had God all to herself. The chapel was tiny but exquisite. Gilles de Rais's passion for beauty had made a jewel of it: a blue back-drop for an altar worked in massive gold and a great gold and ebony crucifix such as Catherine had rarely seen. The vaulted roof was blue, spangled with gold stars, the windows tinted blue with gold patterns, the cushions scattered about on the pews were blue and so, too, were the carpets which gave a

rather too sensual and luxurious atmosphere to the place. It
was more a hymn to the glory of Gilles than of God. He must
come there to dream of a sumptuous Heaven where he would
have pride of place as he did here and rule over a mob on their
knees.

But Catherine's mind was temporarily closed to the beauties
of the place. She knelt with hands folded and closed eyes, be-
seeching God to grant her the courage and strength she so desperately needed. She took communion with fervour and then,
for a long while, remained on her knees praying to the Holy
Mother of God for all those she loved and who were now in
great danger, like herself. At last, feeling somewhat comforted,
she left the chapel just as a bleary-eyed watchman decided,
rather belatedly, to sound his horn for the opening of the gates.
The weather was fine this morning and the puddles rosy with
dawn light. Scullions were idling across the courtyard with
baskets of scraps and left-overs from the night before, yawning
uncontrollably as they went. The château was setting to work
to clear away the traces of the festivities in readiness for a new
day.

Catherine doubted that Gilles would be awake at this hour,
but she set out resolutely in the direction of his apartments.
She soon discovered that this was no easy undertaking. There
was at least one sleeping soldier on every step of the stairs.
They lay, curled up or stretched out on the ground, some of
them still clutching a cask of wine or a flagon. The smell which
rose from the pools of spilt wine was so acrid and nauseating
that Catherine had to hold a sachet of perfume to her nose. All
these sleepers snored resoundingly and the noise they made
sounded like a mad organist. There were a few women here and
there, also sleeping, mouths open and hair sticky with wine.
Some of them, even in the depths of sleep, seemed to be trying
to pull their disordered clothing together. Catherine stepped
over this sleeping multitude with a grimace of disgust without
paying too much attention to where she put her feet.

The great hall was in the same state of chaos. Some nobles
were still there, fast asleep in their high-backed chairs.
Catherine passed through and emerged in the other wing of
the castle. She finally reached the door of Gilles's chamber,
which she recognized because old Anne de Craon had pointed
it out to her on a tour of the building. On either side of the door
a burnt-out torch flickered feebly. There was a figure lying
stretched out across the doorway. The light from a near-by win-

dow fell on the sleeper's face and Catherine recognized Poitou, the page. She prodded him with her foot, and he woke with an oath.

'Who goes there?'

He recognized Catherine and, in an instant, was on his feet. He looked as if he had drunk too much wine. His face was grey, his eyes dulled and there were deep lines of weariness on either side of his mouth.

'Dame, what do you want?' he asked hoarsely.

'To see your master; at once!'

Poitou shrugged and tried rather clumsily to fasten his doublet which was only held together by a belt.

'He is asleep and I fear he could not hear you.'

'If you mean that he is too drunk to understand what I have to say to him, I don't believe it. He was sober enough an hour ago when he had my maid arrested. I want an explanation. Go and fetch him!'

The boy shook his head and his face lengthened.

'Dame, I have no desire to offend you and I beg you to believe me, but anyone entering Monseigneur Gilles's room does so at the risk of his life.'

'What do I care about your life? I want to see him,' Catherine cried angrily.

'I'm not talking about my life, Dame, but yours. He will kill me undoubtedly if I go in ... but the next blow would be for you.'

In spite of her determination, Catherine wavered. Poitou was clearly in earnest and he must know his master well. The young page added imploringly in a softer voice:

'Believe me, Dame Catherine, I am not joking. It would be far better for you to wait till later. I will say that you came and wished to speak to him, but please go now, for pity's sake. Please go!' He said no more. The door opened and Gilles de Rais himself stepped out.

Catherine's first instinct was to run away. He wore nothing but red hose tightly belted round the waist. His muscular torso was bare and it was covered with thick, curly black hair. His appearance and strong smell were irresistibly reminiscent of an unchained beast. A ray of sunshine falling across his face through a red glass pane gave it a touch of the infernal. His bloodshot eyes flashed with recognition when he saw Catherine. He sent the page stumbling with a blow, then he gripped Catherine's arm, his fingers like a vice.

'Come!' was all he said.

As they entered the room, Catherine went cold with fright. The shutters were closed and the curtains drawn and the room was in almost total darkness. A little flickering light came from an oil lamp on a wooden coffer. The room was suffocatingly hot and the smell of wine and human bodies made Catherine feel sick. She tried to free herself, but Gilles held her fast.

'Let me go!' she cried in a voice half strangled with terror, but he took no heed. He pulled her over to the bed which was unmade and spilling coverlets and sheets over the floor. In the lamp's reddish glow, Catherine saw a human form moving amidst the cushions and covers. Gilles stretched out an arm and revealed a naked girl whimpering and trying to hide herself in her long black hair.

'Go away!' he commanded, still in the same strangely absent tone of voice.

The girl mumbled something. Catherine noticed that her adolescent body was marked by curious dark stripes and that she seemed petrified with terror. She must have been very young – barely fifteen. She seemed to be trying to hide herself behind one of the bedposts, but she might as well not have bothered. Gilles snatched up a dog whip and struck her three times.

'I said go!' he roared.

The girl screamed, but ran stumbling towards the door. Catherine saw her white body gleam for an instant in the sunny corridor. Blind panic seized her as she realized that Poitou had not exaggerated and that the Lord of Champtocé was really half-demented at this moment. She tried to run to the door, but once again that terrible hand fell upon her.

'Not you,' he growled. 'You stay!'

He flung the whip away and without more ado snatched her in his arms. For a moment Catherine felt as if she would suffocate. She was crushed against a hard matted chest. It was rather like being hugged by a bear, except that this one smelt of sweat and wine. Catherine struggled desperately, hitting him with her fists and pushing him away with all her strength. It was not easy. He was a strong man at any time and drunkenness had redoubled his strength. She felt his hot lips against her neck and lost her balance. He was pulling her off the floor towards the bed. He writhed against her and murmured something unintelligible. He was beyond coherent speech or thought. Only cunning could procure her escape. . . .

All at once she stopped struggling and allowed him to drag her on to the bed, but no sooner had her back touched the mattress than she took advantage of his momentary loss of balance and rolled over like an eel so that she fell off the bed on the far side. The bed creaked as Gilles flung himself upon her – as he imagined. Finding her gone, he gave a howl of rage, but, by now, Catherine had run to the window and flung back the shutters. Sunshine, flooding into the room, blinded him for a moment as he lay stretched out on the bed.

He leapt to his feet and Catherine blenched as she saw him pull out a dagger. His face was contorted like a madman's. She had imagined that the daylight would have sobered him and that chasing away the darkness would have chased away the devils too, but she saw that she had guessed wrongly and that his worst instincts had now been unleashed. He strode towards her, grinding his teeth. His eyes were murderous. She gazed around her frantically for a weapon, for something to defend herself with. . . . Then she saw a basin full of dirty water standing beside an ewer on top of a chest. It was her only chance. . . .

She snatched up the basin – a heavy thing of wrought silver – and flung it with all her strength at Gilles's head. It crashed to the floor while the man himself, half-blinded by this unexpected deluge, stumbled and fell. Catherine did not wait to see what he would do next. She ran to the door, drew back the bolt and ran out. In the gallery, she found herself face to face with Poitou.

'You were right. He is mad!' she whispered.

'Not mad, but strange. Go back to your room, Dame Catherine, and I will calm him. I know what to do. By Heaven, you have been lucky. I never believed you would come out of there alive.'

It was Catherine who almost went out of her mind during the hours which followed. The jaws of the trap which held her had never looked more terrifying. What use were courage and a clear head when dealing with a creature like Gilles? She had come up against the most fearful obstacle of all – mental illness – and she was appalled by the sinister stranger she had discovered in Gilles.

When Anne de Craon came into her room towards midday, she felt almost relieved. The inhabitants of this accursed castle all seemed to her so weird and abnormal in the distorting glass of fear that Anne de Craon struck her as extraordinarily wholesome and welcome in comparison. She found, however, that the old lady was herself in a state of acute agitation.

'Why did you do it? Why did you go to see Gilles? You foolish child, didn't you know that no one, not even his grandfather, has the right to enter his room after he retires for the night?'

'How could I have known?' Catherine protested. 'And how was I to know the man was half mad?'

'I believe he is quite out of his mind and darkness seems to release all sorts of uncontrollable evil forces within him. The girls and boys he takes are too frightened to admit it, but it is rash to try and inquire too deeply into another person's secret soul, even when that person is a member of one's own family.'

'But what about his wife?'

The old countess shrugged.

'Since the birth of little Marie, Gilles has never entered her chamber. When he is here, he spends the night with his favoured companions – Sille, Bricqueville and that insolent page whom he showers with gifts and favours. My granddaughter and the child are better off at Pouzauges where we have sent them. But enough of that! I am here to get you to appear at supper. Gilles insists.'

'I don't have to obey him! I won't go! All I want is for him to release my servants. That is why I went to see him this morning.'

'And you only succeeded in stirring up a terrible scene. I am not exaggerating, Catherine, when I tell you that you owe your life to my husband. Now please, I implore you, come to supper. Don't provoke him too far ... especially if you care for your servants' safety.'

Catherine sank down on her bed, despairing, and looked at Anne de Craon with eyes swimming with tears.

'Can't you understand how I feel? I know you are kind and sympathetic. I am held here against my will, a prisoner for quite imaginary crimes; my loyal followers are taken from me; then, on top of everything else, I am expected to be charming to my jailer. Isn't that too much to ask?'

The old lady's sharp-featured face suddenly softened into an expression of amazing sweetness. She bent and embraced Catherine.

'My dear, I have learnt from many long years of experience that, in this century, we women must be prepared to fight right through our lives, whatever our rank or wealth. And our worst enemy is not war, plague, death or ruin, but man him-self. We must fight him with such weapons as we possess! Sometimes it is better to bend like a reed than stand firm and risk being broken. Believe me. Come to dinner tonight and make yourself as beautiful as possible!'

'I don't want Messire Gilles to think I am trying to capti-vate him!' Catherine protested.

'That isn't the idea at all, but beauty of any sort has a strange power over Gilles. He makes such a cult of it that one might almost say it awes him, especially when he is starved of it. I know him well. Take my advice. I shall send my women to you.'

At the hour when the night watch sounded the all-clear from the battlements, Catherine appeared in the great hall, framed like some unearthly vision in the dark doorway. She had never looked so pale ... or so beautiful! A beauty at once tragic and wistful! Her crimson velvet gown framed her dazzling shoulders and bosom, unadorned by a single jewel. Her match-ing horned headdress trailed a misty-red, long silken veil behind her. She looked like a tongue of flame, but, in her narrow, frozen face, only the huge eyes and tender mouth seemed alive. A silence fell as she advanced slowly between a double line of footmen, as if everyone present had been put under a spell. Gilles de Rais was the first to break the charm. He stepped down from the high table and strode swiftly towards her to offer her his hand. Together, they went up to the table where Jean de Craon, his wife and the captains of the house were already seated. Gilles motioned her into the place next to his own.

'You are very beautiful tonight,' he said abruptly. 'I must thank you for accepting my invitation. I trust you will forgive the incident of this morning.'

'I had already forgotten it, monseigneur,' Catherine murmured.

They did not speak again during the meal. Catherine felt Gilles's eyes on her from time to time, but she never looked up from her plate except to speak to old Craon who was doing his best to keep the conversation alive. The fish and venison which was set before her she barely tasted, but the Sire de Rais, on the other hand, fell on his food like a wolf, devouring slices of pâtés and pies, whole fowls and an entire haunch of venison. He washed it all down with great draughts of Anjou wine with which the cup-bearer standing behind his chair kept his goblet filled. The wine gradually began to take effect on him and his face grew flushed. As the sweetmeats were being carried round, he suddenly turned to Catherine and addressed her.

'Poitou tells me you wanted to speak to me this morning. What did you want?'

Catherine inclined slightly towards him. The moment had come. She gave a little cough to clear her throat, but she looked Gilles full in the eye.

'This morning, at dawn, you had my maid, Sara, seized and taken from me. What am I saying? She is much more to me than a maid: she brought me up and is my most faithful friend. After my mother, she is the person I love most in the world.'

Her voice trembled slightly as she tried to express her feelings for Sara, but she forced herself to go on, gripping her fingers tightly to help control her emotions.

'Furthermore, my squire, Gauthier Strongitharm, was thrown into prison the very night of my arrival here. They have always refused to release him, because they said you must give judgement on him first. So now it is to you, monseigneur, that I address my request for the release of my servants.'

Gilles struck the table so forcefully that the cups and plates rattled.

'Your squire interfered in matters which did not concern him! He wounded one of my men and normally he would have been hanged long ago. To please you, however, I have decided to give him a chance to save his miserable skin and get himself strung up somewhere else.'

'What chance?'

'Tomorrow he will be taken out of the castle and given a head start. Then I and my men and dogs will set off after him. If we catch him, he will be hanged, but if he gets away, he will be allowed to go free.'

Catherine sprang to her feet so violently that her tall chair crashed to the floor. She drew herself up and glared at him with blazing eyes, her face ashen.

'So! A man-hunt! A most delicate treat for a bored nobleman! That is how you honour my request! That is how you respect the code which says that my servants are my own responsibility!'

'You are in my power! It is only kindness which prompts me to give him this chance at all. Let me remind you that I could easily have strung your fellow up in an instant and have done with it. You could be handed over to the King's men.'

'Don't try to pretend – you mean La Trémoille's men! I would have nothing to fear from King Charles's men.'

Now Gilles too had risen to his feet. His face was twisted with rage and his hand groped about on the table for a knife.

'You will doubtless change your tune before long, fair lady! My mind is made up. This Gauthier will stake his life against my hounds tomorrow. If you refuse, I shall have him hanged at once. As for your witch – she may thank her master, Satan, that I have certain questions to put to her, otherwise she would be tied to a stake now with a good pile of firewood under her. I need her and I'm keeping her! Later on I shall decide what to do with her.'

Catherine looked the Sire de Rais up and down with inexpressible scorn and contempt. Her voice rang out cold and hard as steel as she replied:

'And you *dare* to wear the golden spurs of a knight? You *dare* to call yourself a Marshal of France and carry the *fleur-de-lis* on your coat of arms? The meanest lackey in this hall knows more of honour and loyalty than you! Hang and burn my servants and kill me – kill too, now that you have handed your companion-in-arms, Arnaud de Montsalvy, to your cousin. With my last breath, I shall call on Heaven to witness that Gilles de Rais is a traitor and a felon!'

Amidst the shocked hush which had fallen upon the hall, where even the footmen held their breath, she snatched up Gilles's great golden cup and dashed the contents in his face.

'Drink, Monsieur Maréchal, this is the blood of cowards!'

Ignoring the startled murmur which greeted this action, she turned and swept out of the room, the red veil on her headdress floating out behind her like the head crest of an oriflamme. Gilles de Rais slowly wiped the drops of wine off his face and beard with the back of his hand.

Once outside the room, Catherine paused for a moment to take breath. Such violent emotions were bad for her in her condition and she was suffocating in her dress. Then, feeling a little calmer, she turned and began slowly climbing the stairs which led to her room. She had mounted a few steps when she heard running feet behind her. The next moment, she flattened herself against the wall with a cry of terror. Gilles de Rais sprang towards her, black with anger, and seized her by the throat so brutally that she could not help moaning with pain. His hard hands hurt her. . . . He must have noticed for he tightened his grip.

'Now listen to me, Catherine! Don't ever repeat what you have just said; not if you set any store by your continued existence! I am not the man to submit to a public humiliation. One more display like that and I might well strangle you!'

It was strange, but suddenly she felt not the slightest fear of him. He looked dreadful with his face deformed by fury and she was sure that he was going to kill her, but she answered him calmly:

'If you knew how little I cared. . . .'

'What?'

'It would not matter to me at all, Messire Gilles. Consider my position. Arnaud is probably already dead. Gauthier will no doubt be torn to pieces by your dogs tomorrow and then, I suppose, it will be my good Sara's turn. How can you expect me to feel much interest in life under these circumstances? Kill me, messire. Kill me at once, if that is your wish. You would be doing me a service.'

This was not vain bravado, but true sincerity, a sincerity so impressive that it pierced the veil of fury which blinded Gilles. His face, under Catherine's resigned gaze, slowly relaxed. He opened his mouth, but no sound came forth. Then he let his hands fall, turned away and heavily descended the steps again.

Catherine had not moved. When Gilles's footsteps died away in the depths of the great hall, she gave a great sigh and went on up the stairs, rubbing her bruised throat with one hand.

At dawn, Catherine, who had not slept all night, sprang out of bed. She knew that the hunt would leave the château at first light and she wanted to climb to the watchtower to follow the gruesome expedition as far as she could. Her fire had gone out and she shivered in the chilly air, but there were already sounds of movement coming from the courtyard. She snatched up a hooded cloak and wrapped it hastily about her.

She was about to leave her room when she noticed a slip of paper pushed under the door. On it were traced seven words which Catherine had some difficulty deciphering in the faint dawn light: 'I will do what I can. A.' Catherine's torment eased a little as she read this and the weight on her chest seemed to lift a little. If the old countess was on her side, Gauthier might still have some chance of escaping from this hideous affair with his life. Suddenly she made up her mind: she would follow the hunt herself, even if it killed her!

She tore off the cloak and hurriedly pulled on a thick woollen dress and stockings and stout leather shoes. She braided her hair tightly over her ears and once more flung on the voluminous cloak. She did not forget her little reliquary either and tucked it into her bodice after addressing to it a somewhat curious prayer:

'If you really are St James, help me, because you are so powerful, but if it was you who made this, Barnaby, then you must help me to save a friend whom you too would have loved.'

She stepped out into the courtyard as the prisoner was being led out. Gauthier was smeared with dirt and mud and a thick, reddish beard hid most of his face. He wore nothing but his breeches and a shirt laced up the front and the chill air made him shiver, but he seemed in reasonably good health. He was chained at the wrists and ankles. He paused a moment on the threshold to take a breath of fresh air.

'By Odin! That smells good!'

A blow from a pikestaff silenced him, but he managed a smile despite the pain, because just then he caught sight of Catherine. She went over to him, but then a sergeant stepped forward and barred her way.

'Monseigneur Gilles had forbidden anyone to talk to the prisoner.'

'I don't care what Monseigneur Gilles says . . .'

'Perhaps not, Dame, but I do. Come on now. Quick march . . .'

'Don't be afraid,' Gauthier cried, thus earning himself another blow from the pikestaff. 'I haven't been turned to dog food yet!'

The horses were being led out from the stables together with a huge pack of enormous mastiffs all barking like demons and straining at their leashes. They were strongly-built brutes, wild beasts whose snarling jaws revealed rows of sharp white teeth.

'They have not eaten since yesterday morning,' Gilles de Rais announced coldly behind Catherine. 'They will be all the more eager in the chase!'

He stood, smiling, in the entrance to the turret staircase, negligently pulling on a pair of gloves as he watched the dogs being brought out. The Dame de Craon stood behind him dressed in her usual hunting green and with her was the old Sire de Craon leaning on a stick. He had come to watch the hunt set out. He seemed to have aged considerably of late and his stoop was much more pronounced.

'Free the man!' Gilles cried.

At once the sergeant struck off Gauthier's chains and he

stretched out his long limbs with evident relief. The men-at-arms prodded him towards the drawbridge at lance point. With a parting wave to Catherine, he bounded out towards the open. Gilles called after him:

'We will give you half an hour's start, bumpkin! Make the most of it!'

Then he turned to Catherine and said conversationally:

'See how the dogs are straining at their leashes! They are raring to go! I gave instructions this morning for your friend to be rubbed down with the blood of an old buck which had been slaughtered some time ago. He stinks like a rotting corpse and the dogs will have little difficulty in picking up his scent.'

'If he knows anything about hunting,' old Anne interjected with a shrug, 'he will give you the slip, grandson! Your hunting dogs are strong and eager, but they are not infallible.'

'What do you say to this? It is a recent gift from my dear cousin.'

Catherine's eyes widened in horror. A gigantic kennelman, dressed from head to toe in stout leather, had just emerged from a dungeon leading behind him a long, supple form whose black and yellow coat rippled as it moved. It was a magnificent leopard, its oblique, green eyes flashing as it looked about. At the sight of this creature, the servants ran for shelter, squawking like a clutch of startled hens, but the beast ignored them and the dogs which growled ferociously at the sight of the big cat. The leopard took one look at them, spat warningly with a gleam of needle-sharp fangs and stretched itself out calmly along the ground.

'Well, what do you think?' Gilles asked Catherine, looking at her narrowly. 'Do you think a man could escape from a hunter like that, however fleet he were?'

She forced herself to look up and meet his eyes.

'Give me a horse. I want to follow the hunt!'

He drew back, astonished. Clearly he had not been expecting this request.

'What is the idea? Are you hoping to use the hunt as a cover for your own escape?'

'And leave Sara in your hands? You don't know me very well,' she said, shrugging contemptuously.

'Must I then remind you that you are pregnant ... almost five months pregnant?'

'Women of my class ride till the day they are brought to bed!'

Gilles's eyes narrowed to black, shining slits.

'And what if you were to lose your child: the precious child of your dear Montsalvy?'

'He'll give me others!' Catherine retorted. There was so much arrogance in the bold shamelessness of her reply that Gilles turned and beckoned to Sille.

'A horse for Dame Catherine. Or, rather, a saddle hack. Give her that mare, Morgane, then I can be sure she will not leave me. Morgane follows Nutcracker about like a shadow.'

A small white mare with slender legs and a long tail was led out and trotted over beside Gilles's great black war-horse. He gave her his hand to help her to mount, then sprang into the saddle. The others were already mounted and Catherine noticed Anne de Craon's curious behaviour. She seemed oblivious of what was going on around her and sat, absently stroking her horse's neck as it pranced and pawed impatiently at the ground. She did not appear to have noticed that Catherine was joining the hunt. Her eyes were fixed upon the gateway through which the countryside beyond could be glimpsed. Catherine tried to catch her eye, but failed. She longed to feel that she had an ally but she had to content herself with stroking Morgane's neck. There was still some time to wait. Gilles gazed up at the sundial on the north tower. Behind him were ranged all his captains, wearing leather under their armorial tunics, waiting with the patience of a highly disciplined body of troops.

Suddenly Gilles raised his gloved hand.

'The half-hour is up. The hunt begins!'

Horses and riders jostled together. The dogs set off in front, almost dragging their handlers with them. The air was full of their baying. The Dame de Craon sped after them.

'My noble grandmother does not care a fig for the quarry so long as she gets a good day's hunting,' Gilles commented dryly to Catherine. 'You may be sure that she will give chase to your Norman as passionately as though he were an old boar!'

Side by side, the little white mare and the black charger bounded across the drawbridge.

As she left the château, Catherine saw that the road to the village and the river was barred by a cordon of soldiers. They must have feared that their quarry would head for the river and attempt to swim across it, thus putting an insuperable barrier between himself and his pursuers. The men, all chosen for their height and girth, their faces expressionless beneath their helmets, stood out in strange contrast to the sandy, flat countryside from which arose the ghostly towers of Montjean and the masts of ships which had sailed up-river from Nantes.

'You leave nothing to chance,' Catherine ground out through clenched teeth.

'I did not want our day's sport to be unfairly curtailed,' Gilles answered with an amiable smile.

Meanwhile, the dogs were making for the shores of the lake. Deep footprints sunk into the muddy shore showed that the man must have run that way making for the forest. The forest! His own kingdom, woodcutter that he was of the great virgin forests of Normandy! Despite the recent rains, the grass was turning yellow and did not show up green again till they were deep among the trees. Beyond the lake, the autumnal forest glowed like a great golden pelt with patches of scarlet, already beginning to moult on to the forest floor. High above, a flight of migratory birds flew past on their way south. Catherine envied them their freedom and their wonderful gift of being able to leave the earth behind them and fly up into the blue in search of sun and warmth. More cruelly than ever she felt the terrible danger which threatened Gauthier, and her own helplessness!

The dogs followed the man's track like the good hunters they were. The leopard was much more indolent. The great beast seemed to find the expedition tedious, and his indifferent eyes glanced around him, totally ignoring the howling, struggling pack of mastiffs who were like the disordered advance guard of some phlegmatic prince. Deeper in the forest, the trees thinned out and there was more light. Sometimes the pack stopped, sniffing the wind; then a huntsman would sound the horn to show that the scent had been picked up again and the party set off once more.

'Unleash the dogs!' Gilles cried.

The dogs sprang forward like arrows; the horses broke into a gallop. In front of her, Catherine could see Nutcracker's black tail tossing and gleaming. The little mare followed him like a shadow. A little way ahead, she saw Anne de Craon's green veil floating between the russet leaves. It was a long time since Catherine had been hunting, but she found all her old skill returning automatically as she rode. Philippe of Burgundy had been an exacting master where horsemanship was concerned and he adored hunting like all the Valois family. Under his tutelage, Catherine had learnt all the finer points of the chase

and knew precisely what could be done with a horse. There
wasn't a woman alive, and few men for that matter, who rode
as skilfully, or as elegantly. The Duke Philippe had been very
proud of her in those days, but she had taken care that Gilles
should have no suspicion of this and contented herself with
appearing merely competent. Meanwhile, she studied her
mount. Morgane was clearly much attracted to the great black
stallion, but, on the other hand, she was finely bred and her
mouth was sensitive. She would not resist if the hand on the
reins was firm enough.

If Gauthier's life had not depended on this barbarous hunt,
Catherine would have enjoyed her gallop in the open air. The
baying dogs and the huntsman's horn filled the forest with a
cheerful din.

The pack paused for a moment in the middle of a little clearing where one magnificent oak stood alone. One of the mastiffs
stood, nose raised, for a moment, then he snorted and went off
to the right of the gigantic tree. The rest followed. Gilles
sneered.

'He won't escape! We'll soon find him shivering in a corner
somewhere ... waiting for the dogs. I just hope they leave
something of him. ...'

Just then a terrifying uproar filled the wood, sending the
birds into a panic and a cold shiver running down Catherine's
spine. She felt a cold sweat breaking out all over her. The
leopard growled and, with one powerful spring, broke free from
the man who held him. Catherine saw a streak of yellow
lightning flash through the undergrowth in the opposite direction from the one the dogs had taken. Anne de Craon stopped
first with a look of astonishment, followed by Gilles, swearing
horribly. Catherine's eyes met those of the old lady. The latter
made an imperious gesture towards her which she understood
with a flash of inspiration. She snatched a pin from her bodice
and drove it fiercely into Nutcracker's black haunch. The
horse whinnied with pain and then sped off like a thunderbolt
on the heels of the dogs. Catherine dragged on her reins with
all her strength so that the little mare was forced to remain
where she was, willy-nilly. Anne de Craon was already beside
her.

'Quick! We must follow the leopard. I hadn't counted on
that confounded beast!'

As they hastened after the great cat, Catherine asked:
'What did you do?'

'One of my servants was waiting here for the pack with a
young buck, a two-year-old which had been caught a couple of
days ago. I sent word to your peasant to make his way here
and then climb into the oak where he would have been hidden from view while the dogs set off after the buck, but that
damned cat saw through that ruse. He is off on the right track
and we must catch him before he reaches the man.'

The wind dispersed Catherine's words almost before they
were out of her mouth, but she just managed to make herself
heard.

'But what about Gilles and the rest?'

'They will all follow the dogs – and my young buck – for a
moment until they discover their mistake. That gives us a little
time.'

'But how ... will you stop the leopard from attacking?'

'With this!' Anne de Craon drew a sharply-pointed ash boar
spear from the pommel of her saddle. The two horses sped on,
foaming at the bit, through a brilliant autumnal setting, ankle-
deep in fallen leaves. Soon they reached a delightful little clearing carpeted with moss, enclosed by ranks of trees and opening
out into a rock defile at the far end. Thin spears of sunlight
pierced the leafy dome, sparkling here and there on a dewy
blade of grass. The spot was peaceful and charming, but, to
Catherine, it spelt nothing but horror and anguish. At the far
end, Gauthier and the leopard were face to face. ...

The tall Norman stood with his back to the mossy rocks,
legs straddled, hands half-open, ready to make a grab. He stood,
leaning forward slightly, panting from his efforts, eyes riveted
on the beast's every movement. The leopard crouched down
among the dead leaves, snarling ferociously, its great claws
sunk into the ground as it growled softly and studied the defenceless man with its brilliant, cruel, green eyes.

Anne was about to spur her trembling horse forward when
Gauthier called out:

'Don't move!'

A second later the animal sprang. Its long, supple body flashed
through the air and landed on Gauthier. Man and beast rolled
together in the moss. The Norman had succeeded in getting
both his hands round the creature's throat and he was just able
to hold its open jaws out of reach of his face, every muscle
straining in the effort. His face was twisted with pain, because
the leopard's claws had slashed his shoulders and were struggling to reach him again. The animal's angry growls mingled

with the man's heavy breathing. At a little distance, the two women fought to control their mounts, terrified by the battle.

'My God ...' Catherine prayed mechanically, half under her breath. 'My God!'

She could do no more. In such a perilous situation, only Almighty God could do anything.... Gauthier's arms were two pillars of solid flesh, bulging with muscles and veins which writhed like blue snakes as he fought to keep the beast off. With a powerful movement, he suddenly reversed the positions, forcing the leopard down beneath him at the cost of some more scratches. The beast was panting hard, struggling furiously to free its throat from the murderous grip. The smell of blood was driving it mad, but Gauthier held firm. His huge hands squeezed, squeezed, taking good care not to slip on the smooth fur. ...

The giant's face was scarlet, twisted, grimacing like a demoniacal mask. Blood streamed from his wounds, but he uttered not a sound of complaint. Suddenly there was a crack followed by a plaintive mewing. Gauthier staggered to his feet. The black and yellow cat lay outstretched at his feet, its spine broken. The long body arched once and then fell back motionless and both women gave a sigh of relief. Anne de Craon laughed nervously.

'Od's Blood, my boy! You would make a mighty animal-tamer! How do you feel?'

She sprang from her horse, throwing the reins to Catherine, and ran towards him. Catherine too dismounted and came towards them. As the old lady examined his lacerated shoulders, he stared at Catherine and murmured in great astonishment:

'You are weeping, Dame Catherine! For me?'

'I was so frightened, my friend,' she said with a brave attempt at a smile. 'I never could have believed you could master that beast!'

'Bah! If you forget the claws, he was no more formidable than an old boar. I've often had to fight bare-handed against the wild boars in the forests of Écouves.'

Catherine took out a handkerchief and tried to clean his wounds with water from a little spring near by.

'What are we going to do with him?' she asked Anne who was tearing up her veil and handkerchief for bandages. 'Listen!'

The distant sounds of the hunt seemed to be drawing closer through the forest. The huntsman was sounding his horn as loudly as his breath would permit.

'They are coming closer,' said Anne. 'We haven't a moment

to lose. Jump up behind me, my friend. Dame Catherine's mare is too small to take your weight. . . . Quick now! Your ordeal is not yet over, but we can at least try to save you from the dogs. You could never hold them off in the state you are in now!'

Catherine remounted while Anne leapt back into the saddle, Gauthier getting up behind.

'Off we go!' the old lady cried gaily. 'Follow me, Catherine.'

In spite of its double burden, the great golden chestnut leapt forward like an arrow, followed docilely enough by little Morgane. The mare had ceased trying to rebel. Like all thoroughbreds, she recognized the hands of a master. They resumed their headlong gallop, fording a freshet of clear water, glowing amber in the sun, russet in the shade. Beyond it was a slope of low rocks which the horses climbed easily.

'No hope of picking up the scent on rock,' Anne cried. 'Don't hold me so tight, my friend. I can't breathe. I'm no leapard, you know!'

Gauthier had girdled the elderly amazon more tightly than he realized and her face was red under her green cap. Catherine heard her chuckle:

'It's a devilish long time since anyone clipped me about the waist!'

Nevertheless, the two riders did not pause for a moment. The sound of the hunt died away presently and they found themselves approaching a pool of silvery water set among sparse trees. The horses thundered out of the forest limits, steam rising from their nostrils.

'It's a little tributary of the Loire,' Anne said. 'We shall have to ford it. It's not deep. . . .'

She spurred her horse into the water. It scrambled across easily and up into a field where sheep grazed. A little way off stood an old shepherd in a cloak. They soon reached the river proper, which stretched before them, broad, yellow and turbulent, swollen from the recent rains. On the opposite bank stood a cluster of little houses, a château and a small port in which a fleet of little round boats were drawn up, rather like a clutch of eggs under a hen. Anne de Craon drew up her horse on the bank and pointed to the village.

'That is Montjean, the fief belonging to my daughter, Beatrice, the mother of the Dame de Rais. She has never had cause to love her son-in-law. Gilles's men have never set foot on her lands since the time he threatened to seize them from her and throw her into the Loire. Can you swim, young man?'

'Like a salmon, noble lady! Who ever heard of a Norman who could not swim?'

'Possibly, but you have lost a great deal of blood. Are you strong enough to get across? The Loire is treacherous just here, but, unfortunately, your safety depends on it.'

'I shall be strong enough,' said Gauthier, his eyes on Catherine who smiled back at him. 'But what shall I do once I am there?'

'Go to the castle. Tell the seneschal, Martin Berlot, that I sent you. Then wait.'

'What? Not ask for help for Dame Catherine?'

Anne de Craon shrugged.

'There are hardly ten soldiers there and the mere mention of Gilles's name sends them scuttling for cover. It is enough that Berlot should take you in without argument. If he makes a fuss, tell him that I shall have him hanged at the first opportunity. That should silence him! As for the rest, the best thing would be for you to wait till your mistress succeeds in extricating herself from the wasps' nest in which she finds herself. Unless,' she added haughtily, 'you would prefer to return home without her.'

'Where Dame Catherine is, there is my home!' Gauthier affirmed with a haughtiness to match hers. She smiled briefly.

'Stiff-necked, eh? You are not a Norman for nothing, my friend. Now, quick! We must be on our way home.'

By way of answer, Gauthier knelt and looked at Catherine, who looked down at him from her saddle with tears in her eyes.

'Dame,' he said fervently, 'I remain your loyal servant and I shall wait so long as it pleases you. Take care of yourself.'

'Take care of yourself,' Catherine replied, her voice rough with emotion. 'I should hate to lose you, Gauthier.'

Impulsively, she held out her hand and he snatched it up a little clumsily and pressed it to his lips. Then, without a backward glance, he ran to the river bank and plunged into the water. They watched him ploughing through the flood, his mighty arms flailing the water like a thresher at harvest. Slowly he reached the middle of the stream. . . . Catherine made the sign of the Cross.

'May the Lord protect him,' she said quietly. 'Although he doesn't believe in Him.'

Anne de Craon gave a bark of laughter. Her sharp eyes dwelt on Catherine in amusement.

'I'd love to know where you recruit your servants, my dear.

You may only have two, but they are mightily picturesque: a gipsy woman and a pagan Norman!'

'Oh,' Catherine said sadly. 'I had an even better one – a Moorish doctor . . . a marvellous man!'

A moment later, the Norman's sandy head had been swallowed up in a bank of mist lying on the water. Anne turned her horse's head.

'It is time to go home,' she said. 'We still have some way to go, and we must catch up with the hunt before they leave the forest.'

Hard-pressed by their riders, the two horses flew like the wind across the flat pasture land. The old shepherd, motionless as a brown statue, watched them pass. Anne turned to smile at Catherine.

'I'm hungry,' she exclaimed, '. . . and I'm anxious to find Gilles again to see how he is taking it all!'

Catherine smiled back. She felt relieved of an immense weight. To her left, the cry of a wild duck rang out like the trump of victory. Gauthier was out of Gilles's clutches. That left only Sara and herself. But this first success was highly encouraging. She felt for the little reliquary and pressed it.

'Thank you,' she whispered. 'Thank you, Barnaby.'

CHAPTER SIX

A November Night

After a wide detour designed to bring them back from a different direction, the two women finally caught up with the hunt in the very clearing where Gauthier had so valiantly done battle with the leopard. They galloped straight into a scene of extraordinary savagery. Gilles de Rais stood beside the dead beast, raining blows on his dogs. He was mad with rage and the creatures crouched whimpering at his feet as he lashed them with his whip. His companions stood watching impassively, still as equestrian statues. As the two women appeared, Gilles addressed them angrily:

'Where have you come from? Where have you been? Were you as useless as these ninnies?'

Anne de Craon raised one eyebrow haughtily and shrugged as she stroked her horse's neck to calm it.

'I don't think we were any more incompetent than yourself, Gilles. I saw your horse take the bit between its teeth and follow the dogs. Mine chose to follow the leopard and Dame Catherine's followed mine, as you see.'

Gilles's eyes narrowed as he went up to Catherine and laid a hand on Morgane's neck.

'Isn't it a little odd that Morgane should suddenly have decided to go after Korrigan instead of Nutcracker? Or was I wrong about your equestrian skill?'

'I cannot be held responsible for the caprices of a mare,' Catherine retorted icily. 'Morgane followed whom she chose and I, perforce, went with her. I did not even see you leave. I thought you were behind us, but the horses seemed determined to follow the cat.'

'As a rule, they are terrified of cats, big or small! You amaze me! May I ask whether you found the fugitive?'

Gilles's voice was silky soft, in a strange contrast to the blood-stained whip which he still held in one hand. His grandmother took it upon herself to reply.

'When we reached this spot where you are standing now, grandson,' she said, a trifle stiffly, 'we found the beast dead, but still warm, and not a trace of the prisoner, except those left by his struggle with the leopard. He might have vanished into thin air. We searched the forest round about and followed the stream a little way, but found nothing.'

'You, perhaps, but what about her?' Gilles hissed, pointing a trembling finger at Catherine. Anne de Craon did not falter.

'Dame Catherine did not leave my side for an instant,' she said calmly. 'I had to keep an eye on her since you had disappeared. What exactly did happen?'

Gilles flung down his whip in a fury.

'These cursed dogs suddenly took it into their heads to chase off after a young buck and led us a pretty dance as far as the abbey! Now they are worn out and my leopard is dead. You will have to pay for this too, fair Catherine. A hunting animal is beyond price.'

'I really don't know what there is left for you to take,' Catherine answered curtly. 'Except my skin.'

She forced herself to meet the cruel eyes and behave normally. Above all, she must hide her delight in her friend's escape. She did not believe that he could have perished in the river. He would have mastered it just as he mastered the leopard, she was sure of that.

'Who knows?' Gilles said gently. 'I may even think of that. You have won this round, but it won't always go your way. I still have your witch and, if she doesn't tell me what I want to know, I shall make her pay for you both. Hola, Poitou! My horse!'

The page brought up Nutcracker, whom one of the servants had hastily rubbed down. The stallion's black coat still glistened with sweat and his eyes burned wildly. Gilles climbed heavily into the saddle and set off again into the forest without a backward glance at the rest of the hunt. Anne de Craon brought her horse up near to Catherine's.

'You must be on your guard tonight,' she murmured, keeping her lips still, because Roger de Bricqueville was watching her closely. 'Bolt your door, Catherine, and do not open it for anyone.'

'Why?'

'Because the devil himself will be the lord of Champtocé tonight. Gilles has suffered a defeat; he will seek to avenge it. . . .'

Catherine was, in fact, forcibly confined in her room for three days. Gilles de Rais sent word that he did not wish to see her.

She did not even see Anne de Craon who had taken to her bed with a feverish chill. The strange thing was that, during all this time, the château seemed to be wrapped in slumber. A profound silence enveloped it. They did not even lower the drawbridge and, if the servants went about their duties, they did so as silently as shadows. Catherine asked the little maid who brought her meals what was happening.

'I cannot tell you, gracious lady. Monseigneur Gilles has shut himself up in his apartments with his boon companions and it is forbidden, on pain of death, to disturb them for whatever reason.'

The maid, a plump, pink-cheeked little Breton girl, was almost too frightened to open her mouth. She seemed to be afraid that the echo of her words might penetrate the stone walls and reach her master's sharp ears.

'And Lady Anne?' Catherine asked. 'How is she?'

'I don't know. She is also locked up in her rooms and no one but Alienor, her tiring woman, is allowed to enter. Excuse me, gracious lady, but I must hurry....'

The girl was anxious to be off and Catherine did not dare question her further. Sara's fate was a matter of cruel anxiety to her and she despaired of finding out about it, but what could she do while her door was barricaded and the occasional metallic tread of an armour-shod foot proved that it was also guarded?

On the evening of the fourth day, however, the bolts were slid back to admit someone other than the maid. The door opened and Gilles de Sille, the Sire de Rais's cousin and companion in debauchery, entered. He was of the same age as de Rais, but looked quite different: shortish, stocky, with massive shoulders and a flat belly. His brick-red face had a flat nose and a pair of astonishingly cold, expressionless pale blue eyes. He was inelegantly clad in purple breeches and a maroon doublet embroidered with a golden lion, but there was an impressively large dagger thrust through his belt. He stood for a moment on the threshold, thumbs hooked over his belt, feet straddled, staring arrogantly at Catherine. Then, as she turned away with a shrug, he laughed aloud.

'I have something to show you,' he said, after a pause. 'Take a look in the courtyard....'

Catherine had closed her shutters some time ago, because it was already dark outside. The day had been a melancholy one; misty and dank, smelling of rotting vegetation and stagnant

water: All Saints' Day. Catherine, who had not been permitted
to attend Mass, had tried to make herself comfortable in her
own room and shut out the dismal scene outside. She went
across to the window and threw back the shutter. Flickering
torchlight from the courtyard below danced across her face
through the leaded panes. She opened the window and leant
out. Men went to and fro carrying faggots and logs which they
were piling up around a wooden stake to which dangling chains
had been secured. Catherine drew back with a cry of horror,
white to the lips. Sille looked at her slyly.

'Ah, yes! Gilles has decided that there should be another
death tomorrow – All Souls' Day – so your familiar is to go up
in smoke.'

'I don't believe it!' Catherine whispered to herself. 'I don't
believe it! He can't do that!'

'Your witch behaved like a fool, my beauty,' Sille remarked
with a coarse laugh. 'If she had been more dangerous, she would
never have come to this pass. But at least you will have the
consolation of witnessing the event. . . .'

He picked up a partridge from the table where Catherine's
untouched supper was growing cold and bit into it as if it had
been an apple. He poured out a cup of wine for himself, drained
it at one draught, then wiped his mouth on his sleeve and went
to the door.

'Sweet dreams, fair lady! A pity you are in this condition
and that my cousin has forbidden anyone to touch you! I
should have liked to keep you company a little longer, eh?'

Catherine stayed motionless, looking out of the window, until
she heard the door close behind Sille. Then she fell on her knees
on the floor and buried her face in her hands.

'Sara!' she sobbed. 'My poor Sara!'

She remained there till the last sounds in the courtyard had
died away, the torches put out and the candles guttering in
their wrought-iron holder. She crouched, prostrated by grief
and horror, praying and weeping, not knowing to whom she
could turn for help. She felt as though she were at the bottom
of a deep well whose walls were so smooth that she could not
get a foothold. The well was gradually filling up with water and
she knew it must end by drowning her, but there was no way
out. . . .

It was the cold, damp air blowing through her window
which finally drew her from her despair. It wrapped itself

around her like a shroud. She rose painfully to her feet and, taking a new candle from her dresser, lit it at the guttering flame in the sconce. Then she closed the window. The fire, too, was dying in the grate. She took some logs and threw them on the embers, then rekindled the flames with the bellows standing near by. Simple, familiar domestic actions these, and they took her back to the happy times long ago in the house on the Pont-au-Change, or at Uncle Mathieu's draper's shop in Dijon before a princely caprice had removed her from her humble background and made her into a great lady. She sat with her arms locked around her knees, staring at the flames as they leapt up again in the chimney and warmed her cold body.

She shut her eyes. These glowing flames had brought back the nightmare! The terrible hungry fire which would swallow up Sara tomorrow and hurl her, screaming in agony, into eternity! And she, Catherine, was helpless, a prisoner, forced to submit to an implacable destiny! Suddenly her eyes flew open again in great astonishment. Swiftly she pressed both hands to her belly where she had felt a faint fluttering. The babe! Arnaud's son had just shown his first sign of life! She was washed over by a wave of joy and tenderness and she felt her courage returning. Her child! Would he really see the light in this accursed place? What if his life should be that of a wretched prisoner! And his first cry that of a captive soul! Gauthier the Norman must be peering through the mist from the other side of the river, waiting for news from Champtocé. She must try to do something, go to Gilles and throw herself on his mercy, humiliate herself if necessary, but make one last effort to secure Sara's pardon. She ran to the door. She must first speak to the guard and either persuade him to let her go, or to fetch Gilles and bring him here. She seized the door handle. To her astonishment, it turned and the door opened. The corridor outside was pitch-dark and empty. The whole castle must be asleep.

Catherine had no idea of the time. The only clock was in the great hall and in her present frame of mind she had not heard the chapel bell, but her resolve was unshakeable. Offering silent thanks to Heaven that Sille had forgotten to re-lock her door, Catherine went back into the room to fetch her cloak and a candle. The sound of her footsteps in the deep silence awoke faraway echoes. She set out calmly and resolutely for the staircase. She would have to traverse nearly half the château to reach Gilles's apartments, but something told her that she would not meet any obstacles in her path. The night was hushed about her. When she reached the gallery, she was able to see round most of the courtyard; there was neither light nor movement.

She crossed the gallery and the great hall and began to climb the spiral staircase which led to Gilles's room without meeting a living soul. From time to time, however, a snore from behind a closed door proved that this was not a place under a spell. Then, as she climbed higher, strange sounds began to reach her ears, half-smothered by the thick walls, human sounds which were difficult to place ... laughter? ... or death cries ...?

Catherine was just about to set off down the passage which led to Gilles's room when a dark, hunched form suddenly emerged from the inky shadows. She stepped back with a smothered cry, but there was nowhere to hide herself. Old Craon stood there looking at her.

Seeing him blinking in the dim light of the stairway, she thought he looked more than ever like an old owl. She could not understand why he seemed in such an agitated state ... he looked at her blankly, as if her appearance there, at that time of night, was the most natural thing in the world. He leant against the wall, breathing hard. She saw him tug his collar as if to loosen it. He seemed to be choking and closed his eyes.

'Seigneur,' she whispered. 'You are ill!'

His heavy lids fluttered. Catherine stared, astounded, as a great tear rolled down beside his great, beaked nose. In Jean de Craon's customarily hard glare there was a look of despair and an almost childish bewilderment. She leant forward and touched him on the shoulder.

'Is there anything I can do?'

Catherine's voice seemed to penetrate the old man's somnambulistic trance. As he looked at her a little life kindled in his gaze.

'Come!' he whispered. 'Don't stay here!'

'But I must. I want to see your grandson.'

'See Gilles? See that ...? No, come. Come at once! Your life is in danger ...'

His gnarled old hand gripped her arm and drew her after him. His hand was trembling. Then, all at once, he let go of her arm, leant his head against the wall and was violently sick. The old, wrinkled face had taken on a greenish tinge and Catherine was alarmed.

'You are ill, very ill, seigneur! Let me call for help.'

'No ... do nothing. I implore you! But come ... come with me!'

His voice was barely more than a whisper, but the old man had regained control of himself and was beginning to descend the stairs. He stopped at the floor below and glanced up nervously as if expecting to see some sinister silhouette at the window. Then his wavering gaze sought Catherine's once more.

'Dame Catherine,' he murmured, 'I beg you not to question me. Chance and ... curiosity have driven me to discover the secret of my ... of Gilles's nights. It is a horrifying secret. In one instant, everything I have ever believed in lay smashed at my feet. All that remains to me now is to beseech the Lord to take me to His bosom ere long. I am ...'

He stopped and gasped for breath. Then he continued with infinite sadness:

'I am an old man now and my life has never been exemplary ... far from it, but, nevertheless ... I did not deserve *that!* That ...'

His bony old face darkened under the pressure of a rage which he could not bring himself to express. Catherine nodded and spoke very gently.

'Seigneur, I do not wish to pry into your family secrets, but I have a human life to defend. Tomorrow at dawn ...'

'What is that?' Craon said, with a distracted look. 'Ah ... your servant?'

'Yes ... I implore you ...'

She leant against the wall, her eyes filled with tears.

'I would intercede with Satan himself to save her. ...'

'Gilles is worse than Satan ...'

The old man's eyes travelled from Catherine's pale face to her belly and rested there as if he had only just noticed her condition. In his eyes she read all the bewilderment of a moment ago.

'That's true,' he muttered. 'You are to be a mother. ... You are carrying a child! A child. ... My God!'

He seized her by the shoulders and thrust his face, twisted with pain, close to hers.

'Dame Catherine,' he gasped. 'You mustn't stay here! This is an accursed place. You must leave ... quickly ... tonight!'

She stared at him, dumbfounded.

'How can I? I am a prisoner. ...'

'No, I shall find a way of getting you out ... at once! Let there be at least one good action in my life ... at least allow me to save you!'

'I will not go without Sara. ...'

'Go and get ready. I will fetch her. Hurry! Then go down and wait for me by the gatehouse.'

He turned and was about to descend when Catherine stopped him.

'But what about Monseigneur Gilles?' she asked. 'What will he say? Won't he ...?'

For an instant, the old Craon became the haughty, hard old man she had first met.

'Never!' he exclaimed. 'However low he may have sunk, I am still his grandfather. He would not dare! Now hurry! You must have reached safety by dawn.'

Catherine did not need to be told twice. Weariness and fear suddenly fell from her like magic. She picked up her skirts and ran to her room, praying that this hope should not prove a vain one and that nothing would come between the Sire de Craon and his generous gesture. She made a hurried bundle of her more precious possessions and Sara's few clothes, slipped what gold remained into the pocket under her skirts, wrapped her cloak around her and took Sara's over her arm. Then she slung the bundle over her shoulder and ran, for the last time, from the room which had witnessed so many miserable hours. She had not felt so carefree for a long time!

When she reached the gatehouse, she saw Craon approaching from the direction of the dungeons followed by a stumbling form. Catherine recognized Sara by the glimmering torchlight, but a Sara grown terribly thin and white. She ran to her with open arms.

'Sara ... my beloved Sara! At last I find you again!'

The gipsy clasped her without speaking and burst into tears. Catherine had never before seen Sara weep and she realized that the poor woman's nerves must have been severely shattered.

'It's all over ...' she murmured tenderly. 'You will be safe now!'

Jean de Craon looked round nervously.

'There is no time for conversation. Come. We must fetch some horses from the stables. Hurry, I am going to open the postern gate.'

He took a key from the immense bunch which dangled at his

waist and opened the door into the smaller courtyard.

'But ... what about the guards?' Catherine whispered.

'If you keep close behind me, they won't see you. I shall put out the torch. We must take every precaution not to alert them. Nothing would save you once Gilles got to hear about this!'

The darkness was total. It swallowed up the imposing architecture of the great courtyard together with its sinister pile of faggots, a sight which lent wings to the women's feet, but the door did not open. Catherine heard Jean de Craon breathing hard and became anxious.

'Why haven't you opened it?' she asked.

'I was thinking. I have decided to change my original plan. The stable guards would see you. Now, listen carefully. I shall open the door and you must slip through alone. The lesser courtyard is only lit near the stables themselves and the guard-post, but the light is very feeble. You are to slip along the wall till you come to the buttress close by the gatehouse and wait for me there. I shall go openly to the stables and take two horses, telling them I am going to the Abbey. I do sometimes fetch the Abbot to hunt heron at dawn – that is the one sport I can still follow. Besides, I sometimes go out alone at night. I suffer from insomnia and I like wandering along the banks of the Loire. You are to slip out at the same time as the horses. The men will not see you. Then you must leap into the saddle and cross the drawbridge. On the other side of the tongue of land, you will find a ferry. You will be safe enough at Mont-jean, provided you do not tarry overmuch.'

'But the guards on the drawbridge will not let us through!'

'Yes, they will if you show them this.'

He drew a ring from his finger as he spoke. Catherine had observed that he wore his coat-of-arms engraved on a ring like all noblemen, but the ring was not always the same one. He had several: cornelian, agate, onyx or plain gold, and it was a vanity of his to change them frequently. He slipped the ring into her hand.

'I shall not be able to return it to you.'

'Keep it. It is a small enough repayment for all you have endured beneath my roof. I respect you, Dame Catherine. You are not merely beautiful, but brave, noble and honourable. I learnt that too late, I should never have obeyed Gilles. Will you forgive me? This night marks for me the beginning of a time of penitence and remorse. God is punishing me cruelly, you see, and I feel that little time remains to me to seek to avert his wrath.'

'But how will you enter the castle again, seigneur?' Sara asked. 'The men will be surprised to see you return so soon, on foot.'

'There is a subterranean passage not far from here which leads from the castle cellars to the countryside outside. I shall return by that means.'

'Why not let us use it for our escape, then?' Catherine queried. 'It would be simpler . . .'

'Possibly, but there are two reasons against it. Firstly, you will need horses and no horse could pass through the tunnel. And the second, which I hope you will not take amiss, is that I have not the right to entrust the defence secrets of this castle to any outsider. The whole safety of the place would be jeopardized. Now, not another word! I am going to open the gate. . . . When you are some distance down the courtyard, I shall light the torch.'

The door opened with a slight creak, its lintels framing a patch of lighter sky beyond.

'Now . . .' Craon hissed. 'Follow the wall to your left.'

The two women, supporting each other, slipped through the gate. Catherine had her arm round Sara's waist and groped along the wall with her other hand. It was none too easy a matter, because she was also encumbered with her bundle. The stone felt rough, cold and damp to the touch. She stumbled on the uneven cobbles at first, but her eyes gradually became used to the dark.

A few moments later a torch glowed ruddily beneath the archway through which they had come. Jean de Craon was carrying it high enough for his face to be clearly seen. He walked sturdily towards the far end of the courtyard.

'Here is the buttress,' Catherine whispered, feeling the wall take a sharp turn. She could just make out the darker bulk of the gate-tower overhead. The slow tread of a guard could be heard and her heart beat began to thump uneasily. She held her breath, alarmed to find that Sara was leaning much more heavily against her. The poor woman must have come to the end of her strength. Now the clanking tread had ceased. The man must have halted. Catherine heard him cough. Then he set off again and Catherine dared to ask:

'Are you sick? You seem so weak.'

'I haven't been able to sleep for nights because of the rats and I haven't eaten for two days. And then . . .'

'Then what?'

Sara shuddered. Her whispering became more sombre.

'Nothing. I'll tell you one day . . . when I grow stronger. I also know the Sire de Rais's secret. You have no idea how I long to get out of here, even if I have to crawl.'

Catherine, by way of answer, clapped a hand over Sara's mouth. She had been observing old Craon as the gipsy spoke. He had gone into the stable and come out on horseback, leading a second horse by the bridle. Now he came towards them, the horses' hooves ringing over the cobbles. Soon, he was between them and the guardhouse, from which a man came running.

'Open!' cried Craon. 'I have business at the Abbey.'

'Yes, monseigneur.'

The gate creaked as it opened, but the little bridge swung down soundlessly. Catherine dragged Sara after her right under the horses' noses, so that the man-at-arms could not see them as he closed the gate behind them. The darkness protected them and they had soon crossed the bridge. The soldier's voice followed them:

'Are you sure you don't want an escort, monseigneur? The night is very dark.'

'I like dark nights. You should know that, Martin,' the old man answered.

The wind was rising and Catherine took a long, deep breath. It was colder out here, but the wet countryside smelt good. She was free! She pulled the trembling Sara after her and raced down the village street till they were out of sight of the château. The tranquil rhythm of the horses' hooves behind them was reassuring. The two women stopped in the shadow of a flying buttress by the village church and there the old nobleman joined them. He sprang to the ground.

'Now, quick! Someone might see us. Here, Dame Catherine, I have brought you Morgane. I hear you have an understanding with her . . . and she will be a sort of farewell gift. She is a good, strong animal. Now, be on your way and may God protect you!'

Catherine could just make out his features in the gloom. He towered above her and the wind stirred his plumed hat. She murmured:

'I am afraid for you, monseigneur. When *he* knows . . .'

'I've already told you I have nothing to fear from him. Even if he were to attack me ... all I want is rest, eternal rest, and, I trust, oblivion.'

There was such despair in his voice that Catherine could not help saying:

'I do not know what happened tonight, messire, but I wish I could do something to help....'

'No, no one can help. What I saw in Gilles's room goes beyond the bounds of horror. I am an old soldier, Dame Catherine, but I have never seen such a diabolical sight. I am not squeamish, but ... those drunken, raving men; that orgy, whose centre-piece ...'

He hesitated a moment, then the words seemed to burst forth irresistibly:

'... whose centrepiece was a child ... a young boy whose stomach had been torn out ... and Gilles was gorging himself on his blood as if to slake a monstrous thirst! And *that's* the creature of whom I hoped to make a man and a soldier! There you have Gilles de Rais, a man with the right to enter the cathedral of Reims on horseback as escort to the Precious Blood! My grandson ... a monster spewed forth by Hell and vowed to damnation! My grandson ... the last of my line.'

The old man's voice died away in a strangled sob. Catherine stood, petrified with horror. She sensed that Craon would never recover from this blow. She saw him raise his hands to his eyes to wipe them, but before she could say a word, he went on hoarsely:

'Now you understand why I don't want any child to see the light in this accursed and dishonoured place. A Montsalvy should not be born on a dunghill. ... Now, go, madame ... go quickly! But swear to me that you will never reveal a word of this to a living soul!'

Catherine seized the old man's withered hand and pressed it to her lips. It was wet with tears and she felt it tremble in her own.

'I swear!' she vowed. 'No one will ever know! Thank you for myself and for Sara and for the child, who, thanks to you, will be born in freedom. I shall not forget.'

He interrupted her with a brusque gesture.

'Yes, yes, you must. I want you to forget ... forget us all as soon as possible. Our house is damned and must now decline. But you, Dame Catherine, must follow a different road. Try to be happy!'

Before she could reply, he had vanished in the darkness.

The two women heard his footsteps making towards the forest. The horses pawed the ground impatiently. As Catherine slipped the Sire de Craon's ring on her finger, she looked up at the cloudy sky. The melancholy cry of a night owl sounded through the gloom. She fastened her bundle to Morgane's saddle while the beast whinnied softly in recognition.

'There ... there ... my beauty! We are just about to set off ... Wait, quietly.'

The old man had chosen a quiet, powerful horse for Sara, one that would make light of the gipsy woman's considerable weight. It was a good animal with an amiable disposition and it was called simply Rustaud. Old Craon's bad leg would have explained the choice of this particular animal, which, though less dashing, was stronger than the fiery war-horses.

Somehow Catherine managed to hoist Sara on to Rustaud's back. Then she mounted Morgane.

'All right?' she asked Sara.

'Yes,' Sara answered, 'but I wish we were on the other side of the water already....'

They slowly descended the hill towards the river. The night was beginning to grow paler and, though daybreak was still far off, the bells of the village church were already tolling the first summons to Mass on All Souls' Day. The turret of the guard post over the bridge appeared before them. Catherine pressed Morgane forward boldly and called:

'Hey there! Guard!'

There was a muffled exclamation of rage from within. Then the door slowly swung open to reveal a disgruntled, bleary-eyed soldier holding a candle. He blinked crossly at Catherine.

'Open!' she ordered. 'I must be allowed to pass through. Monseigneur's orders.'

The cold air had roused the man and he looked more closely at Catherine.

'Why should Monseigneur Jean be sending a woman across the bridge. Who are you? And who is that with you? Your servant?'

'That is none of your business, dolt! I've told you to open, so open! Take a look at this if you don't believe me and remember that every minute you delay shall be measured across your back in strokes of the cat!'

She flung out her hand so that he should see the ring. He stepped back, apologizing humbly, then crammed his helmet over his head and ran to pull up the chain.

'Excuse me, noble lady, but you understand that I am obliged to be careful. My position is one of trust. . . .'

'I know. Good night.'

She passed across with Sara at her heels. The planks of the bridge drummed hollowly under Morgane's neat hooves, but the Loire was not wide at this point and in no time at all they were cantering along a broad highway. Catherine's breast swelled with joy.

'Faster! . . . We must go faster than this,' she cried, spurring her mare to a trot. They soon crossed the tongue of land between the two branches of the river and reached the ferry which formed the only link between themselves and Montjean at the widest point in the Loire's course. A reed hut served as a shelter for the ferryman. It stood a little way above the shore in a field. Catherine saw with relief that the great flat boat was moored on their side of the river. It was the work of a moment to go into the hut and waken the ferryman.

'Quick!' she said. 'I, my servant and our two horses must get across and rapidly. I have to see the Seneschal of Montjean, Martin Berlot, with all speed.'

'But lady . . . at this time the castle is closed. You will never enter now.'

As he finished speaking, the bells of Champtocé started to toll a knell. The melancholy sounds echoed hollowly through the damp night air. A moment later, the bells of Montjean answered them across the black water. The sound was like a file scraping over Catherine's highly strung nerves. She almost screamed. This could only mean that it was close on five o'clock and that they would soon be up and about in the château of Gilles de Rais – and their flight discovered! And, so long as they had not crossed the Loire, it would still be possible to recapture them. They were still on Gilles's land. The dreaded outline of the stake passed before her eyes.

'It is five o'clock,' she said. 'The people of Champtocé and of Montjean will be going to Mass by now. You can take us across, my good man. The towns open earlier today – it is All Souls' Day. And besides . . .'

She fished a gold piece out of her purse and flashed it in front of the man.

'Here,' she said, slipping it into his callused hand. 'This is for you, but for God's sake, make haste!'

The ferryman had heard of gold pieces, but this one was the first he had ever seen. He could not possibly refuse such a reward. He put on a sheepskin jacket and started off down the bank towards his boat.

'Will the horses keep still?'

'I'll make sure of that. ... Hurry!' Catherine answered, eyes fixed on the watchtower.

A few moments later, the great flat boat was heading out from the shore and Catherine, the reins of both horses in one hand, stood watching the black ribbon of water grow wider as they drew away from the bank. ... The river was swollen but relatively calm, and the man wielded his mighty pole vigorously. Sara had collapsed on her knees in the bottom of the boat, utterly exhausted.

This being the hour before dawn, the night air was full of swirling mists and seemed more opaque than ever. For a moment, Catherine feared that the ferryman might lose his way, but he knew the river as well as he knew his own boat. After what seemed an interminable space of time, the two fugitives saw the shapes of ships rise up out of the misty darkness, masts and rigging, bare of sails at this early hour, then the stocky tower of a church and finally the roofs of Montjean itself. A little château with crenellated towers guarded the river port. Somewhere a cock crowed. Then they heard the slap and gurgle of water against the little stone quay. Steps led up into the gloom beside a great iron ring.

'There,' said the ferryman. 'You have arrived.'

An hour later, Catherine and Gauthier held a council of war round a table in the Seneschal's quarters. Sara, worn out by the terrors and anxieties of the past few days, had fallen asleep on a bench before the fire. On the far side of the table, across a repast consisting of cold meat, bread and cheese. Gauthier sat gazing at Catherine with a look of joy mingled with concern in his blue eyes. Her face bore the marks of great fatigue. There were deep blue rings under her eyes, lines at the corners of her mouth and her pale skin had a waxen look about it in the candlelight. Outside, day was breaking. The sky was a dirty grey towards the east. Martin Berlot stood beside the window, one foot resting on a stool, surveying his guests. It was hard to read what was passing behind that placid face whose chief distinction seemed to be a nose quite three times the normal size. But his brown eyes were sharp.

The Seneschal hardly spoke; he preferred to listen. Since Catherine's arrival, he had not taken part in the conversation, but, when the young woman seemed to be unsure of what to do next, clearly desirous of a little rest, he said quietly with a glance at the lightening sky:

'If I were you, noble lady, I would leave here at once. When they find out that you have crossed the bridge – and they will know ere long – they will send men after you. It would be impossible to resist here if Monseigneur Gilles decided to take you by force.'

'He did not come after Gauthier,' Catherine replied.

'Because he believes him dead and does not know he is here. No one saw him arrive, but with you it's different. The guard will talk and this time Messire Jean will not be here to help you. You must flee, lady, while there is still time! I am not refusing you asylum, but I am in charge of this village and château and I haven't the men to defend them. You must be a long way from here when de Rais's men come seeking news of you. Naturally, you and your maid are weary – that is only understandable – but you would not have far to go: only two leagues farther. If you travel on up the Loire, you will reach Chalonnes which belongs to the Duchess of Anjou.'

'The Duchess is in Provence and can do nothing for me, and there is no one there who can protect me in her absence.'

She buried her head in her hands. Before, in the excitement of the escape, she had forgotten Gilles's words but now their threatening significance came back to her. Throughout the King's lands – and Yolande's too, no doubt – she was now a hunted criminal. Arnaud was mouldering in La Trémoille's dungeons and that all-powerful nobleman had only to reach out his hand and snatch her up wherever she set foot in these regions.

'At all events,' Berlot resumed with an anxious glance towards the river, 'at Chalonnes you will find the Prior of Saint Maurille. He will receive you and you can rest there for a while. As you know, Church property is a place of asylum.'

'The Church,' Gauthier muttered. 'Always the Church!'

Catherine placed both hands on the table and pushed herself with difficulty to her feet. She had observed the note of panic in Berlot's voice. The Seneschal was frightened. There was but one thought in his mind: to be rid of these undesirable guests by the time Gilles's men arrived, so he could pretend he had never seen them.

'Very well, we'll go,' she sighed. 'Wake Sara, Gauthier, if it's possible.'

She went over to the window to glance out at the rapidly

paling sky, stretching to help chase away her fatigue. Gauthier, who had failed to wake Sara, merely flung her over his shoulder. He turned his icy blue eyes on Berlot.

'Have you got a horse for me?'

'I have one,' the man grimaced. '... My own. I need that. Monseigneur Gilles would find it strange...'

'There are moments when I wonder,' the Norman said with a slight sneer, 'why you don't cross the river. Whom do you fear most? Gilles de Rais, the Dame de Montjean who hates her son-in-law, or, perhaps, the Dame de Craon?'

'... Or the Devil!' Berlot snapped. 'But I shall be grateful to him the day he takes you away with him!'

'Amen!' said Gauthier, who was acquiring a smattering of ecclesiastical vocabulary. 'Now, let's be off, Dame Catherine. I hope Sara's horse is strong enough to carry us both. Anyway the poor woman would never stay in the saddle unaided. By Odin, I think we shall have to bang her head against the wall to wake her!'

They found Morgane and Rustaud, both of whom had been fed and watered, waiting outside the gates. The little mare whinnied with pleasure at seeing her mistress again. Gauthier helped Catherine into the saddle and then, carrying Sara, mounted Rustaud. The horse did not flinch at the giant's great weight.

'I think that will do,' the Norman said. He took a deep breath and cried out joyfully:

'I shall be glad to be quit of this damned country! We shall have better company where we are going. Let us be off!'

A cry of anguish from Berlot reached them.

'De Rais's men! There they are! Go ... go quickly!'

Just then the ferry came in sight laden with soldiers. Ten or so horsemen, who had chosen to swim across, followed behind and Catherine recognized the Sire de Rais's purple trappings at their head. If he had seen them, they were lost! The Seneschal stammered, green with terror:

'Take this alleyway, down here. You will reach the country-side unseen. I will detain them as long as possible.'

'If you were not so frightened for your own skin, I would say you were a good man!' cried Gauthier. 'Farewell, Martin. We may meet again some day!'

Catherine spurred her horse down the steeply sloping lane, then, at the risk of breaking her neck, she broke into a gallop. Morgane's hooves clattered gaily over the beaten earth track and she could hear Rustaud's more ponderous hoof-beats behind. Soon they found themselves in a small wood, out of sight of Montjean. The road veered away from the Loire and plunged beneath the trees where it became a muddy puddle. Gauthier caught up with Catherine.

'I was wondering whether we should go to Orleans,' he said. 'I am sure Maître Jacques Boucher would take you in, he is such a good friend of yours.'

'True,' Catherine agreed. 'But Treasurer Boucher is above all a loyal and faithful subject of King Charles. He is as straight and rigid as a sword blade, and he would never disobey an order from his sovereign, however friendly he might feel towards me. And the King is La Trémoille now, though Jacques Boucher may not know it.'

'Where can we go then? I trust you don't intend to rush off to Sully-sur-Loire in the state you are in? You must remain alive, madame, if you are to get the better of your enemies.'

'I don't much mind whether or not I get the better of them,' Catherine replied, tight-lipped. 'But there is Arnaud ... and the child. I could return to Burgundy where I have friends and would be relatively safe, but that would mean cutting myself off from Arnaud. I must remain on the King's territory and risk falling into his favourite's hands. We must find someone who will take us in and hide us. Then I can try to contact the only people who can help us – Messire de Montsalvy's brothers-in-arms, all of whom hate La Trémoille.'

'And where do you think you will find this refuge?'

Catherine shut her eyes for a moment as if to summon up an image from the depths of her memory.

'If I am any judge of men, I think I know of a place. If I am wrong ... well, I should be beyond help. But I'm sure I am right!'

'Where are we going then?'

'To Bourges. To Maître Jacques Coeur.'

They rode out of the wood. A broad grassy pasture land stretched before them with the Loire glinting in the distance. They spurred their horses and set off across it at full gallop

Catherine had sometimes wondered whether her situation were really as desperate as Gilles had made it out to be, or whether that evil man had exaggerated it so as to have her more surely in his power. This turned out to be a vain hope. Gilles's words had had the ring of truth about them and they were soon amply confirmed.

She and Gauthier had agreed that, for the present, they would travel by night and hide by day. This way they were less likely to fall in with undesirable or dangerous company. There were other reasons – the November nights were much longer than the days, the King's forces were unlikely to be abroad then and the road to Bourges was easy to follow, even in the dark. They simply had to follow the Loire and then the Cher which would bring them within a few leagues of their destination. They spent All Souls' Day at Chalonnes where the Prior charitably gave them food and shelter, but they left Saint Maurille again at nightfall. By daybreak, they had covered some twenty leagues which must have been a record for Rustaud with his double load. When the mist dispersed and they could see the country-side more clearly, they found themselves standing before an immense abbey, stout walls encircling a quiverful of steeples and towers which stood at the junction of the Loire and the Vienne. The place was so formidable that Catherine was nervous of entering and, when a peasant came trudging along a near-by path, she hailed him:

'That is a fine big abbey, good fellow. To whom does it belong?'

'Dame,' the fellow replied, doffing his cap, 'that is the royal Abbey of Fontevrault and the Abbess is cousin to King Charles, may God preserve him!'

'Thank you,' Catherine murmured as he put his cap on again and went off.

She and Gauthier exchanged brief but eloquent glances. An abbey was certainly a place of asylum, but it would scarcely be wise to venture into this holy fortress famed for providing a refuge ... often a compulsory one ... for repudiated queens, undesirable daughters of great families, rebellious princesses ... a place whose abbess was always chosen from princely, if not royal houses! Five religious communities were ruled over by the Abbess of Fontevrault, including a hospital and a leper house, and the strange thing was that three of these five were masculine. The inner tensions and strife of Fontevrault were notorious and Catherine felt it would be rash to set foot in such a hotbed, noble though it might be.

'I think we had better look for a woodcutter's hut where we can seek shelter for the day,' she said at last.

This was easily done. They spent a peaceful day, thanks to

Gauthier who caught a hare and roasted it over a wood fire. The Norman was completely at home in the forest. The horses were fed from a sack of fodder provided by Martin Berlot. When the forest grew dark, they went down to the river again, making a prudent detour so as to avoid the abbey itself. The night did not pass uneventfully. First, the travellers lost their way and followed the Indre river instead of the Cher and they had just got back on the right road when Rustaud went lame.

'We shall have to stop at the first priory or abbey we come to,' Catherine said worriedly. 'That animal needs care.'

But this was easier said than done. They had still found nowhere when, towards dawn, they came in sight of a large village. They were beginning to feel hungry, for by now both animals and humans were in need of a meal.

'We are a long way from Champtocé,' said Gauthier. 'We might, perhaps, take the risk of entering this town and finding some food.'

'Let us try,' said Catherine, whose stomach was aching with cramp and hunger. Her pregnancy made her extraordinarily sensitive and she felt a desperate need of calm and repose. The child moved about within her so vigorously that it frightened her.

But, just as they were about to set foot over the village boundary, a trumpet call shattered the air. Gauthier, who had gone on ahead, turned and looked back at her.

'Dame Catherine,' he said, 'the whole village is gathered in the square at the end of the road. They are listening to a herald in blue and gold livery who is reading from a scroll.'

The man's powerful voice reached Catherine, clear and threatening in the cold morning air.

'Good people!' the herald cried. 'By order of His Majesty, Charles VII, may God defend him, you are informed that two escaped criminals, both women, are currently fleeing across your district. One of them, Catherine de Brazey, is accused of conspiring with the enemy and of the heinous crime of seducing one of the King's captains in order to win him over to the English. The other is a gipsy sorceress called Sara, under sentence of death for witchcraft and evil doings. Both women have escaped from the prison of Monseigneur Gilles de Rais, Marshal of France. One of these women is blonde and several months with child. The other is very dark. They have, moreover, stolen two horses to assist their escape: a white mare and a chestnut percheron. Twenty gold pieces reward for anyone who can assist

in their arrest and one hundred gold pieces from either Monseigneur de Rais at Champtocé or Monseigneur de la Trémoille
at Loches to the person who hands over the two women alive.
And the gallows to anyone found guilty of helping them or
giving them shelter.'

Catherine sat frozen in her saddle. The man was now silent,
but she still seemed to hear his words re-echoing. She could just
see him in the distance rolling up his scroll and wearily tucking
it into his doublet. He turned his horse's head and set off for
the other end of the village. The peasants were about to dis-
perse when Gauthier, quick as a flash, snatched the reins from
Catherine and pulled her into the shelter of an oak wood just
outside the village. She sat passively, eyes filled with tears, as
she thought over what she had just heard. Criminal! She was
an escaped criminal now, prey of the first ruffian who came
along. Who would be likely to resist the temptation of so much
gold?

When they reached the shelter of the trees, Gauthier stopped
and leapt to the ground. He helped Catherine to dismount, for
she was sobbing like a child, worn out with despair.

'Kill me,' she faltered. 'Kill me, Gauthier! It would be so
much quicker and easier. . . . You heard? They are hunting me
up and down the land as a common criminal!'

'Well, and what does that prove?' the Norman said gruffly,
cradling her against his chest like a child. 'That Gilles de Rais
has stirred up his fine cousin and that they are both after you?
But you knew that already! Come, come, Dame Catherine, you
are tired and that loudmouth's tale was the final blow. You
need rest and then we must make plans. Do you think this pro-
clamation would influence the man we were going to ask help
from?'

She stared up at him through her tears.

'I . . . I don't know! I don't think so, but . . .'

'No buts. Then we go to Bourges as before. The thing is to get
there. There is one thing you haven't thought of.'

'What?'

'That damned scroll spoke only of two women. There is
no mention of me, so I have plenty of elbow room and
that's something. And there are certain changes which can be
made.'

He handed Catherine over to Sara who was laying out their
cloaks on the ground under a tree and went up to Morgane,
unsheathing his dagger.

'My God, what are you doing?' Catherine cried.

'I shall have to kill her,' Gauthier replied sadly. 'I hate to do it, but this pretty little horse betrays your rank more clearly than a banner.'

With more energy than she would have believed herself capable of a moment earlier, Catherine leapt up and flung her arms around the giant.

'No ... I forbid it! It will bring us bad luck to kill Morgane. I know it! I would rather be captured because of her than saved by her death!'

Morgane, meanwhile, watched Gauthier with a look midway between uneasiness and anger. Anger took the upper hand and she started to rear up dangerously, but Catherine seized her bridle and spoke softly to her.

'Hush, there's nothing to be afraid of. . . . We will look after you, my pretty. Be good now!'

The little mare gradually calmed down. At last, by way of pardon, she nuzzled Catherine's hair. Gauthier looked on uneasily.

'You are being unreasonable, Dame Catherine.'

'Maybe so, but she loves me. I don't want to kill an animal which loves me. You *must* try to understand!' She was on the verge of tears again.

'Very well. In that case, stay here. We are some way from the village. I don't think anyone will think of looking for us here. I shall go and see what I can do for the time being.'

'You are not leaving us?' Catherine cried, instantly alarmed.

'Aren't you hungry? Besides, I must see what can be done to disguise you both till we reach Bourges. You must sleep, meanwhile. How do you feel, Sara?'

'How do you think?' the gipsy grumbled. 'Perfectly well, so long as there is no talk of roasting me alive.'

'Then take this. And don't hesitate to use it if some nosey fellow should come too close.'

'This' was the long knife which always hung at the giant's belt. Sara took the knife and passed it through her own belt as coolly as though it had been a newly-plucked rose.

'Rely on me!' she said. 'No one will come near.'

Catherine slept the sleep of a hunted animal. When she awoke, it had grown dark and Gauthier was bending over her, shaking her gently.

'Hey, Dame Catherine . . . wake up . . . it's time!'

A little way off, Sara sat gravely turning a fowl on an improvised spit. This sight, together with her sound sleep, restored Catherine's spirits. She stood up and smiled at Gauthier.

'I feel better,' she said.

'I'm glad. Now put this on. And then we shall eat.'

He held out something dark and heavy. Catherine felt a length of coarse stuff and looked at him uncomprehendingly.

'What is it?'

Gauthier gave a savage grin which made his white teeth flash.

'A monk's habit. I have another one here for Sara. What luck that I came across those two friars before they reached the village!'

Catherine went pale. She remembered her companion's strange religious beliefs with a stab of terror. Gauthier was a pagan! Neither God nor God's servants meant the least thing to him. A dreadful thought flashed through her mind and she let the robe drop. Gauthier laughed and handed it back to her.

'Don't worry, I didn't kill them! I just stunned them a bit and put them in a nice quiet spot. When they come to, they will have but one thought in their minds – to get back to their monastery as fast as they can!'

'Why?'

'Because I left them as naked as newly caught fish,' Gauthier said, so solemnly that Catherine could not help laughing. She slipped on the thick, brown habit and tied the cord round her waist. The Norman watched approvingly.

'Now you look like a plump little monk!' he said and went off in search of the horses. While Sara and Catherine devoured the chicken which he must have stolen from some farm, Gauthier submitted Morgane to a treatment which was just the opposite of a good grooming. He carefully rubbed the little animal's coat with mud from a near-by stream. By the time he had finished, the horrified little mare was no longer any definite colour, but something between grey and dirty yellow.

'Let us hope it doesn't rain too much and that she stays like this till we arrive,' he said, standing back to admire the effect like a painter with a newly completed work. Catherine reflected with amusement that he was just like her celebrated friend, Van Eyck, when he stood back to look at one of the marvellous Madonnas for which she had so often modelled, his head on one side, eyes narrowed and his face tense with thought.

That done, Gauthier polished off the rest of the chicken,

washed it down with a gulp of river water and then lifted
Catherine into the saddle.

'Come along now, Reverend Father, we must be on our way!'
he said cheerfully. 'The Devil himself would not recognize you
in that attire! And when I say "Devil" I am thinking of a certain
Messire Gilles de Rais, otherwise known as Bluebeard.'

Night was falling. The frail notes of the Angelus reached
them from beyond the trees. Catherine's anxious fears were
gradually fading. The monk's robe smelt unpleasantly of sweat
and dirt, but it was warm and so thick that it would need a
torrential downpour to penetrate it. Catherine soon had the
opportunity to put it to the test because, just as the three travellers left the shelter of the wood, heavy rain began to fall.
Catherine pulled her hood over her head till it covered her as
far as the chin. Then she rolled back the sleeves which were a
little too long. She felt rather like a snail in its shell, protected if
not invisible.

'Oh, Lord God,' she murmured to herself. 'Forgive Gauthier
his terrible sacrilege in stealing these two monkish habits. Remember only that he wished to save our lives! ... And please
guard your servants against catching cold in this rainstorm!'

After which, feeling eased in spirit, she spurred Morgane to a
trot and caught up with Gauthier who had gone on ahead.

CHAPTER SEVEN

Nothing is Impossible to the Brave

The last stroke of the Vespers bell rang out as Catherine, Gauthier and Sara came at last to the end of their journey. It was almost dark. Jacques Coeur's house stood before them at the intersection of the rue d'Auron and the rue des Armuriers: a large house composed of three different buildings under three pointed roofs. The shop took up the entire ground floor on the corner itself, but by now the heavy blackened oak shutters had already been put up. The road was dark, lit only by one brazier burning before a statue of St Ursin.

Catherine's heart was still thumping painfully after seeing the Royal Standard floating above the guard post at the city gates. This meant that the King, and, consequently, La Trémoille, were in residence. She had lived long enough in Bourges to run the risk of being recognized. To give herself enough courage to brave the entry into the city through the old Ornoise gate, she had drawn her monk's hood over her face so far that she could see nothing but Morgane's ears in front of her. She was terrified lest anything should go wrong now that she was so near the end of her journey and she clutched the little reliquary under her robe. . . . As it happened, her fears proved groundless, because, either from weariness or indifference, or a desire to get back to a warm room as soon as possible, the soldiers had taken no notice of two monks escorted by a peasant who claimed to be on their way to the Jacobin monastery. But they were only just in time! They were barely through the gate when Catherine heard the clanking of the drawbridge being raised behind them. The town was closing its gates for the night. . . .

There were few people about in the street which climbed steeply towards the palace. The three travellers passed unnoticed by a few homeward-bound housewives and one or two merchants talking business in the doorway of a shop. As a precaution, however, Catherine reined in her horse several times before nearing the shop and then she pointed to it with her chin.

T—E

'That's it!' she said.

'But it's closed!'

'Only the shop, I imagine, for it is late. I think I see light in the floor above. The curfew has not yet sounded. There seems to be light under the door.'

As if to confirm what she said, the door opened and two men stepped out. They wore long, fur-lined greatcoats. One was tall and thin and the other short and round. Catherine instantly recognized the former whose clear-cut profile stood out sharply against the lighted room behind him.

'Maître Coeur!' she whispered to Gauthier. 'The tall one.'

As she spoke, she slipped off her horse and crept towards them, taking care to keep in the shadow of the walls. The furrier was taking leave of his visitor.

'That is agreed, then. I shall have those ten Mongolian squirrel skins sent to you, Maître Lallemand. They are the last I shall be able to supply you with for some time. God knows when the Venetians will let any more through!'

The small, fat man murmured something Catherine did not catch, touched his black cap and vanished up the rue des Armuriers. Catherine took her courage in both hands and ran forward. She stopped the furrier just as he was about to enter his house.

'Maître Jacques,' she said in a voice hoarse with emotion. 'Will you extend the hand of charity to an outlaw?'

As she spoke she threw back her hood and raised her pale face and haggard eyes towards him. The candlelight from the shop shone for a moment on her golden hair which she wore strained back from her face. Jacques Coeur's eyes widened. He gave a start.

' 'Od's Blood! The Dame de . . .'

He bit his lip and then, without a moment's hesitation, took Catherine by the arm and pulled her into the house.

'Come in quickly! But I see two people on horseback over there and two horses.'

'My servants,' Catherine said. 'They are waiting for me.'

'I will have them taken into the courtyard. Wait here a moment.'

He closed the door carefully and bolted it, then he swept the skins off a little stool for Catherine to sit on before he vanished through a small door.

'Wait,' he repeated. 'I'll be back!'

Catherine collapsed onto the stool. The shop was pleasantly

warm, thanks to a great bronze brazier which glowed in the middle of the floor. A long, wax-polished counter ran along one wall, behind which were ranged the tall locked cupboards in which the furs were stored. In one corner a wooden desk held an inkwell, several goose quills and a huge parchment-bound book. The strange musky smell of the furs mingled with the odour of hot wax from the candles. The house was perfectly quiet. Catherine was sharply aware of it. The tight feeling in her throat relaxed and she breathed more freely than she had for weeks.

Jacques Coeur was returning. At once he ran to her, took both her hands in his and pulled her to her feet.

'My poor friend! How did you ever manage to get as far as this? The town is full of spies and treachery lurks round every corner while the Sire de la Trémoille is here. But come with me. We shall be more comfortable in my study. My assistants are all in the warehouse, but they will be returning soon to put everything in order.'

He slipped an arm gently through Catherine's and led her to the other end of the shop where a stairway rose up between the dark beams. She was so tired that she stumbled and would have fallen but for the stout arm which supported her.

'You are kind to take me in, Maître Jacques.'

She looked up at him, happy to see his fine face with its long nose and firm lips again. The high, broad forehead denoted a considerable intelligence, as did the well-set, but stern, dark eyes. The firm line of his lips was belied by a certain sensuality in the expressive face and still more by the warmth of his voice.

He smiled and laid a reassuring hand on her.

'I trust you were not in any doubt as to your reception,' he said.

The 'den' to which he took her opened off the stairway opposite the communal room. Despite its name, it was a sizeable room whose windows overhung the street below. With its narrow windows giving on the shining rooftops of the Jacobin convent on one side and the rue d'Auron on the other, it was more like a captain's cabin than a merchant's study. There were, of course, heaps of tawny skins here and there and samples of cloth on the great round table, but what struck one most about the room was the number of books strewn over the chairs and dressers, and ranged in open cupboards – thick books in worn leather covers, their pages yellowed and pitted with worm. One stood open on a reading-stand, next to a great brass-studded chest which appeared to be full of parchment scrolls tied with ribbons. However, the most outstanding thing was a huge old nautical map, richly illuminated, spread out on the table, and, near it, a large globe which spun easily in its bronze cage.

Catherine's astonishment made Jacques Coeur smile. He ran one finger over a red and gold ship sailing over the blue waves of the chart.

'I have dreams of travelling,' he said. 'My furs and the fabrics which my partner, Pierre Godart, sells are no longer enough for me. But let us talk about you. Come, sit on these cushions and tell me what miracle brings you here and where you come from ... and why you are so pale! I have believed you dead these many months, Dame Catherine!'

He gently put back the hood so that her head appeared in the full blaze of the candlelight, with her tight braids and tired eyes.

'Haven't you heard the King's edicts, then ... or heard me proclaimed a common criminal at every street corner ...?'

'Yes,' Jacques interrupted, 'I know all that, but I simply couldn't understand what could have happened. They accused you of having lured Captain de Montsalvy away with you and handed him over to the enemy. But then there were other rumours ... that you were both dead, at Rouen ... that you had died with the Maid whose soul is now with God.'

Catherine's nervous laugh gave the full measure of all she had endured. She had had enough of being afraid, of trembling at every glimpse of a helmet or coat of mail. The bad roads and ceaseless trotting of her horse had shaken her badly and there wasn't a fibre of her body which didn't ache.

'Don't you share the general opinion, then, Maître Jacques?' she asked. 'Don't you think she was a witch whom they were right to burn?'

'Only a knave or a coward would dare to suggest such a thing!' Here the furrier lowered his voice. 'Only a Messire de la Trémoille, or a Messire Regnault de Chartres, Archbishop of Reims, and it was an evil day for France when those two gained control over the King's mind and conscience. Alas, it is La Trémoille who reigns and not Charles VII. But what is it you require of me, Dame Catherine?'

She looked at him with limpid eyes which awoke stirrings in his heart which had long been still. Suffering had made Catherine's face more delicate than ever, shadowing it tenderly here and there, and she had the look of a trapped animal, a look which would have aroused the chivalry in any man.

'Can you hide me and my two servants? I am hunted, cornered ... and I am pregnant. And you can help me find either Xaintrailles or La Hire ... assuming that they are not in prison, too.'

'Why should they be ... unless it were by the English?'

'Arnaud de Montsalvy is!'

'Arnaud de Montsalvy went over to the English,' Coeur replied curtly.

'That is a wicked lie!' Catherine declared, stamping her foot. 'Arnaud did everything in his power to save Joan, as I did, too. We even got into Rouen and lived there, he and I ... we left the town sewn into a sack thrown into the Seine. If that's what you call going over to the English ....'

She was trembling all over in indignation. The merchant seized her hands in his.

'Calm yourself, my dear. I beg you, calm yourself! There are a thousand things you will have to explain to me. But first, I am going to get you something warm. You are soaked through. Macée, my wife, is at Vespers. When she returns, she will prepare a room for you, for of course, we shall take you in. You were right to come here and I am touched that you should have thought of us. Now, wait here a moment.'

He vanished and Catherine was alone once more. She leant her weary head against the back of her chair. Something within her relaxed and grew quiet. At last she had reached port – no more roads and highways, cold, rain, fear and hunger; an end, for a while, of nights of journeying on and on, not knowing if there would be shelter at the other end. There was a lump in her throat when she thought of Arnaud in his prison, but she knew he was both proud and courageous. Besides, she felt an overwhelming confidence in this man who had taken her in without a qualm and offered her refuge.

Maître Jacques Coeur returned in a moment with a steaming bowl which he handed to her. Catherine's hands closed gratefully round it and a comforting, spicy smell met her nostrils.

'Wine and cinnamon,' said the furrier. 'Drink it while it's hot. Then you may talk. Don't worry about your servants. ... They are in the kitchen where my old Mahaut is taking care of them.'

Catherine sipped the hot drink and felt better. Coeur stood

watching her, chin in hand, one foot resting on the corner of the table. When she had finished, she set the bowl down. Her cheeks were a little pinker now, and she managed a smile.

'I will tell you the whole story now,' she said. 'It's rather long, but I'm feeling much better.'

She clasped her hands around her knees and began her tale, speaking in a quiet voice which was strangely moving. Coeur listened without moving a muscle. His stooping silhouette against the candle glow was as still as a wooden statue, but his eyes never left her face.

Catherine was just finishing her recital when there were sounds from below, followed by a noise like the crashing of thunder. Someone was running up the stairs four at a time. The furrier stood up and smiled encouragingly at Catherine.

'Don't be frightened. I think this is a visitor for you! I sent for him a short while ago.'

A tall figure was framed in the doorway: broad shoulders under a black ponyskin coat which was thrown back carelessly to reveal a short leather doublet and hose of the same colour; above that, a face at once hard and joyous, dancing brown eyes and a flaming shock of red hair. With a cry of delight, Catherine ran towards him. It was Xaintrailles! Xaintrailles of the fiery crest! The faithful follower of Joan of Arc and Arnaud's best friend!

He gave a roar of delight as he recognized her. None too gently, he swept her off her feet and kissed her soundly. Then he set her down and held her at arm's length to look at her.

'By the Lord's Intestines! Where have you sprung from, Catherine? You look like a wet rabbit! By God, it's good to see you again! What have you done with Montsalvy?'

'Arnaud? Didn't you know?'

The captain's hands tightened on her shoulders and his face darkened angrily.

'Know what? What some lunatics are noising up and down the land? That Montsalvy has gone over to the English? The greatest patriot in the country? One of the heroes of Agincourt? One of Joan's trusty followers? *My* friend?'

It was evidently the last title which conferred the most prestige on Arnaud in Xaintrilles's eyes, but Catherine was in no mood for laughter. She turned away.

'Others believe it. Messire de Rais . . .'

'May the plague take him, him and his damned cousin, La Tré-moille! I spend all my time tearing down those cursed posters from the town walls and I run anyone through who dares to stop me. As for those who try to read them, I give them a good box on the ears! What incredible stupidity! The idea that a man like that could be led to betray his country, especially by a woman he hates. . . .'

'It's not true! He loves me!' Catherine protested. 'There is no longer any barrier or cloud of mistrust between us. And if you want proof, messire, look at my belly!'

The violence of her attack left Xaintrailles gaping, but he soon recovered himself and burst out laughing.

' 'Od's Blood! That's good news! A little Montsalvy! We'll have a great baby and I'll be godfather. You owe me that, Catherine, and . . .' He stopped short and looked at Jacques Coeur who had not spoken since he came in. Then he cleared his throat and went on:

'Yes . . . I know. You were thinking that this is no time for celebration when this poor child is being hunted down like an animal and Arnaud . . . Where is he, by the way? Do you know, Catherine? Since the King paid my ransom and I was freed from the Earl of Arundel's highly civilized prison, I have been searching high and low for him without success.'

'He's not far, my friend, but you aren't likely to find him easily. La Trémoille has him prisoner in the château of Sully-sur-Loire.'

'By God . . .!'

Xaintrailles was purple with fury. He clenched his fists and Catherine saw his jaw bones jutting as he gritted his teeth. His brown eyes flashed and his anger exploded in the peaceful study.

'That scurvy dog dares to imprison a Montsalvy? He dares to tell the world that he deserted? He dares . . .'

'He dares in the King's name!' Jacques Coeur interrupted dryly. 'Calm yourself, Messire de Xaintrailles. Remember that, if you attack La Trémoille, you attack the King!'

'The King knows nothing of such intrigues. . . .'

'The King does not want to know about them,' the furrier corrected him. 'Believe me, sire, I know him well. Our King hates worries and complications. And then . . . he is in a delicate situation. His favourite loses no opportunity of reminding him that he owes his crown to a witch!'

'You don't believe that!' Catherine cried.

'Of course not, but La Trémoille makes good use of the trial at Rouen.'

'An English trial.'

'No, a Church trial. That's infinitely more irksome.'

Xaintrailles's fist crashed down, making the things on the table dance.

'What does all that matter? Arnaud is not going to stay in prison a moment longer. I give you my word, or my name is not Xaintrailles. I am going . . .'

Coeur's hand fell restrainingly on his arm.

'Where are you going, messire? To the King? You would be losing your time and probably signing your friend's death warrant. His Majesty would appear amazed and summon his favourite who would swear by all the gods that this was an abominable lie. . . . And, before tomorrow, Captain Montsalvy's body would be thrown down some *oubliette* or into the Loire.'

Catherine's moan reminded the two men that they must be more tactful. Xaintrailles looked anxiously at her, but Coeur smiled.

'Don't worry,' he said. 'I'll look after her. She will be safe here.'

The captain heaved a great sigh which might have been relief or annoyance. Then he slowly drew his heavy sword from its scabbard and brandished it in the candle flame before holding it out to the furrier.

'Very well! That only leaves this! Look at it well, Maître Jacques,' he said with a threatening smile. 'Mark my words. If I do not get Montsalvy out of that cursed place alive and whole, I shall sheath this blade in La Trémoille's rotting belly. I swear before God!'

He sheathed his sword again, then turned and kissed Catherine on both cheeks.

'Pray for me, fair lady! I shall make sure that your child has a father!'

She stood on tiptoe to kiss his cheek which smelt of lavender and horses.

'Look after yourself, Jean . . . I am frightened for you!'

'Bah!' cried the captain in high good humour again at the thought of the coming fray. 'I have several companions who will gladly help me play a trick on that fat pig. Besides, as La Hire says, the best way to stop yourself feeling afraid is to strike first. That's what I'm going to do and that's what I recommend in future. If Queen Yolande were here I would take you to her, but there is no one in the palace but that poor Queen Marie who doesn't know how to do anything but pray and make royal babies.'

With that, Jean Poton de Xaintrailles bounded down the stairs as fast as he had mounted them earlier. Jacques Coeur turned to Catherine. She stood watching from the window as the captain jumped onto his horse. Her eyes shone with a happiness that she had not felt for a long time.

'How good it is,' she murmured, 'to have friends like him ... and you! How wonderful it is to be confident once more!'

'It's time you thought of taking rest, my friend,' the furrier said gently, taking her by the hand. 'Let us see if Macée is back from church.'

Jacques Coeur's wife seemed to have been brought into the world expressly to be the wife of a man of high worth and an adventurous spirit. During the twelve years or so of their marriage, she had never once permitted herself to reproach him or make the slightest criticism. She contented herself with admiring him with all her heart and loving him proportionately. Catherine had always been very fond of Macée. She had come to know her while she was acting as lady-in-waiting to Queen Marie, and she had been on her way to visit her when Xaintrailles had come to fetch her to Arnaud's sick bed. She had often spent the afternoon with her friend, Marguerite de Culant, under the lime tree in the company of that sweet and gentle young woman.

Macée was blonde, shy, small and delicate-featured. She had pretty hazel eyes, a charming smile and a little pointed nose which in no way detracted from her charm. A daughter of the Provost of Bourges, Lambert de Leodepart, she had been carefully brought up and knew how to dress. Jacques Coeur had fallen in love with his pretty neighbour after seeing her on her way to Mass one day, dressed in scarlet velvet with a border of squirrel's fur and a matching cap on her pale blonde hair. He had at once asked his father to demand her hand in marriage for him. Pierre Coeur, a wealthy furrier from Saint-Pourcin, had been a little nervous of asking for the daughter of so notable a man, but Leodepart was an intelligent man. He sensed that Jacques was out of the ordinary and accorded him his daughter's hand in marriage without more ado.

Since then, the family had lived happily ever after, apart from a few financial troubles. Five children, Perrette, Jean,

Ravand, Henri and Geoffroy, had been born to the young couple. After his father's death, Jacques had willingly taken on the business and the happiness of the Coeur family had continued unclouded.

As Jacques had expected, his wife welcomed Catherine with great sweetness and touching solicitude. When they had first met, Macée had been a little apprehensive of the beauty and fame of the Dame de Brazey, knowing how susceptible her husband was to pretty women. Indeed, once or twice she had caught Jacques looking rather too intently at Catherine. But now, finding her so thin and pale and pregnant into the bargain, she stifled her doubts and let her warm heart speak for her. Catherine loved Arnaud as she herself loved her husband and this was all that Macée needed to make her welcome her guest as devotedly as a sister.

She installed Catherine and Sara in a room on the second floor with a window just below the eaves of the pointed roof. It looked out over the garden and faced a corresponding room which was used by the children.

The room was longer than it was wide, and an immense bed draped in blue serge and big enough to accommodate three or four people took up most of the space. Catherine liked it because it reminded her of the one she and Loyse shared in Uncle Mathieu's house in Dijon. It was above all tranquil, and she spent her first two days there in bed and fast asleep, except when she was roused for nourishment. She was so weary that she felt as though she could never have enough sleep. She did not even stir when Sara slipped in beside her. She had never felt so tired before in her whole life, not even the time she walked to Orleans. The child she was carrying was beginning to make itself felt.

On the morning of the third day, she was woken by the sound of childish voices singing. They were so near that the words impressed themselves clearly on her drowsy brain.

> And so my heart bemoaned
> The great grief it bore
> In this pleasant solitude
> Where the sweet wind blows . . .

Sung by these fresh young voices, the words of the old love song which Catherine knew well took on a new and unexpected charm and innocence. Without opening her eyes, she sang the next lines:

So softly one feels it not.
There did my lady go. . . .

'How long is it since I heard you singing?' Sara's voice inquired. Catherine opened her eyes and saw the gipsy sitting on the foot of the bed, waiting for her to wake as she had done so many hundreds of times before. She smiled and Catherine noticed that she had lost the half-starved bedraggled look she had after her escape from Champtocé. The food must be good at Maître Jacques's, because Sara's dusky cheeks had already filled out.

'I don't know,' the young woman answered, sitting up. 'But it must be a long time. Marguerite de Culant and I used to sing that song during Queen Marie's interminable embroidery sessions. I believe it was Messire Alain Chartier, the King's poet, who wrote it. Help me dress now, will you? I feel wonderful.'

Her sleep had done Catherine a world of good; she threw back her covers and scrambled to the foot of the bed like a sixteen-year-old. As she began washing, she asked:

'Is there any news of Messire Xaintrailles?'

'None! All that Maître Coeur was able to discover was that he left town yesterday with several companions shouting at the top of his voice that he was going hunting. That's all we know.'

'Pray heaven he arrives in time ... and that nothing bad has happened to my lord. . . .'

She stared at herself for a moment in the polished tin mirror, her eyes wet with tears.

'Help me finish dressing as soon as possible, Sara. I want to go to the church to pray.'

'In broad daylight? You can't be serious! Maître Coeur advises you not to go out before dark. There are too many people who might recognize you.'

'That's true,' Catherine said sadly. 'I'd forgotten that I was still more or less a prisoner.'

The children's voices struck up a new song next door, but this time a deep, masculine one joined in. Then another, so deep that it sounded like a cathedral bell – a bell which rang out of tune.

'Lord!' Catherine exclaimed. 'What's all that?'

'Gauthier,' Sara said, laughing. 'He has won the hearts of all the children and he often goes up to play with them when they are with their tutor.'

'Fancy! A tutor! I would never have supposed our friends lived in such style.'

'To tell the truth,' Sara said, picking up a comb and starting to dress Catherine's hair. 'He is a rather curious tutor – the most house-loving man you ever saw. He never leaves his room except to take a turn in the garden after dark.'

'Do you mean to say that I'm not the only person to seek refuge here?'

'By no means! One might almost say that Maître Coeur has taken it upon himself to give succour to everyone La Trémoille is persecuting! His household is the oddest imaginable. For instance, the famous tutor is none other than Maître Alain Chartier in person. La Trémoille does not like his "Ode on the Deliverance" written in honour of Joan of Arc and has had him banished.'

'So all you have to do is to sing Joan's praises to get into trouble?'

'Or have been one of her followers. So long as that fat creature is alive and in favour there will be no safety for those who lament her death and publicly maintain that she was a holy and virtuous girl. But there is more to come! In the house opposite, which belongs to Messire de Leodepart, you will find Messire Jean Pasquerel, Joan's almoner, and Imerguet, her page, both of whom are in hiding till times are easier. And there are others on the farms belonging to them.'

Catherine was flabbergasted. Not that it was surprising that Jacques Coeur and his father-in-law should have made their homes cells of resistance against the favourite; both men were high-minded and audacious enough for that. But their coolness was, nevertheless, amazing. To harbour all these people in Bourges itself, under La Trémoille's nose and not two paces from the Royal Palace, was proof of a courage far out of the ordinary. But apparently Jacques Coeur was not lacking in that . . .

Catherine had met Alain Chartier two or three times when she was in attendance upon Queen Marie. In those days, he followed Charles about everywhere as his secretary and official poet. He was a pleasant, well-educated man whose court life and post near the King had won him a few conquests and who therefore considered himself irresistible. Finding Catherine sitting at the Coeur family table, he shot her a significant glance.

'I thought Heaven would not abandon me entirely and would send me some charming feminine presence to help me endure

my exile! Oh, matchless woman, my heart was empty waiting
for you! The two of us together will create a secret garden, a
pleasant solitary spot.'

'And will there be a sweet wind in your solitary place, too?'
piped the childish treble of Geoffroy, aged five, the youngest
Coeur child. The poet shot him a stern glance under his greying
eyebrows.

'It is well that you should remember fine poetry, Master
Geoffroy,' he chided. 'But a child should not speak before
grown-ups.'

Geoffroy blushed and hid his face in his bowl while the rest
of the family repressed a laugh with difficulty. Catherine met
Jacques' eyes full upon her, sparkling with mirth, while Macée,
noticing the poet's air of chagrin, hastily set a portion of stuffed
carp before him. Chartier was sensitive, but he was also greedy
and the carp smelled good. He took a large mouthful and his
good humour seemed to be restored. Catherine thought affec-
tionately that he was rather like her Uncle Mathieu.

'You aren't eating a thing, Catherine,' Macée said, smiling.
'Are you still feeling unwell?'

'Dame Catherine is amazed at her good fortune!' the poet
intervened, momentarily abandoning his carp. 'She can't take
her eyes off the prophet and seer whom God has set in her
path. . . .'

He launched into a monologue and Catherine might well have
enjoyed it, if, just then, a sound of cries, followed by the rattle
of arms and horses' hooves, had not reached them from the
road outside. Jacques Coeur was on his feet in an instant, running towards his study. He appeared to have nerves of steel and
he was always on the alert. Catherine ran after him while
Macée sympathetically banged the poet on the back to dislodge
the piece of carp which had got stuck in the excitement and
was threatening to choke him.

The two study windows gave an oblique view up the rue
d'Auron. The street was full of archers under the command of
an officer on horseback. Several of them stood shoulder to
shoulder barring the way with their lances held crosswise, while
others were occupied in battering down the door of a house
three doors away from the Coeurs'. Jacques frowned.

'That is Naudin, the spurmaker's place. I wonder if . . .'

Before he could finish his sentence, the archers had rushed
into the house and were emerging again pushing before them
three men, one old, the others younger. The last was fighting

like a demon, using his feet and elbows and butting with his head in an effort to escape from the two men who held him. Catherine watched spellbound.

'What is happening?' she asked.

'Naudin was hiding a cousin of his wife's who had made the error of refusing to surrender a piece of land which the Lord Chamberlain had his eye on. Someone must have denounced them. It's a scandal! La Trémoille loots, steals and kills and the King takes no notice.'

In a sudden passion of resentment, Jacques snatched up a fragile blue glass vase from the table and dashed it to the floor where it shivered into a thousand fragments.

'But I am just as much a risk to you,' Catherine said dully. 'How can you be sure that someone won't denounce you to-morrow?'

'It's possible,' Coeur answered firmly. 'But I refuse to be intimidated. La Trémoille's real grudge against Naudin is that he loved, admired and supported the Maid and he publicly stated that it was wrong to have abandoned her so cravenly. All who talk like that are in danger. Even a respectable woman like Marguerite de Touroulde, with whom Joan lodged, is no longer safe. The favourite simply wants to wipe out anything in the kingdom which could remind him of the Maid. He was always against her and now he feels he has to get even with her in the grave, and that at a time when the kingdom needs peace above all else. We are short of money, culture is languishing and business dead. The great fairs are no longer held and merchandise avoids passing through France on its way from Venice to Bruges when it can go through the German States and Bavaria instead. What little remains goes into La Trémoille's coffers.'

'What are you going to do about it?'

'Nothing for the moment. The favourite is like a wild boar who must be hunted down with the weapons of war. I leave that to the Constable de Richemont and Queen Yolande when she returns. But once La Trémoille has been dispatched, it will be necessary to rebuild, to get commerce back on its feet and make money. That is why I am off when spring comes.'

'Off? But where?'

'To the Eastern Ports,' said the furrier, glancing at the great chart now hanging on the wall. 'When the equinoctial gales are past, the galley of Narbonne will set off on its annual tour of the Mediterranean. I shall go with her taking merchandise with me: enamels, fine fabrics, wine, coral from Marseilles to barter for silks, spices and furs, all of which are becoming impossible to find. And I shall forge new commercial links which the King will find very useful. Finally, when it is all under way, I shall re-open the old silver, iron, lead and copper mines which the Romans worked and which have been abandoned ever since. The kingdom will rise again, far richer . . . far, far, richer!'

Catherine looked at the merchant in amazement. He seemed to have forgotten her as he stood there, his gaze far away, imagining his ambitious dream come true. There was something of the prophet in this man. For an instant she seemed to go back in time and hear her husband, Garin de Brazey, talking. He too believed in the importance of trade with the East. The one-eyed Treasurer would have understood and appreciated this bold merchant, so like him in so many ways. A deeper silence fell in the quiet little room. The uproar in the street outside had died away. One or two passers-by hurried past, darting frightened glances at Naudin's splintered door. A few drops of rain began to fall. . . .

'Don't you see,' Catherine pleaded, 'you just haven't the right to run the risk, however small, of keeping me here? Your future is too important, Maître Jacques. Once people start informing, you are no longer safe. Can't you take me to some country cottage or farm where I could wait till Xaintrailles returns?'

But anger had roused him from his usual reserve. He leant over to Catherine where she sat, hands folded in her lap, and took her soft face between his palms.

'There are few rare and precious things left in this poor country of ours, Catherine. You are one of them and I envy the man you love with all my heart. I have only the right to your friendship, so let me deserve it. If it means a little danger, so much the better – it will prove my devotion to you. You shall remain here.'

He leant over further and, before he could stop himself, placed his lips against hers. But it was a light, tender, soft kiss, the sort of kiss which comes from the spirit rather than the flesh. Catherine shivered slightly, however, and involuntarily found pleasure in the touch of his lips. The furrier's hands trembled a little on her shoulders and she knew he was deeply moved. Then he pushed her gently away to arm's length.

'I forbid you to move from here, Catherine. You must trust me.'

'Of course I trust you! My fears are all for you and your family.'

'Don't worry! I can look after my family as well as protecting you.'

Jacques's fingers gripped Catherine harder than he knew in his eagerness to persuade her to share his confidence in himself. He had quite forgotten the scene in the street and he started when a quiet voice spoke from the doorway:

'You must go down to the shop, Jacques. The Dame de la Trémoille is asking for you, and you know how impatient she gets.'

They both turned to where Macée stood, apparently quite poised and unruffled. Catherine felt herself blush. How long had she been standing there? Had she seen her husband kiss his guest? Nothing in her behaviour suggested it. She must have only just arrived! Still, Catherine felt guilty and could not help lowering her eyes.

'I was telling Maître Jacques how much I disliked endangering you all by my presence, Macée,' she said. 'I was asking him to let me go.'

Macée came forward with a smile.

'I'm sure he reassured you on that point. Any guest here is regarded as sent by God, and as such, is sacred. Anyway, where could you go, Dame Catherine? Come, Jacques, you must go down. She is growing angry.'

Macée's arrival had made them forget momentarily the seriousness of her message. Catherine shuddered as she thought of the woman who stood below her at that very moment. The Dame de la Trémoille! The lovely Catherine de la Trémoille! The woman who had Arnaud in her power, whom he had always spurned and whom Catherine had once deeply offended. She went pale and turned to the furrier.

'Quick, Maître Coeur, I beg you ... you mustn't give her the least cause for suspicion. If she had the slightest reason to think I was here we should all be lost. She would recognize me even under a monk's robes and she hates me.'

'I know,' said Jacques. 'I'm going. ...'

Macée and Catherine were left alone, face to face, speechless. They did not look at each other, but, with one accord, strained their ears to hear what was happening below. They did not have long to wait. First came the firm, slightly ponderous tread of Jacques Coeur descending the stairs, then a high-pitched woman's voice addressing him. Catherine de la Trémoille had never bothered to lower her voice throughout the whole of her chaotic and malodorous existence. Wherever she went she made herself heard. Macée and Catherine had no difficulty in following the conversation.

'Maître Coeur,' said the Grand Chamberlain's wife, 'how is it that I have not yet received the sables I ordered from you? The cold weather is coming and you know I can't stand those bulky furs.'

'I thought I had convinced you that I don't like them either, madame. As for the sables, I would willingly deliver them to you if I could, but the fact is, they have become unobtainable. The caravans of merchants who used to travel from Nijni-Novgorod to the fair at Châlons no longer come to this country. They go on to London or stop at Venice.'

'Then get them from Venice . . .'

'We no longer have the means, madame. The country is bled dry. No ships are available and the boats which ply between Venice and Bruges no longer call at our ports. As for going to Bruges, you know very well that is forbidden to King Charles's subjects by order of the Duke of Burgundy!'

The lady's sigh was so dramatic that both Macée and Catherine heard it. Catherine's nerves were so taut that her head ached. Listening to the voice of the woman she hated, now only a few paces away, was something of an ordeal. She stepped to the window and glanced out. The Dame de la Trémoille was getting exasperated.

'Very well, then, I shall have to be content with what you have got. I want you to come to the Palace and show me your finest furs. Or, better still, now that I am here, show them to me at once. You can have the ones I choose sent to me!'

'How is it we didn't hear her arrive?' Catherine whispered, looking out at the crowd of horsemen and ladies-in-waiting who jostled each other in the street outside and who made almost as much noise as the soldiers had earlier.

'You were too absorbed,' said Macée, her voice so gentle that Catherine could detect no double meaning in her remark. 'You couldn't have heard, but I don't like this woman staying here too long. She has sharp eyes and ears and nothing escapes her. . . .'

'And my presence here doesn't help,' said Catherine bitterly. 'If she only knew!'

'We don't risk any more hiding you here than Maître Alain Chartier,' Jacques' wife said quietly. 'Anyway, how can one ever feel safe from spies nowadays? You should go back to your room, Catherine.'

She shook her head. She felt she had to stay. She had often noticed that the close proximity of danger was less frightening than a distant menace. Moreover, she took a sort of wry pleasure in defying, by her invisible presence, this dangerous woman who would stop at nothing to take Arnaud from her. The Grand Chamberlain's wife was apparently going through the entire stock of the shop. They could hear the thud of bundles of skins being thrown onto the counter and the even voice of the merchant commenting on them. Catherine stood, with her face pressed against the window, waiting for she knew not what. The departure of the dangerous customer? The return of Jacques's comforting presence? Both perhaps . . .

All of a sudden, her absent gaze sharpened. A cart drawn by a huge, lazy horse was coming from the direction of the Porte d'Auron and was slowly climbing the hill. It stopped outside the Coeurs' house. It was one of those peasant vehicles made of rough-hewn planks with clumsy wooden wheels which jolted over the furrows left in the alleyway by the recent rains. Its cargo consisted of a somewhat unsteady heap of firewood which threatened to fall off at any moment.

It was, in fact, a perfectly ordinary cart with nothing about it to catch the eye . . . except, perhaps, the figure of the man who was driving it. Seeing him sitting there on the front seat, knees wide apart, shoulders hunched under a wretched little cloak, Catherine had a powerful sensation of having seen him before . . . he wore a black hooded jacket which concealed all but a small part of his face with its short beard. Could it be something familiar in his bearing which had caught Catherine's eye? She had no sooner asked herself this when the man turned and looked at her. Catherine's hand flew to her mouth. The peasant on the cart was none other than Xaintrailles! Catherine ran to Macée and dragged her to the window by her arm.

'Look!' she said. 'Do you see who that is?'

Macée went pale.

'Heavens!' she exclaimed, clasping her hands. 'He's only too easily recognizable!'

Then, as the peasant climbed down off his perch with the evident intention of going over the threshold of the shop, Macée flew off like an arrow and Catherine heard her running down the stairs. She must have raced through the shop, because, in no time at all, Catherine saw her burst out into the street and only just in time to prevent Xaintrailles entering, all unaware of the danger which awaited him. Jacques's wife planted herself in front of him, tossing her head in its high, horned headdress so as to conceal the man's face as much as possible. She cried out angrily:

'What are you thinking of, my man? One doesn't bring a load of firewood through the shop, but into the yard. Back up your horse, please, and I will have the gate opened.'

'Sorry, ma'am,' the man answered with a fruity Berrichon accent. 'Didn't know, y'see. It was Robin, your bailiff, sent me, seeing as he's twisted his knee and that . . .'

'All right, all right,' said Macée crossly. 'Now, back to your horse. Can't you see it's in the way of these gentlefolk?'

The Dame de la Trémoille's escort in their red and blue livery had fallen back disdainfully to get out of the way of this coarse rustic and it was doubtless this which had saved the impudent captain from being recognized. Catherine felt the icy sweat trickling down her back. Her hands were frozen and she trembled with an inexplicable impatience. Why should Xaintrailles, who was free to come and go in the town as he pleased, choose to enter in disguise, and such a wretched disguise, too? What was hidden in the cart?

She felt a rush of blood to her face. A servant had opened the gate and Xaintrailles was turning the cart, dragging his feet like a true peasant. Catherine could no longer contain herself. She picked up her skirts and ran through the main room to the wooden gallery overlooking the inner courtyard which Xaintrailles and his cart were now entering. He saw her standing there and smiled — a smile which entered her cold heart like a ray of sunshine into an empty room. The captain would never smile like that if anything had happened to Montsalvy.

At the other end of the courtyard, old Mahaut, the Coeurs' faithful maid, was flapping a cloth to frighten away the hens while Sara helped Macée open the barn doors to admit the cart. Gauthier and a servant were shutting the double doors of the gateway. By the time Catherine reached the courtyard, both horse and cart were safely hidden. The captain did not even look at her.

'Quick!' he cried. 'Help me!'

He was pulling the logs out of the cart with furious haste and flinging them on the ground.

'What's in that cart?' asked Catherine.

'Don't ask silly questions! What do you think?'

She flung herself on the logs with a moan. They uncovered a sort of compartment at the bottom of the cart, but, as Catherine reached out for the lattice-work grille which covered it, Xaintrailles pushed her aside and almost threw her into Sara's arms.

'Don't let her see him now,' he muttered. 'He's not a pretty sight! We were only just in time . . .'

As he lifted off the cover, a human form was revealed. It was indescribably filthy, its haggard, waxen face half hidden by a straggling black beard. Its eyes were shut and it looked so much like a corpse in its immobility that Catherine tore herself from Sara's grasp with a wild scream and flung herself on the inert body sobbing frantically:

'Arnaud! . . . My God! Arnaud, what have they done to you?'

CHAPTER EIGHT

The Ghost

She was so convinced that the body she was clasping had yielded up the ghost, that Xaintrailles had to drag her off by force.

'He needs immediate attention, Catherine. No tears now. Is there a room where we can put him, Dame Macée?'

'There is mine,' Catherine cried, drying her eyes.

'Good. Go and see if the coast is clear.'

Xaintrailles swung his friend's body up in his arms with no apparent effort and Arnaud's head lolled back against his shoulder. He seemed neither to see nor hear anything around him. He was like a great puppet whose strings had been broken. Catherine covered her mouth with her hands and her eyes filled with tears.

'He is going to die . . .' she wailed. 'He's going to die!'

'I hope not,' Xaintrailles snapped. 'I came as fast as I could. Open that door.'

'It might perhaps be better to wait till the Dame de la Trémoille has left the house,' Sara ventured.

The captain glared at her, his face contorted by anger.

'There isn't a minute to lose, do you hear! As for that red-headed whore, I'll strangle her if I get my hands on her! I swear it by my father's sword and my mother's honour! Open, I tell you! We need a bed and a doctor.'

Just then the door opened and Gauthier's imposing bulk filled the doorway. His pale eyes went from Xaintrailles to the tearful Catherine and back.

'Give him to me, messire! I can carry him more easily than you. Maître Coeur sent me to say that the lady has gone.'

Arnaud looked like a child cradled in the giant's huge arms. Gauthier strode across the courtyard. A fine drizzle was falling and night was beginning to fall. Old Mahaut and Sara had gone on ahead to prepare the bed and open doors. In spite of Xaintrailles's efforts to detain her, Catherine broke free and raced along after the Norman. She heard Xaintrailles call out behind her:

'Wait, Catherine! Don't go up yet!'

But she was deaf to everything save this voice inside her repeating: 'He is going to die. . . . He is going to die!' The noise pounded in her ears and her heart beat painfully. She saw Gauthier lay Arnaud on the bed as she arrived, panting, at the head of the stairs, but then Sara tried to bar her way.

'Let us see to him first, my dear,' the gipsy said gently. 'He is in a bad way and in your condition . . .'

'What does my condition matter?' Catherine ground out between clenched teeth. 'What does the child matter if Arnaud is dying? He belongs to me, do you hear? To me alone! No one has the right to stand in the way when he needs me. . . .'

Reluctantly Sara stood back and let Catherine pass. She shook her head and murmured:

'I don't really know if he is in pain. His eyes are open, but he is unconscious. He doesn't seem able to see. . . .'

Gathering up her courage, Catherine steeled herself against the flood of misery which threatened to overcome her. She must not lose control of herself . . . not now! She must be brave and look the truth in the face, however unpleasant. An inner voice whispered that only thus would she have any chance of saving Arnaud. She clasped her hands together, as she always did in a crisis, and went towards the bed where Mahaut was bustling about.

Now Gauthier was blocking her way. The Norman stood in the middle of the room looking at her with a strange expression in his face compounded of anger and grief. He opened his mouth as though to speak, then shrugged and went to the door. Catherine had not even noticed him. All she could see was Arnaud and old Mahaut's hunched form bending over him.

'What a state he's in, sweet Jesus! What a state he's in! Poor gentleman!' the nurse wailed.

With Sara's help, she stripped the sick man of the stinking, muddy rags wrapped round his skinny body. It looked as though the prisoner must have been cast into a dungeon full of liquid manure. As they tried to remove the last rags from his chest and back, they found they were stuck and the flesh beneath began to bleed.

'He is hurt,' Catherine whispered, horrified. She laid a trembling hand on his forehead and pushed back his long hair.

'We'll never do it like this,' Mahaut murmured. 'Sara, go down to the kitchen and tell them to bring up a tub and several buckets of hot water. Quick! We'll have to give him a bath.'

Sara vanished just as Xaintrailles and Jacques Coeur appeared in the doorway. The former came and stood behind Catherine who had begun, in her turn, removing the strips of rag with infinite care. She glanced up at him.

'Where did you find him, that he should be in this state?' she asked. 'In an *oubliette*?'

'Almost! At the bottom of a disgusting ditch where the water of the Loire trickled in. The mud floor was never dry. He was chained down by manacles on his hands and feet, in total darkness. His food – or what passed for it – was pushed through a hole. The door was sealed; we had to break it down. The guard was a monstrous brute, a black hunchback as strong as a Turk. It took three men to overpower him.'

'What did you do with him?'

'What one does with a rat: we exterminated him. I cut his throat and threw him into the hole before removing Montsalvy. I swear I thought he was dead at first. He didn't move. But then I saw he was still breathing, though faintly. I would have given anything to have laid my hands on a doctor. One of my men had picked up a bit of knowledge from the monks. He forced a little milk and broth into him, but there was no time to do more. We had to hurry. We wrapped him as well as we could in a cloak and brought him on horseback as far as the outskirts of Bourges where I got this cart from one of Maître Jacques's stewards. As God is my witness, Catherine, I was in mortal terror all along the way that I was bringing back a corpse to you. La Trémoille and his gang will pay for this!'

'For the moment,' Catherine said harshly, 'he has suffered nothing worse than a dead gaoler.'

'... and twenty dead men and a château in flames!' Xaintrailles added calmly. 'What do you take me for? I did what I could, naturally. I was in a hurry, but I found the time to set fire to the place all the same. . . .'

'Forgive me,' said Catherine, without looking up.

Now two servants appeared carrying the huge tub. A cloth was placed in it and it was filled with hot water. Meanwhile, Maître Jacques had been standing looking at the sick man without a word. His eyes moved from the long, motionless body on the bed to Catherine's pure profile silhouetted against the candlelight and the long lashes which cast such soft shadows on her cheeks. Mahaut caught his eye and shrugged her shoulders.

'We need a doctor,' she said. 'As soon as possible.'

Jacques Coeur started like a man brutally awakened, and went to the door.

'I will go myself,' he said, stifling a sigh.

Catherine had not given the slightest sign of being aware of his presence from the moment he entered the room. She seemed totally absorbed in the sufferings of the motionless man who was but a shadow of his former self. . . .

With infinite care, Catherine, Xaintrailles and Sara lifted Arnaud from the bed and lowered him into the tub into which Mahaut had tipped a little phial of aromatic oil and a small bunch of marshmallow root. The greyish body whose skin clung to the wasted muscles disappeared beneath the foaming water. At this, Arnaud opened his eyes which were red and oddly marked and spotted. His lips moved and curious sounds came forth, so curious, indeed, that Xaintrailles went pale with fright.

' 'Od's Blood!' he cried, seizing his friend's head and forcing open the mouth to look inside it. 'I was afraid,' he stammered. 'I thought they had cut out his tongue.'

There was a cry of horror from Catherine. She was not looking at him, but was passing her hand slowly to and fro in front of Arnaud's wide open eyes.

'He . . . he can't see! His eyes don't move, even when I put my hand near them!'

'I know,' said Xaintrailles. 'I noticed that several times during the ride here. But . . .' he added hastily, as Catherine started to sob, 'you mustn't give up hope, my sweet. This may have something to do with the weakened state he's in. We must wait for the doctor.'

The bath took a long time. Little by little, the oil-streaked water darkened with dissolved filth. Greasy dirt, wisps of adhering cloth, lice and vermin gradually sloughed off the body whose skin was slowly returning to a more normal hue. Long, swollen weals appeared now on his chest and back, and beads of blood stood out along them.

'What have they done to him?' Mahaut asked with an accusing glance at Xaintrailles. The latter turned away and fumblingly dealt with a smoking candle wick.

'They whipped him!' he said hoarsely. 'The fair La Trémoille knows how to avenge herself when she is slighted. They treated him worse than an animal. . . . This is the result of his loyalty to his love!'

Catherine ground her teeth. She stepped forward, eyes flashing, and impetuously tossed back a straying lock of hair.

'She'll have to pay for this!' she cried. 'One of these days, she will pay for all this ... for my sorrow and his suffering! She will pay in blood and tears!'

She trembled like a leaf as she sank down on her knees beside the tub. Xaintrailles raised her gently and held her against him for a moment as if to pass on some of his own vital warmth to her.

'Wait till Montsalvy is strong again,' he said gravely. 'He has always known how to settle his own scores. There are some women who must be fought as you would a man!'

Catherine sniffed into the captain's jacket, then spoke in a tiny, sad voice:

'But he is quite wasted away. You can see ...'

'Don't you believe it! I've seen Arnaud so often half alive – and most of my other friends, too, if it comes to that – that I shall never think of him as finished till I see him stiff and cold. And not even then!'

They had just put Arnaud back to bed after drying and dressing him when Jacques Coeur appeared and announced that the doctor was on his way. Gauthier and two servants took away the tub of dirty water. Now that he was clean, the young man's tragic pallor showed up more clearly than ever. Xaintrailles had shaved his friend in the bath and his smooth face was so emaciated that the bones seemed to be covered only with thin parchment marked with the fine scars of old wounds.

He looked younger this way and his complete immobility gave him a touching, helpless air. Catherine recalled the wounded knight they had found years ago on the road to Flanders. He had been still and unconscious that night too, but then he had been struck down in the fullness of his powers. One felt that life was bubbling up within the damaged body and that, as soon as he regained consciousness, he would be off to the wars again. But now Arnaud seemed to be lost in a sleep without end ... and Catherine, in her despair, would have given several years of her own life to see him open his eyes and smile.

The arrival of a new personage in the room put an end to her painful train of thought and brought her sharply back to reality. In truth, the newcomer was the sort of figure which would arrest the most wandering attention. He was tall, thin and slightly stooping. His long, yellow face had full, red lips, a big, hooked nose and small eyes set deep beneath beetling brows. Long, curiously plaited hair fell about his bony shoulders and mingled with a beard which might have been composed of

ebony shavings. A thick black robe billowed round him with
a sinister yellow roundel sewn on the breast on which
Catherine's eyes lighted with amazement. The man caught her
eye and laughed wryly.

'Are you afraid of the children of Israel, madame? I swear
that I have never killed a child and ground it to powder, if that
is what worries you ...'

Jacques Coeur's grave voice interrupted before Catherine
could speak.

'Rabbi Moshe ben Yehuda is the most learned doctor in the
town. He studied in the University of Montpellier and there is
no one better qualified to tend my guest. I have often called
upon him myself, for he is both wise and skilled.'

'Isn't there a single Christian doctor in this town?' Xaintrailles said with a grimace. 'I heard that Maître Aubert ...'

'Maître Aubert is a donkey who would kill your friend more
surely than all La Trémoille's torturers. Hebrew science is
second only to Moorish in its learning. It is rooted in Salerno
where the famous Trotula has his practice.'

While Jacques was speaking, Moshe ben Yehuda went up to
the bed and stood looking at the sick man with narrowed eyes.

'He is not conscious,' Catherine murmured. 'Sometimes he
opens his eyes, but he sees nothing. He babbles meaningless
words ...'

'I know,' interrupted the doctor. 'Maître Coeur has explained
it all to me. Will you stand back, please ... I want to examine
him.'

Catherine moved away reluctantly. This tall, black figure
bent over Arnaud seemed like a bad omen to her. He looked so
much like an evil spirit. But she was forced to admire his skill,
as his long, supple fingers investigated the wounded man's body,
lingering on the long weals on his back, some of which were
suppurating. He asked for clean water in a basin, and some
wine. Sara and Mahaut provided both in an instant.

Then he washed his hands before touching Arnaud's face.
Catherine watched him gently lift the eyelids and examine the
damaged eyes. He whistled softly.

'Is it serious?' she asked timidly.

'I can't say. I have often seen these cases of blindness among
people who have been imprisoned for a long time. It is an infection due, I believe, to the bad food given to them. Hippo-
crates called it "keratis".'

'Does that mean that he will be permanently ... blind?'

asked Xaintrailles in a voice so hoarse with pain that Catherine
held out a comforting hand to him. The Rabbi shook his black
plaits.

'Who can tell? Some of them lose their sight, but others get
it back – often quite quickly. Thanks to the Most High, I know
how to look after him as well as anyone.'

He was already engaged upon his task. First he carefully
washed all the wounds with wine. Then he smeared them with
an ointment made of mutton fat, powdered incense and tere-
binthine, finally bandaging them with fine linen. Then he placed
a poultice of belladonna and palm leaves over Arnaud's eyes
with instructions to change it every day.

'Feed him on goat's milk and honey,' he said at last, when
the job was done. 'Make sure you keep him perfectly clean. If
he is in pain, give him a few grains of poppy seed – I will leave
you as much as you will need. Finally, pray to Yahveh to have
mercy upon him, because He alone is the Master of life and
death.'

'But won't you be coming back every day?' asked Catherine
in surprise, moving to the bed and taking Arnaud's hand in
hers.

Rabbi Moshe smiled bitterly, but did not answer. It was
Jacques Coeur who explained in an embarrassed voice:

'Alas, there will not be a second visit. Rabbi Moshe has to
leave the town tonight . . . along with all his co-religionists. The
King has given his orders: by sunrise, all the Jews must be out
of the town under pain of death. I have already delayed Rabbi
Moshe in his departure!'

A deathly silence greeted these words. Catherine rose slowly
to her feet and looked from Jacques to the doctor.

'But . . . why?'

Xaintrailles answered cuttingly:

'La Trémoille never has enough gold! Therefore, it appears,
he has finally obtained this edict concerning the Jews. *They*
may be chased out, but not their gold! They have to go without taking a thing with them. Tomorrow, La Trémoille's
coffers will bulge! And once they are empty again, I dare say
he will turn his attention elsewhere – to the Lombards,
perhaps.'

Though this news affected her only indirectly, it was the last
drop in the cup of bitterness for Catherine. Her nerves suddenly
gave way; her body stiffened and jerked as if torn by painful
cramp. Sara rushed to her and tried to raise her, but without

success. She had seized one of the bedposts and clung there, moaning:

'La Trémoille ... La Trémoille ... I don't want to hear that name ever again! ... Never! ... Never! ... Not La Trémoille! He will devour us all! ... Stop him! Why don't you stop him? Don't you see him standing there in the shadows sneering? Stop him!'

The doctor came and knelt down beside her. He took her head in his hands and stroked and rubbed it gently, murmuring words of calming effect, or of exorcism, in the Hebrew tongue. Catherine seemed to be struggling with a demon which possessed her, but gradually, under Rabbi Moshe's treatment, she quietened; her body relaxed, floods of tears poured from her eyes and her breathing became easier.

'This has all been too much for her,' said Maître Jacques's calm voice. 'She has suffered too much already at this man's hands.'

'Unfortunately she is not the only one,' said Xaintrailles gloomily. 'There is suffering and weeping throughout the kingdom because of La Trémoille. . . .'

The furrier smiled bitterly and his voice sharpened.

'And the captains and the soldiers put up with it! How much longer? How much longer, messire, will you and your men allow this man free rein?'

'Not a moment longer than necessary, Maître Jacques. You may be sure of that!' the captain replied stoutly. 'Just enough time to round up all the huntsmen we need to smoke the old boar out of his lair. At the moment, the huntsmen are all dispersed – they have to be summoned back from the four corners of the earth.'

Catherine's attack was over. Now she rose to her feet, leaning on Sara's arm, a little shamefaced. Mahaut wanted to put her to bed, but she refused.

'I'm all right now. I want to stay by him. I won't sleep tonight, I know. If he were to die . . .'

She could hardly bear to speak of her fear of not being there if Arnaud were to die in the night. Xaintrailles understood.

'I will keep watch with you, Catherine. Death would not dare to take him from the two of us.'

All night long, Catherine and Xaintrailles sat by Arnaud's bedside, listening to his breathing and watching for the slightest sign of weakening. Two or three times the sick man's breath-

ing stopped and Catherine's heart seemed to stop too. She spent
hours kneeling in prayer despite her weariness, while Xaintrailles or Sara took it in turns to keep the vigil. This night became a sort of symbol for her. She convinced herself that these
hours, slowly passing away, were of paramount significance.
If he were still alive at daybreak, he would be saved ... but
would he still be alive when the sun came back to warm the
earth? Rabbi Moshe had indicated before he left that his
greatest anxiety was caused by Arnaud's excessively weakened
condition. He had made him take several spoonfuls of milk and
honey and then an infusion of poppy seed to calm him, but it
was the sick man's inertia which alarmed Catherine most. It
would take so little to snuff out the faint spark of life which
still burned in him.

Xaintrailles barely slept either. He sat on a stool, hands
clasped, looking at his friend. From time to time he spoke as if
to keep up his spirits.

'He will pull out of it,' he said with conviction. 'He can't possibly go under now. Think of Compiègne, Catherine! We
thought he was dying then, too!'

But sometimes he closed his eyes and brushed them with the
backs of his hands. Was it to brush the tears away, or just that
he could no longer bear the sight of that motionless figure with
bandaged eyes? Outside, they could hear the footsteps of the
Jews going into banishment, shuffling along towards the gates
under the weight of the few possessions they had been allowed
to take with them. How many of them would reach Carpentras
or Beaucaire, the southern towns where Jewish colonies were
powerful and protected?

The cock crowed to herald the dawn. The bells of the Jacobin
convent sounded and soon a little light began to steal into the
sky. A band of light appeared in the east and spread till it overcame the night. A trumpet sounded on the ramparts to
announce the opening of the gates and the changing of the
guard. ... And then, Arnaud moved.

His hands groped over the coverlet and then stretched out
before him in the habitual gesture of the blind. Xaintrailles and
Catherine stood watching him, not daring to breathe.
Catherine's heart was pounding so hard that it was painful.
Would the charm be broken if she moved? He mumbled like
someone in a dream:

'Night! ... Always night!'

CHAPTER NINE

'*I, Arnaud!*'

On the night of December 28th, 1431, a little group of people left the house in the rue d'Auron long after the curfew had sounded, on their way to the near-by church of St Pierre-le-Guillard. The night was black as the snow was white, but the bitter cold which had gripped the town for some three weeks showed signs of relenting a little. Ever since Christmas, Bourges had been shrouded in white and silence, so hushed it might have been listening to its own heart-beats. The joyful festivities which annually celebrated the Christ Child's birth had brought an end temporarily to La Trémoille's extortions and the house-to-house raids of his soldiery. But the city had been too deeply wounded to do more than savour the great feast of Christmas in an unaccustomed silence and tranquillity.

It was the first time Catherine had left the Coeurs' house since her arrival there some two months earlier, and she plunged her fur-lined boots into the crisp snow with an exclamation of delight. She squeezed Arnaud's arm a little tighter.

'The town looks more bridal than I do,' she murmured, smiling.

In reply he pressed the slender fingers which were ungloved despite the cold so that they might be clasped the more readily.

'She has attired herself in our honour,' he said tenderly. 'I have never seen her look lovelier. And I have never loved you so deeply, my beloved.'

They were still intoxicated by the simple joy of being together at last and they clung to each other in the street like any loving couple. For Arnaud the joy was redoubled by the fact that he had at long last regained his health.

Ever since the morning his raging fever had subsided, his convalescence had been swift. The young man's robust constitution, which had saved him from death so many times before, had once again accomplished a miracle. He was still thin but he could walk steadily now and lead a normal life again, although the lack of exercise and cloistered life was a sore trial to him.

'I'm really not made for life between four walls,' he told
Catherine with a comical grimace as he strode up and down
his room trying to strengthen his wasted muscles.

'You know you will soon be out on the great highways
again,' she said, with a touch of regret. 'We shall leave the
moment Maître Coeur thinks we can do so without too much
risk.'

'Risk? That's a funny way for a soldier to look at things!
Risk has always been a part of my life, fair lady, and . . .'

'. . . And you miss it now, I know!' Catherine said with some
resentment. Both she and Jacques Coeur had had the greatest
difficulty in the world in restraining the impulsive young man
from rushing to the Royal Palace the moment his strength
returned. He spoke of nothing but flinging himself at the King's
feet and demanding a hearing, of challenging La Trémoille to a
duel, of slapping his face in full view of the Royal Council,
and other equally rash projects which his sense of honour suggested to him and which put Catherine through hours of
anxiety.

It was for this reason that she had not dwelt at too much
length on her sufferings at the hands of Gilles de Rais, when
telling him of her experiences at Champtocé. In the first place
her promise to Jean de Craon not to reveal Gilles's degrading
secret to a soul obliged her to keep silent about most of what
had occurred, and secondly it would have been pointless, if not
dangerous, to excite Arnaud's wrath any further in their present situation. He had already sworn to seek out the Sire de
Rais and tax him with his outrageous behaviour towards
Catherine, but she finally succeeded in making him understand
that the Gilles de Rais affair was closely bound up with the La
Trémoille affair. They were in fact interdependent, and there
was little point in attacking the fat Chamberlain's allies till
the man himself had been brought down. It had been Xaintrailles, once again, who made his friend see reason.

'Your honour can wait, my son, and La Trémoille will have to
wait too. When will you understand that one doesn't hunt a
fox the way one hunts wild boar or wolves! You don't know
what the Palace is like at present. You wouldn't get anywhere
near the Grand Chamberlain; you would be seized, loaded with
chains and thrown into the deepest and darkest dungeon. La
Trémoille knows you of old and he knows that the very first
thing you will do now you are free is revenge yourself. He will
accordingly have taken his precautions. As for your notion of

seeing the King, that sounds to me like the ravings of a deranged mind.'

'I am a Montsalvy and my patents of nobility give me the right to speak to the King when I want without seeking an audience.'

'Your friend La Trémoille knows that too. But he is more powerful than you begin to imagine: did you know that he laid a trap for the Constable de Richemont in August and had three of his emissaries arrested: Antoine de Viyonne, André de Beaumont and Louis d'Amboise? The first two were beheaded and the third was put to ransom. I would remind you that while you may be a Montsalvy, Viyonne was a Mortemart, and therefore every bit as noble-blooded as yourself. And I might add too that Richemont himself would have suffered a similar fate if La Trémoille had succeeded in laying his hands on him. When are you going to realize that La Trémoille enjoys absolute power nowadays and has no intention of letting it slip through his fingers in a hurry! He has made himself rich, he has satisfied his monstrous pride and conceit, and can at last indulge his appetite for power. He cares little whether we are French or English so long as he rules the country! No, I beg you, stay quiet for the time being. Get back your strength and wait till Queen Yolande returns ... and leave La Trémoille to pile idiocy upon idiocy. His men are searching for you and would be only too happy to lay hands on you.'

Arnaud ground his teeth.

'You mean that Richemont allowed this to happen? And the King said nothing?'

'The King is completely under his thumb and Richemont has retired for the moment to wait till the moment is ripe for retaliation. Do as he does ... and begin by getting back your strength.'

Catherine had thanked Xaintrailles warmly for this timely homily. Had it not been for him God alone knows what follies Montsalvy's hot blood might have urged him to commit. But at last he seemed to understand and no longer spoke of rushing to the Palace. ...

The vast bulk of the church looming before her interrupted Catherine's train of thought. The grey stones of the old chapel were dressed in thick white fur tonight, and there was a little matching cap on the square tower. The black trees and old lichened well seemed to huddle closer to the Roman walls as if trying to warm themselves. Macée Coeur had told Catherine the legend attached to this church, which was already two hundred years old. How the mule belonging to the rich Jewish merchant Zacharias Guillard had knelt one wintry day before the Holy Sacrament carried by Saint Anthony of Padua, and how neither the blows nor curses of the old Jew had succeeded in getting the mule back to his feet again till the saintly monk had passed by. The church had been erected on the site of the miracle with gold given by the repentant Zacharias, now a convert to Christianity.

Catherine had retained a taste for legends and strange tales from her childhood in the shadow of Notre-Dame. Her father, Gaucher Legoix, had enjoyed telling them to her, and sometimes he would engrave the beautiful gold or silver covers for the Holy Books just to see the little girl's face light up with joy.

As she crossed the musty threshold into St Pierre-le-Guillard, Catherine thought of her father with a keen pang of regret. Gentle Gaucher, who hated the sight of blood, had died because Catherine hid the brother of this same Arnaud who would shortly be her husband, in his cellar. The goldsmith of the Pont-au-Change could never have dreamed of such a stormy and brilliant life for his daughter and Catherine reflected that this was probably just as well, because she was not at all sure that Gaucher would have been altogether pleased.

The church was dark but for a faint light coming from a side chapel. Jacques and Macée went over to the chapel confidently, but Catherine shivered. It was cold in here. It reminded her of another wintry chapel one morning nine years earlier. That day she had worn jewels fit for a queen, and sumptuous robes, but her heart had been frozen with fear and despair. That day too the snow had fallen over the gently undulating Saône countryside which stretched away on all sides as far as the eye could see. That day, by order of the Duke, she had married Garin de Brazey, Lord Treasurer of Burgundy, with her soul in tumult and her heart full of thoughts of another man. How different it was today!

This time there was no fairly-like dress, magnificent jewels, glittering guests or brilliantly illuminated chapel. She wore a simple green wool dress banded with black velvet, in which she felt comfortable despite her increasing waistline, and over it an ample black coat lined with squirrel, a present from Macée for this wintry bridal night. But all around her were loving hearts and best, best of all, she was marrying the man she had chosen from all others, adored through thick and thin and won only by superhuman efforts and self-sacrifice. It was *his* arm which supported her over the uneven flags of the church floor, *his* proud, clear-cut profile which stood out against his black hooded jacket with an unusual expression of meditative seriousness, *his* hand which was going to lead her through life, clasping her own ...! It was *his* child, above all, which leapt within her like the first springing of their future happiness!

A priest in a white chasuble knelt in prayer within the chapel, his tonsured head gleaming faintly in the light of a pair of candles standing on either side of the altar. Beside him a little acolyte knelt and swung his censer gently to and fro. Catherine's emotion deepened as she recognized the huge nose and kindly face of Brother Jean Pasquerel who had been Joan of Arc's almoner, and whose loyalty to the memory of the girl he had known better than anyone had exposed him to La Trémoille's persecution and wrath. The Chamberlain's hatred of the Maid was such that one had merely to venerate her memory to become the victim of his attacks.

Hearing her approach Brother Jean stood up, smiled and held out both hands to them.

'I thank God for bringing us together here, my friends, and allowing me to be the instrument of His will in marrying you both. These troublous times force us to remain in hiding but I am sure they will not last for long, and that the time of light will return.'

'If I had my way they would return in a flash,' said Arnaud. 'It makes my blood boil to think that the whole kingdom groans beneath the yoke of one man and that it would need only one sword thrust ...'

'My son,' the monk interrupted, 'you are in the Lord's dwelling here, and He does not approve of violence. Besides,' he added with a smile, 'I imagine that your thoughts tonight must be on something more cheerful than a man's death, guilty though he may be.'

A hurried footstep, setting up echoes within the empty church, cut short his remarks. Xaintrailles appeared in the feeble candle glow, scarlet in the face from running. Under his thick ponyskin coat a steel breastplate gleamed dully. Brother Jean glanced at him briefly and then turned towards the altar saying:

'Let us pray....'

With one movement Catherine and Arnaud knelt together on the altar steps. Jacques Coeur stood behind Catherine and Xaintrailles behind Arnaud while Macée went and knelt a little way off, drawing her blue veil over her face as she did so. The acolyte swung the censer and the only sound to be heard was the priest's murmuring voice as he invoked God's blessing on the couple, before proceeding to the marriage ceremony proper.

This was simple and rapid. Prompted by Brother Jean, Arnaud repeated, in a firm voice: 'I, Arnaud, take you Catherine, to be my lawful wedded wife, to love and to cherish in joy and in sorrow, in sickness and health, now and for ever, till death do us part.' Then it was her turn. 'I, Catherine . . .' But her emotions were overflowing, her voice died away and she finished the ritual phrase in a whisper. Great tears rolled down her cheeks, the ransom of an overflowing heart.

Brother Jean took Catherine's right hand and placed it in Arnaud's. His long fingers closed around hers. His voice rose, like a challenge to adversity: 'Ego conjungo vos in matrimonium, in nomine Patris, et Filii, et Spiritus Sancti. Amen.'

He took a gold ring from the platter which the acolyte held out to him and blessed it: 'Bless this ring, O Lord . . .' then he handed it to Arnaud. The young man took the ring and slipped it on to Catherine's ring finger, then, tenderly, kissed it. Her tear-wet eyes shone like amethysts in the sun. In this obscure, dark, cold little church she had tasted a moment of supreme happiness, the fulfilment of a lifetime. The blessing fell slowly upon the two bowed heads and then Brother Jean returned towards the altar to celebrate Mass.

At this moment a loud explosive sound behind them made them turn their heads. It was Xaintrailles, temporarily unable to master his emotions. Arnaud and Catherine smiled and then, hand in hand, turned their attention piously towards the divine office.

After the Mass the bridal couple and other guests followed the priest into a little sacristy smelling of incense and cold wax, to sign the register. Arnaud appended his signature with a flourish which made the goose quill squeak, then he held it out to Catherine, with a faintly teasing smile.

'Now you! I hope you remember what your new name is!'

Slowly and methodically as a small girl, with the tip of a pink tongue protruding between her lips, she signed 'Catherine de Montsalvy' for the first time. A burst of pride swept through her, flushing her cheeks. She promised herself that she would bear this ancient name which was now hers, with pride and honour, no matter what the cost.

The witnesses, Xaintrailles and Jacques Coeur, signed next while Macée embraced Catherine warmly. Then it was Xaintrailles's turn. He bent ceremoniously before her, sweeping her a low and respectful bow.

'Madame la Comtesse de Montsalvy, I am happy to have contributed, in however small a degree, to a happiness which I would wish as great as your beauty and . . .'

But apparently the formality of his address did not accord with his feelings because he suddenly cut short his elegant speech, seized Catherine by the shoulders and planted two smacking kisses on her cheeks.

'All the happiness in the world, my dear. I dare say your troubles aren't quite over yet, but never forget that I am your most loyal and devoted friend.'

With that he left Catherine to fall upon Arnaud, whom he embraced with brotherly affection.

'We'll be meeting again soon,' he said, 'but for the moment I must say farewell . . .'

'Farewell? Are you leaving?'

Xaintrailles made a hideous grimace which ended up as a sly grin.

'Yes. For the sake of my health. La Trémoille appears to have some suspicions as to who burned down his château. If I stay here I shall be found some fine night with a knife in my back. I prefer to rejoin my men at Guise. No one can meddle with me there.'

'I wish I could go with you. It would be interesting to see how they tried to stop me taking up my former place in the army. I can't think of a single one of my brothers-in-arms who would lift a finger against me or my wife.'

This word from Arnaud made Catherine's heart melt with tenderness. She slipped an arm through her husband's. But Xaintrailles shook his head, his eyes sombre.

'Your brothers-in-arms may not have changed but La Trémoille's gold finds its way everywhere. Come, a sacristy is not the ideal place for such talks as these. And I must speak to you. . . .'

Here, Jacques Coeur stepped in courteously.

'We have prepared a little wedding supper at home. Couldn't you come and share it with us before departing? It would hardly delay you. . . .'

The captain hesitated only fractionally before accepting. Brother Jean had unrobed by now, and he came across to offer his own congratulations to the young couple and take his leave of them. The monk too was leaving the city that very night, taking advantage of the truce of Christmastide to journey to the great abbey at Cluny, the most powerful in Christendom, where he might wait till such time as La Tré-moille's stranglehold on the kingdom had been loosened.

'I shall pray God every day for your happiness,' he said to Catherine, with a final blessing, 'and also to her whom we all loved, for I doubt not that she has taken her rightful place among the elect.'

His brown habit vanished into the darkness and the acolyte followed him announcing that he was about to lock up the church. A moment later they were all out in the snow-covered street again. The wind had risen and heavy lumps of snow came sliding off neighbouring rooftops. A distant music of viols and lutes came to their ears and Xaintrailles shrugged.

'A ball at the Palace! ... or rather a ball as the Chamberlain understands it – which means an orgy that would make a bacchanal look like a convent tea-party, They must all be gloriously drunk by now. La Trémoille is at his least dangerous when drunk.'

An hour later Catherine was sitting on a sort of curule chair in Jacques Coeur's study, with Arnaud on a velvet stool at her feet. They were both listening to Xaintrailles who was giving them an outline of their present situation. The supper had soon been finished partly because the captain wanted to leave the town before dawn and partly also because the shortage of food no longer permitted elaborate feasts. The famine which decimated the countryside – the result of the endless devastations of war – had at last reached the cities themselves, where the reserves of food were beginning to run out. Even a man as resourceful as Jacques Coeur found himself affected by the enforced restrictions and the *pièce de résistance* of the wedding supper had been a huge bowl of cabbage soup, eminently nourishing no doubt, but not very refined. Catherine herself had eaten very little, mostly dried raisins, which had been served to them as dessert.

Now that the last drop of Sancerre wine had gone and the last toast to the couple's happiness had been drunk, Xaintrailles was making one last attempt to make his friend hear the voice of sweet reason. The captain's appearance in battledress had dangerously aroused all Arnaud's fighting instincts.

'The best thing would be for you to stay here, since Maître Coeur is only too willing to keep you. Queen Yolande will be returning and she will certainly be able to convince Charles that La Trémoille is leading him to his own doom. She will see that justice is done. . . .'

'Just a minute,' said Arnaud. 'I am afraid there can be no question of remaining here. I am not being ungrateful to my friends when I say that this inaction is preying upon me. . . . I am suffocating. You know me well enough to know that I abhor what is commonly called tranquillity. I have been attacked – now I intend to defend and avenge myself.'

'That's ridiculous. I've told you that there is nothing you can do!'

'I can at least go home, to my mountains in Auvergne. I have lands and peasants there and a strong fortress. My country needs me. It is there, and nowhere else, that my son shall be born.'

'You are mad . . .! You can't drag a pregnant woman out along the highways. . . .'

But Catherine leant forward and clasped him round the neck. 'If he leaves I leave too!'

He kissed her tenderly and carefully as if she might break.

'My sweet, he is right. And I was speaking like an egotistical fool. It is winter, the roads are difficult and our son will be born in two months' time. It would be better for both of you to stay here in safety while I set forth. . . .'

A piercing regret made itself heard in the young man's voice but Catherine pushed him aside, a deep frown creasing her brow.

'So that's your idea of love? Here we are, barely married, and yet you already talk of leaving me and going away. . . . But only a little time ago you said "Till death do us part. . . ." '

'But the child. . . .?'

'The child? He is your son! He will be a Montsalvy, a man like you, a real one! And I intend to be worthy of you both. You were right – it would be better for him to be born on a straw litter in the land of your fathers than in a soft and comfortable bed far from you. Go if you wish but rest assured that I shall follow you, even if you forbid it, as I followed you to Orleans, to Rouen, as I followed you into the Seine and will do into the grave if need be.'

She stopped, flushed with emotion, panting a little so that her bosom rose and fell under her green bodice. Her large eyes

flashed indignantly. Arnaud suddenly started to laugh, and
caught her to him.

'Morbleu! Madame de Montsalvy, you spoke as my mother
would have done!' Then, more gently: 'You win, my love! We
shall travel together through cold, dark and war, if war should
come, and may God forgive me if I have made the wrong
decision.'

Xaintrailles looked from one to the other.

'Have you made up your minds?'

Arnaud turned towards him, pride flaming in his face.

'Yes. We shall leave.'

'Very well. In that case I may as well tell you all. There is
bad news and it is as well you should hear it now. Strange
things are happening in Auvergne. La Trémoille claims it as
his fief. . . .'

Arnaud started. A slow red flush crept up his forehead and his
black eyes flashed angrily.

'The Auvergne? By what right?'

'By the right he arrogates to himself. You recall that his first
marriage was to the widow of the Duke de Berry, Jeanne de
Boulogne, the heiress to Auvergne? And she, as she lay dying,
bequeathed her fief to her nephew Bertrand de Latour?'

'You don't have to tell me that,' Montsalvy growled. 'Latour
is a relation of mine. His wife, Anne de Ventadour, is my
mother's niece. We are near cousins.'

'Splendid! But, for all that, La Trémoille claims the country
as his first wife's heir. It is quite illegal, of course, but then
legality has never been his chief concern.'

'It is one thing to lay claim to the place, and quite another
to take it,' Arnaud retorted. 'What can La Trémoille do? To
seize the Auvergne would require cavalry, soldiers, artillery ...
and La Trémoille is not very popular with the army!'

Xaintrailles, who had been pacing up and down the room,
stopped and sent the great globe spinning round with a flick of
the hand.

'You know Rodrigo de Villa-Andrade?' he inquired gently.

'The Spanish brigand? Of course. We fought together once
under the command of the Maréchal de Séverac. A good soldier
but a wild beast of a man. He is as cruel as a hungry wolf and he
loves blood the way other men love wine.'

'He also loves gold,' Xaintrailles cut in. 'La Trémoille has
acquired his services together with those of his brigands for a
large sum of money. And the Spaniard is now *en route* for the

Auvergne. His lieutenants, Valette and Chapelle, are already laying waste the lands of Languedoc and Gevaudan. They are moving up while Rodrigo moves down to join them ... now do you understand?'

Arnaud de Montsalvy's face had changed from scarlet to waxen white. His nostrils grew pinched and a hard line formed down each corner of his mouth. He let drop Catherine's hand and got slowly to his feet, eyes fixed on his friend's face. Catherine sensed – as if she could see into his heart – the immense anger which swelled within him. He stood towering above Xaintrailles.

'That jackal from Castille is attacking my own land and you wait till now to tell me? And you were trying to persuade me to stay here, toasting my feet by the fire while my own people ...'

'I only heard the news this morning. Anyway, even if I had known before what use would it have been to tell you? How long is it since you were strong enough merely to mount a horse, let alone fight?'

Arnaud stepped back and bowed his head, but his face remained closed and obdurate. Catherine had the strange sensation that an unknown but menacing spirit had entered the peaceful little room. A black, sharp silhouette whose shadow suddenly seemed to cover the whole room, as far as the rafters. It was as though the Spanish brigand had suddenly burst into the house, bringing with him the afterglow of sacking and burning villages, houses and men. An icy hand gripped her heart as Arnaud turned towards Jacques Coeur.

'Maître Jacques, is there any way I can leave this town tomorrow? I cannot remain here any longer.'

'If you wish, I could give you ten men-at-arms who would join you outside the town, wherever you choose,' Xaintrailles cut in.

He finished buckling on the breastplate, which he had removed for the meal, over his tunic. Then he pulled his hood over his head and wrapped himself in his coat. Catherine was sad to think that they were once more to be separated from this trusty companion of theirs, with his boisterous but generous affection. She turned to him and said so quite simply, with the spontaneity which she had never lost.

'I love you dearly, Jean. Come and see us again soon!'

The blunt face with its scattering of freckles gave a rueful grin and he said gruffly:

'We will meet at Montsalvy! I shall come and dine with you one evening when you are not expecting me. And I shall stay long enough to kill some of those old boars of the Châtaignerie. Farewell, my friends.'

With a kiss for Catherine, a slap on the back for Arnaud and a bow to Macée who stood holding out the hot, spiced wine which traditionally speeded the parting guest on his way, Xaintrailles turned towards Maître Coeur who waited, torch in hand, to guide him down the dark stairway.

'I am right behind you, Maître Coeur! And thank you again for all your help.'

'This way, messire. I will tell you where to send the ten men-at-arms you promised. I heard this news even before you and I had made everything ready for our friends to leave the town tomorrow. I guessed that Messire de Montsalvy would want to leave at once, and that Dame Catherine would refuse to be parted from him.'

The furrier's face was perfectly calm and impassive, yet Catherine had the feeling that he was controlling himself with difficulty. Behind that impassivity she sensed a despair which he himself was not perhaps clearly aware of, but which he instinctively fought to suppress.

The bell of the Jacobin convent struck three, and they heard the door thudding shut behind Xaintrailles, followed by the sound of hurried footsteps departing down the road. Catherine and Arnaud had not moved. They listened to their friend departing as though his footsteps echoed in their very hearts. Macée handed Catherine a candlestick and lit the candle.

'Come,' she said, 'it is time for bed. Tomorrow will be a hard day!'

Sleep? Neither Catherine nor Arnaud had the slightest intention of doing so. They stood hand in hand looking at each other in the large room which Jacques and Macée had given up to them for their wedding night, like two children on the eve of a great adventure. The peaceful room, with its walls covered with red and blue embroideries, a roaring fire dancing in the chimney, and great bed with snowy sheets turned back invitingly beneath the scarlet draperies, seemed to offer them a cosy, secret refuge from the world outside. All around the silence of the night pressed in on them like a protective shell. For a while at least they were safe and these first few hours of their life together belonged to them alone. Tomorrow it would all begin again but for the moment neither harm nor hatred could touch them.

Without letting go of her hand Arnaud carefully shut the door and then led Catherine to the bed, where he sat her down before taking her into his arms. Their lips met hungrily. Although they had been living under the same roof ever since Xaintrailles had brought him there near to death, it was the first time Arnaud had made love to Catherine there. They had made it a point of honour to respect the Coeur family by waiting till they were legitimately wed, but now Arnaud seemed bent on making up for lost time.

His lips moved from her temples to her eyes, her lips, her throat. He crushed her with a passion which threatened to bruise her, but she submitted to him with a savage joy. Occasionally he whispered his delight close to her ear.

'My wife. . . . My own Catherine. . . . My wife for all time!'

She surrendered herself to him as he feverishly untied her white fichu and unlaced the bodice of her dress. He snatched off her starched white coif and tossed it to the foot of the bed.

Suddenly she stiffened. The babe was moving about inside her with unusual violence. Arnaud noticed her recoil.

'What's the matter?'

'The baby. It's moving a lot. Perhaps we shouldn't . . .'

He started to laugh and Catherine thought that no one laughed like he did, with such gaiety and vitality. His white teeth gleamed in the shadow of the red curtains.

'If that little devil tries to interfere with my love-making he will have to reckon with me. Children have never laid down the law in my family. And I want you! I've been hungering for you too long! Too bad for him!'

Tenderly but urgently he clasped her to him and laid her down on the velvet coverlet while he uncovered her shoulders and bosom. Catherine's blood caught fire under his caresses and physical passion snatched her up with the violence of a hurricane. She returned him kiss for kiss, caress for caress and gave herself up to him with an abandon which astonished even herself. It was the first time he had made love to her like this, with controlled violence, and a skill and subtlety she had never suspected in him. For a moment the thought flashed through her mind that something in him had changed, because till then their embraces had been fierce, almost brutally passionate. It had been a sort of passionate combat from which they both emerged exhausted, neither of them the winner. There had been something hard, and almost hurried about his love-making. He was bending her to his will. But tonight she sensed that he was intent on arousing her to new heights of pleasure and desire. Under these slow, subtle caresses which made her cry out with pleasure, she was surprised to find her body reacting with an intensity which only that master in the arts of love, Philippe of Burgundy, had ever known how to arouse in her.

She cried out as he left her to undress, but then she purred with delight feeling his hard body pressed against her and his heart pounding against her breast. The firelight cast tawny lights over his brown shoulders and flickered in his black curls. She thought that this was how it would be every night that God gave them ... and then she forgot all else under the burning wave which rolled over her.

The fire had burned low and the room was lit by a dim red glow where the smell of burning pine cones mingled with the acrid odours of love-making and bodies bathed in sweat. Catherine drowsed happily with her head pillowed on Arnaud's shoulder. She felt deliciously disembodied, as though her exhausted and plundered body had been left behind in the tumbled bed. She was warm, she felt happy and safe and she no longer knew where dream ended and reality began.

From time to time the embers crackled in the grate, throwing out a spark but all around a great silence enveloped them like a protective cocoon. There was nothing in the world but the peaceful breathing of the sleeping man, and the fluttering eyelids of the contented woman. With a deep sigh Catherine pressed herself close to Arnaud who murmured something unintelligible in his sleep. She closed her eyes ... and almost immediately opened them again. Outside a strange sound had shattered the silence, a sound as menacing and sinister as the slither of a serpent's scales – the sound of steel against stone.

Slipping out of Arnaud's arms Catherine left the bed. The room was colder outside the curtained bed but she ran barefoot to the window which overlooked the rue des Armuriers. She half-opened the wooden shutter and peeped out. What she saw made her step back with an exclamation of alarm: armed men, carrying bows and halberds, were massing themselves all around Jacques Coeur's house, forming a cordon right across the rue des Armuriers and doubtless the rue d'Auron. The silence in which this manoeuvre was being conducted showed that the officer in charge was clearly bent on taking them by surprise.

Catherine was galvanized by terror. She ran to the bed and shook Arnaud.

'Quick! Get up! We are surrounded!'

He sprang to his feet with the instant reflexes of a man who lives with danger and ran to the window. For an instant his tall form gleamed against the dark wood shutters and then he was slipping on his shoes and breeches. Without stopping to put on a shirt he rushed towards the stairs, whispering to Catherine who stood with her teeth chattering.

'Dress yourself! I'm going to warn Jacques Coeur.'

Fear had made her clumsy and she groped about looking for her clothes and struggled into her chemise. She had only just managed to get her dress on when Arnaud returned with the furrier, who was knotting a dressing-gown cord closely about him. The officer's mailed glove crashed against the door below. They heard him cry out:

'Open! In the King's name!'

'Messire Xaintrailles must have been recognized and followed when he left here,' Jacques whispered. 'There isn't a minute to lose. Come!'

He led them out of the room as Macée, shivering in her long nightgown, came in carrying a candle and slipped into the unmade bed. In passing she and Catherine exchanged anxious, frightened looks. The banging outside had grown louder. They heard the officer call out threateningly:

'Break the door down if those fools don't hurry up and open it.'

'Yes, you break it down,' Jacques Coeur hissed between clenched teeth. 'That will give us more time.'

They reached the kitchen at the same time as old Mahaut, flanked by Sara and Gauthier. Jacques Coeur's face brightened.

'Take them all into the secret room,' he told the old servant. 'I shall go and argue with the sergeant. Thank Heaven everyone is here . . . and the fire is out.'

This last remark, which seemed incomprehensible to Catherine at first, became intelligible when she saw their host step into the chimney place. The bronze plaque at the back, with its pattern of *fleur-de-lis*, swivelled out of sight as if by magic, revealing a black hole. Mahaut entered carrying a lighted candle. Arnaud took Catherine's arm.

'Come,' he said. 'Don't be afraid!'

Her teeth were chattering as much from cold as from fear. After the happy calm earlier on she now seemed to be living in a nightmare. Arnaud quickly took off his doublet and wrapped it, still warm from his body, round his wife's shoulders.

'Quick,' Jacques said impatiently. 'You will find something to wrap yourselves in downstairs. This time it's serious!'

Just then they heard the front door splintering under the soldiers' blows. It sounded as though it would give way any second. Sara and Gauthier entered in their turn and the plaque slid back into place. Catherine found herself surrounded by darkness so intense that Mahaut's candle barely lightened it. The rough-hewn stone steps were steep and slippery and there was a strong smell of cold smoke. Oddly enough not a sound from the house could be heard.

'Where are we going?' Arnaud whispered.

'The master told you. To the secret room. That's where he hides away his precious wares which he doesn't want to fall into the Grand Chamberlain's rapacious hands ... and also the things he plans to take on his journey to the East.'

'But what about the hiding-place in the roof?' Catherine asked.

The Coeur household, like all the houses in Bourges, had received fairly frequent visits from the King's men, but various hiding-places concealed among the attics had served as a refuge for their unofficial guests.

Old Mahaut did not answer at once. They had reached the foot of the stairs and her candle flickered in the musty air. Mahaut busied herself lighting a candelabrum which stood against a round stone pillar. When she spoke she avoided looking at Catherine.

'If they have serious grounds for suspicion, and the master thinks they may have, the soldiers might set fire to the house. That's what they did a little while ago to the apothecary Noblet's house. Here we shall be safe even if the house does burn.'

Catherine remembered the brutal way in which the apothecary's home had been burned to the ground because he was suspected of hoarding rare and valuable spices. The whole town had been in an uproar that night and they had only just managed to stop all the neighbouring houses going up in flames too. It had been luck which prevented the entire district of Notre-Dame de Fourchaud being set ablaze. . . .

The young woman felt sick at heart. What terrible dangers

were those brave people who had taken her in going to suffer
on her account? But she forgot her anxieties for an instant as
she took stock of their strange surroundings. Gauthier stood
holding up the candelabrum so that it lit up the long narrow
room in which they stood, its low vaulted roof made of faded
pink brick. The walls were pierced with rectangular niches at
regular intervals, some of which stood empty while others had
been sealed off with oddly carved stones. The most frequent
inscription seemed to be something like a stylized fish. At the
far end a low, narrow door stood ajar.

The Norman's harsh voice boomed under the low vaulted
roof. 'What a strange place! These niches look as if they were
made to take human bodies. . . .'

'Quite so,' Mahaut affirmed, crossing herself superstitiously.
'The master says it is some kind of cemetery. Oh, it is very old
. . . it dates from a time when the country was still barbarian.'

'In Italy, a long time ago, I saw a Roman necropolis,' Sara
said. 'It looked like this.'

'Whew!' Mahaut interrupted, visibly anxious to escape from
this place. 'Let's go on. It's cold here.'

It was scarcely any warmer beyond the door but the two
rooms which led out of it were a great deal larger, and their
ceilings were roofed with fan-vaulting. They were both stacked
high with bulging sacks and bundles wrapped in coarse sacking.
These helped to dispel any mysterious or sinister atmosphere
the place might have had. A strange smell blended of new sacking, spices and incense, filled the place. In spite of the shelter
of Arnaud's doublet Catherine's teeth were still chattering. Just
then Gauthier spied some furs piled up in a corner. He rum-
maged among them and drew forth a sort of loose mantle lined
throughout in red fox. He held it out to her.

'This will be warmer for you. Besides, Messire Arnaud is in
danger of catching cold.'

Catherine completely vanished in the mantle. It was far too
wide and long for her but she felt a little cosier inside it, and a
little comforted. She went off and sat down on a sack at the
foot of a pillar.

She did not see Arnaud's gaze darken as he watched the Norman enveloping his wife in the fur-lined mantle. He put his
doublet on again, but curtly refused to supplement it with a fur
from the pile in the corner. Gauthier was kneeling in front of
Catherine, carefully arranging the folds of the mantle so that
they covered her feet.

'There,' he said with satisfaction. 'You will be better like that!'

'What an excellent ladies' man you are!' Arnaud said sarcastically. 'Did you pick it up on your journey here? And what was Sara doing all that time?'

Sara was sitting next to Catherine, huddled up for warmth. She looked coldly at Arnaud.

'When I was not in prison threatened with being burned alive,' she said, 'I had my work cut out simply to prevent her going out of her mind with grief and despair.'

Catherine followed this brief skirmish with astonishment. She could not understand Arnaud's sudden attack of bad temper; the giant's attentions seemed perfectly normal to her. However, she did not wish any conflict now; if the two men were to start quarrelling the future would be black indeed. She put out her hand and drew Arnaud towards her.

'Come here, beside me ... I shall always be cold without you.'

He calmed down at once and came and sat at her feet.

'Forgive me ... but it drives me mad to be cooped up down here like a rat in a cage, while up there, perhaps ...'

There was no need to complete the sentence; they could supply the rest themselves. What was happening above them now? Here, in this cellar which was as silent as the tomb, they were completely cut off from the world. How could they know if the house were burning down, or whether the plaque might not have been pinned down by fallen beams when they tried to open it to make their escape? Had they escaped the vengeful fury of La Trémoille only to die buried alive in this well-concealed hiding-place of theirs? The horrifying thought flashed through Catherine's mind and she felt her blood run cold. She already felt as if she were stifling below these low arches. ... As if to lend substance to her thoughts the sound of a distant thud reached them, muffled but unmistakable. Old Mahaut crossed herself hurriedly.

'Sweet Jesus, it couldn't be ...?'

All five companions in misfortune were seized by the same fear. They hardly dared look at each other, as though ashamed of their secret fears. The silence grew oppressive until Arnaud could bear it no longer. He stood up, clenching his fists, and began pacing nervously up and down like a caged beast. Catherine did not dare try to stop him. Dismal though the regular sound of his footsteps might be, it was still better than the alarming silence. It was at least a living noise, just as old Mahaut's wavering, uncertain glance, flickering from face to face as if in search of reassurance, was part of the living world too. She had drawn a wooden rosary from her apron pocket and the polished beads slipped through her gnarled fingers. The minutes followed each other, leaden and intolerable to the anxious people waiting in the cellar. Catherine had to fight down an overpowering desire to scream.

And then, as suddenly as it had come, the agony lifted, Jacques Coeur suddenly appeared within the circle of yellow candlelight. He was smiling, but it was not till he spoke that Catherine would accept that he was a real creature of flesh and blood and not a phantom.

'It's all over,' he said calmly. 'You can come up again now.'

'But what was that noise we heard?' Arnaud demanded. 'We thought it was the sound of the house crashing down.'

'No, simply a dresser full of pewter plates which the sergeant pushed over because he was convinced it hid the entrance to a secret passage. I wouldn't be surprised if the noise was heard as far away as the Royal Palace! Now come, because it will soon be light and we have much to do, even though the danger is temporarily over.'

'I suppose someone informed on you?'

Jacques Coeur nodded.

'Yes. Xaintrailles's mistress appears to be greedy for gold, and he was foolish to pay her a last visit before coming to the church. He was followed here. I have managed to persuade the sergeant of my innocence for the time being, but he could change his mind suddenly. Anyway, what does it matter – you will soon be away from here!'

'When do we leave?' Catherine asked.

'Soon.'

'In broad daylight?'

The furrier laughed.

'Day or night will not make much difference. This cellar where you are now extends farther than you might think. These two rooms communicate with the ancient chapel of the Chevaliers du Temple which stands beyond the Porte Ornoise, and they are but a tiny part which the Templars restored for their own use of an important underground network built by the Romans, which I have explored. Some of the passages which link up burial chambers, like the one you saw, to the stone quarries are partly destroyed and dangerous to walk through, but there are still many which are usable. One in particular passes under the old amphitheatre and follows the ancient water conduit connected to one of the four aqueducts. That is the one you will take, because it passes beneath the rue d'Auron and my house. It will take you outside the city, some way off, to the tower of Bruyères, an old ruin on the road to Dun-le-Roi. And it is there that you will be met by Messire Xaintrailles's men.'

He held out a hand courteously to help Catherine to her feet but they were all too thunderstruck to move.

'A town built over underground passages ... It's like a dream!'

Jacques Coeur gave a faint smile.

'Wherever the Romans passed they left behind them things which seem almost magical to us now. One cannot conquer the world without genius. And a genius which has turned out highly useful to a humble merchant like myself!'

CHAPTER TEN

The Caverns of Ventadour

Seeing Arnaud leap into the saddle the next day by the Tower of Bruyères, Catherine could not help feeling a pang of regret. By the simple act of gripping a horse's flanks between his knees Arnaud seemed to throw off the last traces of the exhausted pitiful creature who had been brought to Jacques Coeur's house. Over his black leather suit he wore a light coat of blue steel armour which the furrier had found for him, and over that a voluminous black ponyskin coat. The hood was thrown back and his dark head, with its close-cropped cap of black hair, gleamed in the light. He stood in the stirrups with his head flung back proudly and there was no trace left of the wretched captive of Sully, or of the hunted quarry of some greedy, unscrupulous lieutenant. He was once more the proud image Catherine had always had of him: the Lord of Montsalvy again; and Catherine was not altogether sure that she was pleased. She had never felt so close to him as during those days of physical weakness and mental and moral uncertainty.

The ten men sent by Xaintrailles, who had joined up with them at nightfall, had instantly recognized the quality of this man. He was a warrior and a leader of men, and they unquestioningly, with tacit accord, bowed to his commands. And yet, judging by their arrogant demeanour and the scars which decorated their tanned faces, they must belong either to the military élite of the day, or to the lowest type of brigand – which amounted to much the same thing. Catherine had not much liked the odd way they had looked at her.

They were all Gascons, and all, with the exception of their gigantic leader, Sergeant Escorneboeuf, small wiry swarthy men with pointed moustaches and black eyes. But they were magnificent soldiers. Perpetual contact with the English-occupied territory of Guyenne had made the war against the invader their daily occupation since they were old enough to carry arms. When he reached the Bruyères tower with the four horses destined for the fugitives, Sergeant Escorneboeuf had handed Arnaud a sealed document. He opened it and found to his amazement and amusement that it was no less than a pass duly signed and stamped by the Lord Chancellor of France, authorizing the departure of the Baron de Ladinhac, with his wife and servants and ten soldiers, for Lectoure where he was to rejoin his sovereign lord the Comte Jean V d'Armagnac. It seems that Xaintrailles had done his task thoroughly and was leaving nothing to chance. The Great Seal of France appended to this forged document was proof, all at once, of his loyalty to his friends and his gift for intrigue. Catherine addressed a mental thank-you to the strapping red-headed fellow whose boisterous good humour was only equalled by his devotion to his friends. Then she sighed, Heaven only knew when the Montsalvys would see their friend again!

Now the little band was riding peacefully along the ancient Roman road which ran from Bourges – or Avaricum in Roman times – across Berry and Limousin, towards the mountains of Auvergne. Arnaud rode at their head, mounted on a tall black charger, and he had to fight against a wild desire to spur the beast to a gallop. It was such a long time since he had last ridden thus with his cloak flapping behind him and the wind in his face, but Catherine's condition demanded that they go more slowly and he was forced to curb his natural impetuosity. Catherine rode behind him with Gauthier and Sara on either side of her. She and Morgane had been delighted to find each other again. The little mare trotted along gaily, ears pricked, her white plume of a tail rivalling the whiteness of the snow. As for Sara she had taken possession of Rustaud once more with considerable satisfaction. The gipsy woman's by no means inconsiderable weight perfectly suited that animal's peaceful and leisurely nature, and at this moment Sara was dozing off happily, apparently indifferent to the cold. But Gauthier was far from tranquil. From time to time he would glance behind to where the huge Escorneboeuf and his Gascons rode bunched close together. These two men, who appeared to be evenly matched in their prodigious physical strength, had taken an instant dislike to each other. One look had been enough, a look Catherine had intercepted and understood. Accustomed as they were to dominating everyone around them by the sheer threat of their physique, the Norman and the Gascon were clearly itching to trade blows with each other. She confided her doubts to Arnaud.

'Sooner or later those two will come to blows,' she whispered, looking at Escorneboeuf, who was wiping his nose thoughtfully on his sleeve as he watched Gauthier saddling up Morgane.

'If it were a purely formal trial of strength it might be amusing to see those two giants fight it out. But if they really start fighting I should know how to deal with them. The only way to train animals is with the whip and I've been accustomed to using it since I was a child.'

This characteristic reply had only increased Catherine's anxiety. She vowed to keep her eyes and ears open, but she could not help thinking how much simpler and pleasanter life would be if only men could get rid of this unholy passion for killing each other. Instinctively she laid a hand on her belly. Would the child sheltering there grow into one of these lucid, ruthless war machines too? Would the fiery Montsalvy blood in him stifle the more peaceful nature he inherited from his mother and grandfather, good Gaucher Legoix, who had been hung simply because he loved peace above all? For the first time Catherine felt afraid of this living mystery which she carried within her.

To this anxiety another added itself inevitably: fear of the unknown future before her. What would she find at the end of this road? What awaited her in this country of Auvergne of which she knew nothing? Mountains, of course, and a new aspect of nature for a daughter of the plains like herself ... strange faces, a new home, a mother-in-law. ...! It was this last thought which really tormented her most – Arnaud's mother! Catherine knew very little about her except that her sons adored her. A long while back, in the Legoix cellar, before his massacre by the Parisian mob, Michel de Montsalvy had described his mother to the attentive little girl she was then: a tall lady who had been widowed at an early age with two sons to rear, and a large household and great estates to manage. She almost seemed to hear Michel's voice: 'My mother will be left all alone again when my brother becomes a soldier in his turn. She will be sad, no doubt, but she will not say a word of what she feels. She is too great and too proud to complain.' How, Catherine wondered, would this high, proud lady receive her unknown daughter-in-law, a commoner's daughter to boot? And if they should have to live side by side how would this life unfold?

'What are you thinking about?' Arnaud asked suddenly. She had not noticed him come alongside her, so absorbed had she been in her thoughts. She smiled at his anxious expression and when he added:

'Aren't you well? Are you tired perhaps. . . .?'

'No,' she replied. 'I was just thinking.'

'What of?'

'Of what lies ahead . . . your countryside . . . your family.'

Arnaud's teeth flashed as he leant forward in the saddle and dropped a swift kiss on her brow.

'You can tell me, you know!' he whispered. 'You are a bit frightened of it all, aren't you?'

'Yes . . . a little.'

'You mustn't be. If you learn to love the Auvergne, it will repay you a hundredfold. As for my mother, since she's all the family I have left, I think she will take to you. She prizes courage above all things. . . .'

Reining in his charger to Morgane's sedate pace, Arnaud talked to her about his native country. She gradually lost sight of the softly undulating countryside through which they were passing and imagined herself in a high windy plateau, tumbling down in rocky wooded slopes to a deep valley where a river flowed, mountains which were blue in the morning mists, violet at sunset, black rocks and white torrents. She found herself suddenly longing to reach this strange place where, perhaps, happiness at last awaited her, hidden behind the ivied walls of an old fortress which no longer served its martial purpose. She even forgot the threatening shadow which the Spanish brigand cast across her husband's native land. But Arnaud could not forget. . . . After a pause he added sombrely:

'And now it's all in danger because that rapacious dog of a La Trémoille decides to seize a fief against all the feudal laws. Ah, how time lags on this journey of ours!'

So long as they remained in the Berrichon country, which was relatively protected by the King's residence and was mostly still under cultivation, their journey was peaceful enough. Food was scarce and expensive, but the gold which Jacques Coeur had so generously lent them (Arnaud had been quite unable to persuade Jacques to accept any surety against their debts to him) opened many a poultry-run and oven to them in the various inns where they stopped. But the scenery changed and everything became a great deal more difficult as they entered the wild and savage country of Limousin. This was a region of vast deserted plains and steep hills intersected by deep valleys made almost impassable in winter. The marshes had been frozen by the cold, and dead reeds protruded here and there from the cloudy ice. The few villages they passed were huddled down in the valleys as if trying to shelter from heaven itself. They were so impoverished that the little simple grey churches were roofed over with nothing more pretentious than straw thatch. In more peaceful times the peasants there used to grow barley, beetroots, cabbages and a little wheat, as well as vines in the dried regions farther south. But so many armies had crossed and re-crossed the countryside, English, Armagnacs, Burgundians, brigands and robbers, each one more rapacious than the last, that the Limousin countryside had reverted to its wild and primitive state. The soldiery had looted most of the livestock that had survived illness and famine, and now the whole countryside was gradually starving to death.

The happiness which Catherine had felt on leaving Bourges, at the outset of this long journey to her new home, had slowly evaporated during their trek through this despairing land. With each step of Morgane's dainty feet the weight of misery and sorrow upon her breast seemed to increase. The oppressive silence of these deserted wastes, and the hills crowned with black, mute castles, affected her more than she could say. When by chance they came across a human being, he invariably fled at the sight of this band of horsemen, and such times as they passed close enough to see their faces clearly there was no comfort to be found there. Hunger and cruelty had turned these poor peasants into human wolves. But however wild they might be it did not take Catherine long to discover that Escorneboeuf's Gascons were more cruel and savage still.

As soon as the provisions they brought with them were exhausted the search for food became a daily adventure. They had to find what they could along the way and their journey was delayed accordingly. The days were short and night came on early, which meant they had to halt because the marshy lands were too dangerous to cross in darkness.

Catherine, moreover, was anxious about herself. This slow and arduous journey was tiring her out more than she had ever imagined and she found it harder and harder to snatch some sleep when she and Arnaud at length found somewhere to spend the night. Her nerves grew tense and unreliable in consequence. One evening Catherine and Arnaud had their first quarrel.

They had stopped for the night in a half-ruined chapel in the heart of the great forest of Chabrières, and, as was his wont every evening, Gauthier had set off with his trusty axe in hand to see what he could hunt down for food. The Gascons lit a fire for Catherine and Sara to warm themselves by and then they set off likewise, to see what they could forage, leaving three of their number to keep guard. Since the day before, they had eaten nothing except a mess of boiled chestnuts found in a deserted barn. Everyone was hungry and tempers were short. In the dry-stone walled enclosure where they had tethered the horses Arnaud was trying to see to Rustaud who had gone lame in one foot. Catherine held her hands out to the fire while Sara tried not to think how hungry she was.

Suddenly the silence was shattered by oaths and cries of pain. Two of the Gascons burst out of a thicket dragging a peasant who was struggling with all his might. Two trapped hares hung round his neck. The man begged and implored them to spare him the fruits of his hunting, saying that his wife and four children were starving to death in their cabin, but the men paid no attention. Their brutal laughter drowned the unfortunate man's cries. Catherine leapt to her feet and ran towards them but Escorneboeuf got there first. The Gascon's huge fist rose and fell. There was a cracking noise, like a nutshell being cracked, and the peasant collapsed on the ground at Catherine's feet with his skull split open. She stumbled for an instant, weak with horror at this outrage. Then a wave of anger hurled her furiously upon one of the two men bending over the corpse. She snatched the hares away from him and turned towards the murderer in a fury.

'Wretched brute! What right did you have to attack this man? Who gave you the order? You have killed him ... killed an innocent man who never did you any harm. . . .'

Half crazed with anger, she was about to fling herself upon the massive Gascon, claws out like a wild cat, when Arnaud ran up and pinned her arms to her sides.

'Catherine! Are you mad? What has come over you?'

Hot tears started from her eyes and she looked at her husband with a face convulsed by sobs.

'What has come over me? Haven't you seen! Don't you see that corpse lying there? That man killed an unfortunate peasant for no reason at all, for *this*. . . .'

She pushed the dead hares away with her toe as if they had been a snake.

'He was shouting too much,' the Gascon interrupted. 'God's Blood! I don't like shouting!'

'And I don't like men killed for no reason, my friend!' Arnaud interrupted coldly. 'In future you will await my orders before attacking anyone, otherwise I shall be forced to teach you a lesson. Now take the corpse away. Two of the men shall dig a grave here in the chapel. This is sanctified ground. And Sara shall skin and cook the hares.'

Catherine had been leaning against him, sobbing quietly, but now she pushed him away and stood back staring at him, wide-eyed.

'What! Is that all the punishment you are going to give a murderer? Is that all the funeral oration you can spare for that poor man there? Bury him and then don't mention it again?'

'What more can I do? I am sorry the man is dead but since he is there is nothing to do but bury him. At least that is better than finishing up as food for wolves or vultures!'

Possibly because he had noticed the ironic glance Escornebeouf cast him as he moved away Arnaud answered her with a note of harshness which further increased Catherine's exasperation.

'I have never confused a soldier with a murderer!' she cried heatedly. 'That man murdered in cold blood, without provocation. He should be punished according to the law.'

'Don't be silly, Catherine,' Arnaud said wearily. 'We haven't too many men as it is, and Heaven knows what awaits us in the Auvergne. When all's said and done he was only a peasant. . . .'

The remark struck Catherine like a blow. She suddenly felt crushed and sad, but then she roused herself to face him proudly.

'Only a peasant!' she echoed bitterly. 'A creature of no real importance! Or not to people like yourself, perhaps – but to those like me a peasant is still a man!'

'People like myself? And doesn't that include you?'

She shrugged despairingly. Was their life together always going to be founded on deep mutual incomprehension? Would their love always bridge the gulf between the hereditary Lord of Montsalvy and the Pont-au-Change goldsmith's daughter? Had he but known, at this instant she felt much closer to that murdered peasant than to the man whose name she now bore.

'I wonder,' she said, turning away. 'Yes, I really do wonder. Do whatever you please. For my part I will not touch that meat. The price was too high for me.'

Arnaud's black eyes flashed with anger. He opened his mouth to reply angrily, but just then Gauthier emerged from the wood carrying a wild boar across his shoulders. With one eye on Arnaud he came across and dropped it at Catherine's feet.

'You will not have to go hungry all the same, Dame Catherine. . . .'

The two men, Norman and knight, stood facing each other for a moment, black eyes gazing into grey ones. Arnaud's hand slowly descended as far as his sword, then he thought better of it, and turned away.

'Do as you wish,' he said to Catherine before going off again to where Rustaud was tethered.

She watched him go in silence, afraid that Gauthier might have wounded his pride, but she did not dare follow him. At that moment they could not understand each other. When he returned some time later she was sitting a little apart, wrapped in her long cloak, watching while Sara roasted a haunch of boar on an improvised spit. He came across to her and knelt down and laid his head on her lap.

'Forgive me,' he murmured. 'I am afraid you will need a great deal of patience, but I will try to understand . . . to understand you!'

By way of reply she bent over and pressed her lips to his thick black curls. For a moment they were able to forget the cold, the night and the war, and savour a magical moment of peace. He raised her gently in his arms and carried her off to a quiet spot where the others would not be able to see them. The shadow of the little chapel lay about them, cutting them off from the world. Arnaud wrapped Catherine up carefully in several blankets, then he lay down beside her, flinging his own coat over them both.

'Are you all right?'

'Quite all right . . . but Arnaud, I'm frightened. I do wish we could get there quickly . . . because of the baby! He's moving a great deal now, you know.'

'We will try and go faster. Now try to sleep, my love. You need some peace and quiet.'

He kissed her cold lips passionately and she fell asleep at last. He stayed for a long time looking at her, not daring to move for fear of waking her, and felt himself stirred by a profound emotion. Each night that passed made her dearer and more precious to him.

A little way off the Gascons were grouped about another fire where the two hares were roasting. They too seemed peaceful enough. For them life and death were logically intertwined, following each other in an unbroken chain. . . .

But when they set off the following morning across the

scrubby countryside, swept by a cutting north wind, Catherine
noticed that Escorneboeuf's features had suffered certain altera-
tions. The giant was vainly attempting to conceal his face between his helmet and coat collar, a face which had clearly been
in the wars. One black eye, some recent scratches and a whole
series of bruises ranging in colour from blue to deep purple,
made up a somewhat curious physiognomy. Trying to catch
Arnaud's eye she saw that it was likewise fixed upon the sergeant and that it sparkled with a gaiety which was not, however, visible on his lips. He smiled at his wife and then turned
towards the Norman. Gauthier was riding peacefully along,
hands folded across his stomach, with the satisfied expression
of a big cat which has just lapped up a whole bowl of cream.
He looked so innocent that he must almost certainly have been
the cause of Escorneboeuf's ravaged appearance. . . . One more
look satisfied Catherine on this point and this was the murderous glance of pure hatred which the giant flung at Gauthier.
He had evidently suffered a drubbing that night which he
would not forget in a hurry. Catherine was pleased about this,
but it worried her to think that there were deep enmities springing up about her which could endanger their journey and lead
to serious conflict.

The granite plateau came to an abrupt end and the road
wound downhill towards a small village from which there came
not a sign of life. No smoke rose from the chimneys, nothing
moved . . . but a little way off a confused mob of people seemed
to be struggling with one man, who was putting up a frenzied
fight. As usual Arnaud was ahead of the rest and Catherine saw
him stand in his stirrups to get a better view of what was going
on. She spurred Morgane towards him, but by now he had galloped off at full speed, the sun's last rays glinting on his drawn
sword.

'Some disbanded mercenaries, no doubt,' came Gauthier's
voice beside Catherine. 'They are attacking a man. I must go
and help your husband.'

'No, stay here. I think he would prefer not to have any help
this time!'

Arnaud sprang to the ground, disdaining the advantage of
horseback, and fell upon the vagabonds like a thunderbolt. It
was done swiftly and well. The first fell without a cry, his throat
slit from ear to ear; the second drew a long knife and made as
if to fight, but as he struck, Arnaud's left hand rose, a dagger

flashed, and the man fell with a terrible scream. The sword dispatched the third just as he tried to leap on Arnaud's horse and make his escape. It was not till then that Catherine saw a man lying on the steps of the wayside cross. He appeared to be wounded. Arnaud laid his bloody sword aside and knelt beside him.

'Quick,' Catherine breathed. 'He needs us now!'

She dug her heels into Morgane's flanks and behind her the whole troop swung down the hillside at a canter. Catherine and Sara dismounted in front of the cross and went up to Arnaud.

'It is a pilgrim,' he said, 'and a poor enough one by the looks of him. How could they attack anyone so wretched?'

'Bah!' Escorneboeuf's coarse voice exclaimed behind them. 'These pilgrims sometimes have more gold pieces hidden under their rags than you might imagine. I have known some who made fine pluckings . . .'

'Enough!' Arnaud cut in harshly. 'God's wanderers are sacred, or should be! Now go and see if it is possible to stay somewhere in this hamlet. It looks deserted, I know, but it may not be. And remember my orders: you are not to lay a finger on anyone!'

'Yes, lord,' the Gascon growled sulkily. 'On your feet, you lot!'

While Sara opened up the leather casket containing their supply of nostrums and herbal poultices, Catherine took the unconscious pilgrim's head upon her lap. He was an old man, and so skinny that his papery skin seemed stuck to his very bones. A large beaky nose protruded from a thicket of grey beard and hair. There was certainly nothing about him to excite the covetous. The long cloak he wore over his patched and tattered doublet and hose was torn by thorns, faded by innumerable suns and mildewed by countless rainstorms. His feet were swaddled in bundles of rags stained here and there with dried blood. An old felt hat with a cockleshell sewn to the brim lay a little way off in the mud.

While Sara mopped the blood which ran from a wound on the old man's forehead Catherine passed a tremulous hand over the cockleshells sewn here and there about his mantle. The man reminded her of her old friend Barnaby, but this mantle spoke of more genuine repentance and self-sacrifice than Barnaby's ever had.

'He comes from Compostela,' she said, looking at a little metal figure of St James sewn to his collar.

'He comes from farther away than that, my love,' said Arnaud's voice gravely. 'Look. . . .'

He pointed to a little lead palm tree and crucifix hanging on a string round the man's neck. Then, to Catherine's astonishment, he knelt respectfully and kissed the bloodstained bandages round the pilgrim's feet.

'What are you doing?'

'Paying him the homage he deserves. He comes from Jerusalem, Catherine. He is a pilgrim from the Holy Land, a Great Pilgrim, and these feet I kiss have trodden the same soil as Our Lord.'

Catherine and Sara fell back, mute and awed. The old man seemed suddenly to have grown to supernatural dimensions, and they stared at him with deep veneration. The great Christian sanctuaries drew crowds of pious pilgrims, but men who had been to the Holy Land itself were few and far between. He must be a very great saint . . . or have committed a very black crime to go so far, through so many dangers, to seek grace and pardon!

The pilgrim was regaining consciousness. His eyelids rose and disclosed eyes as blue as a summer sky. He tried to get up and finally managed to struggle to his feet with Sara's aid. Then he looked at the couple kneeling at his feet with great sweetness.

'Jesus Christ be praised!' he said. 'And may you be showered with blessings for thus coming to my help. Had it not been for you I believe that . . .'

He stopped. He had just noticed the three corpses of the robbers and tears came into his eyes.

'Was it necessary for them to die that I might be saved? And in a state of sin?'

'It was them or you,' Arnaud said gently. 'Those who attack God's wanderers deserve neither pity nor mercy.'

'They were hungry, no doubt,' the pilgrim said. 'I shall pray for them when I reach the end of my journey.'

'Isn't it yet time for you to rest? You come from afar, it seems.'

The pilgrim's pale eyes grew so luminous that Catherine felt as though winter had vanished and a ray of sunlight had fallen upon them.

'Yes . . . from afar,' he said. 'I have seen the Master's grave, and prayed all night under the olive trees of the Garden of Gethsemane. I did so because of the great grace accorded to me, wretched and unworthy sinner that I am. I was merely a humble mason who worked on building cathedrals when God ordained that I should lose my sight. In my despair I sank so low that I cursed and reviled God, and doubted Him. And then I grew ashamed and I decided to go to the tomb of St James to pray for pardon, for St James has the power to sweeten bitter souls. At Puy I joined up with a caravan and so I made the long journey to Galicia. And there . . . can you imagine my joy? . . . There, all of a sudden, my sight was restored! I saw the blue sky and the immense cathedral, the white town and the tomb with its flashing candles massed all around. Such a favour from on high seemed to merit a greater act of gratitude. So then I decided to go to the Holy Land. . . .'

'Blind!' Catherine stammered, marvelling. 'You were blind and your sight was restored?'

The old man smiled at the pretty face upturned towards him. He placed a hand on her forehead.

'Yes, my child. Faith is love, my daughter. There is nothing, wretched as one may be, which one cannot obtain from Heaven if one has faith and knows how to ask for it. Remember, in the hours of pain and sorrow which still await you, the old pilgrim from Compostela . . . to whom you brought help, and who will pray for you. Remember Barnaby . . .'

'Barnaby!'

The blood drained from Catherine's cheeks, and her hands trembled. By what strange quirk of fate did this man too bear the name of Barnaby? Was this a sign, and if so, what did it mean? She knelt there watching with unseeing eyes as Sara finished bandaging the pilgrim's wounds and Arnaud devoutly unwrapped the old man's torn and bleeding feet and washed them in some water which the Gascons had hastily warmed. She barely heard what her husband was saying to the old man.

'Where are you going now?'

'I have just been to Saint Leonard's tomb and I shall now go to the great house belonging to Monseigneur Saint Michel, in Normandy, girded round by the sea. When I returned to France I heard of the wonders he had accomplished, and how he had spoken to Joan the Maid when she was but a child. . . .'

'Joan is dead,' Arnaud said sadly, 'and there are many who believe she was a witch. And we who served her and loved her are outlawed and persecuted like criminals.'

'That will not last,' Barnaby asserted stoutly. 'God does nothing by halves. But I bless Him for having allowed me to fall in with you along the road. You knew the holy shepherdess, then? You shall tell me of her this evening, before our ways part once more.'

Catherine never forgot that memorable evening. They installed themselves for the night in one of the abandoned houses in the village. All her life long she was to see that circle of faces seated about the fire, gazing up at the pilgrim's tall figure. He and Arnaud talked for hours and exchanged memories. Barnaby spoke of his long journey and the beauty of the hot countries through which he had travelled. Arnaud countered with tales of Joan the Maid and her sufferings, and he spoke with such fire and devotion that those who listened held their breath and stared at him with rapt eyes. Even the Gascons, as impious and godless a group as ever breathed, stayed as still as stone and listened with glowing eyes. When they separated at last to seek a little rest the old man looked thoughtfully at Arnaud and Catherine who sat close beside him, hand in hand.

'Much more will be demanded of you,' he said, 'but you have received the grace of love. If you can keep it you will conquer the world. But, will you be able to keep it?'

He smiled suddenly and rubbed his eyes as if awaking from a dream. Then he made the sign of the Cross rapidly over each of their heads.

'Peace be with you. Sleep well.'

In spite of this blessing Catherine did not fall asleep for a long time. She lay with her cheek pillowed on Arnaud's shouder. There was something about this meeting with the old pilgrim, something elusive and undefinable which suggested to her that it was a sign from Heaven. A puzzling sign, no doubt, and one which she would not decipher till many long years had passed. But one thing she was sure of : the encounter had been pre-ordained.

At daybreak they set forth once more along their respective roads. But as the pilgrim's tall figure was swallowed up in the morning mist Catherine noticed that Gauthier stood looking after him, lingering a little way behind the rest. And as he rose up beside her again he was frowning deeply. She guessed that he was deep in thought and did not disturb him. Then, abruptly, he spoke:

'The God you serve must be a powerful one to command such servants as that one.'

'Were you impressed by him, then?' Catherine asked gently.

'Yes ... no ... I don't know. All I know is that I felt a great longing to get up and follow him!'

'Because he was going to Normandy?'

'No ... just to follow him! He gave me the feeling that while I was with him I would be safe from all misfortunes and pain?'

'Are you so afraid then of misfortunes and pain?'

He looked at her briefly, with that hungry look in his eyes which she had seen there two or three times before.

'You know very well that I'm not,' he murmured, 'as long as you are the cause of them!'

With that he spurred his horse to a trot and rode up to join Arnaud who rode on ahead, arguing with Escorneboeuf.

Arnaud had deliberately chosen the difficult and dangerous route across the Limousin which would permit him to reach Montsalvy without having to cross the Auvergne, but not, as he explained to Catherine, out of love of difficulty for its own sake. He explained to her that the county of Auvergne, which was the subject of so much litigation, was in effect governed by two bishops: the Bishop of Clermont, who supported the King and La Trémoille, and the Bishop of Saint Flour who, for some reason, was hand in glove with the Duke of Burgundy.

'I take it you are not particularly anxious to fall into the hands of the noble duke?' Arnaud said with a sidelong smile.

Catherine flushed and shrugged. This allusion annoyed her, but she had realized long ago that she would have to reckon with Arnaud's jealousy, and in any case this was a case where a little jealousy was understandable. She replied peaceably:

'Why ask a question when you already know the answer?'

He had not pressed the point. In any case he wanted to make a short stop with one of his cousins, at the Château de Ventadour, where his mother, who belonged to that powerful Limousin family, had been born. He described Ventadour as an awesome fortress and a safe refuge where they could learn all the latest news, and where they could eventually set forth with extra reinforcements. Vicomte Jean was rich, powerful and wise. Catherine, for her part, was beginning to long for this stop with all the strength left in her exhausted body. The cruel journey was taking an increasing toll of her strength. She grew visibly thinner and the long hours on horseback were torture to her. She was shaken by violent pains which darted through her as sharply as a lance thrust, and she had terrible cramps in her back and legs when she set foot on the ground. And to make matters worse she could no longer stomach the food, chiefly game, which was all they could find.

As her face grew thinner Arnaud's dismay increased. He reproached himself for having brought her with him and imposed this interminable journey upon her. He would let Gauthier ride on ahead nowadays, trusting to his almost sixth sense to warn them of any impending dangers, while he himself rode next to Catherine. Sometimes, seeing her tremble with cold, he lifted her from Morgane's back and sat her in front of him, so that she might have his arms and a fold of his coat over her to help protect her from the north wind. In spite of her weakened condition and discomfort, Catherine loved riding like that, leaning against him. It gave her a deliciously safe feeling and the journey suddenly seemed less arduous. Soon she travelled no other way and Morgane fell into the habit of trotting along by herself, led only by her bridle, behind the black charger.

When Catherine finally caught sight of Ventadour, towards the end of a wet grey day, she gave a great sigh of relief. Arnaud called out gaily : 'Look, my love, the Vicomte's château at last! There you will be able to rest in comfort and safety! If you aren't safe there you won't be anywhere!'

It was certainly a formidable-looking spot : high walls rose sheer above a rocky prominence round whose foot a deep gully ran, with a foaming torrent tumbling in it. The walls were topped by granite towers and bright painted wooden hoardings, and above these a giant keep towered. It looked ancient enough to have seen the departure for the first Crusades.

'They say,' Arnaud said, laughing, 'that all the straw in France would not fill the moat of Ventadour!'

It was a strange sight, this great cleft between the mountains whence the fortress soared as if issuing from the bowels of the earth. A path led up from a tiny village scattered on the escarpment, towards the immense doorway set at the top of the mighty castle mound. This doorway was as large as the gateway into a fortified town. The weary little group set off up the winding path. In a suddenly joyous mood Arnaud cradled Catherine against him and started to sing :

'My heart is full of love and gentleness,
The ice is like a flowering mead and all the snow is
    green. . . .'

She smiled tenderly and laid her head against his warm cheek.

'That's a pretty song . . . . I didn't know you liked singing.'

'I'm quite as civilized as Xaintrailles, if that's what you mean,' he laughed. 'My mother taught me that song. It was composed here a long time ago by a miller's son called Bernard. He became a troubadour and loved the châtelaine. He nearly lost his life as a result but managed to escape in time, and they say that a queen loved him.'

'Sing some more,' Catherine said. 'I like hearing you.'

Obediently Arnaud began to sing again and his exultant voice rang from the four walls of heaven.

'When I see the lark soaring in the sunlight . . .'

But here he broke off and reined in his horse. High above them the castle gateway had opened and a body of horsemen issued forth and were now riding straight towards them. Arnaud watched them, frowning. Something about his expression alarmed Catherine.

'What's the matter? Aren't those the vicomte's men?'

He did not answer but called to Gauthier :

'Gauthier!'

The Norman hurried up, and without a word Arnaud transferred Catherine from his horse to the giant's arms.

'Quick! Go back and take Sara with you. Find a safe place for them.'

'But, seigneur . . .'

'Do as I say . . . quick, save her, and if I am killed . . . take her to my mother. . . .'

'Arnaud!' Catherine cried. '*No!*'

'Take her away, I tell you! That is an order! Those men riding towards us are not the men of Ventadour. They are Villa-Andrade's mercenaries!'

Deaf to Catherine's cries and despairing entreaties, Gauthier turned his horse, snatched Sara's bridle up on the way and led both horses towards the village. Catherine was craning her neck to see over his massive shoulder. The Gascons had grouped themselves around Arnaud who was standing in his stirrups, with his sword drawn, watching the enemy approach. These latter were now riding post-haste down the slope and their armour, swords and lance-points flashed sinisterly.

'Leave me here!' Catherine cried. 'Go and help them . . . they will never manage alone. There are too many men against them . . . they must be at least five to one!'

'Your husband is a brave man and he knows how to fight! For once, Dame Catherine, suffer me to obey him . . . this is a situation where you can only submit . . .'

T—G

In order to prevent her seeing the beginning of the battle and also to hide her from the mercenaries, Gauthier suddenly plunged off the path into the thick trees and tangled undergrowth of the ravine. He was heading straight for the Luzège, the little river which encircled Ventadour. But he could not prevent her hearing the clash of arms and the ferocious war-cries shouted by either side.

'My God .... they are going to kill him ... I beg you, leave me here, my friend.... At least let me see!'

But Gauthier rode straight on down to the bottom of the gully, pulling Rustaud and the terrified Sara along behind him.

'See what? Blood flowing and men dying? I am going to find you as safe a place as I can and then I shall go back and see what I can do. Try to be reasonable. . . .'

He found the shelter sooner than he expected, a narrow cave overhanging the foaming torrent. It seemed to be cut deep into the rock and after a quick glance round to make sure the place was deserted the Norman carried Catherine into it. It was less cold inside and it looked as though it sometimes served as a refuge for shepherds and forest folk because there was a great heap of straw against one wall. And furthermore, despite the near-by torrent, it was not damp.

He laid Catherine upon the straw and then turned to Sara.

'Light a fire and stay by her. I will return.'

Then he turned on his heel, leaving the two women alone together. Sara rubbed her back, wincing with pain.

'It won't be long before that brute is giving me orders!' she grumbled. But the diatribe died on her lips when she saw how pale Catherine had become. The young woman was crouching with her back against the rock wall of the cave and in the faint light her face was ashen-pale and pearled over with a fine sweat. Fear and pain showed in her eyes and this told Sara all she needed to know.

She swiftly pushed back Catherine's blonde hair which had fallen over her forehead and examined her haggard face. A sudden brutal pain made Catherine writhe in agony for a moment. Then she fell back, panting :

'It hurts, Sara! ... It hurts terribly! ... It's as though some-one stuck a knife in my side.... That is the second.... A little while ago when Arnaud passed me across to Gauthier was the first . . . I . . . I don't know what it can be. . . .'

'I've got a shrewd idea,' said Sara. 'We've been travelling for so long we've lost track of the time.'

'You don't mean . . . that it's the child already?'

'Why not? All this riding may have made you give birth pre-maturely. Lord, this really is the last straw!' But she wasted no time in vain words. She hurriedly removed the baggage Rustaud was carrying: the medicine casket and a roll of clothing. Gauthier had left the things his own horse had been carrying and these included some more clothes, a sack of fodder and a large cauldron. In the twinkling of an eye Sara wrapped Catherine up in two coverlets and a thick cloak. Then she set to work to light a fire with some of the straw and some branches she gathered up outside. Catherine watched her with wide eyes. The pains had abated for a moment and she strained her ears to catch some sound of the battle, but the roar of the torrent drowned everything else.

Catherine tried to summon up a prayer but her memory seemed curiously empty. She could think of nothing but Arnaud. Her whole being yearned towards him and she tried to detect the flash of agony within herself which would mean that he was dead. If that close bond which had united them for so long were suddenly severed Catherine knew that she would be warned of it by a secret and terrible pang. . . .

The fire was now roaring merrily and it put up a welcome screen of warmth between her and the cold outside. Night was coming on fast and Sara was building up a screen of branches and stones over the entrance to the cave to cut down the risk of being seen from without. Occasional confused sounds reached them – a howl of rage or a long groan of agony. A trumpet sounded somewhere, presumably on the ramparts.

'What can Gauthier be doing?' Catherine moaned. 'Why doesn't he come back to tell me . . .'

'He almost certainly has other things to do,' Sara said crisply. 'The combat may drag on for hours because they are all seas-oned warriors.'

'And Arnaud? Do you think he is quite recovered from his illness yet?'

'We shall soon know. . . . For the moment we must think of you and the baby, if it *is* the baby coming.'

As if in reply, Catherine's body was wrenched by another more violent spasm of pain, and an unpleasant damp feeling spread over her. . . .

Catherine had no idea whether the pains which followed lasted for ten hours or one. All her consciousness of time passing vanished and with it her awareness of things around her. Even her anxiety about the near-by battle had gone. All that was left was this unbearable pain. It continued without a moment's respite and Catherine, in her agony, felt as though the child were a giant trying to break out of its prison, bursting and breaking everything inside her in its haste to reach the light. The one real thing, apart from the suffering, was Sara's anxious face bent over her and her warm hand which she gripped convulsively when the pain grew unendurable. She did not cry out, but a sort of long continuous moan escaped her lips. She panted in the grip of this agony which she could do nothing to shorten and which was fated to continue till the birth was accomplished. From time to time Sara bathed her forehead with a handkerchief dampened with eau-de-Cologne, and the coolness revived her for a moment but then the infant returned to the attack and Catherine was submerged in a new sea of pain. She longed for a moment's respite, one moment only, which would allow her to rest. She was so terribly weary. She longed to sleep ... to sleep, to forget, to stop suffering! Would this agony never stop? Would she never be able to sleep again? Her consciousness was growing dimmer, almost without her realizing it. But suddenly there came a stab of agony so much crueller than the others that she gave a real howl of pain, a howl so loud and high-pitched that it could be heard across the valley, in the countryside wrapped round by darkness, and it struck terror into the hearts of those who heard it. But there was only this one cry because immediately Catherine relapsed into the blessed unconsciousness which she had prayed for. She did not even hear the angry roar which echoed her great shriek of deliverance, or hear Sara's joyful laugh. She had fainted away.

When she regained consciousness everything still seemed cloudy and confused. Catherine felt as though she were floating through a light mist through which sparkling pairs of eyes stared at her. She was incorporeal. She had miraculously broken all the chains which bound her to this earth with its griefs and agonies. She felt so light that for a moment she wondered whether she were not dead and transported to Heaven. But then a thoroughly earthly noise shattered her blessed torpor: a baby's wail. ...

Then quite awakened, she opened her eyes wide, raised her head on the rolled-up cloak which had been placed under it as a pillow, and saw a tall black shadow kneeling between her and the fire, a shadow which was saying joyfully:

'Look, my love . . . look at your son!'

A great wave of happiness rolled over her. She tried to stretch out her arms but they felt as heavy as lead.

'Wait,' Sara whispered at her ear, 'I am going to lift you up. You are worn out.'

But that did not matter. She wanted to clasp the little bundle which she could now see clearly in Arnaud's big hands.

'A son. . . . Is it a son? Oh, let me see. . . .'

He slipped her baby next to her. Gauthier appeared then, carrying a good luck torch made from a blazing branch. He looked enormous from where she was lying on the floor but there was a broad smile on his face. Thanks to this light Catherine was finally able to see her son: a tiny red wrinkled face peeping out from the woollen swaddling clothes in which Sara had wrapped him, two tightly clenched little fists, and a light fluff of blond hair over his little round skull.

'He is superb!' Arnaud's joyous voice rang out. 'Tall, strong and magnificent . . . a real Montsalvy!'

In spite of her weakness Catherine had to smile.

'Are all the Montsalvys as ugly as that when they are born? He is all wrinkled!'

'He will get rid of his wrinkles,' Sara intervened. 'Remember . . .' She bit her lip, just in time. She had almost reminded Catherine of little Philippe, the child she had had of Philippe of Burgundy, who had died at the age of four in the Château de Châteauvilain. It would have been foolish, and Sara cursed herself mentally. But Catherine had caught the allusion. Her face darkened and she instinctively held the new-born child a little closer. This child was the son of the man she adored and she would protect him from all evil. Death would never take him! But her movement had roused the sleeping babe. He began to protest at once, his tiny mouth opening in a roar. All that was left of his face was this round hole below a minuscule nose, a hole which communicated with a particularly fine pair of lungs.

' 'Od's Blood!' Arnaud cried. 'He has a good cry, the little devil!'

'He must be hungry,' Sara said. 'I shall give him some sugared water till the milk comes. And I shall give some to Catherine too. Then she can sleep. That's what she needs most: sleep.'

It was true. That was the one thing she wanted. But now

that the first moment of joy and relief had passed, memories of their present situation came crowding back. She clung to Arnaud, who had sat down beside her.

'What about the combat?'

'We were victorious ... in a manner of speaking ... by which I mean that we are safe enough for the moment, so long as we have that hostage over there.'

Now, for the first time, Catherine noticed a stranger sitting at the far side of the fire, guarded by huge Escorneboeuf and two of the Gascons. He was tall, thin and lean as a rapier and dressed entirely in red. His thin face was remarkable chiefly for its huge beaked nose. He had an arrogant chin and red sensual lips and might have been about forty. There were a few grey streaks in his flat black locks which he wore rather long. He sat on a stone, with his long legs drawn up, looking at the fire with an expression of weary boredom. But his captive status did not seem to worry him unduly.

'Who is it?' she asked.

'Rodrigo de Villa-Andrade, in person! I came upon him in the thick of the battle and threatened him with a dagger at his throat. That is how I managed to stop the fight. He is a wild beast but his men are loyal to him. I brought him here knowing that the people in the château will not attack us so long as we have him for fear that we might put him to death.'

At this the Spaniard yawned hugely and looked at them.

'I hate to destroy your illusions, Montsalvy ... but my men know me and they know that I am not afraid of death. They will do everything possible to rescue me and unless you slit my throat in cold blood you will not be able to take me with you to the death which awaits you. Remember ... you have but four men, even if two of those are worth three ordinary men each.'

'It's true,' Sara whispered to Catherine. 'Almost all the Gascons were killed. We only have the sergeant and two soldiers left ... and to make matters worse, we have nothing to eat.'

'In other words,' Catherine said despairingly, 'this cave which gave us shelter is really nothing but a trap!'

Catherine had the unpleasant sensation that the cave was shrinking and drawing in upon them, slowly but inexorably. Why had her child come into the world in this living tomb?

The sound of whispered feminine voices must have reached Villa-Andrade's ears because he stood up abruptly and walked to the far end of the cave, followed closely by Escorneboeuf.

'Stay where you are!' Arnaud cried roughly.

'Why? Would you have me shout when we could talk in civilized tones? You ought to realize, before too late, that your situation is not as good as you suppose and that . . .'

He stopped short. The Spaniard had just caught sight of Catherine by the flickering light of the blazing branch which Gauthier had managed to fix to the wall. She lay outstretched beneath her covers, pale and exhausted but enveloped in the sumptuous silky mass of her hair which hung about her like a royal mantle, surrounding her with an aureole of light. Villa-Andrade's sarcastic smile vanished from his lips in his astonishment. For a second the mercenary leader and the young woman examined each other. . . . She perceived a look of undisguised admiration in the man's eyes and in her heart of hearts she found him an interesting character. That thin, bony face, with its look of stony arrogance, was strangely at odds with the warmth which shone in his eyes. Bird of prey he might be, but a handsome bird for all that, and Catherine's feminine intuition whispered to her that he belonged to the category of men whom women always look at more than once, if not many times! But for the moment Villa-Andrade was in transports.

'Rose of May!' he murmured, 'full of sweetness,
    You are comely and fair
    The Queen of flowers. . . .'

'What's that?' Arnaud demanded threateningly, placing himself between the Spaniard and Catherine. 'Do you think you are some sort of minstrel, or do you imagine my wife enjoys listening to these effusions?'

Rodrigo stared at Arnaud with the eyes of a sleep-walker.

'Your wife?' he murmured. 'I did not know you were married, Montsalvy. And now I see a child there. . . . I don't understand.'

'I thought you were more intelligent,' Arnaud sneered. 'There is nothing so complicated about it all. We were making all haste to reach my own lands but the rigours of the journey were too much for my wife. We hoped to find our dear cousins at Ventadour, as well as the rest and repose which Madame de Montsalvy is sorely in need of . . . but all we found was a pack of carrion, and brandished swords! You and your men, sir knight, have obliged my wife to give birth to a son at the bottom of a mole-hole! And she was lucky to find *that*! Now do you understand?'

Arnaud's harsh voice struck Catherine oddly. Weak and

anxious though she was, she did not fear the Spaniard. A man who could look at her with that bedazzled expression could not possibly be a serious threat. So why did Arnaud deliberately seek to provoke him? It could only mean that jealousy had taken hold of him, and as she knew, his jealousy was fierce and formidable.

But Villa-Andrade did not seem upset. With an ease and grace which bespoke the great nobleman, he knelt before Catherine with one hand placed over his heart and his eyes fixed on her pale face in its golden frame.

'The noblest and saintliest of women also gave birth to her son on a bed of straw. That precedent should be some comfort to you, madame. But the glow of your beauty makes even that memory grow dim. You are fairer than the evening star, madame!'

This was more than Montsalvy could stand. His hand fell and seized the Spaniard by his collar and forced him back onto his feet.

'That's enough! You know me well enough to know that I will not tolerate such language in speaking to my wife!'

The Castilian's thin lips curled in a smile and his eyes sparkled. Catherine was convinced that he was mocking Arnaud.

'In that case you should oblige her to go about veiled, like Moorish women, because wherever she goes your wife's beauty must dazzle the night and bend men's backs under the weight of their desire. But,' he added treacherously, 'I congratulate and envy you, Montsalvy. You seem to have a gift for attracting exceptionally beautiful women. Isabelle de Séverac, whom you were once engaged to, was outstandingly beautiful and I envied you then. But compared to your wife, she is but a pale ray of moonlight compared with a summer dawn.'

The allusion to Montsalvy's former engagement was a deliberate piece of gaucherie and it was not lost on Catherine. Although Isabelle's name was disagreeable to her she was too sensible to go in fear of the dead. Besides, had Arnaud ever really loved Isabelle? But Villa-Andrade's calculated insolence made her fear that the two men would come to blows, and dagger blows at that. She sensed that there was an old rivalry here and the Spaniard's tone suggested that they had now found a new battlefield. Arnaud was scarlet, and his fists clenched and unclenched, ready to strike this mocking face with its sardonically gleaming eyes. But he did not have time to reply. One of the Gascons on guard at the entrance to the cave sprang forward.

'Messire . . . men are approaching under cover of darkness. I hear footsteps all around us, steps which they are trying to keep silent.'

'Many of them?'

'It is hard to say precisely, messire . . . but certainly more than twenty men.'

Instinctively Catherine clutched at her husband's hand and drew the baby closer to her. Her fear had returned. He must have sensed her anguish because he held the trembling fingers firmly and his cold voice did not betray the least sign of nervousness.

'Very well, then . . . let them approach! Escorneboeuf! . . . You and your men and Gauthier are to stand by the entrance! I don't think anyone is likely to get through. I will stay here to dispatch this gentleman here if need be . . . his life is not worth a farthing!' He smiled ominously at the prisoner. 'If his men grow too threatening, that is.'

Villa-Andrade shrugged with an air of exasperation.

'They will not come nearer! Chapelle, my lieutenant, is far from being a fool. He knows how to smoke a boar from its lair . . . As for your threats of killing me in cold blood, I do not believe them. You have never killed an unarmed man, Montsalvy. I know you . . . and so does Chapelle! The most stubborn, obstinate, difficult character in the whole French army, but the most perfect expression of chivalry.'

The Spaniard's mocking tone robbed this compliment of much of its force. Arnaud disdained it in any case.

'I might have changed . . . particularly as I now have a wife and child!'

'No . . . men like you never change! Madame,' he added, with a quick look at Catherine whose anxious eyes went from one to the other, 'tell your husband he is being a fool. Now that I know you are here I am no longer your enemy! I, too, know the laws of chivalry and the respect due from a Castilian noble to a woman of your rank . . . and beauty!'

'Messire,' Catherine replied in a trembling voice, 'everything my husband does is well and wisely done in my eyes. It is his decision to make and if he decides to die here I shall die with him, without regrets.'

'Have you brought a child into the world only to remove him from it again so quickly?'

The young woman had no time to reply. Sara had jumped up with a scream of terror, which echoed the howl of pain given

by one of the Gascons. A shower of arrows was falling about
the entrance to the cave. One of them had pierced the soldier's
chest. But the remarkable thing about these arrows was that
each of them carried a packet of blazing hemp fixed to the tail
in lieu of feathers. Gauthier and Escorneboeuf both rushed forward to try to put them out but there were so many that the
cave was brilliantly illuminated as far as the rocky roof and the
place was soon filled with dense smoke. Catherine clutched her
son to her breast.

'They are trying to smoke us out, or burn us alive!' Gauthier
growled.

But Arnaud had leapt forward, so swiftly that he took Villa-
Andrade by surprise. The Spaniard found himself pinioned by
the knight's iron-hard hand, and at the same moment the cold
and disagreeable edge of a naked blade was pressed against his
throat.

'Tell them to stop!' Arnaud growled, 'or by the liver of an
Auvergnat I'll cut your throat like a chicken's, chivalry or no
chivalry! Such refinements do not apply to carrion like you!'

Despite his danger Villa-Andrade managed to smile.

'I'd be delighted to ... but I don't think it would help. Until I
rejoin him, Chapelle will continue the attack. After all ... he
must have thought he could lead the men as well as myself
for a long time now. My death would mean his promotion!'

The dagger bit closer, nipping a little way into the skin so that
a thin trickle of blood appeared. Catherine's eyes were smart-
ing in the thick smoke and now she began to cough, and this
exasperated Arnaud past endurance.

'Do something then, or you die!'

'I am not afraid of dying to some purpose but I have a horror
of useless actions. Let us both go out there, you and I. When
Chapelle sees me he will hold his fire. He would be prepared
for you to kill me, I am sure, but I do not think he would risk
doing so himself.'

Without a word, and without removing his dagger, Arnaud
pushed the Spaniard outside. Catherine stretched out a hand to
stop him but they had already reached the entrance with its
hail of blazing flying torches. The arrows stopped falling.

'Carry me outside!' Catherine cried to Gauthier. 'I want to
stay with my husband!'

She could hardly breathe. She was on the verge of fainting
away but the Norman hesitated. The two men were out of sight.
But she could hear the Spaniard cry out:

'Stop, Chapelle! That's an order! Stop firing!'

This was followed by another voice, one which sounded un-couth and hoarse through too many years spent shouting orders.

'Not for more than a quarter of an hour, messire! After that I shall attack again, even if it means you have to lose your life! I know there are women there. Tell these people that if they don't release you I shall show the women neither pity nor quarter. The men will be skinned alive, and the women disembowelled after they have provided the men with a little amusement. And then . . . I shall say a De Profundis for your soul!'

Catherine was shaken by such a violent fit of coughing that Gauthier hesitated no longer. He gave the child to Sara and then picked Catherine up, coats, coverlets and all, and carried her out into the open air. She drank in the fresh night air. He set her down on a flat rock where Sara soon joined her with the baby. From where she was she could see the foaming torrent and shadowy shapes of men among the trees, and an occasional gleam of armour. The moon was rising behind the mountains, lighting up the countryside more each minute. She also saw Arnaud still grasping the Spaniard, standing a few paces away. She heard Villa-Andrade's voice speaking urgently:

'Killing me would be a small triumph, Montsalvy, and little comfort to you when my men were raping your wife beneath your eyes. These are men of Navarre and the Basque country half-savage mountain people who love blood and do not know the meaning of pity. You are in an impasse now from which I alone can save you.'

'How?'

Arnaud's voice was as harsh as ever and from where she sat Catherine could see his profile clearly, etched black against the moonlight. The strange group he formed with Villa-Andrade stood out clearly against the darker masses of the woods, and suddenly she was afraid of what Arnaud's pride might do, afraid for herself and the child. He would never give in, even if their lives depended on it.

'Set me free! Soon it will be too late. They will never stop once they have smelt blood.'

As if to lend force to his words, the lieutenant's voice reached them and Catherine was in such torment she almost cried out.

'Time passes, messire. You do not have much longer,' said Chapelle.

The Spaniard now spoke again, more urgently than before. 'I have promised for the sake of your wife and son to forswear all

warlike action. I give you my word as a Castilian and a knight.
I will only remember that, once long ago, we fought side by
side. . . .'

The dagger withdrew the fraction of an inch from his neck.

'You swear by the Cross?'

'I swear by the Cross and the Holy Name of Our Saviour who
died for us!'

Then at long last Montsalvy withdrew his arm, and he released the Spaniard's wrists which he had been holding in his
left hand. Catherine heaved a great sigh of relief.

'Very well. You are free. But may you roast in an eternity of
hell fire if you have lied to me,' Arnaud said.

'I have not lied. . . .'

The Spaniard stepped forward to meet the soldiers who had
begun closing in around them. Their iron-clad ring now completely encircled the mound where they stood, and Catherine
could see their battle-axes, halberds and pikes. And this barbarous apparatus threatened the frail life of her own helpless
babe!

Villa-Andrade spoke out. His voice was powerful and reson-
ant and the echoes gave it something of the quality of a last
trump.

'Peace has been made, and I am free,' he said, 'thanks to you,
Chapelle!'

'We don't attack?' said a skinny, wiry little man who had
stepped forward out of the group and who stood a good head
shorter than the tall Villa-Andrade. It could only be the famous
Chapelle and Catherine felt uneasy, sensing the regret in his
voice.

'No. We shall not attack.'

'But ... what if we *preferred* to attack, my men and me?
Have you forgotten that the Seigneur de Montsalvy is a traitor
and criminal against the state?'

The blow fell in an instant. The Spaniard's fist crashed down
and Chapelle rolled downhill towards the stream.

'I will hang anyone else who argues with me! Now, carry out
my commands! I order you to return to the château to fetch a
litter and make a room ready. You, Pedrito . . .!'

The rest of the conversation was in Spanish and Catherine did
not understand a word but now Arnaud interposed:

'One moment. We may not do battle together but I still refuse
to accept your hospitality. I will not enter Ventadour until its
rightful owner awaits me there.'

'Your wife needs rest and food . . .!'

'Stop worrying yourself about my wife! We shall leave at daybreak. Now return to your lair and leave us here. . . . But please accept my thanks.'

Villa-Andrade's swarthy face turned aside, and he sought Catherine's eyes and then turned away in a sort of confusion.

'No. You do not owe me anything. . . . You will understand soon enough why it is I do not want your thanks. Farewell then, since you wish it. No one will molest you while you remain on the lands of Ventadour.'

He stepped forward and bent one knee before Catherine. He gazed at her with an ardour which made her blush.

'I would like to have welcomed you as a queen, fair lady. Forgive me for leaving you here like this. One day perhaps I may have the pleasure . . .'

'That's enough!' Arnaud cried roughly. 'Now, go!'

Villa-Andrade got to his feet, shrugged, laid a hand over his heart in salute to Catherine and turned on his heel. She watched the tall red-gowned figure vanish into the trees in the pale moonlight. This odd man intrigued her, and she did not feel the least aversion to him. He had behaved like a gentleman, and she was a little cross with Arnaud for refusing his hospitality. She would have dearly liked a comfortable bed and roaring fire, something warm to drink and more shelter too for the baby who was sleeping now in Sara's arms. The night cold penetrated her clothes and she shivered. Sara had noticed her sigh.

'Well, those are fine sentiments,' she said crossly to Montsalvy. 'But what do you propose to feed your wife on in her present delicate state of health? It's all very well putting up objections and talking about pride and honour, but Catherine must eat, otherwise the baby will have no milk. . . .'

'Peace, woman!' Arnaud interrupted wearily. 'I did what honour demands. When will you understand?'

'I understand this . . . that Catherine and the babe are like to perish for the sake of your precious honour! Truly, messire, you have a strange way of loving!'

The barb went home. He turned away from Sara, bent over Catherine and picked her up in his arms.

'Did you too think I didn't love you, my darling? Perhaps Sara is right, and I am too hard and too proud! . . . But it would have been painful for me to accept that man's hospitality. I don't like the way he looks at you. . . .'

'I think you were right to act as you did,' she said, twining her arms round his neck and laying her head against his shoulder. 'I am strong, as you know ... but I'm cold! Take me back into the cave. Perhaps the smoke has dispersed. I'm so afraid the baby might catch cold!'

The smoke had gone, and there was nothing left but a faint smell. While Arnaud settled Catherine down again Sara set about lighting the fire at the mouth of the cave. Gauthier had gone off to see if any of the horses killed during the combat had been left on the spot, so that he might cut off a haunch or two to roast. He had barely gone when three men appeared. Two of them were carrying a large basket covered with a white napkin while the third held a little silver pitcher. They were all dressed in tunics bearing the Spaniard's armorial device of bars and crescent. They bowed and placed their basket on the ground. The tallest went up to Catherine, took a rolled parchment from under his tunic and handed it to her on one knee. Then, without waiting for a reply he bowed, turned and departed with his companions before either the astounded Arnaud, Catherine or Sara could say a word. But the surprise did not last long. Sara ran to the basket and lifted up the napkin.

'Food!' she cried joyfully. 'Pâtés, roast chickens, white bread! Sweet Jesus! How long it is since we tasted anything like that! And here in the pitcher there is some milk for the child! Thanks be to God!'

'One moment,' Arnaud interrupted dryly. He took the parchment roll which Catherine had not yet thought of opening, and read it. His handsome face grew crimson.

'The devil!' he cried, 'that damned Castilian is making a fool of me. ... How dare he!'

'Let me see,' Catherine said. He handed her the scroll with bad grace. The message written thereon was brief.

'Fairest of women,' Villa-Andrade had written, 'even a man as rigorous as your husband could not wish to starve to death. Please accept these modest offerings, not as charity but rather as a homage to a beauty which even hunger could not destroy and which I hope to have the pleasure of contemplating again before long. ...'

In spite of herself she blushed, and let the parchment roll itself up again. Arnaud snatched it from her and flung it into the fire.

'Does he think he can pay court to my wife under my very nose, that stinking dog? As for his gifts ...'

He walked across to the basket with a determined look but then he found that Sara was barring the way, with a look of blazing defiance on her face.

'Ah, no, that's too much! You are not going to touch these heaven-sent provisions in here, messire! You will have to kill me first. I've never seen anything so ridiculous! I swear to you that Catherine will eat this whether you like it or not.'

She stood there challenging him, eyes flashing, ready to leap at his throat if need be. He raised his hand in a fury and would have struck her, but Catherine stopped him:

'No . . . Arnaud! You must be mad.'

His hand fell back slowly to his side, and gradually his face lost that dark flush. At last he shrugged.

'Well, it seems you were right after all, Sara. . . . Catherine and the baby must have everything they need. Give some to the men too, they need it.'

'And you?' Catherine asked sorrowfully.

'Me? I shall share Gauthier's haunch of horse meat.'

The Norman, like Montsalvy, refused to touch the contents of the basket, but Escorneboeuf and the one remaining Gascon, a little fellow whose monkey-like face was always twitching nervously, and who was known as Fortunat, fell upon their food like men who had not assuaged their hunger for a long time. There was feasting that night in the caves of Ventadour. Then Arnaud organized the night watch and took the first for himself. He went and sat by the fire, with his long legs folded up under him, and his arms clasped round his knees. The baby slept soundly on Sara's opulent bosom, and Catherine herself, after swallowing the last mouthful of food, finally dropped off into a dreamless sleep. The men slept too, heavily, lying on the bare earth, like tired animals.

In the countryside all was silent. The danger was past. Now the voyage would not be long. At daybreak Arnaud would take Catherine on his own horse once more, to spare her the cold and the rudest jolts and bumps, and soon the rooftops and crenellations of Montsalvy would rise up beyond the vast plateau where all the winds in the world had their kingdom. The old seignorial dwelling, rich in an eventful and glorious past and warm, fond memories, would fold its walls about this new family which its master had brought back with him like a gift offering. . . .

Forgetting his hatred and his desire for vengeance for a moment, Arnaud de Montsalvy smiled tenderly into the fire which protected these two beings who were now his whole life from cold. Then his gaze went to the dark sky beyond the mouth of the cave.

'Praise be to Thee, O Lord, for Brother Fire who lights up the night! He is handsome and gay, and strong and unconquerable. Praise be to Thee, Lord, for the wife and son Thou hast given me. . . .'

CHAPTER ELEVEN

Return to Montsalvy

Six days after leaving Ventadour, the little party, reduced to six horsemen, was crossing the high plateau of Châtaigne, south of Aurillac, against incessant squalls of wind. Now, the very heart of the Auvergne had been reached and Catherine's eyes lighted upon the ancient mountains, black and stark, whose winter bleakness was softened by the unchanging, sombre green of the pines. She saw torrents tumbling down the hillsides, midnight blue lakes, which made her uneasy with their dark, silent waters, and seemingly endless forests.

Thanks to the invigorating air and the provisions from the Spaniard, some of which they had brought with them, and not least to her sturdy constitution, she had recovered her strength with amazing rapidity. Two days after the birth of her son, she mounted Morgane despite Arnaud's protests.

'I feel perfectly well,' she told him, laughing. 'We have been delayed long enough on my account and I am anxious to get on.'

They stopped for a day at the Benedictine Abbey of St Geraud, which overlooked Aurillac and whose abbot was a relative of Arnaud's. There the infant was baptized. His parents, by mutual consent, had given him the name Michel after Arnaud's brother, who long ago had been murdered by the Parisian rabble after Catherine had tried desperately to save him.

'He will take after him,' Arnaud maintained, gazing at his son with joy. 'He is fair like he was . . . and like you,' he added, looking at his wife.

To have devoted a day to this child whom Arnaud swore would become a second Michel de Montsalvy – a man whom Catherine had adored at first sight – filled the young woman with profound joy. The infant became even more precious to her.

For a week-old baby, little Michel was wonderfully lively. The journey, despite the cold and snow, did not seem to worry him. He nestled in the vast lap of radiant Sara for whom winter had no meaning except for its effect on the infant. Warmly wrapped, his tiny face covered by a light shawl, he slept with

clenched fists most of the time, only waking to demand food in
a piercing voice. The travellers then halted in a sheltered corner and the child was passed to Catherine. These moments were
unfailingly wonderful for the young mother. She had a deep
feeling of unity with this creature of her own flesh and blood.
The miniature fingers fastened on the swollen breast she offered
to him and the little round mouth sucked with an ardour which
disturbed Arnaud.

'Young rascal,' he grumbled. 'When we get to the castle, we'll
get you a wet nurse. If you go on like this, you'll eat your
mother up!'

'There's nothing better for a baby than his mother's milk,'
pronounced Sara dictatorially.

'Nonsense! At home the boys were always given out to nurse.
We've great appetites in our family and our mothers can't
cope as a rule. I had two nurses myself,' he concluded triumphantly.

These little skirmishes amused Catherine who knew quite
well the real reason why her husband was in favour of nurses.
Arnaud had little time for the convention which obliged a man
to be separated from his wife until weaning. When night came,
he reluctantly allowed Catherine to sleep with Sara and the
baby. Then, in spite of the fatigue of the ride, he would stride
about the neighbourhood for hours. Catherine could tell his
desire from his expression as he watched her feeding Michel.
He would stand in front of her, his gaze fastened on her bare
bosom, hiding his hands behind his back so she would not see
them trembling.

Things had come to a head that morning when Arnaud
knocked down Escorneboeuf whom he had surprised hiding
behind the door while Catherine suckled Michel. The huge man
had not realized Montsalvy was coming. His face crimson, he
was squatting with his eye to the keyhole, while the young
woman, believing herself alone with Sara in the monastery cell,
opened her bodice to the waist, smiling as the gipsy sang a lulla-
by to the infant. The blood was pounding so loudly in his ears
that Escorneboeuf was not aware of Arnaud's rapid steps under
the cloister arches. The next moment, the huge sergeant was
rolling in the dust with a yell. With a mighty blow, Montsalvy
had crushed his nose. Then he lifted him with a kick in the back-
side, roaring:

'Get out! If ever I see you again, I'll kill you!'

The other went, cringing like a beaten dog, muttering curses between his teeth. Arnaud paid no attention, but Catherine was worried.

'He's a bad man! He will pay you back. . . .'

'He wouldn't dare! I know his sort. Anyway, once at Montsalvy, nothing would be easier than to put him in a cell to calm down.'

When they were ready to depart, however, Escorneboeuf was nowhere to be found. In spite of his enormous height, he seemed suddenly to have evaporated. No one in the monastery had seen him, but Arnaud refused to be upset.

'Good riddance! After all, we had no further use for him.'

All the same, he advised the Abbot d'Estaing to throw the Gascon in irons if ever the town constable laid hands on him. Of the men supplied by Xaintrailles, only the slender Fortunat remained, but Fortunat appeared to miss his superior no more than did the others. Since the incident in the Forest of Chabrières, he had conceived a deep admiration for Gauthier, equal to that he reserved for Catherine whom Fortunat regarded as a supernatural being. His was a simple nature, rough and cruel more by habit than by disposition, and henceforth Fortunat followed the Norman like a shadow.

Night was falling and the eight leagues separating Aurillac from Montsalvy slipped away beneath the rapid hooves of the horses. Arnaud could not conceal his impatience and the great black stallion broke into a gallop when his master saw the Roman tower of a church above dark walls, floating on the misty horizon, unreal as a mirage. Behind him, Morgane literally flew, her tail streaming gaily behind her as the stones sped beneath her hooves. Gauthier and Fortunat stayed in the rear with Sara. Burdened by Michel, the good woman could go only at the most gentle pace. In any case, Rustaud had never galloped in his life.

Carried away by the mad ride, Catherine spurred Morgane. The mare surged forward, catching up with the black horse. Arnaud turned to his wife who was rosy and radiant with excitement.

'You won't beat me, my fair equestrienne. In any case, you don't know the road,' he cried into the wind.

'Is that the château down there?'

'No . . . that's the abbey. The village houses are clustered between it and the Puy de l'Arbre, the hill where our house stands. We must take a road on the left under the walls of the monastery which runs through the woods, and the castle is on the flank of the hill. From the tower it commands a wide view. You'll see. ... You'll get the impression that the world is at your feet.'

He fell silent as the speed of the ride took his breath away. Catherine smiled and again urged on her mare. Morgane gave of her best, passing the stallion. Catherine shouted with laughter as, out-distanced, Arnaud swore like a trooper. Cruelly spurred, his horse leapt forward like a cannonball. They approached the walls of the abbey. Catherine could make out the slate roofs of the little houses of the hamlet. Suddenly, Arnaud veered to the left, leaving the main road for a narrow track which lost itself in the trees. She turned back and saw that the others were far behind.

'Wait for us,' she cried.

But he did not hear. The air of his native land which he had not breathed for more than two years went to his head like wine. Catherine hesitated for a moment. Should she follow him or wait for the others? If she followed him, the others, Gauthier, Sara and Fortunat, could not fail to see which way she had gone. She leaned forward, patting Morgane's mane.

'Come on, my pretty, let's catch up with the runaway who has abandoned us!'

The little mare whinnied as a sign that she understood, and sped forward on Arnaud's trail. The black shadows of the evergreens engulfed them both. All of a sudden it was like night, but a lighter streak lit up the end of the road. The form of a rider appeared in profile for a moment and then Arnaud vanished.

Catherine and Morgane passed along the little forest road, refusing to be distracted by the faint scents of burgeoning spring. They came out into the fading, violet light and Catherine could almost believe she saw the world open before her. The slope of an extinct volcano dominated an unfolding landscape of valleys and mountains, rocks and water, trees and fields: a scene of such fantastic, savage grandeur that it made one giddy.... Pulling hard, Catherine reined in Morgane at the edge of an outcrop of rock and then turned her head towards the summit of the puy to search for Arnaud.

She glimpsed him at last and stifled a cry. There he was, his back towards her, straight as a lance in the saddle and as rigid. Before him towered a huge ruin, a mass of blackened, riven stone ground almost to powder, a field of titanic rocks which still gave the distant impression of the shape of a tower, the

line of a turret, the shattered curve of an arch: a prodigious
mass of masonry crushed by some giant's fist. Long, blackened
stains spoke of fire, while rafters still strained towards the sky
like a cry for help. Stones tumbled down into what had lately
been a moat and fragments of chain hung derisively over the
blackened ruins and twisted iron, the remains of the drawbridge. This was all that remained of the Castle of Montsalvy.
. . .

The funereal cry of a crow spiralling in the pale sky dragged
Catherine from the stupor into which the sight had thrown her.
She looked at her husband. Arnaud was like a man struck by a
thunderbolt, his pallid face expressionless, pupils dilated. Only
the black locks of his hair, stirred by the wind, gave him the
semblance of a human being. Otherwise, he was a stone
statue – blind and dumb.

She approached him with dread and touched his arm.

'Arnaud . . .' she whispered. 'My dear lord.'

But he neither heard nor saw her. He dismounted, still staring
before him. Catherine watched him approach the ruins with the
jerky steps of a sleepwalker. He turned towards something
which, in her shocked state, she had not immediately noticed:
a great parchment where a scarlet seal dripped like a wound
from the end of a cord transfixed by four arrows to the rubble.
Her heart missed a beat and she held her breath. . . . She saw
Arnaud mount a pile of stones, tear down the parchment and
scan it rapidly. Then, like an oak uprooted by the wind, he fell
face downwards with a hoarse cry which struck to the depth of
Catherine's soul.

The woman's moan echoed that of the man. She jumped
down from her mount, ran to her husband and fell on her knees
beside him, trying to loosen his clutching hands which were
tearing at two tufts of dry grass. A vain effort! Arnaud's body
was torn by a nervous spasm which the young woman's strength
was powerless to overcome. Blindly she groped about, trying to
prevent the wind from blowing the parchment away. She seized
it and tried to read it, but night had fallen and she could only
decipher the first line written in large letters: 'By order of the
King . . .'

Now Arnaud sobbed, his face buried in the grass, and Catherine, overcome, tried again to lift him and cradle him in her
arms.

'My love . . .' she beseeched, almost in tears herself. 'My love
. . . I beg you!'

'Leave him, Dame Catherine,' came the rough voice of Gauthier next to her. 'He doesn't hear you! The weight of sorrow upon him makes him blind and deaf to the outside world. But tears are good for him. . . .'

The Norman's firm hand helped her to rise. Still, grasping the parchment between her fingers, she found herself in Sara's arms, the baby having been entrusted to Fortunat. The gipsy was trembling like a leaf, but her embrace was warm and her voice steady.

'Be strong, little one,' she whispered in Catherine's ear. 'You must be brave enough to help him. He will need it.'

She nodded, wishing to go back to Arnaud, but Gauthier restrained her.

'No. . . . Leave him to me!'

Little by little, the convulsive sobs which shook Arnaud were calmed. This was the moment the Norman chose. He took little Michel from the careful hands of Fortunat and, in his turn, knelt by the man.

'Messire,' he said in a voice vibrant with emotion. 'The ancient sagas of my people say, "When your burden is heavy, cast it off and seek to help yourself." There still remains vengeance . . . and this!'

Michel woke and began to yell. Catherine freed herself from Sara's arms. Her heart beat as though it would break and her hands stretched out instinctively towards the prostrate man. All at once, Arnaud stood up. He looked at Gauthier and then at the child, his face distorted by his paroxysm of grief. He took the screaming morsel in his hands and it became quiet as though by magic. He pressed the infant to him fiercely, then his gaze returned to the Norman, a wild resolve shining in his eyes.

'You are right,' he said harshly. 'I still have a son and a wife . . . and hate! Cursed be the King who thus repays my loyalty and the blood I freely shed! Cursed be Charles of Valois who has given what was mine to his servant, destroyed my house and killed my mother! I forswear my oath of allegiance from this moment hence and I will not rest until . . .'

'No!' cried Catherine, shocked by this voice which roared like a hurricane, by this terrifying anger which swelled Arnaud's veins like the flow of lava tracing its way from the crater of a volcano. She flung herself on him, snatching the child from his arms and folding it in her own.

'No,' she repeated more quietly. 'I do not want curses round my child. You must not, Arnaud, you must *not* say such things!'

For the first time he turned on her, his face black with fury.

'My mother, doubtless, lies dead under the ruins of our home. I am an outlaw ...' he seized the parchment which she still held and shook it in his fist. 'You can read? Traitor and felon! I? Traitor and felon as Joan was a heretic and a witch. Shame, despair and the executioner: that is how Charles repays his servants!'

'It is not he,' said Catherine wearily, 'and you know it. . . .'

'He is King! If it is thus he exercises his sovereignty, it were better that he take the tonsure and enter a monastery. The Duke of Burgundy should have the throne!'

A cloud of despair invaded Catherine. Was it possible that Arnaud, in the extreme of sorrow and anger, should come to wish as overlord the man whom, all his life, he had hated and fought? Would be now turn to his enemy, to the man from whom Catherine had torn herself so painfully to rejoin him, Arnaud? She shook her head. Huge tears rolled from her eyes onto little Michel's cheek. She pressed her lips passionately to the tiny face and drew her cloak closer so she could wrap the child more snugly. The upland wind blew strongly, coming from the black trough of the valleys filled with night. The torch which Fortunat had just lighted flared and dimmed in the damp gusts. Catherine shivered, looking round at the figures frozen in this painful tableau. Her eyes rested on her husband. He was still standing before the ruin, straight as a spear, his wild eyes riveted on this new destruction which the firelight made even more sinister. ... Discouragement gripped the young woman. Once more he had escaped her and she did not know how to reach him through the wall of fury which enclosed him. He could not understand calm words, because, for the time being, he knew only rebellion.

Believing that her womanly weakness was her best weapon, she approached him and leant against him.

'Arnaud,' she murmured. 'Can't we find some shelter? The wind is rising and I am chilled through. I am anxious about Michel, too.'

When his eyes fell on her, Catherine saw that the anger had left him, but that he was filled with a tragic despair. The young man's arm went round her shoulders and pressed her to him.

'Poor little thing. You are tired and cold! The child needs your attention, too. Come, we can do no more here for the time being.'

The reassuring contact of his hard muscles restored Catherine's courage. She lifted a confident face towards her husband.

'The ruins will be rebuilt, Arnaud, and time will efface the tears!'

'But it will not bring back the dead! And my poor mother . . .'

His voice broke and Catherine felt his fingers tighten on her shoulder, but he pulled himself together and repeated mournfully:

'I'm sure she defended her home until the end! Tomorrow I must get the people of the village to help me shift the rubble and recover her body to give it proper burial. Now, we'll go to the monastery. The abbot and I have not always seen eye to eye, but he can't refuse us asylum.'

The sorrowful party remounted, turned about and, following Montsalvy, again entered the tunnel of trees through which they had ridden so joyfully only an hour before. The ruins of Montsalvy were left to their solitude and the moaning wind which seemed to come for the express purpose of weeping over them.

The rosy-yellow point of light which had appeared in the path was growing rapidly. Catherine perceived that it was a lantern swinging at the end of the arm of someone walking to meet them. Fortunat's torch and the lantern soon reached the same level and stopped. Half-hidden by Arnaud's back, the young woman saw a peasant, so weather-beaten and brown, but so vigorous, that the smock and woollen hose he wore seemed to clothe an old, gnarled tree. His stiff, grizzled hair hung below the brown cap pulled down to his ears, but, under bushy grey eyebrows, his hazel eyes shone with a cheerful gleam. The face was rough-hewn with tight lips which would not smile easily, a chin like a boot and a nose like a knife-blade, but the creases and folds around the mouth gave his face an expression of roguish cunning.

The peasant, ignoring Fortunat and his torch, went straight to Arnaud and stopped, his face raised, just under the horse's head. He lifted his lantern up to his face and pulled off his cap.

'Milord!' he said. 'I thought I recognized you on the heath when you galloped past as though the devil were after you! Blessed be the Good Lord for bringing you back to your homeland!'

His narrow mouth stretched in a huge grin which showed his toothless gums and his old face was lit with such a shining joy that the night was illuminated. Catherine saw two tears glistening in the corners of his eyes as the good man knelt in the mud, still gazing at Arnaud as though he were an archangel. The latter, meanwhile, jumped down from his horse, grasped the peasant by the shoulders and kissed him on either cheek.

'Saturnin! Old Saturnin! 'Od's Blood! How glad I am to see you again! You can tell me . . .'

Now, under Arnaud's embrace, the old man wept for joy.

'Ah, now that you are back, Messire Arnaud, all will be well! At last you have come back to deal with those god-forsaken dogs who descended on our countryside like carrion crows!'

As he spoke, Saturnin's sharp eyes noticed Catherine on Morgane and Sara, upright on Rustaud, the baby in her arms.

'Oh!' he said with open admiration. 'What a lovely lady! In truth, milord, never have I seen anyone so lovely. . . . She's like . . .'

'This is my wife, Saturnin,' replied Arnaud with a touch of pride which made Catherine smile. 'And here is my son! You may kiss her hand. . . . My dear, Saturnin is the bailiff of Montsalvy and our most faithful servant. He looks like a peasant, but there is more to him than meets the eye. He brought us up, Michel and me . . . almost like our own mother. . . .'

Once more, Arnaud's voice broke at the mention of his mother. Saturnin, who had kissed Catherine's hand, turned back to him, crying:

'Old fool that I am to keep you here instead of taking you straight off to find her! Our poor mistress will be so pleased!'

'My mother! You know where she is? She isn't . . . ?'

'Dead? Is that what you thought? If I hadn't succeeded in making her leave the castle when those savages set it on fire, you would never have seen old Saturnin again! I couldn't have looked you in the face.'

Arnaud once more took him by the shoulders.

'Alive! She is alive! Where is she? At the monastery?'

Saturnin spat on the ground and shrugged his shoulders.

'At the monastery! Valette and his men are there, the ones who burnt your home. Where else would Madame la Comtesse be but at my place? At the farm, because Valette's men are in the best houses in town. Come now, it's getting late. At night, you understand, the roads are dangerous. . . .'

As he spoke, Saturnin took Morgane's bridle and turned the little mare. Before putting on his cap, he bowed to Catherine with an unconscious dignity.

'Milady,' he said with great respect. 'It will be an honour for old Saturnin to conduct you to his house, unworthy though it be to receive you. But you will be as much at home there as if the walls of Montsalvy were still standing.'

She thanked him with a smile. Innumerable conflicting feelings agitated the young woman. This peasant, at once so proud and so simple, whom Arnaud treated as a friend, threw new light on her husband's character. She had a fleeting glimpse of the child he had been and also of the intensely human side of him which he hid under his haughtiness. She was happy to think that she and hers would soon be safely sheltered; however, under this same roof would be the woman she so much dreaded: Arnaud's mother! As the moment of their meeting drew near, Catherine felt a pang of anguish. Would the great lady who was Isabelle de Montsalvy accept a common girl, or would the young couple have to face reproaches and a bitter scene? The young woman was ashamed to admit that when she first beheld the ruins of the manorial mansion she had, for a brief moment, entertained the shameful thought that fate had granted her a reprieve. In spite of her misgivings, she reproached herself for this thought as for a crime. She had too much courage and was too accustomed to adversity not to look facts in the face.

'The ordeal will come, my girl,' she said to herself as Morgane retraced her steps towards the Puy de l'Arbre. 'And that is as it should be: a well-deserved punishment for what you dared to think!'

But, in spite of this inward reprimand, Catherine's alarm increased with each hoofbeat.

Saturnin's farm sheltered its great tiled roof under a copse of pines on the side of the hill. The faint, narrow road which passed it petered out a little below the ruins, but a rocky spur hid them from the eyes of anyone not searching the valley. As they drew near, Catherine could hardly believe it was there: a darker swelling against the black rock. In the façade there opened, like two dull, red eyes, two narrow windows which she stared at defiantly. The house crouched in the shadows as though lying in wait for them. . . .

The hollow drumming of the horses' hooves brought out the short, black silhouette of a peasant woman in a white cap with a torch raised above her head.

'Who's there?' demanded the woman roughly.

'It is I, Donatienne,' replied Saturnin.

'But you're not alone. . . .'

The woman had come forward and now halted abruptly. The torch trembled in her hand, then slowly she fell on her knees, her face alight with joy.

'Sweet Jesus! Messire Arnaud . . .!'

He was already out of the saddle and, while Saturnin helped Catherine to dismount, lifted old Donatienne to her feet and kissed her on both cheeks.

'It is indeed I . . . My mother? . . .'

'She is in there, milord! Oh, she will be so happy!'

But Arnaud was no longer listening. He had seized Catherine by the hand and dragged her towards the house so quickly that the young woman's heart had no time to beat faster. She found herself in a low room with a floor of beaten earth. A woman in black was sitting on the stone hearth. She rose with a cry.

'You!'

'My God!' thought Catherine. 'How alike they are!'

In truth, the tall, dark, slender woman who supported herself against the chimney-piece bore a striking resemblance to her son: the same high forehead, the same almost aggressively clear-cut features, the same pale complexion and black eyes, but, under the lawn wimple which enclosed her face in almost conventual fashion, the thick black hair was streaked with white. The violet-shadowed eyelids were wrinkled and the delicate mouth had a weary droop absent from the man's firm lips.

Already Arnaud, releasing Catherine, had thrown himself at his mother's feet and was covering her trembling hands with kisses.

'Mother, darling!'

Leaning against the frame of the door where she had recoiled, Catherine surveyed the tableau formed by mother and son, hardly daring to breathe.

Heavy tears slid down the cheeks of Isabelle de Montsalvy as she cupped her son's face in her two hands and raised it to her lips. For a moment which, it seemed to Catherine, lasted a century, they remained locked together. The mother's tears showed no sign of ceasing.

Behind her, Catherine was aware of the bated breath of those who, from respect, had remained outside. Suddenly, she heard Michel wail. She turned and almost snatched the child from Sara's arms, clutching him to her bosom as though demanding protection from this unknown woman whose first words she awaited so fearfully. The warmth of the small body nestling in her arms gave her courage. She swallowed and lifted her head. The dreaded moment had arrived.

Against Arnaud's shoulder, Catherine saw Madame de Montsalvy open the eyes which she had closed in order to savour her joy the better. She saw them rest on her in surprise. Then came the question from Arnaud's mother, spoken gently:

'Who is with you?'

Catherine moved forward two steps, but already Arnaud was beside her. His arm enfolded the young woman's shoulders.

'Mother,' he said gravely. 'Here is my wife, Catherine.'

One of those sudden impulses which she had never been able to control impelled Catherine forward. She found herself kneeling, in her turn, before her husband's mother, offering up the child in both hands.

'And here is our son,' she murmured in a voice husky with emotion. 'We have named him Michel!'

Her violet eyes fastened on those of her mother-in-law, begging her to accept him. Her heart pounded and she fought back the tears. Isabelle de Montsalvy stared incredulously at the young woman at her feet. She opened her mouth, but no sound came. Then she leant forward and peered at the baby's tiny face.

'Michel . . .' she stammered. 'Will you give me Michel?'

She took the child from Catherine's hands and went to the fire to see him better. Catherine could see her lips trembling and her eyes filling with fresh tears. She expected to see her burst into sobs, but it was a smile which came, bright and young: Arnaud's smile. The grandmother caressed with a cautious finger the little tuft of golden hair which sprang from Michel's head.

'He is fair!' she said ecstatically. 'He is fair like my poor child.'

Catherine felt Arnaud's hands slip round her waist and raise her to her feet. Without releasing her, he said:

'We are glad you are happy, Mother, but have you nothing to say to my wife, the mother of your grandson?'

The Lady of Montsalvy turned and her eyes dwelt on the couple standing there. Then she approached them slowly and smiled.

'Pardon me, my daughter. Coming after our misfortunes,

this great happiness has made me lose my head a little. Come here, so I may look at you.'

She held out her left hand to Catherine, cradling Michel in the crook of her right arm. Obediently, the young woman came to the fire, throwing back the hood which covered her head. The flames made her tresses gleam and reflected golden sparks in her eyes. She stood there, very straight, her small, delicate head held with unconscious pride, awaiting the verdict which could hardly be delayed.

'How lovely you are!' breathed Isabelle de Montsalvy. 'Almost too lovely!'

'The most beautiful lady in the kingdom,' said Arnaud tenderly. 'And the best-beloved.'

His mother smiled at the warmth which he gave to those few words.

'You could only have chosen a beautiful wife,' she said. 'You were always hard to please. Come and kiss me, my child.'

Catherine's constricted heart swelled. She bent her neck slightly to offer her forehead for her mother-in-law's kiss before touching her lips to the smooth cheek presented to her. Then the two women bent over Michel who was becoming restless.

'He is beautiful, also,' exulted the grandmother. 'How we shall love him!'

A cry from the doorway interrupted her. A young, dark girl had appeared, pushing Saturnin, Donatienne, Gauthier, Sara and Fortunat aside impatiently.

'Arnaud! Arnaud . . . You're back! . . . At last!'

As in a dream, Catherine saw the young girl run to her husband, throw her arms around him and, stretching on tiptoe, press her lips to his with a passion which left no doubt of the depth of her feelings. Arnaud had been too surprised to react immediately, but Catherine felt a sharp, searing anger. Where did this creature come from and what right did she have to embrace her husband with such ardour? She stepped up to Arnaud who, meanwhile, had recovered himself and was vigorously pushing his assailant away.

'Marie!' said he. 'You should learn to control yourself! I didn't know you were here.'

'Her brother entrusted her to me,' said his mother. 'She was so bored at Comborn!'

'And this place,' said Arnaud with a crooked smile, 'is so much more gay! Get along! Calm yourself,' he snapped impatiently, beating off the arms which were wound round his neck once more. 'You are too big to behave like a hoyden. My dear,' he added, turning to his wife, 'this little pet is our cousin Marie de Comborn.'

Catherine suppressed a twinge of apprehension and forced herself to smile. She received the full force of two dark green eyes charged with fury. Marie de Comborn had a slight, but unmistakable, resemblance to a goat. Small and nervous, one sensed that under her rather shabby black dress was a wiry body, taut as a bow-string. Her triangular face was strange, pointed and widening at the temples to take huge dark eyes. Her black hair, curly as a gipsy's, was untidily plaited over her ears with stray wisps escaping. Her mouth was very red, full-lipped, even sensual, revealing sharp, very white teeth. 'A goat?' Catherine mused. 'Perhaps. ... Or a viper! That triangular face and those weird eyes ...!' She smiled at the object of her thoughts.

'Good evening, Marie,' she said gently. 'I am happy to meet you.'

'Who are you?' the young girl demanded curtly. It was Madame de Montsalvy who enlightened her. Her voice, which was normally grave and musical, had a tinge of severity.

'Her name is Catherine de Montsalvy, Marie ... and she is Arnaud's wife. Embrace her!'

Catherine thought Marie was going to faint at her feet. Her dark face went grey and her nostrils grew pinched. Her green eyes flickered from Arnaud to Catherine, from Catherine to Arnaud. A sort of rictus deformed her young mouth, showing her teeth like a dog about to bite.

'His wife!' she snarled. 'You are his wife and you dare to speak to me? Since I was born, I have been destined for him ... I have loved him since I could feel anything at all, and you have married him. ...? You!'

'Marie!' cried Madame de Montsalvy. 'That's enough!'

Catherine was torn between tears and anger. With a shrug Arnaud turned away.

'Now I think she must be mad!'

Marie turned on him, her face drawn and tense.

'Mad? Yes, I am mad, Arnaud, mad for you! I always have been, and I shan't give you up to this woman. I shall not rest until I snatch you from her.'

Marie's arm, outflung threateningly towards Catherine, fell back to her side. The girl looked about her distractedly, then she burst into tears, flung open the door and ran out into the night. Arnaud moved as though to follow her, but Catherine stopped him with a touch on the arm.

'If you go after her, I shall leave within the hour,' she said coldly. 'I must say, we're in for an agreeable time.'

He looked at her and saw her great eyes glistening with tears and anger. A brief smile twisted his features. He pulled the young woman into his arms and pressed her to him clumsily.

'You are not going to be jealous of that emotional chit, are you, my radiant one? I can hardly be responsible for any dreams she may have cherished and, on my honour, I have never abetted nor encouraged them!'

He closed her moist eyes with a kiss and, turning slowly, met the gaze of Gauthier which was strangely impassive.

'Go and look for her!' he ordered. 'The little fool is capable of falling in the stream in the gloom.'

'That would surprise me,' grumbled Donatienne, who stood, hands clasped in front of the baby, in a trance. 'She has the eyes of a cat . . . she can see in the dark!'

Gauthier disappeared without a word followed by Fortunat. Saturnin, who had taken the horses to the stable, came back into the room. Catherine went to sit on the hearthstone where the grandmother was still crooning to Michel, whispering those tender little words, silly, but touching, which make up the mysterious language used between the aged and the very young. The atmosphere stifled Catherine; the sudden stoop of her shoulders alarmed Arnaud. He came to kneel beside her, took her hands and covered them with kisses.

'Why so sad, Catherine? Our home is destroyed, but the family is intact. We have shelter . . . and I love you! Smile at me, my heart. When you are sad, the world is dark.'

The handsome, stern face which became so tender with her, implored and demanded simultaneously. The knowledge of his love returned to her sharply and almost painfully, driving away the crude surroundings, the bare stone walls, the blackened rafters, sparse furnishings and the pervading odour of smoke. Could she ever resist, or refuse him anything? For when he said 'I love you' nothing mattered except the greatness of their love. With infinite tenderness she gave him the smile he claimed.

'You will never know,' she whispered, 'how very much I love you, too!'

Beside them, impassive and apparently deaf, Isabelle de Montsalvy went on singing to Michel.

Of that first evening at Montsalvy, Catherine retained an

impression of strangeness and incongruity. It was all so different from what she had hoped for and expected. ... Not that she really regretted the lordly château where she would have had to rule, or felt any reluctance in accepting the hospitality of Saturnin and Donatienne, but she had the feeling that she had come to a bizarre world, peopled by creatures she found it difficult to understand. Isabelle de Montsalvy admittedly was much as she had imagined her: proud and a great lady to her finger-tips. And like Arnaud, whose character Catherine knew so well, passionate but intractable. The young woman felt that her mother-in-law had not quite accepted her yet. ... Would she accept her in the future?

When Gauthier returned with Marie de Comborn, Madame de Montsalvy, Catherine and Arnaud were at dinner served by Donatienne. Neither the good woman nor her husband would consider sitting at table at the same time as the nobility to whom they had offered shelter. Catherine felt all her misgivings return when the young girl, after a glance at Arnaud, seated herself opposite her. The anger which she had provoked seemed to have left her and, much to Catherine's surprise, it was to her the young girl spoke.

'I know all the families of Auvergne and thereabouts,' said Marie, 'but I have never seen you ... cousin. You can't be from our neighbourhood, because I imagine that if I had met you, I would remember it.'

'I am from Paris,' replied Catherine. '... But I spent my youth in Burgundy. ...'

She regretted this imprudent remark immediately. Madame de Montsalvy turned pale.

'In Burgundy? ... Why?'

Arnaud did not let his mother finish her sentence. With a haste which betrayed his embarrassment, he flung out:

'Catherine's first husband, Garine de Brazey, was hanged for high treason by order of Duke Philippe. ... You must be satisfied with that, Marie. Catherine does not like to recall such painful memories.'

'Marie did not know,' intervened his mother, her eyes fixed on her bowl of soup. 'Moreover, she meant no harm in inquiring of the origins of her new cousin. The question was a natural one. I, myself ...'

'Mother, if you don't mind, we will broach this subject again later,' cut in Arnaud dryly. 'This evening we are tired out. My wife is exhausted and I desire nothing more than rest.'

Catherine felt some surprise at her mother-in-law's frown and the mocking gleam in Marie's eyes, but no one spoke again and the frugal supper was finished in silence. She felt a gradual thickening of the atmosphere, but she did not know how she could dissipate the uneasiness. How would Arnaud's mother react when she learned that her daughter-in-law had been born on the Pont-au-Change, in the humble house of a goldsmith? It was a shame that Arnaud had not dared to tell the truth. The presence of this Marie who was not only suspicious but full of hatred, did not help matters. Catherine had expected one enemy and she found two!

She managed to put a good face on things during the rest of the evening, busying herself with her son with the help of Sara whose uneasy eyes moved ceaselessly from the young woman to the old lady. She calmly presented her forehead to Isabelle and addressed a brief 'Good night' to Marie, but, once in the hayloft where Donatienne had arranged a bed for the young couple as best she could, she gave way to her anger and disappointment.

'You are ashamed of me, aren't you?' she said to her husband who sat musing on the edge of the straw mattress with his hands clasped around his knees. 'How will you ever tell your mother who I am when just a moment ago you were afraid to?'

He raised his eyes and looked at her a moment through his lashes without speaking. Then, calmly, he declared:

'I wasn't afraid. It's only that I prefer to discuss this alone with my mother and not in a farm kitchen before strangers.'

'If you are speaking of Sara and Gauthier, they know me and have nothing to learn. But if it's your precious cousin, I grant that . . .'

He stretched out an arm round Catherine's knees and pulled her roughly down next to him. Then he held her in his arms and kissed her deeply. Then . . .

'You don't grant anything! Marie is a pretentious goose who has never listened to anything but her own desires . . . and you are nearly as silly as she is if you even think of being jealous of her!'

'Why not? She is young, pretty . . . She loves you,' said Catherine with a wry smile.

'But I love you!' he replied. 'You tell me that Marie is pretty . . .?'

With one hand he held Catherine's wrists behind her back, then, with the other, he undressed her with meaningful ingenuity

T—H

and let down the magnificent hair which he wound round
his own neck before gathering the young woman to his breast.

'It is time we tried to find a mirror, my love. Have you forgotten your own beauty and how it has enslaved me, then?'

'No, but ...'

She had no time to say more as Arnaud's mouth crushed
down on hers, stopping her breath. In the moments which followed, she had no further wish to talk. The magic of his caresses
moving over her blotted out everything else, such was the
miraculous accord they realized in their love.

When she roused herself from her torpor a long time later,
with her head on Arnaud's chest, knowledge came back to her
and, in a voice already drowsy with sleep, she murmured:

'What are we going to do, Arnaud? What are we going to do
tomorrow?'

'Tomorrow?' He thought a moment, then, as though it were
the most natural thing in the world: 'Tomorrow I shall go to
the monastery and cut the throat of that Valette. He shan't live
long enough to boast of having destroyed Montsalvy. ...'

Her brief peace brutally shattered, Catherine was about to
protest, but the deep regular breathing of the young man told
her that he was already asleep.

Not daring to move for fear of wakening him, because his
arms were locked about her, Catherine lay there for a long time
with her eyes wide open in the almost tangible darkness, gradually becoming aware of the thousand imperceptible noises which
fill the nocturnal silence of an unknown countryside. She wished,
childishly, that this night in which their two bodies were blended
would never end. For the first time in a long while they had
given themselves unreservedly. The knowledge of her love was
almost suffocating, and tomorrow – when the inevitable struggle
must begin again – terrified her. Beneath her cheek, the young
man's skin was supple and warm and she heard his heart beating calmly, strongly. .... He was hers as he had never been
before. Catherine abruptly thrust aside her terrors and the un-
answerable questions. One thing alone mattered: nothing which
happened to her would ever take Arnaud from her. Her flesh,
her blood were very extensions of Arnaud. She would allow
neither Marie de Comborn, nor Valette, nor life, nor death itself
to separate her from the being who was her only *raison
d'être*.

CHAPTER TWELVE

Bernard the Younger

When Catherine came down from the loft the next morning, Saturnin had let the sheep out of the sheepfold hewn from the living rock. At a little distance, a scrawny shepherd in a black wool cloak waited with two great tawny dogs. The old man bowed deeply to Catherine, a broad smile on his sunburnt face.

'The lodging is not worthy of you, gracious lady, but, even so, have you slept well?'

'Wonderfully! I did not even hear my husband go out. Have you seen him?'

'Yes, he is in the house with Her Ladyship. She is helping him into his armour.'

Catherine's heart faltered. Apparently, Arnaud had not given up his mad idea of attacking, almost single-handed, the mercenary entrenched behind the monastery walls. She let her glance fall on the thick surge of yellow wool as the sheep passed before her. Mechanically she said:

'You have a fine flock, Saturnin. Aren't you afraid to let them out lest they attract the attentions of Valette's mercenaries?'

'They are not all mine. Most of them belong to the venerable abbot, and the bandit who burned Montsalvy wouldn't dare lay hands on the personal property of the abbot. It would cost him dear. It is a benefit to me to mix his with mine since, in that way, mine are protected. But, excuse me, the beasts are going out to graze and I have business in the village. . . .'

Slowly, taking deep breaths of the fresh, morning air, Catherine moved towards the house. The weather had grown considerably warmer during the night, and the countryside around her was glistening with running water. From the slopes of the mountains gushed forth a multitude of little streams which traced their shining path across the brown earth and dry grass. The sky was a pale blue, veiled with white clouds like the strokes of a pen. The earth, freed from the weight of snow, seemed to give a great sigh of relief. Catherine told herself that the country was lovely, that she felt drawn to it and could love it if . . .

The sentence remained unfinished in her mind. Approaching the open door of the farm house, the young woman heard her name spoken in a furious voice. Instinctively she darted behind the old sprawling pine tree which grew against the mud walls of the house, and slipped between the trunk and the building. She was just opposite the narrow window and could see Arnaud standing in front of the hearth where the fire blazed under a huge cauldron. His legs, thighs and hips were already encased in plates of steel armour and the upper part of his body was hidden, for he was struggling painfully into the short coat of mail over which he would put the rest of his armour. When his head emerged from the chain fabric, the angry voice went on:

'I did not dare hope, mother, that you would be overjoyed to learn of the common stock from which my wife has sprung, but I must say, I did not expect such scorn!'

Isabelle de Montsalvy who, to Catherine, was no more than a black shadow at this moment replied dryly:

'Is it so strange? The daughter of an artisan, without a drop of noble blood, for you who could have aspired to a princess!'

'If it had been in Duke Philippe's power, Catherine would have been a princess, and more!'

'The madness which overcomes the Duke in the presence of women is common knowledge, and I don't deny the beauty of this ... this trollop!'

The word was like a slap on the face to Catherine. She had an urge to throw herself into the fray, but held back. She wanted to know, above all, how Arnaud would react, but she had hardly time to ask herself the question.

'I would recommend you to use other terms when you speak of my wife,' flung out Arnaud brutally. 'And I expect you to remember this: you are my mother and I respect and love you, but she is my wife, flesh of my flesh, the breath of life to me and nothing, no one will make me give her up!'

Her legs giving way, Catherine let herself fall against the tree, suffused with a passionate gratitude. 'Oh ... my love!' she breathed fervently.

There was a silence. Isabelle buckled the cuirass round her son's body and Arnaud was deep in thought. Catherine heard him draw the long breath he always took when he wanted to master his anger. Then, calmly this time, he said:

'Try to listen to me without anger, mother dear, and perhaps you will understand. It all began the day Michel met his death in Paris in the worst days of the Cabochian riots. ...'

Hidden behind her tree, invisible from all sides, Catherine held her breath and listened to her husband recall the story of their love. It was done without seeking to stir up any facile emotion, in simple direct words which had all the more meaning. He told of the blind devotion of the thirteen-year-old Catherine for an unknown man whom, at the risk of her life and at the price of her father's, she wished to save. Then, their meeting on the road to Flanders and everything which had, for such a long time, separated them: Catherine's disastrous marriage, Duke Philippe's love and how, in order to die with him in besieged Orleans, the most beautiful woman in the West had renounced everything: fortunes, titles, glory, the love of a prince, to go, alone and penniless, on to the highways infested by brigands. How, at last, to snatch Joan of Arc from her executioners, Catherine had, like himself, attempted the impossible which had made them outlaws and brought about the ruin of Montsalvy.

'That, mother, the loss of our home – you can reproach Catherine for that, and myself too, for, if the price still had to be paid and doubled to bring Joan back to life, we would do it again without the shadow of a hestiation!'

'That she has a great and proud spirit is one thing,' replied his mother obstinately. 'But that she has common blood is another. How can you wish to forget that she comes from a shop. ...?

Arnaud's patience came to an end. The roar of his voice made Catherine jump.

' 'Od's Blood, mother! I always believed you to have the noblest, most magnanimous heart of any woman in the world and I should not like to have to change that opinion. Must I remind you of the first of my noble ancestors, an adventurous friar who, at the time of the First Crusade, was forcibly unfrocked, who joined the following of the Count of Toulouse, Raymond de Saint Gilles, and returned from the Holy Land covered with glory, rich as a sultan and duly ennobled by the King of Jerusalem? The Comborns, if their ancestor, Archibald le Boucher, had not won the sister of the Duke of Normandy at dice, would be, perhaps, at this moment, dirty little lordlings, brutalized by the cattle shed, hardly better than the peasants with whom they shared for so long the carcasses of wild boars. As for the Ventadours from whom you come, my mother ...'

'You are going to say to me, I think, that they were rooted in some pigsty,' cried Isabelle scornfully.

'Nothing is more like a pigsty than a wild boar's lair. And

from what else did they come, these Frankish chieftains, half wild barbarians who emerged from the forests of Germany where they worshipped trees and streams, unimportant men, granted arms on the occasion of some auspicious hunt or when some enemy was well slaughtered? ... And these are the noble ancestors of our noble houses.'

'It was the sword which gained for them titles and honours, not the merchant's scales. Never has our noble blood been debased by commerce!'

In the shadows, Catherine's eyes saw Arnaud's wolf teeth gleam.

'Are you sure of that? How many Knights Templar have been supplied by the Ventadours, the Montsalvys, and what was that bank, so rich and powerful that it threatened King Philippe till he had it crushed, if not a very profitable business? Come now, mother, for once forget your nobility in favour of the one I love, for she is worthy. Catherine is one of those women of such powerful stamina that they founded great dynasties like those Roman empresses, crowned by a chance victory, from whom the Caesars were descended. Queen Yolande, who is known for her humanity, accorded her her friendship and rank next to her; Joan the Maid loved her. Will you be more regal, madame, than the Queen of the Four Kingdoms, who is more proud than a daughter of God?'

'As you love her,' murmured Isabelle bitterly, 'so you defend her!'

There was a metallic clatter as Arnaud dropped to his knees before his mother.

'Yes, I love her and I'm proud of it. Mother, you will love her also when you know her better. Although brave Gaucher Legoix, dead with Michel, did not merit it, forget him; forget that Catherine is his daughter. Forget, too, Duke Philippe and Garin de Brazey. See only in Catherine the lady-in-waiting to Queen Yolande, she who wanted to save the Maid, who was my companion in arms before becoming my wife, Catherine de Montsalvy, my spouse ... and your daughter!'

Catherine closed her eyes. She could no longer see clearly because tears blinded her. If she should live for an eternity, she would never forget Arnaud's words, this appeal which was, rather, a vibrant cry of love. Thrown into confusion by love and thankfulness, the young woman struggled against the weakness which overcame her. There are moments when happiness is too much for the human spirit, when it can be as shattering as

sorrow, and now Catherine was on the verge of swooning. She
clung to the rough tree-trunk as though to draw from its core
the strength she lacked. Inside the house no sound was to be
heard. Isabelle de Montsalvy sat on a bench, eyes closed and
her back against the wall musing, while Arnaud, on his feet
once more, calmly drew on his gauntlets without disturbing
her, respecting her meditation. But in the small room behind,
Michel, probably under Sara's ministrations, began to yell and
Catherine, at the sound of his voice, opened her eyes. She stifled
an exclamation of anger as she saw Marie standing facing her,
on the other side of the door with her shoulder against the wall
of the house. She was watching her, laughing wickedly.

'A fine piece of rhetoric, wasn't it? But don't pride yourself,
dear Catherine ... there will come a day when it has passed
from Arnaud's mind and he will only remember your lowly
birth. And on that day, I shall be there, I ...'

Catherine's inward happiness was so great she did not lose
her temper. Disdain curved her lovely lips in a half smile of
amusement.

'And I cannot help wondering what you will look like when
that day comes! You are not all that pretty now! When
Arnaud ceases to love me, I shall be most surprised if he plights
his troth to an old maid dried up with envy and spite.'

'Hussy!' spat Marie, fists clenched and eyes glittering with
rage. 'I'll scratch your eyes out!'

From her girdle she snatched a stiletto whose narrow blade
flashed. Marie's pupils contracted and, more than ever, she
looked like a cat about to spring. Hatred distorted her features,
the dangerous fire in her eyes made Catherine recoil. She put
the pine tree between herself and her enemy, but she was able
to keep up her banter.

'What a very feminine weapon! Now I understand why your
ancestor was called Archibald the Butcher!'

'You have understood correctly, and I'll tell you this, what's
more: I can kill as well as he could; you'll see!'

Mad with fury, Marie raised her arm and was about to
fling herself on Catherine, when Gauthier appeared around the
corner of the house and jumped on the girl from behind. In a
moment the stiletto left her twisted hand and flew into the
grass, while the Norman's large palm was brutally applied to
her mouth, stifling her cry of rage. ... Catherine breathed again.
Deep inside, she admitted to herself that she had been afraid of
this half-mad girl who would stop at nothing to eliminate her.

Reduced to impotence, she fumed with fury in Gauthier's solid grasp.

'Come along, young lady,' said he in his drawling voice. 'Calm yourself! When you want to kill people, make sure there aren't twenty others watching you.'

As he spoke smocked peasants poured into the meadow, their long hair under woollen caps, clothed in the skins of goats and sheep, some carrying pitchforks, some scythes. ... Resolution could be read on all those brown faces, burned and weather-beaten by sun and snow. Coming out of the wood by almost invisible paths, they advanced on the farm over the grass, silent, slow and implacable as destiny itself. At the head came old Saturnin, a long pitchfork in his fist, his feet shod in clogs which scraped loudly against the clods of spongy earth. Gauthier swept the peasants with a rapid glance. Then he released Marie, but bent to pick up the stiletto which he slipped into his belt.

'The hour has come,' was all he said. 'I'll get the horses.'

Fortunat, also armed, came out of the stable dragging after him a longbow of yew as big as himself. Marie hesitated a moment, then she threw Catherine an uncertain look and went into the house, but bumped into Arnaud as he came out in full armour. He pushed the girl aside without a glance, seeing only Catherine standing with her back to the pine tree. She looked at her husband with surprise. He was not wearing the light armour which had been given to him by Jacques Cœur when they left Bourges, but the black suit in which he had become respected in tournaments as well as on the field of battle. The helmet, crested with a sparrowhawk, was held under his left arm. Catherine felt that time had taken nothing from him, for he looked exactly as he had at the betrothal of the Princesses of Burgundy when he threw his gauntlet at the feet of Duke Philippe. As he bent to kiss her, she asked:

'How have you recovered this armour? Where was it?'

'In the castle armoury which one can still enter by a secret passage. It is a room in the cellar and, luckily, it is always accessible. I haven't lost everything.'

She slipped her arms around Arnaud's neck and clung to him with all her strength in a loving attempt to keep him near her, but she knew in advance that it was useless.

'Where are you going? What are you going to do?'

He gestured towards the invisible heights of the village, towards the monastery whose bells rang out at that moment in the clear morning air. Then his hand indicated the peasants, now gathered in front of the house, resolute under their woollen caps, and then the massive outline of Gauthier, armed also, and finally the frailer one of Fortunat.

'I go there and here are my forces. I shall repay Valette for the ruin of our house.'

'You will attack him?'

'It is my profession,' he said with a small smile. 'I shan't find a better opportunity to exercise it.'

'Are you aware that, by attacking Valette, you are, to some extent, attacking the King?'

Now brutal anger inflamed Arnaud's face. His mailed hand beat his armed chest which resounded.

'What does the King matter to me? Have I still a King when he has outlawed me? I – who am innocent! He has ruined me to please his favourite. No, Catherine, I no longer have a King and, believe me, in attacking this impudent dog, I shall not have the impression that I act against honour and right; on the contrary, if I kill him, I know more than one who will thank me for it.'

For the last time he kissed his wife, then he went to his horse held by Fortunat. Catherine longed to throw herself after him; she wanted to follow him, but she held herself back. He would never allow it. She would let them go and then rejoin them at a distance.

From the house, Sara stepped forth, carrying a gurgling Michel, followed by Isabelle de Montsalvy and Donatienne, who was wiping her eyes on a corner of her apron. Marie had disappeared. With an instinctive movement, Catherine took her son into her arms. He was in excellent humour this morning and smiled at his mother, so that her heart filled with tenderness. The contrast was too cruel between this happy baby and these few poorly armed men who were going to confront a band of hardened brigands, inured to every stratagem, all forms of destruction. ... Her eyes overflowed with tears and she did not see Isabelle watching her closely.

When Arnaud and his men had disappeared into the pines, Catherine turned briskly to her mother-in-law, holding out the child to her.

'Take Michel,' she said calmly. 'I am going to watch.'

'Are you mad? The place for a woman is not alongside the men. Don't you know the risks?'

The young woman gave a sad smile which did not reach her eyes.

'I only know what Arnaud is risking and that is all that matters to me.'

'Has your son no claim on you?' asked Isabelle, a disdainful lift at the corners of her lips. 'A good mother would never leave her child.'

'Perhaps I am a better wife than mother. Moreover, madame, he has you to look after him in my absence: you are his grandmother. And even if misfortune should befall me, I believe it will only simplify things, won't it?'

And without waiting for a reply from Isabelle who stood quite still, dumbly looking at her, Catherine turned on her heel and went to the stable. Without assistance, she saddled and bridled Morgane, then, leaping to the saddle, she too took the road to Montsalvy.

As she climbed towards the village, Catherine heard the bells more clearly and was guided more by them than by the trail left by Arnaud's men. Like Joan the Maid, Catherine had always loved church bells passionately. Their voices, deep or shrill, resounding across the sky seemed to her to speak some mysterious language out of this world and beyond time. But this morning, their tolling struck her as sinister. The bells of the monastery were ringing a knell and Catherine felt a shiver run down her back.

The thought came to her that it was the first day of Lent. The mournful, melodious drops of sound were calling the peasants to Ash Wednesday devotions, but her distressed heart saw in them an evil omen. She twisted her cold fingers for a moment in Morgane's mane to seek a little warmth, to touch something living. Deliberately she turned her eyes away from the Puy de l'Arbre and its blackened ruins, spurred her mare and, head bent, thrust into the undergrowth.

As she came out of the cover of the trees on to the plateau, Catherine reined Morgane in and forced her to stop. From where she was, she could see clearly the fortified walls of Montsalvy and the north gate which was wide open. She also saw peasants hurrying along the little paths, leaning forward with bent backs as if pursued by some calamity. But nowhere was there any trace of Arnaud or his men. Perplexed, Catherine considered the scene before her. The two archers who mounted guard over the gate were miserable looking, their garments shabby, but their arms shining. Bows held in both hands ready to fire, they stared at the peasants morosely. High in the sky on

the monastery towers, Catherine saw the scarlet standard fluttering, barred and crossed, which she had already seen on the
walls of Ventadour: the arms of Villa-Andrade, joined by a
smaller, chequered pennon representing the mercenary, Valette,
his lieutenant. Quick anger rose up in her: it was certain that
Valette had burned Montsalvy on the orders of the Spaniard and
she now understood why Rodrigo had refused Arnaud's thanks;
he already knew what had happened in the lands of his enemy.

Prudently Catherine decided to enter Montsalvy on foot.
Since she could not see her husband, it would be better to pro-
ceed as unobtrusively as possible and Morgane was too easily
recognizable, apart from the fact that she might excite some
ruffian's covetous desires. She dismounted and led the little
mare by the bridle deeper into the wood where no one could
see her. Then she tethered her to a tree and, after telling her to
wait quietly, set out for the village.

Her dress of brown wool and the large grey cloak which
covered it would not attract attention. They were inconspicu-
ous garments, already well-worn on the journey. But, to pass the
gate, Catherine drew her hood over her face. She advanced,
forcing herself to appear natural, although her heart was beating fast. It was unnecessary, however, as the men-at-arms did
not pay her the least attention. One of them merely sneered:

'Come along, clodhoppers, hurry up! Otherwise you're going
to miss the show. . . .'

The show? The young woman did not wait to ask questions,
but pushed on through the rounded arch and found herself in
the single narrow street where, in the shadow of the Benedictine monastery, huddled the lowly houses of Montsalvy. In the
church, the knell still tolled and the lugubrious notes dinned
into Catherine's head. Other people, mostly ragged and down-
trodden in appearance, were following the same road.

Coming out into the little square dominated by the Roman-
esque church, she saw that a silent crowd filled it, enlarged
moment by moment by those who came from outside and those
who, marked on the forehead by grey ash, were coming out of
the church. These last were walking, head down, avoiding looking at the armed men massed in the gateway and the chained
man whom they were guarding. This was a small man, hunch-
backed and deformed, whose grey face was the same colour as
the ash which marked the others. His defeated attitude and
haggard eyes contrasted violently with the chequered finery in
which he was dressed. His hose, parti-coloured green and red,

hung on his twisted legs, a yellow tunic ornamented by little
bells, a large red cloak and a crown of gilded paper made up a
grotesque costume which would have been laughable if the man
himself had not been so pitiable. But no one wanted to laugh
and Catherine no more than the rest. She only saw his gaze fixed
on the ground, his hands with fingers clenched, his cheeks
marked by tears and privation. From time to time a sob broke
the heavy silence which fell between each of the slow beats of
the bell. The ferocious countenances of the drunken and laughing mercenaries contrasted with all the other faces scored by
fear and grief.

Now funereal chanting could be heard in the church and the
flickering of wax tapers could be seen through the open door.
Catherine looked about her, not understanding what was happening. Where ever were Arnaud, Gauthier, Saturnin ... and
the others? She had the absurd idea that she was dreaming
and pinched herself to make sure she was awake.

The crowd murmured suddenly. Under the stone portico,
carved with stiffly gesturing stone figures, an old man in a mitre,
crozier in hand, appeared with another man with a bony, crafty
face whose battered armour and the elaborate silk tunic
covering it could not disguise his frightful emaciation. The
weather-beaten skin barely covered his facial bones and gave it
the terrifying aspect of a death's-head. The man was so appalling that Catherine closed her eyes for a moment. The green
plumes dancing on his helm added still further to his spectral
appearance. The abbot, standing by his side, looking so pale
under the gold embroidery of his mitre, dared hardly turn his
eyes towards him.

Even before he spoke, Catherine realized that this was the
man who had fired Montsalvy, the lieutenant of the Castilian,
the mercenary Valette. He allowed a calculating, evil stare to
rest on the poor people who instinctively huddled together,
then gave a burst of grating laughter.

'A band of frightened rabbits!' he cried. 'Is it thus that you
bury Lord Carnival? Come along, you must laugh and sing ...
It is the first day of Lent and you will be able to make suitable
penance later, but today I intend that you shall be jolly. There
will be singing! That is an order!'

The bells were still and a crushing silence fell on the square.
The rising wind lifted the hair on all the bent heads, obstinately
mute. Somewhere a shutter banged. ... The worn voice of the
abbot came to Catherine from the depths of time.

'My children . . .' he began gently.

But Valette cut in coarsely:

'Peace, abbot! . . . You have nothing to say! Now, you others, haven't you heard? I said "sing"! . . . Isn't there a pretty song you sing to bury Lord Carnival? "Farewell, poor Carnival . . ." And put your hearts into it, I want the whole world to hear!'

The chained man had fallen to the ground, weeping convulsively. Around him and on the monastery walls, the men of Valette bent their bows, aiming at the terrified crowd . . . Catherine's heart missed a beat. An impotent fury rose in her against this brute and also against Arnaud who had not yet appeared. Where was he? What had happened to him? Twenty-five men could not vanish into the mist. . . .

The groan of terror which rose about her, accompanied by the wail of the wind, changed, little by little, to a hesitant song, tremulous and barely audible, coming from throats constricted by fear.

'Louder!' shrieked Valette. 'Otherwise, I swear you will be silent for ever!'

An arrow whistled into the air as a warning. The voices became stronger. A wave of rage carried Catherine away. She was about to throw herself, talons bared, on the ferocious brigand leader without thought of the consequences, impelled by the impulses of her generous nature, when a clutching hand seized hers under the folds of her cloak.

'For pity's sake, Dame Catherine, don't move! You will cause a catastrophe. . . .'

Old Saturnin stood beside her, his grey hair pulled down over his face, his head held high. He opened his mouth wide as though singing as he spoke.

'What are you doing here?' she breathed. 'Where is my husband?'

'Elsewhere! He is biding his time! But you, gracious lady, it's more to the point what you are doing here. . . .? When Messire Arnaud knows . . .'

The voices of the others, lugubriously singing the cheerful Carnival song, covered their words. In front of the church, his rotten teeth bared in a wicked smile, Valette beat time with his sword. His men dragged the unfortunate jester roughly to his feet and forced him to dance by tugging cruelly on his chains.

'Who is that man?' murmured Catherine. 'What has he done?'

'Nothing! Or very little! He is Étienne la Cabrette, our bone-
setter ... a good man, a little simple, and some would say a bit
of a sorcerer, because he understands the uses of herbs. His
great pleasure was to play on his pipes when it was full moon.
Valette seized him because he treated one of his men who was
dreadfully wounded. The man died. Then the martyrdom of
poor Étienne began. It was the day the castle ...'

Saturnin stopped, sliding a rapid glance towards Catherine,
but she did not flinch.

She only said: 'Go on!'

'The men tortured him in a hundred ways and were amused
by him. They crowned him king of the Carnival in place of the
effigy they usually make ... in better times! And now they are
going to burn him, as they do the effigy. Poor fellow!'

With blows of their staves, the solders now pushed the crowd
towards the south gate of Montsalvy, the one which opened
on the deep valley of the Lot. Étienne and his guards were already under the arch. The archers followed, bows at the ready.
Then came Valette, trailing after him the old abbot and a line of
friars chanting the Misèrere. It was an abominable cacophony
which offended Catherine's ears. The impression of a nightmare
was accentuated. In this miserable and tragic world, only Saturnin seemed alive. Discreetly, respectfully, he slipped his hand
under Catherine's arm to save her from stumbling on the stones
of the muddy road. All around them, roughly handled people
jostled her and Catherine had the grotesque feeling that she
was a sheep in a flock.

There was a more violent shove under the arch, then Catherine and Saturnin found themselves propelled out of the town
on to a gently sloping field surrounded by chestnut trees in the
centre of which a bonfire had been built. The unfortunate Lord
Carnival, still wearing his mockery crown, was there, already
bound, dragging heavily in his shackles because his damaged
legs could no longer carry him. His head, with long hair
straggling beneath his crown, hung on his chest. He wept continuously, great, convulsive sobs. An enormous pity filled
Catherine. In spite of the maniacal shrieks of Valette, the
peasants had stopped singing the insulting song, which was
strangled by the sight of the instruments of torture.

Catherine felt herself weaken. ... Since the tragedy in Rouen,
these dreadful piles of faggots on which men dared chain other
men had pursued her with their frightful outline. She saw again
the white body of Joan chained to her stake ... and also, in the

court of Champtocé, the funeral pyre which had waited in
vain for Sara.

'Sing, by the guts of the Pope!' yelled Valette, flourishing his
rapier. 'And you, executioner, do your duty!'

A man in rags, whose muscular arms protruded from a
leather jerkin full of holes and whose massive head was completely shaven, appeared carrying a torch. He swung it in the
wind to make it burn up and was already applying it to the
faggots, when something whistled in the air and the executioner
fell back with a raucous scream. Shot from out of a chestnut
tree, an arrow had pierced his throat.

The song, which had been taken up again, stopped anew.
Catherine saw Valette's eyes grow round with amazement and
she turned to Saturnin, but the bailiff of Montsalvy had disappeared. ... At that moment the crowd let out a growl in
which a note of joy could be heard. Next to Catherine, a
big young man, whose fair face was framed in a full beard,
murmured, almost in ecstasy:

'Heaven and earth! Monseigneur Arnaud! God be blessed!'

Indeed, from the screen of chestnuts which plunged down to
the deep valley, Arnaud had just emerged, his shield on his arm
and a battle-axe in the other hand. Catherine's heart exploded
with joy and pride when she saw him. What knight had ever
such a noble bearing? Gauthier and Fortunat followed three
paces behind, rigid and dignified as befitted the squires of a great
house. Keeping his horse to a walk, Montsalvy advanced as
far as the pyre, raised the visor of his helmet and, without
lifting his voice, indicated the unfortunate Etienne with his arm.

'Martin,' he said quietly. 'Release him!'

The boy next to Catherine leapt out without bothering about
the furious Valette who howled:

'Kill him!'

An archer raised his arm, but had no time to fire. Another
arrow struck him down on the spot while Martin climbed on the
pyre, released the poor sorcerer, now in a swoon, and carried
him down on his shoulder to the acclamations of the crowd.

'Keep quiet, Valette!' warned Arnaud coldly. 'These trees are
full of soldiers and an arrow will pierce you if you move.'

His voice was drowned by the cries of the peasants. They
were flinging their caps in the air and already the men were
rushing to surround their lord, but he kept them in their places.

'Don't move! I have a score to settle with this man here and,
for that, you must give me room.'

Catherine, who was about to run towards her husband, froze in her tracks, then quietly fell back with the others, leaving a large space between them and the bonfire. The sight of Arnaud hypnotized them. If he was arrogant, he was surely himself! His horse curvetted as though he were performing in the most courtly tournament, but he brandished his axe in his mailed fist menacingly. Valette's hideous features were convulsed with hate. He pointed towards his enemy and cried:

'Seize him! He is outlawed by order of the King!'

'By order of King Trémoille,' flung Arnaud contemptuously. 'Get along, Valette, at least pay honour to your master and come and fight ... or would you rather an arrow struck you on the spot?'

As though to underline his words, a third arrow came to strike one of the men who stood nearest to the chief. Valette turned green and Arnaud burst out laughing.

'Don't you laugh any more, Valette? Don't you even want to sing? You sang so well, just now. Come along now! Use that long sword with which you have such facility. ...'

Suddenly Arnaud urged his horse into a gallop, grazing Valette as he passed. The battle-axe whistled round the plumed crest. Then Arnaud struck out abruptly, knocking the mercenary to the ground.

'I said "Come"!' said the young man derisively.

Valette got up almost immediately. His spectral face was twisted with hate and a light foam flecked the corners of his snarling lips. He leant forward, expecting the horse to kick, but, disdaining this advantage, Arnaud dismounted.

'No!' Catherine cried in horror.

'He is mad!' growled Saturnin who had returned to her side without her being aware of it. 'One cannot show chivalry to carrion!'

Terrified, the young woman gripped the old man's arm. Valette's dreadful appearance struck to her soul. It seemed to her that Arnaud was fighting Death in person, though the mercenary did not wield the famous scythe which would have made him an exact replica of that sinister personage. But Montsalvy was not impressed by this in the least. He dropped his visor and, his sword held out to ward off blows, advanced step by step towards his enemy. Above his head, the flail turned, its heavy mass bristling with points of steel. The first blows rang out on their armour like the strokes of a bell. Valette drew back step by step, seeking, no doubt, to reach the gates of the town.

His men, motionless in their places, did not dare move for fear of the arrows which reached their targets so unfailingly. Catherine, her hands knotted together, begged Heaven to spare her husband.

Suddenly, behind Arnaud, someone cried:

'Fall on the sparrowhawk, captain! He has tricked us. In the trees there is only a handful of peasants armed with . . .'

He said no more. Gauthier had wheeled his horse whose hind hooves crashed down on the head of the over-curious soldier who, doubtless, had crept under the trees from the other end of the field without being seen. Alas, the harm was done! The peasants tumbled down from the chestnut trees, while Gauthier brandished his sword and charged on the first wave of soldiers and Fortunat did his best on his side, but Valette dodged behind a wall of armed men, leaving Arnaud alone facing six men. Catherine, half fainting, searched about her for Saturnin, but the old man, pulling his dagger from his belt, had already rushed with the agility of a youngster to his master's aid. The young woman in the midst of the other women, children and dotards, retreated as far as the town wall, driven back by the hopeless combat which was unleashed. The peasants, galvanized out of their terror by Arnaud, were putting everything into the struggle, fighting with their bare hands and with whatever they could find on the field: stones and pieces of wood, against the swords and spears of the mercenaries.

In the thick of the battle, Arnaud, Gauthier, Fortunat and Saturnin accomplished prodigious feats of valour. The huge Norman took two men at a time by the neck and knocked their heads together before letting them fall. The armed flail turned ceaselessly, cracking casques and craniums like nutshells, but the band of mercenaries was numerous and seemed to renew itself without end.

Soon Arnaud and his men were weakening and the issue of the battle seemed to Catherine to be in no doubt: it was the end and, inevitably, death to a brave undertaking.

Ten men had isolated Arnaud from his companions and were engulfing him under their weight of numbers. For Gauthier, twenty were needed, but, a few minutes later, the two men, with Saturnin and Fortunat, securely bound and disarmed, were dragged before Valette who had suddenly reappeared.

'Sweet Jesus!' moaned a woman near Catherine. 'We are done for!'

'Keep quiet,' cut in the young woman sternly. 'It doesn't matter what becomes of us if they die.'

Valette's grating laughter covered her words. The bandit
approached Arnaud, secured by two men as well as the bonds
which they had placed about him. They had snatched off his
casque and a thread of blood ran down his cheek from a split
eyebrow, but his black eyes had lost nothing of their arrogance.
Scornfully he surveyed the mercenary who strutted before him
like a crippled heron, shrugging his broad shoulders. This was
too much for Valette's vanity: with all his strength, he slapped
his prisoner twice.

'That will teach you to respect your master, dog!'

Then Catherine saw red. Blindly she threw herself forward,
claws bared, and before Valette had even seen her coming, she
was on him like a wild cat. The man screamed, holding his hand
to his cheek where the young woman's fingernails had traced
five bleeding stripes. He tried to retreat, but she clung to him
with all her strength, trying to reach his eyes, possessed by an
instinct to destroy as old as the earth: the instinct of the female
whose mate has been attacked.

When two newcomers finally dragged her from her prey,
Valette's face was bright red and he squealed like a stuck pig.
But in the hands of the men-at-arms, Catherine still foamed
with rage, spitting fire like a furious little wild beast and trying
to scratch and bite. Wiping away the blood which was running
down his tunic, the mercenary walked up to her.

'You miserable bitch!' he growled. 'Who are you?'

'My wife,' said Arnaud pleasantly. Then he added, a half-
smile stretching his wounded features: 'When will you learn to
obey me, Catherine, and stay at home when I want you to?'

'When you stop running into all sorts of danger!'

'He will soon stop, you only need a little patience!' grinned
Valette. 'Just a few more moments and you will be for ever free
of your worries. Come on, you others, chain those two on the
bonfire for me! I have a horror of waste.'

The crowd rumbled with anger, but two men raised their
spears: two men fell, transfixed. . . . Irresistibly and cruelly, the
others were dragging Catherine and Arnaud towards the pyre.
The young woman's eyes grew large with terror at the prospect
of the terrible death which awaited them. She cried:

'You won't. . . .? No. . . .! Not that!'

'I beg you, have courage, my love,' beseeched Arnaud. 'Don't
give them the pleasure of hearing you beg for mercy. . . .'

Already they were being hauled up on to the pile of faggots.
Catherine stumbled and fell with a groan. Gauthier made a

terrific effort to break his bonds. His muscles swelled and his chest heaved and the ropes broke. Roaring like a lion, he fell with all his weight and strength on the men-at-arms, hitting one on the head, making another's teeth rattle. He forged a path towards the captives. He seemed possessed by a holy anger. Light flashed from his eyes, his foaming mouth twisted convulsively. His strength was doubled by rage; overwhelmingly, he beat down his enemies about him like a flail in a field of wheat. The peasants were seized with a superstitious admiration and gazed at him with open mouths. . . .

The giant reached the pyre as an arrow struck his shoulder. He fell on to the faggots with a groan which was echoed by Catherine's desperate cry, then by the ferocious scream of Valette.

'Tie him up with the others! Then light the fire!'

Catherine closed her eyes. Against the rough wood of the stake, Arnaud's manacled hand searched for hers, found it and enclosed it.

'It is the end,' she murmured in a choked voice. 'We shall die. My poor little one! . . . My poor little Michel!'

Her eyes filled with tears. She saw, as in a nightmare, the grinning face of a soldier who, at a little distance, was lighting a torch. . . . But in spite of approaching death, everything seemed to her absurd, as though impressed with unreality. This stupid thing could not be true. A miracle would happen. . . .

And the miracle did happen! A trumpet blast suddenly rang out, loud and imperious. The road which rose from the valley was thronged with horses and arms and banners. A large troop had appeared, heavily armed but richly dressed. The ground trembled under the hammer blows of their hooves and, in the field, everyone was frozen in his place, watching, even the man with the torch, even Valette, eyebrows drawn, stared intently at the arrivals. Like a living wall of iron, a squadron of armed men advanced four by four, rank after rank, lances at the slope, their multi-coloured pennons dancing in the wind. They stopped at the edge of the plateau, split in two parts and ranged themselves on either side of the road, giving passage to a herald glowingly adorned in red and white, who bore in an arrogant fist a huge banner of silver cloth on which was a scarlet lion rampant. . . .

Hardly had Arnaud seen this emblem than he shouted at the top of his voice:

'Help me, Armagnac!'

The effect was magical. The beautiful herald had no time to draw himself up; a group of horsemen in shining armour wearing tabards embroidered in red, white, blue, gold or silver, their helmets topped with fantastic emblems, the caparisons of their horses swirling round the hooves which trampled the ground, struck out across the meadow. In the twinkling of an eye, the place was invaded by a warlike multitude, tumultuous and many-coloured. They surrounded a huge red and silver horseman whose casque was encircled by a count's coronet. Other knights followed, then a detachment of archers on foot, pikemen in iron helmets, squires, and lastly young pages fighting to keep control over their huge greyhounds in gold collars, a sight both heraldic and superb. Next to this small army, Valette's men made a pitiful show and they were already making as if to retreat into the town, but the peasants whom they had herded together barred their way. The plateau was still filling with soldiers and Catherine's eyes darted about trying to make out whether these arrivals were friend or foe. She did not have to look for long.

The red and silver count galloped up to the pyre and sprang down on to it despite the weight of his armour. His pointed shoes crushed the faggots and straw and his steel gauntlets broke the chains which bound the prisoners as easily as though they had been rotten stems. Under the raised visor, Catherine could see a narrow face which was red with fury, and the green gaze she met was as menacing as could be, but Arnaud gave a sigh of relief, He cried out with a note of tenderness in his voice:

'Young Bernard! By Our Lady! Saint Michael has sent you!'

'I will build him a chapel,' said the other with a strong Gascon accent. 'Brother Arnaud! What are you doing on this heap of faggots trussed up like a quarter of beef?'

'Ask Valette.'

The two men embraced heartily, Bernard's mailed fist banging on his friend's back. But Arnaud disengaged himself just in time to seize Catherine who had swooned away from the shock and strain. He lifted her in his arms while the newcomer leaned forward curiously over the fainting girl.

'What a beauty! Who is she?'

'My wife! But help me. ... That man must be taken away!' he added, pointing at Gauthier who had not yet come to, and lay face down on the heap of wood. 'He is wounded.'

Already, men had run up and were lifting the giant. A knight

whose helmet bore a silver-gilt dolphin crest with jade eyes held
out his arms to receive the unconscious woman. Arnaud was
about to jump down from the pyre, but the count restrained him.

'Stay here. There is still work to do and this bonfire makes an
excellent observation post.'

Then, raising his voice to a shout, he declaimed:

'Men of Armagnac, forward! Spare the serfs and townsfolk,
but slaughter all that rabble for me! And I want the leader
alive!'

As if awaiting such a command, the armed men and knights
charged at the mercenaries. Swords, cutlasses, épées, daggers
and battle-axes joined in the fray. In a few moments, the
meadow, as far as the chestnut trees, was transformed into a
slaughter-house. The earth drank blood and little streams
trickled away under the trees. The air was full of cries of pain
and moans and gasps of agony. Near the gate, the grey mass of
peasants looked on at the massacre torn between terror and
relief, while Bernard the Younger watched, standing on the
pyre, legs straddled and a face of stone.

It was only when the last mercenary had expired and Valette,
loaded with chains, had been dragged to the monastery, that the
Count of the Scarlet Lion finally descended from his observation
post with one hand on Arnaud's shoulder.

A feeling of lively warmth reanimated Catherine. She opened
her eyes and found herself lying on a mattress in front of an
immense stone fireplace in which a whole tree-trunk was
ablaze. Arnaud knelt beside her rubbing her hands to warm
them, and watching her anxiously. Seeing her open her eyes, he
smiled at her.

'Do you feel better? You had me frightened, you know. We
couldn't revive you.'

'What lady, chained to a stake on a pile of faggots, would
not have lost her senses? I would never have forgiven myself
if I had come an instant later, madame. . . .'

The red and silver count appeared behind Arnaud in the
dancing light of the flames. He still wore his sumptuous tabard
over his grey armour, but his face, without the helmet, was
narrow and cheerful with irregular, but pleasant features. His
eyes were the colour of the sea and a cap of short black hair
over two pointed ears accentuated his faun-like appearance. He
looked at Catherine with a politeness not devoid of admiration
and held out her cloak to Sara without looking at him.

'Sir Count,' she said. 'I owe you more than my life, since I owe you also that of my beloved husband. I will not forget and, for these great gifts, I give you thanks. May I add,' she said with a smile, 'that I would love to know who you are?'

It was Arnaud who presented to his wife Bernard Armagnac, Count of Perdiac, called Bernard the Younger, who had been his childhood companion. Sitting up on her mattress with her back against the chimney-piece, Catherine examined this unknown young man whose name had dominated her youth. So this was one of those famous chiefs of the House of Armagnac who, for twenty-five years, since the assassination of the Duke of Orleans by John the Fearless, had made France an immense battlefield as a result of their hatred of Burgundians? Catherine told herself that Bernard the Younger was a worthy representative of his family.

He was the second son of that Constable Armagnac who, long ago, had taken Paris from Caboche the Skinner before he fell, murdered by the Burgundians in 1418. His blood was of the noblest in France for, by his mother, Bonne de Berry, Bernard the Younger, like his older brother, Count John IV, was the grandson of King Charles V. The blood royal could be seen throughout his elegant and highly bred person, in his slender wrists and ankles and his proud bearing. But, from his ancestor, Sanchez Mittara, founder of the Duchy of Gascony, he got his dark skin, inky hair and that mobility of feature, that teasing nonchalance tinged with wildness which formed the basis of his character. Great warriors, great hunters, the Armagnacs were celebrated equally for their cruelty and their poetic talents. They scorned death and were implacable in vengeance; Catherine remembered having heard it said that Count John IV carried, attached to his banner, the strip of skin which the people of Burgundy had taken from his father's back when they murdered him. However, these same redoubtable fighters held courts of love and composed for their fair ones and for Our Lady the most tender verses. . . .

It was to this last talent of his family that Young Bernard chose to refer. Offering his closed fist to the young woman, he helped her to her feet, then, leading her to a high chair, carved and cushioned, he whispered gallantly:

'Lovely countess, this evening I shall compose a sirvente on the lute in honour of your grace and beauty, but, for the nonce, I must leave you, and deprive you of your husband at the same time.'

'Where are you going?'

Bernard d'Armagnac stood up after having brushed his lips over the fingers of the young woman.

'To see that justice is done! In a minute Valette will be hanging on the abbey gallows. He has amply deserved it. He is only a bandit. He boasts of his service to King Charles VII, but, like Villa-Andrade himself, he only serves La Trémoille. ... Oh, how I hate La Trémoille! Rest while you wait for us. You are in the abbey hospice where your people will come to join you.'

He moved away from her towards the door, gathering up his helmet from the top of the chest where he had placed it as he went. Arnaud bent over his wife to kiss her, but she clung to him.

'Gauthier? ... And the rest of the family?'

'The Norman is in the charge of the brother-physician. His wound is not serious. I have sent someone to fetch my mother and the child ... and all the rest of the family. The venerable abbot offers us hospitality. Now, stay here quietly. You must gather your strength.'

He started to leave her, but she held him back. She had just remembered Morgane whom she had left tied up in the wood behind the town and who would feel herself forgotten.

'Send for her,' she said. 'At least she must be saved.'

'I shall go myself,' promised Arnaud. 'As soon as ...'

A bell ringing in the tower completed his sentence better than he could have done himself. Catherine listened intently. It was another passing bell, like before. From one knell to another, how things had changed! Only a few hours had slipped away, but she felt that months had passed since she had left Saturnin's farm. Closing her eyes, she let herself sink against the back of her chair, and the sound of the funeral bells calling a bandit to his last journey flowed over, over the returned security and her soothed nerves. And, bearing no grudge, she held out her hands to the fire in which, a short time before, she had believed she would perish.

With his long legs encased in grey doeskin outstretched before the fire and the soles of his shoes propped on the andirons, Bernard the Younger sipped his mulled wine with evident pleasure. Under the dark curtain of his eyelids, his green eyes, shining with contentment, gave notice of his alert mind. Leaning forward, his elbows on his knees and his hands clasped, Arnaud watched him silently. As for Catherine, curled up in the depths of her high armchair, she waited to see what would come of this sudden silence which seemed to stretch to eternity. Only the snap of a branch in the hearth disturbed from time to time the monastic calm which surrounded the hospice. The monks of Montsalvy slept in their cells, awaiting the bell for Matins which, in the dead of night, tumbled them, blinking and stupid with sleep, into the icy chapel.

Supper had been a cheerful and plentiful meal, for the stocks of the abbey were still adequate, and had lasted late into the night. Isabelle de Montsalvy had retired over an hour ago to the cell which had been allotted to her, with little Michel over whom she watched with a jealous care amounting almost to an obsession that made Sara frown. Marie de Comborn had also retired to her room on a brief order from Arnaud, followed shortly by Sara whom Catherine had charged to watch discreetly over the young girl. Now, Catherine, Arnaud and their deliverer were alone, in that intimacy which comes in the serene moments which follow a meal taken in peace. Nothing, henceforth, could threaten them. All around the village, Armagnac's men had raised their tents and installed their bivouacs. Occasionally, the echo of a tabor pipe reached as far as the old Benedictine monastery, on the wind from the great plateau.

Catherine relished intensely the novelty of this unexpected peace. She was not sleepy; her faint and the rest which followed it had dispelled her fatigue. For the first time, things took on the colour with which she had invested them in her dreams. It was not long since the singing and dancing of the good people of Montsalvy had ceased, for they had celebrated the end of the birds of prey. Poor Étienne, the unfortunate Carnival of such a short time ago, had come as well with his pan pipes, to give thanks in his fashion. The marvellous peace of a night scattered with stars, a true spring night, filled with hope and life, enveloped the village delivered from a nightmare.

Suddenly, Bernard d'Armagnac stretched himself, giving a jaw-breaking yawn. His body seemed to lengthen immoderately. Then he turned a lazy look on Arnaud.

'What will you do now?'

'What can I do?' replied Arnaud moodily. 'Rebuild? The country is bled white, the land needs every man's hand and there is no time to spare, since the war has ravaged everything. Finally, you forget that I am an outlaw and that my lands no longer belong to me! Auvergne must be reborn, only then can the destroyed castles be rebuilt. ... But only when the towers overlook something besides desert and when wheat dances at the feet of the ramparts.'

'Well?'

'You have told me that you will resume the war against La Trémoille. You are going to rejoin the Constable de Richemont, Bernard. Richemont, like the Duke of Bourbon, my overlord, wants to destroy the wild beast. It will be best, I think, to leave my people in the care of the abbot and follow you.'

'That is what I hoped you would say,' cut in Bernard, 'but I have something better to offer you. Your people will not be safe here. The abbot is old, the monastery out of date and badly fortified, the peasants at the end of their tether. I have hanged Valette, but Villa-Andrade is not far away and the news of the death of his lieutenant will bring him hurrying here. I haven't enough men to leave here. On the other hand, your presence will possibly place de Richemont in a delicate position. For the King, as La Trémoille sees it, you are a rebel and de Richemont will become one if he recruits you. Queen Yolande will no doubt return with the fine weather. She alone will take your part. I will call you when the time comes. . . .'

'Wait! Always wait!' groaned Arnaud who had got up and was pacing nervously about the tiled floor under Catherine's worried eye. 'I am a warrior, not a contemplative! How long must I wait?'

'Until I send for you!'

'I was not made to spin the distaff and watch the horizon.'

'Damned mountain wolf! I know that! I shall soon offer you a distaff in the shape of a lance. I came this way, because I had to go to Carlat. My mother, as you know, brought the viscounty into the family when she married my father. The door of the High Auvergne and the key to the valleys of the south, Carlat is governed by an old soldier, John de Cabanes. Too old, alas! The sword is heavy now for his feeble hand, and the Bishop of Saint Flour, who is all for the Duke of Burgundy, often looks in the direction of Carlat and licks his lips. We must not leave the brightest jewel in my mother's crown in danger. I was going to name one of my knights as governor of Carlat, but now I have a better idea: I shall entrust the fortress to you!'

Since Arnaud had begun to demand a part in the conflict, Catherine's blood had run faster in her veins, sounding the alarm. The word 'fortress' made her explode.

'More battles! Always war! Can't we live in peace, on this land which carries our name, with the people who, a short time ago, would have died for us? The abbey is big enough to hold us all. And I want so much ... so much, a little peace!'

Her voice broke on the last word, and the mocking light in the Young Bernard's eyes silenced her. He came to her and, resting a knee on the cushion which supported her feet, said :

'Peace, lovely Catherine, is an unattainable desire for us all in these pitiless times. How can we wish for peace when the English are so near us, when they still hold Rochefort in the mountains, and Besse, and Tournoel, when the English leopards float from the towers of Auvergne? You would not be safe here. What is more, your presence would put the village in danger, great danger, and they have no means of defending themselves. Carlat is antiquated, but its rock is impregnable. It will close its walls on you like the fingers of a solid fist and protect you. ...'

He had taken Catherine's hand and gently raised it to his lips. 'It was, I think, the poet Bernard of Ventadour who wrote somewhere, "He is truly dead who does not feel in his heart the sweet savour of love." You will be this "savour of love" in the heart of the old hills which live no longer, you will be the treasure Carlat will guard and you will never know how much I envy it.'

Behind Bernard's bent back, Catherine met Arnaud's gaze and thought she saw it darken, but this was a fleeting impression. Already Montsalvy was turning on his heel, hands clasped behind his back, to stare into the flames. Catherine's eyes rested dreamily on her husband's wide shoulders. At the back of her mind she saw a dream castle rise, far away and high in the clouds, but shining with an intense inner luminosity, a home filled with sunlight which would be the hearth where their love would find shelter at last.

'Perhaps you are right, Lord Bernard,' she said pensively. 'Perhaps I shall be happy at Carlat. ...'

Without letting go of the young woman's hand, Bernard rose, turning to his friend.

'You haven't given me an answer. Will you defend Carlat for the House of Armagnac?'

'Against whom?' asked Montsalvy dryly, without turning.

Young Bernard smiled and, between his narrowed lids, Catherine saw a mocking gleam in his eyes.

'Against any assailant, whoever he may be, or wherever he may come from: Saint Flour, Ventadour ... or Bourges!'

Arnaud did not move. There was a brief silence, then he asked:

'From Bourges? Against . . . King Charles VII?'

Bernard's brown hand pressed Catherine's fingers. On his face the smile gave way to an implacable resolution.

'Even against the King!' he spoke roughly. 'As long as La Trémoille rules, we, the Armagnacs, will recognize no other sovereigns than ourselves, no will but ours! If the King himself comes to ask for Carlat, Brother Arnaud, you will refuse him Carlat!'

Arnaud turned slowly. His tall silhouette was etched in black against the burning depths of the fire, making him seem even more redoubtable. In the shadow, Catherine saw her husband's white teeth gleam and the sharp knowledge of her love for him filled her with something akin to sorrow. What man could ever take his place in her heart? She loved everything about him: his virile beauty, surely, but also his burning spirit, his indomitable vitality, his character, forthright, but staunch and proud . . . he was the only master she would ever accept . . . and, gently, she withdrew her hand from Bernard's.

Arnaud rejoined his friend in three rapid steps.

'I am your man, Bernard! Give me Carlat and go in peace! But on one condition.'

'What's that?'

'I want to be there when the Constable de Richemont defeats La Trémoille!'

'You have my word! You will be in at the death!'

Bernard opened his arms. His two hands fell heavily on Montsalvy's shoulders which he pressed.

'Have patience and take care, Brother Arnaud! You will recover your land and your goods and, one day, the castle of Montsalvy will rise from the ashes.'

The two men embraced with rough tenderness. A vague jealousy stirred in Catherine's soul. She realized that, in this moment, they had both forgotten her, rejected women from their universe, a man's universe, an incomprehensible universe where violence and war held such an important place. Quietly she got up and left the room. While Arnaud and Bernard thought only of each other, Catherine felt a strong need to be near her son.

CHAPTER THIRTEEN

The Refuge

Carlat! A steep cliff of black basalt, barring the valley of the Embène, with its long narrow plateau, riven as though by the stroke of a sword with a deep fissure. At the foot, muffled within walls, a cold village, little houses like granite blisters around a primitive church with a separate bell tower. Above, on the proud spur crowned with vertiginous walls punctuated by huge towers, a bristling of belfries, roofs, pepperpot towers and crenellations. The fortress which had been the asylum of so many revolutionaries down the centuries seemed like a city, enclosed and mute, terrible in its total silence, which was so complete that Catherine almost believed as she approached that she could hear the flapping of the oriflamme at the summit of the keep. As she ascended at Morgane's unhurried pace, the young woman saw unfolded at her feet a gigantic landscape of meadows and forests, russet heaths, high fernbrakes, rocks rolling down to the white spume of torrents. The road was so steep and the sky so blue, so pure, that the high crenellated gateway, gilded by the last rays of the sun, seemed as though it would open on Paradise. And the two men who rode with her, the black count with the silver sparrowhawk and the grey count with the scarlet lion, were they not archangels with flaming swords who, in a moment, would turn the shining gates on their azure hinges? This monstrous eyrie whose black stones seemed to scale the sky, this was the place which was to be her hearth, where finally she could live out her love and her life as a married woman and watch Michel grow up. The menacing ramparts took on a reassuring gentleness. What harm could reach them so far away, so high. . . .?

A strident trumpet-call a few feet in front of her made her jump. They had reached the wall already. The black shadow of the rough wooden walls was swallowing up the horsemen. The silhouette of a soldier reared up against the sky holding a horn whose bellowing filled the air. Then, as the first horses reached the plateau, the gate slowly opened releasing a flood of rosy sunlight.

A vast esplanade appeared, ringed with various buildings: a chapel, a kind of large dwelling house with lancet windows, an antique commandery, arms stores, a forge, stables, an old well green with moss, a huge keep dominating with its height the four great corner towers, and, finally, its twisted and stripped branches writhing like black serpents, a large gallows tree which struck fear with its sinister fruit, the rigid corpses of five hanged men.

Catherine looked away as she passed by the tree. From everywhere, soldiers came running, carrying their crossbows, adjusting their helmets, eyes uneasy as they recognized their master's colours. The chapel bells began to ring at the same time as three heralds, on the threshold of the dwelling house, placed long silver trumpets to their lips. An old man in armour appeared, supporting his faltering steps with a stick.

'Sire Jean de Cabanes,' murmured Bernard d'Armagnac to Arnaud. 'He is too old. You see that it was time to bring fresh forces.'

Indeed, the immense courtyard gave an impression of disorder and neglect. The buildings were antiquated, some close to ruin, and many panes were missing from the windows of the lodging. Bernard the Younger sketched a smile at Catherine and she managed a grimace in return.

'I fear you will not be very satisfied with your palace, my lovely Catherine. But your smile will make a place of delight of it.'

The flash was gallant, but Catherine felt that the most beautiful smile on earth would not replace missing window-panes, patch cracks in the walls or stop up draughts. Spring, happily, was coming, but it was not yet warm and her perspicacious eyes were already noting everything which must be done before winter to make this old building habitable for women and a child. While Arnaud and Bernard exchanged greetings with the old chief of the garrison, Isabelle de Montsalvy drew up her mule beside Morgane.

'I am afraid we shall find more rats than tapestries here,' she said. 'If the inside is anything like the outside. . . .'

Her eyes turned towards Sara who was carrying Michel. The child was the only subject of conversation she would admit with her daughter-in-law and their common anxiety for his well-being brought them together a little. Apart from the baby, they could establish no new ties. Isabelle was not prepared to forget Catherine's origins and Catherine could not forgive Isabelle her snobbery. Moreover, she insisted on keeping Marie de Comborn with them after both she and Arnaud wished her to be returned to her brother.

'Marie was a daughter to me during the darkest days,' she had said. 'Her company gives me pleasure. . . .'

The look which accompanied this declaration let it be understood that no other company could replace hers and Arnaud, who had already opened his mouth to remind his mother that, in Catherine, she had a ready-made daughter, closed it again without saying anything. What good would it do to aggravate these antagonisms? By being forced to live together, the two women would end, perhaps, by appreciating each other. Arnaud believed in the soothing power of time and habit. . . .

In spite of everything, Catherine had willingly accepted a life shared with Isabelle, out of respect for her age and for love of her husband, but the idea of living on top of that fiery Marie de Comborn whose malevolent eyes she felt always upon her, made her feel almost physically ill. She found it harder and harder to tolerate the girl and she, with a malign insight, was perfectly aware of it. She played wickedly on these feelings, taking a malicious pleasure in following Arnaud about like a shadow whenever she got the chance.

When the women had passed under the deep, carved doorway of the manorial lodging, Marie glided up to Catherine whose disenchanted eyes were moving from the arched roof black with soot to the broken, uneven flagstones, spotted with grease and covered with muddy tracks which showed how long it was since they were last scrubbed.

'How does the noble lady like her palace?' purred the girl. 'Magnificent, of course! After a merchant's stinking shop, the worst hole would be dazzling, I imagine.'

'Does it please you?' replied the young woman with an angelic smile, pretending to take her enemy at her word. 'You are not difficult to satisfy. It is true that you have not had the opportunity to see anything better in your brother's ruined tower. This lodging is quite good enough . . . for a butcher! It is a hole worthy of a Comborn.'

'You are mistaken,' hissed Marie, darting a fiery look at her. 'It is not a hole . . . it is a tomb!'

'A tomb? What a morbid imagination!'

'It is not imagination, only a certainty that I hope you will share. A tomb, I repeat . . . your tomb! Because, my dear, you will not leave it alive!'

Catherine felt herself flush with anger, but she held it back by dint of a violent effort. She was not going to give this little shrew the pleasure of seeing that she had hurt her! A sarcastic smile drew her lips away from her perfect little teeth.

'And I suppose *you* will be the cause of my passing away? Are you not a little tired of threats, of these grand, tragic sentences? What a pity that destiny had you born in a castle! On the stage at the Saint Laurence Fair in Paris you would be an enormous success!'

Marie glanced round to make sure that no one was listening to them. Isabelle de Montsalvy and Sara had already gone upstairs and the men were gathered in the courtyard. They were alone, apparently, in front of the rustic fireplace.

'Laugh,' ground out the girl. 'Laugh, my beauty! You won't always laugh! Soon you will be no more than a carcass rotting at the bottom of some hole, and I, *I* shall be in your husband's bed!'

'The day Dame Catherine is at the bottom of a hole,' said a deep voice which seemed to come from the chimney itself, 'Messire Arnaud's bed will be empty, because you won't live long enough to get near it, miss!'

Gauthier appeared from behind the column of the hearth, hands held before him, so formidable and threatening that Marie recoiled, checking herself quickly. Her little head held high and her lips curled disdainfully, snakelike, she spat out:

'Ah, the watch-dog! He is always behind your skirts, I know, always ready to fly to your aid. I wonder how Arnaud puts up with it, since he pretends he loves you.'

'The feelings of Messire Arnaud are not in question at present, miss,' rudely cut in the Norman. "For a long time I have watched over Dame Catherine and he knows it. Also, allow me to speak as a watch-dog: if you touch Madame de Montsalvy, I shall kill you with my own hands!'

The enormous paws of the giant stretched out under Marie's eyes, sufficiently impressive to make the girl grow pale. But pride and hatred came to her aid.

'And ... if I tell my cousin that you have threatened me? Do you think he will keep you here for long?'

'For as long as I wish!' snapped Catherine slipping between the two adversaries. 'Remember this, and don't forget it again ... my dear! If Arnaud is your cousin, he is my husband. And he loves me, you hear; he loves me, should you burst with rage and jealousy! He will never hesitate between you and me! Say

and do what you will, but take care, as I shall myself. We shall
see who wins. Come, Gauthier, let us join the others.'

With that, Catherine, with a scornful shrug of the shoulders,
turned from Marie and, her hand resting on the Norman's arm
as though to underline her reliance on him, moved in her turn
towards the stairs.

'Beware, Dame Catherine,' murmured Gauthier, with an
anxious look. 'This girl hates you. She is capable of anything,
even the worst.'

'Very well, my friend, watch over me! Under your care, I
have never had anything to fear. Why should I begin today?'

'All the same, take care! I shall watch, but there are moments
when I cannot be near you. In the meantime, I shall warn Sara.
Faced with that viper, two will not be too many....'

Catherine did not reply. In spite of the confidence which she
evinced, she could not ignore a secret uneasiness. As Gauthier
had said, Marie was one of those reptiles who might raise her
head to strike at any moment. But the young woman had the
impression that if she showed her underlying fear, she would
lose the greater part of her defence.

The soldiers of Bernard the Younger worked late into the
night to render the ancient palace more habitable. The wagons
which followed in Bernard's train were, happily, well supplied
with hangings, coverlets, draperies and everything indispensable
to a comfortable life. The great hall on the first floor and the
three chambers on the second were brought into something
approximating order. The enormous bedsteads, each one large
enough for five people, were fitted out with featherbeds, mat-
tresses and pillows. Arnaud shared one with Catherine; Isabelle
de Montsalvy, Sara and the baby took another; Marie and old
Donatienne, who had not wished to leave her master, the third.
Bernard and his knights erected their tents in the immense
courtyard. As for the old Lord de Cabanes, he no longer lived
in the lodging, preferring the keep where he had his belongings,
because of the unbelievable filth of the lodging where the
ground floor hall served for the men-at-arms. All the rest was
deserted. But several vigorous roars from Bernard worked
miracles, reinforced in echo by furious cries from Arnaud who
was inspecting the defences and the round way.

Happily, wood was not short and great fires were lit in all the
fireplaces.

But when Catherine at last joined her husband in their room,

she was exhausted and depressed. She went to sit on the narrow
stone bench in the window embrasure and let her gaze stray
over the courtyard where the cooking fires of the soldiers still
burned. The dying light of the braziers shone eerily on the
corpses hanging from the oak-tree branches, contrasting harshly
with the elegance of the great tents of silk or embroidered linen
which sheltered the nobles. The young woman shivered and
drew the big woollen stole in which she was wrapped closer
about her.

'What are you doing, Catherine?' asked Arnaud from the
depths of the bed. 'Why don't you come?'

She did not reply immediately. Her mind as well as her eye
was hypnotized by the gallows tree. She was so worn out by
these horrors which continually crossed their path! Blood!
Always blood! Man's savagery effaced everything, even the
pure beauty of nature. How was it that, in hoping to find peace
and goodwill in this place, she at once stumbled on this brutal
recall to their pitiless times? How could one dream of love and
life in the shadow of a gibbet?

'Those hanged men,' she said finally. 'Couldn't someone . . .'

Arnaud's head appeared between the bed curtains, then his
naked brown body, for he was not in the habit of wearing a
sleeping-garment. Decisively, he strode over to his wife, picked
her up and came back to subside with her under the curtains.

'I said "come", Dame Catherine, and you must obey me!
Stop tormenting yourself over those men. I shall have them
taken down tomorrow to please you, although they are not
worth the trouble: a little present from the Bishop of Saint
Flour, some of these "tuchins"* whom he continues piously to
make much of in a poor quarter of his city. From time to time,
he lets loose a band on a castle or city which he covets. This
rarely succeeds. Several are always captured and hanged and
that's that until the next time. Fortunately they are not as
numerous as they were in the time of the great revolt, but there
are enough to do a good deal of harm. . . .'

He stopped speaking abruptly. While talking, he had undressed
Catherine and let down her hair which, as a game, he twisted
around his own neck. It was practically dark behind the curtains

---

*The 'tuchins' were involved, fifty years earlier, in a terrible peasant
revolt resulting from the frightful misery which devastated the country.
The name came from 'Tue-Chiens' because the rebels used to kill dogs to
eat. The Bishop of Saint Flour had given asylum to the tuchins in part of
the city. In a vestigial form, tuchins existed for many years in Auvergne.

and, with an impatient gesture, he slid forward, burying his hands in the thick hair which gleamed softly with warm lights. He held Catherine's head and bent his face to hers.

'I want to look in your eyes,' he said tenderly. 'They grow lighter when we make love ... they become almost transparent.'

'Listen,' murmured Catherine. 'I want to tell you ...'

'Shh. ... Forget all that! Don't think of anything. ... I love you! There is nothing but the two of us, you and I. ... We are alone in the midst of an empty world! Bernard was right when he said you are the most precious of treasures, and all he knows of your beauty is your face. He doesn't know the delights of your body. I love you, Catherine. I love you unto death.'

Tears which she could not hold back filled her eyes.

'Death? It is I who am condemned to death. Marie has told me that I shall not leave here alive, that she will kill me. ...'

She felt Arnaud's hands tighten on her head and saw him frown, but suddenly he burst into laughter.

'I wonder which of you two is the more mad: that unfortunate girl who will say anything to poison your life, or you who believe every word like Gospel. Marie knows me too well to try anything against you.'

'But if you had heard her. ...'

'Come on, Catherine, stop being unreasonable!' Arnaud's voice was stern, but his arms were close about her body. 'I have already told you to forget everything! There is only one reality in the world, you and I, we two, you understand; nothing but the two of us. ...'

Catherine did not reply Only the two of them? In the neighbouring room, Isabelle slept by Michel's cradle. Sara also shared the room, for she refused to abandon the child to his grandmother and defended her rights as a nursemaid, tooth and nail. She realized that Isabelle wanted to detach the boy from his mother completely and understood very well how to prevent it. On the other side slept Marie, and Catherine thought bitterly that in one room as in the other, someone dreamed of dispossessing her: Isabelle of her son; Marie of her husband. ... Where could Arnaud take them where there would be only the two of them?'

'Don't evade me,' scolded Arnaud against her ear. 'You must think only of our love when we are together ...' he kissed her, but under his mouth her lips were cold and trembling. She shut her eyes to try and hold back the tears rolling down her cheeks. Arnaud swore between his teeth, suddenly furious.

'And now you cry! I shall have to tear these stupid ideas out of your head!'

And instantly he released on Catherine such a storm of caresses and kisses that she, brutalized, ill-used, but transported by a pleasure which seemed never to reach its climax, delirious with a passion so violent that she cried out in her transports, could think of nothing but submission to Arnaud's will. When, finally, he subjugated her completely, she heard him murmur, mocking and tender, in a tone of triumph:

'I told you I would make you forget this stupidity!'

He left her suddenly to run to a sideboard standing near the fireplace on which stood goblets and a flagon of wine. Prostrated, crushed by glorious fatigue, Catherine half opened her eyes which had never been so heavy. Her complete exhaustion made the young man laugh. He lifted the silver flagon.

'Do you want a little wine? I have the devil of a thirst!'

She made a negative gesture with her hand, without even the strength to speak. Through her half-closed eyes, she saw him empty the cup to the last drop and wipe his lips on his bare arm. She was closing her eyes when a metallic sound made her jump. The cup had fallen to the ground, but Arnaud did not notice it. He went to the fire and seemed to be looking at something on the inner side of his arm. His absolute immobility struck Catherine who sat up against the disordered pillows, vaguely uneasy.

'What is it? What are you looking at?'

He did not reply or even move. There was something so frightening in this immobility that Catherine cried:

'Arnaud! What is the matter?'

He turned, letting his arm fall; he smiled, but it was but a mechanical stretching of the lips, almost a grimace.

'Nothing, my love! A branch flared up and a spark burned my arm. Go to sleep now. You need it. . . .'

His voice seemed to come from far away. With an automatic gesture, he took from a stool a long robe of green cloth edged with moleskin, slipped it on and tied the girdle about his loins. Catherine watched him stupidly.

'But where are you going now?'

'I'm going to make sure that everything is all right, that the sentries are in their places. The men have drunk a lot tonight and there is always the possibility of a surprise attack.'

He approached the bed, bent down, took up a lock of hair which lay outside the covers and pressed it to his lips fervently.

'Sleep, my angel, sleep . . . I shall be gone for some time.'

This night patrol was normal, after all, for the governor of a fortress. Then Catherine was too weary to ask herself any more questions. Arnaud was the most unpredictable of men. As he crept away from her on tiptoe after having carefully arranged the blankets over his wife's shoulders, she closed her eyes, already filled with a delicious torpor. Still, before slipping into unconsciousness, she again felt a curious uneasiness. Was she already asleep, or had there really been, all of a sudden, anxiety and even fear in the look Arnaud had given her. For a moment, his face had seemed to be chiselled in granite. Nothing was alive in it save his eyes, his eyes. . . . Come, it was a figment of her exhausted mind! Catherine, a smile on her lips, slept deeply.

Sara's voice, humming an old cantilena, woke Catherine. She felt as though she had only slept five minutes, but it was broad daylight. She smiled to see Sara sitting on the foot of the bed in the attitude in which she had seen her hundreds of times when she was a little girl, but now holding Michel in her arms. It was to the baby that she sang, smiling, and the baby, entranced, waved little hands as rosy as shells.

'Is it so late?' asked Catherine, sitting up.

'It is time to feed your son! He is very hungry.'

Catherine held out her arms to take the child with the deep feelings of love and fulfilment which were hers each time she fed him. The little fair head nestled against her and the little fingers, spread wide, pressed the rounded breast which she offered him. Michel began to suck avidly. Catherine burst out laughing.

'My word, how he gobbles! Look, Sara. . . . Isn't he greedy?'

From the child, her thoughts went to the father and she asked Sara where Arnaud was.

'Outside. Count Bernard is getting ready to leave. When the little one is finished, you must be quick.'

Sitting in her bed, Catherine followed Sara with her eyes, astonished at not having noticed the strange stooping of her shoulders before. Sara bent? At hardly fifty years of age? And this violet shadow round her eyes. Fatigue, perhaps? Sara spent herself continuously for Michel and Catherine. At this moment, she was opening a leather travelling-chest and taking out various garments, first of all a tunic of violet velvet appliquéd with grey satin.

'Count Bernard has left several boxes. From these men's

gowns and mantles I can make you several garments. You haven't a thing to put on.'

'We are a long way from the robes of Bruges and Dijon, aren't we?' Catherine gave a small smile. 'And the perfumes and the jewels. ...'

'You regret nothing? Truly nothing?'

Catherine's smile was dazzling as it went from the little boy's downy head to the blue arch of the window through which could be heard Arnaud's voice shouting orders.

'What should I regret? In these two, I have everything. They are far more to me than a palace, brocaded robes and diamonds. You know ...'

The sentence remained in mid-air. Sara, with a furious gesture, was wiping her eyes on her sleeve. Catherine's pupils widened in disbelief.

'You are crying!'

'Certainly not! ... I'm not crying,' said Sara impatiently. 'There is dust in these clothes.'

'It's in your voice, too. ... There, he's finished! Take him; I'm getting up!' she said, putting Michel back in the gipsy's arms.

While she splashed her face with water, put on her clothes and braided her hair, Catherine watched Sara. Dust? Surely not. ... She was crying, or rather, she had been crying and some tears remained. But it was certain that she was not going to say any more about it. Outside, the hurly-burly of a large party about to set off could be heard: the clank of armour, horses' hooves pawing the ground, the rumbling of baggage wagons, brief orders loudly shouted, calls and laughter. Approaching the window, Catherine saw that the silk tents had been dismantled and loaded on the carts. She saw also that Arnaud had kept his word: the branches of the old oak no longer bore their grisly fruit. The courtyard was full of armed men who waited quietly at ease, for the departure.

The knights were already mounted. ...

As Catherine leaned over the stone sill the better to breathe the invigorating morning air, to feel the mild caress of the spring sun which gave sweetness to the countryside, Arnaud and Bernard came out of the chapel. The two men were in full armour, except for their helmets which they carried under their arms. They went towards their steeds which their squires held by the bridle, hoisting themselves into the saddle. Arnaud no doubt wanted to accompany his friend along the road. Bernard

was about to place his casque on his head when he saw
Catherine at her window and turned his horse towards
her.

'I did not wish to disturb your sleep, Catherine,' he cried, 'but
I am happy to see you before I leave. Don't forget me entirely!
I will do everything to ensure that your grace and beauty will
soon return to illumine the Court of King Charles VII.'

'I shall not forget you, messire! And I shall pray for your
success in arms.'

Under his red and silver caparisons, the charger danced with
the grace of a young lady. Bernard the Younger bowed deeply
in his saddle, his laughing eyes fixed on Catherine who, from her
window, made him reverence. Then the horse wheeled and, at a
canter, Bernard of Armagnac took the head of his retinue.
Arnaud followed him with Fortunat, who henceforward served
as his squire, at his heels. As he passed his wife, he lifted his
gloved hand and smiled, and suddenly the strange uneasiness
she experienced the night before returned to her. Arnaud's
smile was sad and his features drawn as though he had not
closed his eyes all night.

Meanwhile Catherine's attention was suddenly distracted
from her husband. Facing her, almost at the same height, a man-
at-arms stood on the wall leaning on a shining lance which
he held in both hands. The steel hood framed a large, olive-
skinned face whose little pig-like eyes were the size of pinheads.
The man smiled automatically as he looked at her, and Catherine, in amazement, recognized the sergeant Esconeboeuf, the
leader of the escort Xaintrailles gave them at Bourges, who had
disappeared so mysteriously from the abbey at Aurillac after
having been punished by Arnaud.

Instinctively she drew back into the shadow of her room,
calling Sara to her with a gesture. She pointed out the man, who
had not moved.

'Look,' she said. 'Do you recognize him?'

Sara frowned, but shrugged her shoulders.

'I've known he was here since yesterday evening. I knew him
at once. It seems he came here straight from Aurillac which is
reasonable since it is the nearest town and the only fortress of
the Count of Armagnac, Escorneboeuf's master. It is not so
astonishing to see him here.'

'Arnaud knows?'

'Yes, nothing escapes him. But Escorneboeuf made his excuses
to him after having asked Count Bernard to plead for him. Oh, I

could see that Messire Arnaud was not pleased, but he could not refuse.'

'Excuses!' murmured Catherine without taking her eyes off the huge sergeant. 'I can hardly believe it!'

It sufficed to see the menacing smile on the hulking man's face to realize that these excuses were but a ruse, no doubt hiding a deep desire for vengeance.

'Nor I,' said Sara. 'And there is something more. Yesterday evening I saw Escorneboeuf near the chapel. He was talking to your friend, Marie, and the conversation was very animated, I can tell you. But when they saw me, they separated. . . .'

'Strange,' said Catherine, twisting the end of one of her plaits in her fingers. 'How could they know each other?'

Sara spat on the ground with undisguised disgust.

'That girl is capable of anything,' she said. 'You know she is a little witch and nothing astonishes me. She will have divined in Escorneboeuf the same sort of ill will against you which she has herself.'

The door opened, although no one had knocked. Isabelle de Montsalvy appeared, clothed in black from head to foot. She was enveloped in a long cloak, and a gauze veil, also black, gave her narrow face an impressive hauteur. In the shadow of her mantle, the ferret face of Marie could be seen. Arnaud's mother halted on the threshold and said without even a greeting:

'Are you coming? Mass is about to begin . . .'

'I'm coming,' replied Catherine simply. She took a hooded cloak in which she wrapped herself, putting back the hood from her bare head, and followed her mother-in-law after dropping a light kiss on Michel's brow. Sara had placed him in a nest of pillows on the great bed.

The sun was sinking when Arnaud returned to the castle. With Fortunat and the dozen men he had taken with him, he had ranged the neighbourhood to assure himself that everything was in order. Finally, he stayed long enough in the village of Carlat to question the leading citizens, inspect the reserves of provisions and try to inject a little hope into these discouraged peasants who had lived in a state of perpetual alarm for years, ready at any moment to flee or fight.

Two things struck Catherine when Arnaud entered the great hall, now thoroughly cleaned and strewn with fresh straw, where the family waited for supper: the worried expression on his face and the fact that he had not taken off his armour. He seemed even more pale than in the morning. Immediately alarmed, she ran to meet him, already stretching out her arms to hold him, but he pushed her gently away.

'No, don't kiss me, my love! I'm filthy and I feel feverish. My old wounds are troubling me. I must have taken a chill and you must not risk becoming ill yourself.'

'What does that matter to me?' cried Catherine, furious at feeling the satisfied smile of Marie behind her back. Arnaud smiled, and lifted his hand to place it on his wife's head, but the movement was not completed.

'Think of your son. You are still feeding him and he needs a mother in perfect health.'

This was logical, even wise, but Catherine's heart was stricken. Moreover, she noticed that he made the same excuses to his mother, only bowing before her and Marie. Isabelle de Montsalvy looked closely at her son with surprise tinged with uneasiness.

'Why are you still armed? How can you take supper with fifty pounds of iron on your back?'

'It's all right, mother. I shall not sup ... not here, at least. I am worried. The peasants have drawn my attention to strange comings and goings by night. Men have been seen approaching the outer walls, others have even tried to scale the escarpment. I must learn the extent of the castle's resources as I must also know my men. I am going to live with them for a time. I have already ordered a camp bed to be made up for me in the Saint John tower, the most exposed of the rocky spurs. . . .'

He turned to Catherine who, pale and heavy-hearted, kept back through pride the protest which spontaneously rose to her lips. Why did he want to isolate himself from her, to deprive himself of what was so important to his happiness: their wonderful hours of intimacy?

'We must be reasonable, my heart. We are at war and I have grave responsibilities.'

'If you want to lodge in the Saint John tower, why can't I go too?'

'Because a woman's place is not in a guard post!' cut in Arnaud's mother dryly. 'It is time you learned that the wife of a soldier must first of all learn to obey!'

'Must the wife of a soldier necessarily have an iron-plated heart, must she arm her soul?' flung out Catherine rebelliously.

'Why not? The women of our family are never weak, even when things are hard – particularly when they are hard! It is evident that you have not been brought up with these opinions.'

Disdain was flaunted in the old lady's tone and Catherine, already made sensitive by her disappointment, felt it cruelly. She was about to reply, but Arnaud interposed.

'Leave her alone, mother! If you can't understand her, at least don't make it so obvious! And you, my love, you will have to be brave, because it is necessary. Sara will sleep with you. I don't want you to be alone.'

He moved away from her with a gesture of the hand and Catherine tried to control her features in spite of a growing desire to cry. This evening things took on again that absurd and disquieting aspect which they had lost for a short time. Had Bernard taken away with him all security, all happiness and all freedom from worry? And the spectres of fear and doubt which her vigorous common sense had dispelled for a time, were they to return? Catherine felt a painful sensation of suffocation. The walls seemed to lean towards her to engulf her. What was she doing in this strange hall, among these hostile women? Why was Arnaud leaving her alone? Did he not know that, without him, nothing had taste or colour? Each of his absences was like a long winter. ... The icy regard of her mother-in-law met her in the depths of her isolation.

'Well, let us take supper now! There is no point in waiting.'

'Excuse me,' said Catherine. 'I am not hungry. I would rather go to my room. I'm sure my absence will not be displeasing. Please accept my wishes for a good night.'

A swift curtsey and she had left the room. On the stairs, the suffocating sensation left her. She definitely breathed better away from Isabelle and Marie. She gathered up the heavy folds of her gown to ascend the stairs more quickly, almost breaking into a run on the last steps, and nearly fell into the arms of Sara who had just settled Michel for the night. Trembling with chagrin and cold, she clung round the neck of her old friend, instinctively seeking the warmth of her sympathy.

'If he leaves me constantly with those two women. I won't put up with it, Sara, I can't! I feel their hatred and scorn as though it were something I could touch. Tomorrow I shall see Arnaud. I shall tell him he must choose, he ...'

'Be still,' cut in Sara firmly. 'You should be ashamed of behaving like a guttersnipe. And for what? Because your husband has other duties and can't spend his time billing and cooing with you? What childishness! He is a man, you know, and he must lead the life of a man. Your duty is to help him. There are moments when this is difficult, terribly difficult, but you must be brave.'

'Be brave! Be brave!' grumbled Catherine. 'Will the day ever come when you will stop demanding courage from me? I tell you, I have no more left.'

'But of course you have!'

In her motherly fashion, Sara made the disconsolate young woman sit down on a bench and put an arm around her. The blonde head came naturally to rest against her shoulder.

'Little one, you'll always need more courage. More, perhaps, than you know, but you will not fail, because you love him . . . because you are his wife.'

Meanwhile, Sara's gentle hand caressed her bent head and Catherine did not see the tears which, once more, were filling the Romany's dark eyes. She did not hear the impassioned prayer which rose from her old friend's heart, a silent prayer that the bitter blow which was looming up would pass away without touching her.

'Noble lady,' said the soldier, out of breath from running. 'Messire Arnaud is asking for you! Quickly . . . it is very urgent! He needs you. . . . He . . . he is sick!'

'Sick?' Catherine threw down the spindle of wool she was spinning near Michel's cradle to occupy herself and leapt to her feet. 'What is it? Where is he?'

'In the keep. He was inspecting the upper defences. Suddenly he collapsed. . . . Come, lady, come quickly!'

Catherine did not wait to ask further questions. Throwing a backward glance at her sleeping son and not even taking the trouble to call Sara who was down in the kitchens, she gathered up her skirts and ran behind the soldier. As she crossed the threshold of the lodging, a gust of wind caught her, winding her gown round her legs like a wet rag. Below, the keep rose from the midst of long ribbons of fog which swirled in the tempest. Catherine paused instinctively to struggle against the damp squalls and then with her head lowered like a little fighting bull, she pushed across the huge barrack square. Anxiety carried her forward, but at the same time she felt a curious joy. At last he was calling for her! At last he needed her . . . !

For more than two weeks, since he had been lodged in the Saint John tower, she had scarcely seen him. Each morning and evening he came to the dwelling house, greeted his wife and his mother, but did not embrace them. He had a sore throat, he told them, and he was coughing. For the same reason he refused to touch his son. Catherine had questioned Fortunat, and what he told her was scarcely reassuring! Arnaud ate practically nothing and he passed the nights on his feet, pacing up and down his room for hours.

'This walking about in the night will drive him mad ...' Fortunat protested. 'Monseigneur has a secret worry.'

Several times Catherine had tried to be alone with her husband, but she was forced to admit sadly that he seemed to avoid her especially. The safety of Carlat and its inhabitants seemed to be the sole interest of his life: he was devoting himself to it entirely. He kept away quite deliberately, Catherine knew, from the house where the three women led their antagonistic lives around Michel's cradle. They watched each other, spied on each other, on the look out for faults or moments of depression to take up arms against each other. Marie was past mistress of this implacable fencing, whereas Catherine was torn to pieces by it. She longed desperately to understand, to grasp this thing, however trifling, which eluded her, but which was the cause of her separation from her husband. But, as she ran across the court-yard, buffeted by this maddening south wind, she told herself that Arnaud's sudden illness would give him into her power: now he would have to tell her the truth!

She reached the low door of the keep and flung herself blindly towards the stairway. No torch burned within as was usual, but an acrid current of air moaned. The wind blowing through the loopholes must have extinguished the flames. Catherine laid her hand against the damp stones, feeling for the worn treads with her feet. Little by little her eyes grew used to the gloom of the spiral staircase, lit at infrequent intervals by narrow slits in the formidable thickness of the walls. A strange sensation of loneliness gripped Catherine. There was no man-at-arms, no one came or went on the stair which was filled with a terrible hub-bub from above as if thunder were crashing on the summit of the tower. Something up there reverberated like a gigantic drum from gigantic blows.

Catherine suddenly noticed that the soldier who had come to fetch her had disappeared. Absorbed by her uneasiness, she had taken no notice of him. It was strange that Arnaud's illness did not cause more commotion. And this stairway was never-ending!

Still running, she passed the door of the main hall and climbed still higher, but now her breath failed her. With beating heart,

she leant back for a moment against the slimy wall to recover.
While she stood there, gasping, her wandering gaze fell through
the loophole near her. ... She was aroused with a start. She
stuck her head over the sill of the long slit window and gave an
exclamation of astonishment. There, below her, coming out of
the old command post, she saw Arnaud, dressed and armed as
usual. He seemed in perfect health and sustained with one arm
the hesitant steps of the old Sire de Cabanes. Catherine screwed
up her eyes to see better. No, there was no doubt of it: it really
was Arnaud!

She lifted her eyes to the summit of the keep where the din
had now ceased. The sudden silence made her sharply aware of
the loud, heavy respiration of someone coming up. All of a sudden, she was afraid and waved her arm through the slit calling:

'Arnaud! Arnaud!'

But she was too far away, too high up! Montsalvy did not
hear her. Without even turning his head, he went towards the
forge with Cabanes.

Shrugging her shoulders, Catherine went back down the stairs,
plunging into the shadows. In her haste, she missed a step,
twisted a foot and nearly fell. She had to stop a moment till the
pain passed away a bit, and it was then, in the shadows of the
stair, that she saw the purple face of Escorneboeuf on his way
up. He mounted heavily, hands in front of him and eyes fixed,
shaking with silent laughter. Catherine's blood froze in her veins
as the terrible knowledge of her danger filled her. The huge body
of the Gascon obstructed the narrow stair completely and he
did not seem likely to give way.

'Come along!' she said firmly. 'Let me pass!'

He did not reply, but continued to come towards her. His
panting breath sounded like a bellows and filled the young
woman's ears. Those staring eyes, this evil, idiot laugh! She
recoiled a step. The man leaned forward, stretching out his
enormous hands to catch her. ... A mad terror possessed her.
She suddenly realized that she was alone in this tower at the
mercy of this brute whose intentions were all too clear. With a
strangled cry, she rushed upwards. ... She wanted to reach the
top floor to shut herself up in the great, round chamber in
which Jean de Cabanes lived. She remembered the massive door
and the solid bolts she had seen there. But she had not recovered
her breath sufficiently and her heart knocked painfully against
her ribs. Behind her, the man began to run. And it was dark, so
dark, on those stairs! Would she never reach the shelter of that

door? Tears of anguish gushed from her eyes.

Above her something seemed to explode. There was a great crash and a shriek of tearing metal. Several steps above Catherine the door fell back with an apocalyptic uproar, letting out a flood of daylight, and Catherine, who was about to throw herself into that miraculously opened room, flung herself backwards so violently that she bruised her shoulder against the wall. Between her and the wide open door, across the sill of which Gauthier, fuming with rage and covered with dust, was about to spring, a chasm gaped ... a black void, terrifying. ... Some iniquitous hand had removed the wooden steps which formed the access to each floor of the keep. These steps acted as traps for the assailant to hold him up in his ascent to the summit. Carried away by the impetus of his attack he would find nothing below his feet but blackness and would crash to the depths of an *oubliette*.

Catherine realized that, by flinging open the door and letting in the light, Gauthier had saved her. One more step and she would have disappeared into the abyss, never to be found. It would suffice to replace the steps ... choked with fear, seized with giddiness, incapable of making a sound, she held out a drowning hand to Gauthier, hardly noticing his terrifying aspect. The large face was convulsed by one of those murderous rages she knew so well. Blood ran from his shoulder under the torn leather of his tunic, and also from his hands. ...

'Don't move, Dame Catherine!' he gasped. 'I'm beginning to understand why I was shut up in there!'

Just at that moment, Escornboeuf appeared. He was so intent on his pursuit of Catherine that he did not immediately see the Norman. He was about to throw himself on the young woman with a grunt of joy when Gauthier thundered:

'This time you won't escape me, you dog!'

Catherine did not have time to press herself against the wall as with one great leap Gauthier bridged the gap, knocking her aside as he passed. She was momentarily stunned while the Norman fell with all his weight on the Gascon who tumbled backwards. The two men, locked together, toppled down the stairs to the next landing.

The cold stones roused Catherine, who was on the verge of fainting. She gritted her teeth and stood up in spite of the pain in her back. Holding on to the wall, with trembling legs, she descended as far as the passage where the two men were rolling. The combat continued, savage, relentless.

Escorneboeuf and Gauthier were so tightly entwined that it was impossible to distinguish one from the other. There was a spasmodic heaving of arms and legs punctuated by cries like wild beasts as they rolled together in the narrow space, and sometimes it was the Norman and sometimes the Gascon on top.

From her panting heart, Catherine sent up a fervent prayer that Gauthier would gain the advantage, because his defeat would cost both of them their lives. But the Gascon was equally strong and the recent wound in the Norman's shoulder handicapped him, particularly since his superhuman effort in forcing open the massive oak door had reopened it. ... Finally, the two combatants were obstructing the passage and Catherine could not get past to seek aid. Suddenly she decided to call out and cried:

'Help! Help!'

'Keep quiet!' gasped Gauthier. 'The devil only knows whom your call will bring here! I'm getting on all right ... better to finish it alone!'

With a powerful twist of his hips, he succeeded at last in getting the advantage. He was able to seize his enemy by the throat and squeeze it with both hands despite the blows the other was raining on him with his fists. Little by little, however, the Gascon was being throttled. His mouth opened, his blows grew weaker and less accurate. Gauthier squeezed more strongly and then, lifting up the Gascon's head, he banged it against the ground. Finally, the other croaked:

'Mercy! ... Don't kill me!'

'Answer my questions first. I'll decide afterwards. Who shut me up in the tower room?'

'I did! Someone asked me to.'

'Who?'

'The young lady ... Marie de Comborn!'

'You did know her, then?' demanded Catherine who was regaining her presence of mind. Between Gauthier's hands, Escorneboeuf's face was the colour of wine lees. He was gasping for air like a stranded fish. The Norman relaxed his hands. Escorneboeuf took two or three breaths.

'Yes,' he said at last. 'I served long ago in the household of her brother at Comborn as a mercenary. She promised me ... one of her mother's jewels ... and to give herself to me ... if I killed you both!'

'So!' grunted Gauthier. 'And the displaced steps?'

'I did that, too. I took advantage of the fact that Messire Arnaud and Messire Jean were inspecting the defences in order to strengthen them. Then ... I sent a man-at-arms to fetch Dame Catherine ... When I saw her running towards the keep, I went in after her. I wanted ... No! Pity!'

The last words burst from him. Gauthier's face had become purple with fury. All his features were convulsed and Escorneboeuf felt the deadly pressure increasing round his neck.

'You wanted to push her over, didn't you? In case, by a miracle she had seen the hole. . . .'

Escorneboeuf heard death in the passionate voice of his adversary and, with a somewhat childlike gesture, he pressed his hands together. He could no longer speak.

'He is begging for mercy . . .' began Catherine.

Gauthier's eyes turned to her with an expression of enormous surprise.

'By Odin! You still have pity? What should I do then?'

Catherine was about to reply, but astonishment had relaxed the Norman's grip without his realizing it. Escorneboeuf, although on the edge of coma, took advantage of this. His reaction was born of desperation. With all his strength he twisted his body, catching Gauthier off his guard and rolling him to one side. In the twinkling of an eye the half-strangled man had jumped to his feet and fled down the stairs. The clattering of his boots on the stone steps was followed by the slam of the door behind him. Gauthier, meanwhile, got up grumbling:

'He has escaped me! But I'll catch him yet. . . .'

Catherine stammered incoherently:

'No ... I beg you! Let him go. ... Don't ... don't leave me alone! I was ... I was so afraid!'

In the dim light her face looked like a pale flower. She was trembling and the Norman heard her teeth chattering. She leaned against him, seeking refuge, her fear giving way to a nervous weakness. Her fingers touched his wounded shoulder. She drew them back sharply, covered with blood, and looked at them in horror.

'Your wound . . .!' she cried.

'It's nothing. It will heal! Let me carry you; otherwise you'll never get down these damned stairs.'

Already he was lifting her from the ground. Like a frightened child, she pressed herself against the giant's chest.

'You saved me,' she breathed. '. . . Once more, I owe my life to you!'

He began to laugh good-humouredly.

'That is what I am here for,' he said. 'You know what Marie said: I am your watchdog!'

Catherine did not reply, but an impulse, for which she had long sought the explanation, brought from her an unthinking movement. Although she was starting to descend the dangerous stairway, she suddenly wrapped her arms about his solid neck and pressed her lips against his. He stopped short and, at first, under Catherine's lips, his remained unresponsive. The unexpected kiss stunned him, but only for a very brief moment. As the young woman was about to draw back, he gathered her to him and returned her kiss with a passion which threw her into confusion. His full lips were warm and sweet as those of a child. A strange emotion possessed Catherine. This kiss had a quality unknown to her; it was tender, with an ardour tempered by devotion. All the freshness of first love was enshrined in it and, in Gauthier's arms, Catherine was suddenly reminded of Landry, her childhood friend, who had become a monk through despair. Landry had loved her like this. He loved her, this man, selflessly and completely with a love as natural as the wind on the fields or the flight of a bird. In him Catherine recognized the same breed, the same race as herself. . . .

Brusquely he set her down, retreating several steps. By the light of the open door of the keep, she saw his face twisted by a sadness she could not grasp. There was suffering in the Norman's grey eyes, in the huskiness of his voice.

'Never do that again . . . for pity's sake! Never do it again!'

'I only wanted to thank you, to let you know how much . . .'

He shook his great, bristly head and bent his shoulders under the torn leather of his jerkin. Turning away, he said:

'You have the power to madden me and you know it quite well.'

He walked away, buffeted by the rising wind. The beating rain slapped Catherine. She watched him go towards the stables his broad shoulders hunched, and she was conscious of having wounded him. He had not understood Catherine's unconscious gesture. How could he, since she had not understood it herself. He had been justified in thinking it a favour accorded to his unspoken love. A line from the strange song he loved to sing came into her mind, that ancient ballad of Harold the Valiant: 'My ships are the terror of the world; I have sailed the seven seas. Yet am I scorned by a Russian maid.'

Gauthier was very much like herself. He belonged, as she did, to the proud and patient people of France. Would there ever come a day when she would truly understand him, this unaccountable son of the Norman forests?

Catherine returned to the lodging in a dream. Empty-headed, her thoughts drifting, she allowed the rain to soak her face, abandoning herself to its violence as though it could wash away her doubts and fears. What was she going to do now? Find Arnaud at once and make him listen to her? If he really wanted her safe, he would make Marie de Comborn leave Carlat before sundown.

'I won't live another day near her,' she repeated between her teeth. 'He must choose!'

A retrospective shiver ran over her as she realized what might have been. At this moment, without Gauthier, she would be a crushed body, a mangled lump of flesh, blood and bone, at the bottom of a stinking pit. . . . She clenched her fists and bit her lips. What had failed this time could succeed another time. She had escaped death by a miracle, but tomorrow . . . ? In what shape would death approach her, secretly, in the shadows?

An exclamation of anger broke from her lips. Some yards in front of her, Marie ran out of the dwelling house and, after looking back to see that no one was following her, hurried towards the corner of the courtyard where the baths were. Catherine gathered herself together in order to follow her, but then she remembered that when she flew to Arnaud's succour she had left her little Michel all alone. No doubt Sara had returned to him, or the grandmother had come back from the village where she had gone to distribute alms, but she had better glance at him before going after Marie. Prisoner as she was herself within the walls of the fortress, the girl could not escape her. With a smile tinged with spite, Catherine told herself that she would always find her. . . .

She ran up to her room, impelled by a sudden urge to see the child again. Perhaps too she should change out of this wet gown which clung to her unpleasantly, hampering her movements. She went into the room and across to the oak cradle. Suddenly she froze in her tracks and her heart stopped beating. The baby was not to be seen. Some murderous hand had pulled the covers up over his head. There was not a sound from the little bed . . .

The cry wrung from Catherine's throat was like an animal's howl, like the howl of a she-wolf before her abandoned lair. It rang through the huge empty halls, and shook the old dwelling

to its farthermost corners. It startled Sara in the basement kitchen, carried as far as the sentries standing guard on the walls
and the peasant delivering straw in his rough wooden cart. Up in
her room Catherine snatched the covers away and lifted Michel
up. The baby's face was blue. His little head lolled back limply
... Catherine sank to her knees.

'My God. ... No! ... Not that! Not that!'

She choked, half strangled with grief and began smothering
her child with wild kisses. This was the cruellest stroke of all!
The atrocity of the crime plunged her in horror and suffering so
abominable she could not bear it. ... She cried out again and
again. ... Sara came running in and saw the young woman
collapsed on the floor, cradling the baby in her arms.

'What has happened?'

'They have killed him! They have taken him from me. My
little one! Someone has suffocated him in his bed! Oh, God!
Oh, my God!'

But Sara was not listening. She snatched up the baby and
ripped off the swaddling bands from the little body which was
as limp in her hands as a rag doll. Then she smacked the baby's
buttocks sharply several times, stretched him out on the
mother's bed and began to blow slowly and gently into the
baby's open mouth. ... Catherine watched her in amazement.

'What are you doing?' she stammered.

'I am trying to revive him. Long ago I saw children born with
cords round their necks, who looked like this. The midwives
always acted in this way....'

She bent over Michel once more. Catherine's feet seemed to
be rooted to the floor. She could not move. One thing alone
seemed to be alive in her, apart from her aching heart, and
that was the despairing gaze which drank in Sara's every movement. Then a black form suddenly appeared before her and she
heard Isabelle de Montsalvy's harsh voice cry out:

'What are you doing, you mad thing? What are you doing
to my grandson?'

She shook Sara by the shoulders. With this Catherine recovered abruptly. Impelled by an ungovernable fury she sprang
to her mother-in-law, seized her by the shoulders and wrenched
her away. As the old lady turned to look at her, open-mouthed,
she screamed at her with violet eyes flashing:

'She is trying to save him! I command you to leave her
alone!' Then she went on: 'They have killed my son, do you
hear? They have murdered him! I found him suffocated under

the covers which someone had wrapped round his head! He
is dead . . . and you killed him!'

Old Isabelle went deathly pale. She staggered and clutched
at the chimney-piece. The shock seemed to have aged her; she
looked stooped and worn. The voice which came from her
colourless lips was barely more than a whisper.

'Dead . . . murdered?'

She repeated the terrible words as if she did not understand
them. When she turned to Catherine her features were sunken,
and her eyes unseeing.

'Who killed him?' she stammered. 'Why do you say it was
me? I kill my little Michel? You must be out of your mind!'

She said this without anger, almost calmly: a simple state-
ment of fact. And there was so much real grief in those few
words that Catherine felt her own anger give way to sorrow.
She was tired all of a sudden, tired to death.

'Forgive me,' she murmured. 'But if you had not kept that
accursed Marie here against Arnaud's will and mine, this would
not have happened. She is the criminal!'

The accusation came from within her and the truth of the
words struck Catherine as she pronounced them. Once more,
she saw Marie leaving the lodging quickly, almost furtively. . . .
Who hated her enough to dare attack her little child, if not the
viper of Comborn? But, on Isabelle de Montsalvy's face, amazement mingled with incredulity.

'It is impossible! She would not do such a thing. You detest
her because she loves my son. But she has always loved him . . .
and it is not her fault. No one is mistress of her heart!'

Catherine shrugged. As she bent over the bed, Sara continued
to chafe the baby and blow into his mouth.

'She hates me so much that nothing matters to her. She tried
to kill me too, not an hour ago! But for Gauthier, I should be
at the bottom of the oubliette in the keep, smashed to pieces!
You say she would not do such a thing. She would do even
worse to efface even my memory from the surface of the earth
and the mind of my lord!'

'Silence! I forbid you to accuse Marie! She is of my blood!
I practically brought her up.'

'Congratulations!' said Catherine bitterly. 'Oh, I never expected to have to be rude to you! But I swear to you that she
leaves this place this evening! If not, I will! At heart,' added
the young woman sadly, 'that is what you would prefer, now
that my child . . .'

As if in reply, Sara's voice rang out:

'He lives! He breathes!'

As one the mother and the grandmother moved towards the bed. Between Sara's strong hands, the baby had lost his tragic blueish tinge. His mouth opened like a little fish out of water. His hands and feet moved feebly. Over her shoulder, Sara flung out at Isabelle:

'Warm his swaddling bands in front of the fire!'

The grandmother obeyed her with dispatch. Her eyes were full of tears, but they were shining.

'He lives!' she stammered. 'God be praised!'

On her knees beside the bed, Catherine laughed and cried simultaneously. Michel regained consciousness more and more quickly as Sara continued to administer little slaps to him. This treatment ended by displeasing him deeply, for, all at once, he went bright red, opened his mouth wide and began to scream loudly. No music could have been more beautiful to Catherine, who sat back on her heels and listened ecstatically while Sara quickly took the warm bands from Isabelle's hands to wrap the little kicking body. Catherine caught one of her old friend's hands and pressed her tear-wet face against it, covering it with kisses.

'You have saved him!' she stammered. 'You have given him back to me! Thank you! Oh, thank you!'

Sara bent a look full of tenderness upon the young woman. Leaning over briskly, she kissed her on the forehead and drew away her hand.

'Come, come,' she grumbled. 'Don't cry any more! It's all over now.'

She rapidly completed the swaddling of Michel and then gave him to his mother. Catherine took him in her arms with a deep feeling of joy. He was like a warm flame in the centre of her being. It was as though life itself had been given back to her and was now returning in a great warm flood. She covered the silky blonde hair with kisses but, over the child's head, her gaze met that of Isabelle. She stood on the other side of the bed, arms dangling, and watched the mother and child with a hunger which pained Catherine. She was too happy not to be generous. She held out the infant with a lovely smile.

'Take him!' she said gently. 'He's yours!'

Something moved in the frozen face of the old lady. She stretched out adoring hands and looked Catherine in the eyes. Her mouth opened, but no sound came. She smiled tremulously, then pressed the baby to her heart like a treasure and went slowly to sit beside the hearth. Catherine contemplated for a moment this black Madonna bending over a blond, cooing babe. Then she turned away from Isabelle and took off her soaked gown which she replaced by another. It was the gown of wool with black velvet ribbons which she had worn the night of her marriage. When she had put it on, she did her hair, carefully smoothing her braids, rolling them in a crown around her head. Finally, she took a cloak and wrapped herself in it. Sara watched her without a word. When Catherine was ready, the gipsy asked:

'Where are you going?'

'To settle my accounts once and for all. What has happened today must not be repeated.'

Sara let her gaze slide to Isabelle and then back to Catherine. She lowered her voice.

'With whom will you settle your account? With that girl?'

'No. It will be enough to send her away. I wish to discuss the matter with Arnaud. He must be told what has happened to us, to Michel and myself. I think that this time he will believe me. At least this time he won't flee from me as he has been doing lately.'

The anguish in Catherine's voice touched Sara. She took the young woman by the shoulders and crushed her in an embrace so fierce that Catherine felt her faithful friend's heart beating in great regular strokes. For a brief moment, she leaned her forehead in the crook of that welcoming shoulder and let herself go.

'I don't know, Sara! What should I believe? What should I think? He has become so strange lately. What have I done to him? Why does he run from me?'

'I don't think it is only from you.'

'No, but it is mostly from me and I love him too much not to feel it to the depths of my being. And why? ... Why?'

Sara was silent for several seconds. Over Catherine's head, her face reflected a great compassion. Her lips pressed warmly against the fine skin of the young woman's temple. Then she sighed:

'Perhaps it is not so much from you that he flies. You see, he is a man seeking to fly from himself. That is much more serious!'

CHAPTER FOURTEEN

The Enemy

The bath-house at Carlat was antique and rudimentary. It could not be compared with the vast rooms, painted and hung with brocade, where the inhabitants of the palace of Burgundy bathed in tubs of polished pewter or chased silver. There was but one low vaulted room in the centre of which stood a bath of stone. Next to the bath, a great cauldron held water heated on an iron tripod placed under a ventilating hole. In another corner, a bare wooden plank resting on trestles served as a massage couch. A gutter, chiselled in the floor, served as a drain. The place was very dark. One descended into it by three steps cut into the living rock and the room was lit only by a fire-pot in an iron grille.

When Catherine got there, the door was half open and the ruddy-faced lusty wench who served as bath maid was just slipping through it. Finding herself face to face with Catherine, she became even redder.

'Where are you going?' asked Catherine. 'I was told that my husband was bathing. Has he finished already?'

The girl, with uneasy glances at the door, became redder still. Before answering, she moved away several steps.

'No, noble lady! He is still there.'

'Well?'

The bath maid bent her head. Her thick fingers nervously twisted the blue apron soaked with water. She looked at Catherine slyly, then said quickly:

'The young lady gave me a silver piece to let her take my place and rub monseigneur with oil. She . . . she was hiding behind the big pillar at the back.'

Catherine's pretty face reddened in its turn, but with fury, and the frightened girl raised her arm instinctively to protect her head against possible cuffs. The young woman made do with a pointing finger.

'Get out! . . . and hold your tongue!'

She fled without more ado. Catherine approached the half-open door. From inside no sound could be heard save that of water pouring into the tub. Catherine glanced in. What she saw made her clench her fists, but with a violent effort she kept silent. She wanted to see what would happen.

Arnaud was stretched out on his belly, head buried in his folded arms. Standing beside him, Marie was pouring oil on his back from a phial of blue glass. Slowly she began smearing it all over his body. He did not move. The girl's narrow brown hands faithfully followed the contour of the muscles which stood out in sharp relief in the rosy light of the lamp. The skin shone like brown satin and Catherine could not take her hypnotized eyes away from it. She was sharply, almost painfully, aware of those hands caressingly moving over Arnaud's body. The flames of the torch glistened on the beads of sweat on Marie's neck and face. The girl's breath was short and panting. The sensual passion aroused in her by the man stretched before her was so blatantly apparent that Catherine was devoured by jealousy and gritted her teeth. She saw Marie moisten her dry lips with the tip of her tongue. . . .

Suddenly the young girl lost her head. She bent forward and pressed her lips to Arnaud's left shoulder. . . . A flame of blind fury exploded in Catherine's head at the sight, driving her forward with talons bared. Arnaud, in surprise, had leapt up, but Catherine was already on Marie. She tore her from Arnaud and threw her to the ground. Marie shrieked and tried to get up, but Catherine fell on her with all her weight. Carried away by a primitive frenzy, the young woman had lost all control. She set about hammering at her rival's face with her fists, aiming at the eyes or the throat, trying to kill.

One idea obsessed her overheated brain: to destroy that insolent face, scratch out those green eyes, crush the viper once and for all. But Marie had recovered and was now defending herself. The girl's slenderness hid a whip-like strength, and lifting her legs, she kneed Catherine in the chest so violently that the latter was winded and lost her grip. With a supple bound, Marie got up and leapt, in her turn, on her. . . .

Arnaud, on rising to his feet, had at first stared in amazement at the ferocious struggle in which the two women were engaged. He quickly regained his self-control, grabbed a linen cloth thrown on the table and wrapped it round his loins. Then, taking hold of Marie who was on top, he pushed her behind him, but without losing hold of her. Just as roughly, he lifted Catherine up and set her on her feet. Hatred so blinded the two furies that he had to use all his strength to keep them at arm's length.

'That's enough!' he shouted. 'What has got into you? And, first of all, Marie, what are you doing here?'

'Ask her,' fumed Catherine. 'That strumpet has bought the right to rub you with oil like a bath woman. She was hiding here while you were bathing. . . .'

The idea seemed so comic to Montsalvy that he began to laugh. This was the first time in two weeks that Catherine had heard him laugh, and it only emphasized the emaciation of his face. The laugh, however, did not reach his eyes which remained sad and lustreless. In spite of that, Catherine was hurt.

'You find it amusing? Will you still laugh when you learn that today she tried to kill me, first me and then Michel. . . . Without Gauthier, I should be dead. Without Sara, you would no longer have a son!'

Arnaud blenched, but, without giving him time to reply, Marie shrieked:

'I try to kill her? I should like to know how! If you still doubt your wife is mad, this will convince you.'

'Don't worry, I'm going to tell him. . . .'

Forcing herself to regain a little calm, Catherine told the story of all that had happened since the soldier had come to her room to fetch her, omitting nothing. When she mentioned Escorneboeuf's confession, Marie shrugged her shoulders and sneered:

'The man's a liar. He would say anything to save his life. As for the affair of the keep, you would do better to tell the truth.'

'What truth?' cried Catherine.

'Only,' retorted Marie with a malicious smile, 'that you had a rendezvous in the keep with that lout. Everyone knows he is your lover!'

Arnaud released Catherine in order to grip Marie with both hands. His face was black with fury.

'Don't say that again, Marie,' he ground out. 'Unless you want me to strangle you!'

'Strangle me! What difference will that make? I know very well that the truth is disagreeable.'

'Leave her to me,' screamed Catherine, beside herself. 'I swear to make her swallow her lies and choke on them! I'll . . .'

'Enough!' cut in Arnaud. 'I intend that you shall obey me! I shall know the truth of this affair. I shall get the truth out of that miserable Escorneboeuf if I have to torture him.'

'If you want the truth,' Catherine flung out, 'put Escorneboeuf to the torture, but don't forget his accomplice! She'll
confess on the wooden horse!'

'And you!' screamed Marie. 'If they put you on it ... there
would be nothing left to show what has been going on in your
room since your husband left your bed!'

The young girl's hysterical voice had risen higher and higher
to a shriek of laughter so shrill that it was unbearable. With a
lunge Arnaud boxed her ears so violently that she fell against
the stone bath into a puddle of water.

'Get out!' he roared, fists clenched. 'Get out unless you want
me to kill you! You will hear more of this!'

She got up painfully, covered with thick mud, and held out
a hand which still sought to hold on to him, but he took her
arm, forced her to climb the three steps and threw her outside
without ceremony. The heavy door fell back and slammed
behind her. ... Slowly, Arnaud came down to Catherine who
was sitting on the stone rim of the bath settling the gown
which had been disarranged in the battle. The treatment which
Arnaud had meted out to Marie had restored her serenity and
she raised a luminous smile to her husband. She took up a cloth
and damped it in a pail of water to mop up a thread of blood
which her enemy's nails had left on her right cheek. Standing
a few feet away, Arnaud watched her sombrely, arms folded.

'What happened to Michel?'

'Oh, my love ... I thought I would go mad!' Holding back
her tears with difficulty as she relived those minutes of agony,
she recounted how she had found the infant dying and how
Sara had saved him. The memory was still so painful that she
rose and ran to her husband to throw her arms around him for
comfort. But, gently pushing her away with one hand, he burst
out:

'No! Don't touch me!'

Catherine stopped short, thunderstruck. Her face was frozen
and her eyes wide with the startled look of a soldier who has
been struck by an arrow and thrown into the arms of death just
when he believed he had attained glory. Arnaud's rebuff pierced
her to the heart and, in the terrible silence which followed, she
listened to the dying echo of those unbelievable words. To free
herself of it, she repeated incredulously:

'You *said* ... "Don't touch me"?'

Again silence! Crushing, unbearable! Arnaud turned and

picked up his clothes which were piled on a stool, and began dressing himself again. Catherine followed each movement with her eyes, waiting for him to speak, to give some explanation of his behaviour. ... But he said nothing, not a word! He did not even look at her! Eventually, she asked in a small voice:

'Why?'

He did not reply immediately. Head bent, one foot on the steps, hands buckling up the leather belt of his jerkin, he seemed to be considering. Finally he lifted his head.

'I cannot tell you ... not now! Everything which has happened today is so unbelievable.'

'Don't you believe me?'

'I haven't said that! Only, I have to think! I must be alone for that.'

Catherine stiffened, and lifted her head with a surge of pride. Where was their sweet intimacy, their marvellous confidence in each other? Now an abyss gaped between them whose depth Catherine could not fathom, but which seemed terrifying. He spoke to her as to a stranger. He wanted to *reflect* on 'all this'? ... on this double murder attempt which he should have punished immediately by the most extreme measures! A bitter wave of disappointment filled her, but she refused to give utterance to it.

'And the girl, Marie? What are you going to do with her?'

'I must think about that, too!'

'You must think!' articulated Catherine disdainfully. 'Very well, but first, listen to me: that girl must leave here this very evening. Otherwise I shall go, with my child.'

'Where would you go?'

'That is my affair. But you won't find me however hard you search! I will not live another day under the same roof as that murderess!'

Arnaud took a step towards Catherine. In the full light, the appearance of his face and his hollow eyes struck her.

'Wait till tomorrow, I beg you! Only tomorrow! Tomorrow I shall speak. I shall have made my decision. Only a single night!'

He passed a feverish hand over a forehead beaded with sweat. He seemed so distraught all of a sudden that Catherine forgot her pride. All her love for him rose to her lips. She held out supplicating hands to him:

'I pray you, my sweet lord, stop! For days and days you have not been yourself and I seem to be living in a bad dream.

Have you forgotten everything? I am Catherine, I am your wife and I love you more than the whole world! Have you forgotten our love, our kisses . . . our nights of passion? That last night when I cried out with pleasure in your arms . . . ?'

He turned his back abruptly, as though he could not bear to look at her, covering his ears with trembling hands.

'Be quiet, Catherine! Be quiet. . . . And, for the love of God, leave me alone! You, too! Tomorrow, I swear it on my honour, I will relieve all your uncertainties . . . I will make a decision! I promise you this! But, till then, leave me!'

Catherine's hands fell back limply to her sides.

'Very well, I shall wait till tomorrow. Send for me when you want to see me! But no later, Arnaud! I shall not wait one more day!'

All night Catherine was unable to sleep for a moment, listening to the storm swirling around the walls of the fortress. Sitting on the hearth stone with a blanket round her, she stayed motionless for hours. She sat with her legs folded under her and her hands locked round her knees, staring at the flames beaten down by the wind without seeing them. The storm raged over the countryside, but seemed to beset the lordly rock like wild ocean waves rushing on a great galleon. Now and then, between the shrieks of the wind, could be heard the rattle of a shutter, the crack of branches or tiles falling from the roof. All the demons of earth and sky were loose that night, but Catherine welcomed this turmoil so like the one which raged within herself. Her heart cried out with anguish and sorrow. She tortured herself seeking an impossible answer to all the questions which she asked herself. From time to time, Sara, sitting opposite her, heard her murmur:

'Why? . . . But why?'

Heavy tears rolled silently down her cheeks and fell on the green cloth of her gown. Then she lapsed again into her trance. This mute despair was so poignant that Sara tried to alleviate it.

'You are martyring yourself in vain, Catherine,' she whispered. 'You cannot understand the incomprehensible. Why don't you wait quietly for tomorrow?'

'Tomorrow? And what will tomorrow bring me, if not more sorrow? Yes, yes, I know! . . . I feel it here,' she said, a finger pressed to her heart. 'I want to know what has happened, why Arnaud has suddenly changed. He loved me. I'm sure of it. Oh!

How he loved me! And yet he turned away from me as though we were strangers. We were one flesh, one soul ... and now?'

'Now,' said Sara placidly, 'you are letting your imagination run away with you. Has your husband said that he no longer loves you?'

'He shows me. That is worse.'

'By not strangling Marie merely because she implied some nastiness between you and Gauthier? By seeking everywhere for that cursed scoundrel, Escornebouef, to hang him? He, by the way, has disappeared again. If this is not jealousy ...'

'He has a sense of fitness, that's quite different!'

Sara sighed and got up, going to the window. Shortly before curfew, she had seen the Lady of Montsalvy going to the chapel, no doubt for a final prayer. That was at least three hours ago and now she saw the old lady's tall silhouette.

'Your mother-in-law is only now coming from the chapel,' she said. 'I wonder what she has been doing all this time. Oh, come and see!'

Reluctantly, because she was not interested in anything, Catherine joined Sara and glanced into the courtyard. Isabelle's behaviour was strange. She zigzagged like a drunken woman. The wind made her great cloak crack like a flag. Her veil flew away, but she did not notice it. Catherine saw her put one hand to her head as though she were giddy. As she reached the wall of the lodging, the reflection of the guard-room fire fell on her wrinkled face through the leaded windows. It was ashen, the eyes staring. Isabelle clutched at the wall and leant against it for a moment. Her jerky movements seemed to cost her a terrible effort.

'You must help her,' said Catherine. 'She must be ill.'

But the old woman had already disappeared beneath the doorway. A moment later, in the neighbouring room, they could hear the bed creak under the weight of a heavy body. Then there was the sound of desperate sobs. Catherine and Sara stood face to face and listened dumbfounded.

'Go and see!' ordered Catherine. 'Something has happened to her.'

Sara went out without saying a word, and came back a little later. Her face was sombre and deep creases were etched between her brows. At Catherine's questioning look, she replied by a shrug of the shoulders.

'She won't say anything! I suppose it is reaction from the terror she suffered a little while ago. She hoped to find some sort of peace in church, to my mind, but it didn't help her.'

Her quiet voice allowed nothing to be lost of the sounds which came through the wall. ... In her room, Isabelle de Montsalvy still wept. ... But suddenly, it no longer interested Catherine. The reason for those tears, after all, could mean nothing to her. Each for himself and God for all! She had enough sorrow of her own. Slowly, she turned to take her place in the corner of the hearth. In passing, she bent for a moment over Michel's cradle. The little one slept like an angel. ... A little sweetness penetrated his mother's heart and at the same time a plan came into her mind. If Arnaud refused to believe her, if he refused to send away that Marie, she would go away as she had threatened! She would return to her home. ... To Burgundy!

As it came into her mind, the word astonished her. Burgundy! She had bound herself so closely to her husband, she had assimilated his thoughts and his hatred so well, that Burgundy had become for her the enemy's country. ... Yet her mother, her sister and her Uncle Mathieu lived there. She had not seen them for three years and she suddenly missed them cruelly. In this castle battered by the wind, she conjured up for a moment the shop in the rue du Griffon in the shadow of the towers of Our Lady of Dijon, the house in the fields, crouching in the folds of the hills of Marsannay amid the sprawling bounty of the vines, the grey-blue sky of Dijon or the clouds flying quickly over the plain of the Saône, the changing sky of Burgundy to which Dijon flung the fantastic jagged backdrop of its roofs and towers and church steeples, black, blue and gold. Catherine closed her eyes, seeing again the sweet fair face of her mother, the fat, ruddy one of Uncle Mathieu under its travelling hood, the narrow, pale profile of her sister, Loyse, a nun in the convent of Tart. And under her closed lids came tears of a sudden desire to see them again so acute that it was painful, to find again the tender refuge of maternal arms. What was Jacquette Legoix thinking now without news of her daughter for so long? She must cry and pray often. ... Behind her image, so tenderly evoked, Catherine saw another shape rise up, tall, slender, austere, the unyielding form of Duke Philippe. He was a just man but so haughty! Would he have vented his spite as an abandoned lover on innocent people? She hoped not. All of a sudden she longed to know what had happened to them all ... Ermengarde de Châteauvilain, stout, formidable and adorable in the crimson gowns she loved, the elegant shape of

Jacques de Roussay, the young captain of the Guards who loved her so tenderly, Jean Van Eyck, the painter who never wearied of painting her, and the outlandish silhouette, gilded, bedizened and dazzling, of her friend Jean de Saint-Rémy, who had become Messire Golden Fleece, King-at-Arms of Burgundy.

Now came the ghost of a slender shape in a blue silk robe, wearing a mammoth turban, the colour and size of a fine pumpkin, on his head. He had two bright eyes above a beard as white as snow ... and he was, perhaps, the dearest friend of all ... Abou-al-Khayr, the little Moorish doctor.

He had always had some philosophic dictum, or some poetic truth up his sleeve to underline the meaning of each moment of one's existence. What was it he had said when she had emerged bruised and battered from her first encounter with Arnaud at the wayside inn? Something which had struck her forcibly then and which seemed even more valid today. ... Ah, yes! He had said: 'The path of true love is paved with flesh and blood. You who pass over it, lift up your skirts!' O Lord! What road had ever been so thorny and difficult as that of her love? So much pain and blood! And even now what new wound was she about to receive at the hands of the man for whose sake she had left everything and everyone, abandoned love, riches and fame, and whom she could not possibly stop adoring?

With a weary gesture Catherine pushed back the hot, heavy mass of hair which had tumbled over her face and looked at Sara with eyes brilliant with tears.

'Sara,' she murmured, 'I want to go home. I want to see Maman again and Uncle Mathieu and all ... the others.'

'And the Duke Philippe too?'

Catherine collapsed with a cry at Sara's feet and buried her head in her lap. She began to sob desperately.

'I don't know! I don't know anything any more! ... I'm so unhappy. I wish this misery would stop and we could be as we were before!'

Sara did not reply. She was listening to the muffled sounds coming from beyond the closed door, which seemed to be a counterpoint for Catherine's – it was like a dialogue of tears between mother and wife. They were both weeping for the same man, and Sara knew that the reason was the same for both women. She knew Arnaud's secret, which he had confided to her one night making her swear never to reveal it to a soul.

If she could have said anything to alleviate Catherine's distress
she would gladly have broken her promise but she knew if she
did sorrow would only become despair. Better to let things go
on as they were, praying God that her poor girl would not suffer
too much.

'My God,' she prayed silently, 'My God, You are all justice
and all goodness. She has done nothing wrong other than love
this man more than everything, more than herself, more than
You even! Do not break her heart!'

Just then the wind howled and roared in the chimney with
such force that the flames flared up and Sara was almost
scorched and had to move out of the way. Her superstitious
soul read this as an answer to her prayer. Surely an evil omen?
She crossed herself quickly, still caressing Catherine's hair with
her free hand.

When cold dawn lit the stormswept countryside Fortunat
came and scratched at Catherine's door. Sara opened it. The
little Gascon edged into the room, cap in hand, and tiptoed
across to Catherine as though approaching an altar. He had
not had much sleep either. His face was grey under its tan, his
mouth drooped with fatigue and his eyelids kept dropping as
though he could hardly keep awake. He bowed painfully before
Catherine.

'Milady,' he said, 'Monseigneur has sent me to tell you that
he will see you about the hour of tierce after Mass, and he asks
whether that time will be convenient to you.'

The formality of this procedure brought a bitter smile to
Catherine's lips. Had they come to *this* then – the interchange
of messages and requests for an audience? The faint hope
which Sara had awoken in her was quenched again.

'Why should it not be convenient to me? This time or any
other. ... Where am I to meet my husband? Will he come
here?'

The poor squire's embarrassment was easy to see. He bowed
his head and twisted his cap in his fingers.

'No, he will send me to fetch you. Since dawn there have
been suspicious movements in the countryside and monseigneur
cannot leave the defences.'

This courteous and formal address exasperated Sara. She
took Fortunat fiercely by the shoulders, pulled him to his feet
and turned him to face her.

'Enough of this ceremonial, my boy. I have a few questions

to put to you myself. I don't suppose you have left your master's side since yesterday evening?'

'No.'

'What has he done since leaving the bath-house?'

'He reviewed the guard and gave them their night's instructions. Then he went to his room where I served him some cold venison. Then he went to the chapel. His mother joined him there. I don't know what they said but they talked for a long time.'

Sara nodded. Then: 'Go on ... what then? Did he see the Demoiselle de Comborn?'

'Yes,' Fortunat answered, instinctively lowering his voice and looking about him uneasily. 'He sent me to fetch her after chapel. She was asleep and I had to wake her up. I don't know what they said either but I heard weeping.'

'Weeping? Who was weeping?'

'The young lady! I did not know why, of course, but I knew a moment later when the door opened and monseigneur came out. ... He was carrying ... a whip in his hand still ... and he must have been using it because the young lady was cowering in a corner with her clothes torn, trembling like a leaf. Monseigneur pointed to her: "Shut her up in the Guillot Tower," he said. "She may have what she needs but she is not to come out under any pretext. Put two men at her door. No one must go near her. ..."'

Catherine and Sara exchanged puzzled looks. Why Arnaud should have used her so violently was easily explained in view of what had happened, but why had he imprisoned her like this when the simplest thing would have been to hoist her up on a horse and send her under escort to Comborn?

'He must want to keep her here!' Catherine remarked acidly.

'Fortunat said that there had been suspicious movements in the valley,' Sara interposed quickly. 'Messire Arnaud could hardly send her away today or spare the men to escort her.'

'Why doesn't he send her on her own?' Catherine raged. 'Why such precautions for a murderess? Let her go ... in the Devil's care, and if anything befalls her it would only be what she deserved!'

The squire spread his arms wide in a helpless gesture. Catherine's anger seemed reasonable to him, but he had a boundless admiration for his master, and an almost religious devotion which forbade him to offer even the slightest criticism

of him. He merely bowed again and repeated: 'After Mass at
the hour of tierce,' and then disappeared.

Catherine started pacing up and down the room, finding it
hard to keep her rebellious feelings under control. She longed
to relieve her feelings by some violent gesture – to cry out,
swear like a man, revile heaven and earth, relieve the misery of
her own heart by calling upon herself the criticism and dis-
approval of others. She suddenly understood the almost sensual
joy in doing evil when suffering has grown intolerable, maddening the soul.

'I know,' Sara said, reading her thoughts. 'But women can
only resort to tears or silence. You must see to your baby now,
and then I shall help you prepare for Mass.'

The castle was coming to life around them. The sentries'
calls echoed across the battlements. Cattle-shed and stable doors
creaked open. The horses were being led out to be groomed. The
courtyard resounded with clucking chickens and the servants'
ribald jokes. The blacksmith was already hammering on his
anvil in the forge and the chapel bell was ringing for the dawn
office.

Catherine loved this dawn hubbub as a rule but today it exasperated her. She would have preferred a silence so deep she
could listen to her own heartbeats. After changing and feeding
Michel, she asked for a tub of hot water to be brought, and
plunged into it, trying to dissipate the weariness which resulted
from her sleepless night. Sara scrubbed her with a brush till
her skin glowed, and after some minutes of this treatment
Catherine felt better. Her body was relaxed and her spirits restored. Her old fighting spirit came back to her, and with it the
desire to escape from this dismal torpor into which she was
plunged. Before abandoning everything and returning home,
however, she was now resolved to fight to the end.

Sara gauged this change of attitude from the way Catherine
proffered her head for the coif of fine embroidered lawn held in
place by a short hennin of starched linen. Her long graceful
neck reared proudly and there was a belligerent gleam in the
large shadowy eyes.

'There, that's better,' she said, not making it clear whether
she referred to Catherine's headdress or the change in her
spirits. 'Now go! I'll stay here with the babe.'

Catherine picked up her great black cloak and wrapped it
round her as the chapel bell began to ring for Mass. She went
down the stairs and crossed the guardroom where Fortunat was

busily polishing a long sword while two soldiers strove to rekindle a dying fire. On the threshold she stopped to breathe in the fresh morning air. The storm had passed and the sky was perfectly clear and a lovely limpid blue. The air fragrant with the scent of wet trees and new grass, and the courtyard, even the old gallows tree with its twisted branches, and the countryside all about were washed clean. Catherine soaked herself for a moment in this atmosphere of rebirth and then slowly betook herself to the chapel. She glanced at the Saint John Tower, still and silent now, and then at the Guillot Tower, which was just as quiet. The servants stood back to let her pass; among them she recognized the fat bath woman but she passed by without looking at her.

The chapel was damp and smelt like a cellar. The thick walls of rough-hewn stone oozed water which had rusted the ironwork and left long black mildewy streaks on the rough wooden crucifix. Catherine shivered as she reached the seignorial pew. The curé of Carlat, who generally officiated at the castle, started Mass after she arrived. He was a timid, frail old man who seemed to be in fear of some permanent threat, but he had gentle, compassionate eyes. Catherine, who had been to him for Confession, knew that he had a saintly soul which overflowed with compassion for wretched mortals crushed under the weight of their sins.

She knelt and opened the heavy, silver-bound Missal and forced herself to follow the service; but her thoughts were elsewhere. They dwelt on the absent Arnaud, on the captive Marie and on her mother-in-law. What had kept that almost fanatically pious woman from Mass? Catherine still seemed to hear the old lady's sobs. These had not been, as Sara unkindly suggested, tears of self-pity and guilt, but of despair and distress. ... But why?

Impatience for battle to be joined possessed her and she heard the *Ite, Missa est* with a sigh of relief. A last sign of the Cross, a final genuflection and Catherine turned on her heel, walking quickly out of the chapel. Fortunat was pacing up and down in the porch. He came up to her.

'Monseigneur is waiting for you, Dame Catherine ...' he began, but she interrupted him with a curt gesture.

'Go on, I shall follow you.'

She followed him silently. She felt that by speaking now she might squander the strength she had built up since dawn, when she had started preparing for this interview. As she walked she muttered a prayer under her breath. It was a little incoherent perhaps but if God could not read a poor human's heart, who could?

She crossed the courtyard at Fortunat's heels and started up a narrow stone stairway which led to the battlements. They soon left the open air for the rough walls of the interminable covered passageway which ran right round the ramparts, following the curve of the tower walls and crowning the fortress with a circlet of fire when the enemy attacked. They found Arnaud on this roundway. He wore full armour and stood leaning against a loophole with a sombre air, examining the valley where the morning mist was lifting, revealing velvety furrows, pale green streamlets, rosy roofs with smoking chimneys, and the dark russet oxen plodding to the pastures yoked together, two by two.

He stood with his back to them and did not move as their footsteps approached down the roundway. Perhaps he was trying to snatch a final moment for reflection? Perhaps he did not yet feel ready for this moment when he must meet his love head-on, in open battle?

Fortunat went ahead, murmuring something in a low voice. Then the steel-clad statue slowly turned towards her while Fortunat slipped away. She saw her husband's dark eyes gleaming under the raised visor of the black steel helmet. He looked at her without speaking. She summoned up her courage, and to break this interminable, suffocating silence she said gently:

'You sent for me? Here I am. . . .'

He did not react; he stood playing with a crested dagger which he had taken from his belt and the sun struck sinister reflections from his steel casque. Suddenly he seemed to make up his mind. He raised his head and looked at his wife.

'I sent for you to say farewell.'

'Farewell? Do you want me to leave?'

His faint smile faded at once.

'No, Catherine, I want you to stay here! It is I who must leave. Leave never to return. I want you to know . . .'

'You want to go away? To leave?' she repeated the words as though they had no meaning for her. A crushing fatigue weighted her limbs like lead and she sank down between the huge arms of the embrasure. Then, at length, the real meaning of this strange declaration pierced the fog which seemed to envelop her mind.

'Leave?' she repeated. 'But why? Where would you go?'

He turned from her, resumed his contemplation of the countryside and shrugged.

'I don't know where yet ... but perhaps Provence! One can live well down there, beside a blue sea bluer than a summer sky, where the white castles are surrounded by exotic flowers.'

'But if you want to live there, so do I! And if you want to go away, we can go. I am quite ready.'

Again that sad smile. He bowed his head and his voice was mournful.

'I know that I am treating you harshly. But you must be brave, Catherine. I know you are courageous. When two people have made a mistake I think they should have the courage to end it before it is too late. It is not you I shall take with me. I shall take Marie!'

Catherine fell back stunned against the stones. Arnaud's face was haggard and drawn as a martyr's in the arena, but he did not look round and his voice was steady. He had said 'I shall take Marie' quite coldly and calmly. It was a carefully-thought-out decision.

'Marie!' Catherine faltered. 'You wish to take Marie? But why?'

The reply struck her like a thunderbolt.

'I love her!'

Catherine was too numbed by these words to react, and he went on heavily:

'Look, people make mistakes in their lives, Marie and I have known each other for a long time ... and I never thought of her as anything but a little girl. You dazzled me, and I desired you ... but .. when we came back, I saw that she had changed. We are of the same blood, she and I. You must try to understand, Catherine.'

The furious surge of anger boiling up in her heart brought Catherine to her senses. The terrible words pounded in her head like hammer blows. They were not, *could* not, be true! They did not even sound convincing. She raised her clenched fists.

'You love her, you say? You dare to say so to *me*? Have you forgotten everything which has bound us together for ten years? *Ten years!* Are you mad, or don't you know what you are saying? If it is true you love her, then you have a strange way of making love! With a whip?'

He paled and the shadows on his face deepened under the raised visor. His nostrils were pinched and his mouth so tightly shut it looked like a thin red line.

'One beats a dog which has done something wrong even though one may love it! I have told you – she and I are of the same race. She understands why she must be punished. It was for disobeying me. I ordered her to leave you alone.'

Catherine started to laugh, and went on and on . . . harsh bursts of dry, metallic laughter which echoed along the wooden gallery. It was a hateful laugh, uglier than sobbing.

'So?' she went on after a moment. 'You call her attempted murder of myself and Michel *disobedience*, do you? If that is the case you really must be of the same blood. You have no heart! None! The stones of this wall and the wolves howling at night in the woods are more human than either of you. You want to leave? Wonderful, my lord! Then get you gone with your new love! And I shall return to mine!'

Had her life depended on it, Catherine could not have explained what had called this particular remark forth, unless it was a desire to return blow for blow, injury for injury. She saw with bitter joy that the shaft had struck home – Arnaud fell back against the wall.

'What did you say?' he asked angrily. 'What love?'

'The one I never should have left: Duke Philippe. I too will leave here, Arnaud de Montsalvy. I will return to my home, to Burgundy, to my lands, my castles, my jewels. . . .'

'And the reputation of a fallen woman?'

'Fallen?' She gave a short, infinitely sad laugh. 'Am I not lost enough already here? Do you expect me to stay in this ruin of a castle wasting my youth and beauty in contemplating the heavens, praying with your mother and occupying myself with good works, while I pray Heaven to bring you back to me when you have finished with your bag of bones? No, if you think that, sire, you are mistaken! I shall go home . . . and I shall take my son!'

'No!'

Arnaud's voice carried so far that one of the sentries pacing up and down on the next door tower stopped in mid-step, lance at the ready . . . searching for the origin of the cry. Then more quietly, but with savage determination he repeated: 'No, Catherine! You will not leave. You will stay here whether you want to or not.'

'While you go off with *her*! You must be mad. I won't stay here more than an hour. By nightfall I and my people will have left this unhappy spot. I shall take Sara and Gauthier . . . and my child!'

Her voice faltered at this word. She could already see this departure, the horses' hooves clattering away over the hard earth, and the castle vanishing in the mist, blotted out like a dream ... a dream which had lasted ten long years!

'That way,' she said, 'you won't have to break with your past. You can stay here with your mother and that ... and you won't have to betray your honour as a knight!'

'How so?' Arnaud asked dryly.

'By abandoning a castle entrusted to you by a friend. You must look after Carlat! You must love this girl very much to treat me like this and destroy your military career as well!'

Catherine might tremble all over as she spoke, but Arnaud seemed more than ever a steel statue. The visor shadowed his face so Catherine could not see the despair in his eyes. He stepped back a few paces so as to make it harder still.

'Listen to me, Catherine,' he said in a faraway voice. 'Whether you like it or not you are the Lady of Montsalvy, the mother of my son, and no Montsalvy shall ever live in Burgundy. Faith is a sacred duty.'

'Except where your wife is concerned,' Catherine said bitterly. 'You might perhaps have let me go had I been alone. But you are base enough to take advantage of me through my son, to force me to remain as your captive, in spite of myself, in spite of everything, of your own treachery. ... And you want me to stay here alone, abandoned in a foreign country, in the midst of dangers, while you depart to live with I don't know what stupid paramour. ...'

Suddenly her sorrow overcame her anger. She ran to her husband and threw her arms round his neck, resting her tear-wet cheek against his cold polished steel breastplate.

'This must be a nightmare. I shall soon awake. Or are you testing me to see if I am truly faithful? Yes, that must be it! This girl has angered you with her slanders and you wanted to be sure. ... But you are sure now, aren't you, you *are* sure I love you? Then stop torturing me for pity's sake, stop doing this cruel thing to me ... you see how it torments me! Without you my life is meaningless ... I am as lost as a child at night in a storm. Have pity on me, stay with me ... we loved each other too well for there to be nothing else left. ...'

Under her head she could hear his heart beating, below the steel carapace. It beat strongly: great, heavy, powerful beats, but surely they were too fast? Could it be that this heart on which she had so often slept had ceased beating for her? The

pain of tearing her heart asunder from his made her want to
cry aloud. Catherine tried to tighten her clasp, but Arnaud
gently loosened her arms and moved away.

'What use is it trying to awaken what is now dead,
Catherine? I can do nothing about it and neither can you ...
we were not made for each other, after all. Now listen to my
words because they are my last. I am not deserting this fortress.
I have sent to Bernard and asked him to relieve me of my command and send a captain immediately. ... As soon as he comes
... and that should not be long, I shall leave. To you I recommend my son, my family name, my mother.'

'Everything which might be a burden to you,' Catherine
cried. 'But you can't keep me here ... not you nor anyone else.
As soon as your back is turned I shall go! And the name of
Montsalvy shall soon shine in the arms of Burgundy! Of *Burgundy*, do you hear? I shall teach Michel to hate the Armagnacs. Later on I'll make him a page to Duke Philippe, a soldier
of Burgundy who will know no other master but the Grand
Duke of the West!'

'I'll soon put a stop to that ... even when I'm not there!'
Arnaud threatened.

'No one has ever stopped me doing what I wanted – not
even Philippe of Burgundy, and he was more powerful than
you!'

'Guards!'

The word struck like a blow. Suddenly the husband and wife
standing facing each other were enemies.

The sentries were not far away. Two ran up. Arnaud pointed
to his wife who stood with her back to the loophole, fists
clenched and deathly white with rage and misery.

'Conduct Madame de Montsalvy to her room. She is not to
leave it on any pretext. Take good care. This is an order and
you will answer for it with your heads. Put two men at her
door and one in her room. She must be followed if she goes to
her mother and she is not to go anywhere else. Her servant,
Sara, may have access to her and also the man named Gauthier.
Now go, and tell Monsieur de Cabanes to come to me.'

He turned towards Catherine.

'I am sorry to have to treat you with such severity, madame,
but you force it upon me. At least give me your word that
you will not try to escape!'

'Never! Imprison me then, messire. This will be the crowning honour you have heaped upon me.'

Upright, head held high, she turned and went towards the stairs with the guards at her heels.

Her movements were those of an automaton. She walked like a sleepwalker, her brain clouded, eyes burning and her head heavy and sore. She had the curious feeling that she had just been condemned to death and been executed and, though dead, still managed to descend the steps of the scaffold ... the immensity of the tragedy which had struck her was so great she could not yet measure it. She was crushed, numbed ... later on, when this blessed numbness wore off, pain would return in double strength. For the moment her anger and indignation was mingled with a feeling of contempt which eased it somewhat.

Reaching the threshold of her room, she stopped. Sara, who had been standing next to Michel's cradle, turned and saw her, standing there as pale as a ghost, between the two men-at-arms in the doorway. She gave a cry and ran towards her.

'Catherine! 'Od's Blood!'

Catherine held out her arms in a pitifully appealing gesture and opened her mouth to say something ... a wave of heat rose to her head, and it seemed suddenly as though her brain were on fire. A terrible pain swept her and she fell at Sara's feet with a faint moan, writhing in the grip of a terrible convulsion. Her eyes rolled upwards, her teeth clenched, foam appeared on her lips and her arms and legs jerked spasmodically. She rolled on the cold flagstones, to the great terror of the men-at-arms who fled as fast as their legs would carry them. She did not hear Sara's cry of dismay or see Gauthier burst into the room like a cannon-ball, or the other servants running to her. The physical pain which had taken hold of her was so grievous that for the moment at least she was unconscious of the outside world. She was spared the knowledge that her love was ended. It was perhaps a form of divine mercy, but Sara could not help feeling that, in trying to bring succour to Catherine, they would just be prolonging her calvary.

CHAPTER FIFTEEN

The Dagger of the Montsalvys

How long did Catherine float in the abyss of unconsiousness, in those black waters of terror and pain which lie in wait for a woman driven to the utter limits of despair? Even Sara, who never left the bedside of the one being dearer to her than life itself, could not have said. The gipsy remembered that terrible evening when Paris was torn by demented rioters and Barnaby the Cockleshell Man had come to ask her to tend an unconscious child. Once again she saw the little inert form, the pale face under the gleaming mane of tangled hair, that tragically blank stare. . . . She had fought, inch by inch, night and day, to snatch that child from death and madness. That was the night Catherine had tried to save Michel de Montsalvy from the mob and her own father had paid with his life for his daughter's reckless generosity. Would it all begin again and must Catherine be snatched to the brink of death the day the Montsalvys were taken from her as on the day they had first entered her life? How would this young woman who had been so deeply hurt ever survive the shock?

Meanwhile Catherine, deep in the cloudy realms of fever, rose now and again to the surface of consciousness. She recognized Sara and also a tall black figure which stood there silently and cried when it looked at her. And it was this which surprised her most of all – why should the Dame de Montsalvy cry at her bedside? Was she really dead and were they going to bury her? The idea washed over her, sweet and peaceful as a draught of spring water, and then the demons returned and Catherine drifted back into the shadows.

In reality only five days had passed when Catherine finally regained her senses. Her eyes opened on the glory of sun and blue sky outside her open window. A hand rested on her forehead and she found things as they had been each time she regained consciousness: Isabelle de Montsalvy was standing at the foot of her bed, in her black robes.

'The fever has left her!' Sara's voice trembled with joy, as she stood at the foot of the bed.

'God be praised!' exclaimed the silhouette in black leaning over the bed in its turn. Then a strange, almost incredible thing happened: Isabelle de Montsalvy took Catherine's limp hand which was lying on the sheet and pressed it to her lips. Then she turned and moved away as though she feared that the sight of her would upset the sick woman. For a moment Catherine breathed in the delicious mild air of the room, let her eyes drink in the pale golden splendour of the sun, and her ears the sweetness of Michel's baby gurgle as he lay in his cradle waving his fists at the beauty of the day, like tiny pink birds ... how sweet and lovely he was!

Then suddenly the truth came back to her. A bitter wave of sorrow swept over her. She made a desperate effort to sit up. Sara intervened at once.

'Lie quietly. You are too weak.'

'Arnaud,' she faltered. 'Arnaud ... where is he? Oh, I remember ... I remember it all now! He doesn't love me any more. ... He never loved me! He loves someone else ... someone else!'

Her voice became an anguished shriek and Isabelle de Montsalvy came towards her, fearing a relapse. She took the transparent hand which beat the air like a pigeon's wing.

'Be calm, my child ... you must not think or talk ... you must think of yourself, your son!'

But Catherine gripped her hand and half raised herself. Amidst the glowing mass of her loose hair her face was flushed across the cheekbones and there was a visionary light in her eyes.

'He has gone, hasn't he? Tell me, I beg you. He is gone? Oh, oh ...!' She loosened her hold suddenly and fell back on her linen pillows. 'Don't tell me,' she said, with an expression of poignant sadness. 'I know he has gone! I feel it by the emptiness around me ... he has gone ... with her!'

'Yes,' Sara murmured in a heavy voice. 'He left yesterday.'

Catherine did not reply. She was struggling with all her feeble strength to keep back the rising tears. She closed her eyes.

'There is too much light, Sara,' she muttered. 'I don't like it. Why is the sun shining? It must be my enemy too. ...'

But she still saw the sun below the screen of her lowered lids. She saw it glowing along the path of two riders who travelled a green shining road side by side, a road so loud with bird-song that even the horses' hooves did not drown it. She heard the hoof-beats ... clattering along the road, sending stones flying in the haste of their elopement ... the two riders were going far away, fleeing like malefactors to hide their guilty, stolen joy. And the hoof-beats and the stones all seemed to pound remorselessly at the young woman's head. Sara saw her cross her hands, which had grown transparent during these five days of sickness, over her breast and press it tight as if she would drag her heart out. Sara could not know that a broken heart hurt so terribly. Catherine's breathing filled the room, strong and stertorous like a man's after running a distance at full stretch. Sara heard Catherine murmur:

'I want to see him again so much ... just once! And hear his voice again ... feel his lips on my cheek once more, and then die! Only once more. . . .'

She was so weak and miserable in this humble prayer that Sara sank down beside her and folded her in her arms and pressed her cheek against hers.

'My little one, don't torment yourself any more. Try to win ... for your child's sake ... and for mine! What would become of old Sara without you? There is still so much left in the world, so much happiness for you. Life is not ended.'

'He was my life. . . .'

Never had the bond of a promise weighed so heavily on Sara. She longed to tell what she had seen during those five days and nights. The man who stood, crushed with grief, motionless in the window embrasure where the sick woman could not see him. He stood there dry-eyed, hands clasped, without eating or sleeping. . . . So long as danger had remained he had not wavered, but then, when at last the apothecary of Aurillac had pronounced her out of danger, he had risen and left the room without a backward glance. An hour later, in the crimson glory of a windy sunset, he left the castle on horse-back, leading another horse behind him on which sat Marie de Comborn, heavily veiled. Sara had gone up to the Black Tower to watch them depart, entrusting Catherine to her mother-in-law. Not once during the descent did Arnaud turn to speak to his companion, who looked, riding along with bowed head, more like a captive than a woman riding to a happy destiny. . . . But Sara kept all this to herself because she felt that it would only make Catherine's pain more grievous if she knew.

The two women stayed for a long while clasped together, mingling their tears. Catherine found relief in tears at last. They

seemed to wash away a little of the bitterness and heal the
wounds, and Sara's maternal tenderness itself had strange
healing powers. With her head leaning against her friend's
capacious bosom Catherine felt like a little fishing-smack which
reaches harbour by a miracle after being dismasted and damaged by a storm.

'Sara,' Catherine said, after a moment. 'When I am quite well
we shall go back to our home, to Dijon!'

The gipsy woman did not answer, for just then a bizarre and
terrible sound broke loose in the castle courtyard. Strange,
strident music, which spoke of fog and rain with its piercing,
keening note. It resembled nothing in melodic form that
Catherine had ever heard. It seemed to wring the nerves and
yet it had a sort of power and vitality. Catherine listened in
astonishment.

'What can that be?' she asked. 'It is like the pan pipes poor
Étienne played at Montsalvy. . . .'

She spoke the name with difficulty; it seemed to stick in her
throat. Sara, seeing that her attention was temporarily diverted,
quickly replied:

'They are not pan pipes but something like them. The Scots,
who play the instrument, call them the bagpipes. They are
composed of a sort of skin sack from which several pipes pro-
trude, and it is on these the musician plays. The music is outlandish but their dress is even more so. They fight with bare
legs in strange, short skirts patterned with checks and stripes,
and they look barbaric and terrifying.'

'Scots?' Catherine asked in amazement. 'Scots here?'

'For two days,' Sara replied. 'The new captain sent by Count
Bernard brought a little company of these men. They are all
down there with him.'

Catherine had often seen Scotsmen at the court of King
Charles, come to serve France in the train of the Stuarts and of
Constable Buchan, predecessor of Richemont. ... Arnaud had
pointed them out to her and there had been some in the retinue
of Joan the Maid. But, suddenly, Catherine lost interest. Thinking of them had reminded her of Arnaud and brought back
sweet memories which could only wound her now. As Sara
went on talking about the new master of Carlat, she asked, to
silence her:

'What is he called?'

'Kennedy,' Sara replied. 'Messire Hugh Kennedy. He looks a bit
wild but he is a true knight.'

Down below the shrill music of the pipes faded till it was no louder than a wail. A faint wail which, before long, put her to sleep.

The sickness left Catherine as suddenly as it had come. It had in part been brought on by exhaustion and rest soon cured it. Two days after recovering full consciousness the sick woman left her bed to sit in the ingle-nook in a huge chair well padded with cushions. But when Sara brought her a russet silk gown to wear she pushed it away.

'No! From now on I shall wear nothing but black!'

'Black? But why?'

A faint smile contorted rather than illumined Catherine's pale face.

'I am still the Lady of Montsalvy and now I have no husband. Therefore I can only be a widow. Give me a black gown.'

Sara did not answer. She went to fetch the dress she asked for, feeling, in her heart of hearts, that Catherine's beauty would only be enhanced by black. So it was, dressed in a black velvet gown with a quilted cap of the same material from which hung a muslin veil, that Catherine waited to receive the new governor of Carlat. She has asked him to come to see her, not out of curiosity, but to raise various points about her personal situation. Sorrow could keep the realities of life at a distance for a time but Catherine was too well accustomed to facing up to these bravely to be able to ignore them for long. Besides, it was essential for her to bestir herself in some way or other. If she had to live idle in this castle, watching the time slip by, she knew that she would go out of her mind.

When Kennedy entered the room she remembered having seen his striking figure at King Charles's court. He stood almost as tall as Gauthier and quite as ruddy, but while the Norman's hair was fair with reddish lights in it the Scot's was the dark red of pear-wood, matching his face, tanned to the colour of an old brick. His features were heavy but his expression was cheerful. A slightly retroussé nose and a pair of flax-blue eyes predisposed her in his favour. But when he smiled, his lips curled back from his fine white teeth in a way which suggested that one could not always rely on his good humour.

In fact, Hugh Kennedy, who had come from the Highlands of Scotland with James Stuart, Earl of Buchan and Constable of France, was a redoubtable adventurer. He had always fought the English fiercely because his hatred for them was innate and

he still continued to do so. ... After the rude life of his own
mountains the French countryside, ravaged as it was, seemed
attractive enough for him to wish to remain there. The Stuarts
possessed the fief of Aubigny, north of Bourges, by royal gift
and all the other Scots tended to gravitate there. To the good
folk of the Loire valley this meant constant raids from Kennedy and his like, raids which they would gladly have been
spared because this friend of France maltreated them as badly
as the English invader.

All this went through Catherine's mind as the new governor
bowed before her, gracefully enough for so ponderous a fellow,
almost brushing the stone floor with his plumed bonnet. He
wore the strange dress of his country: close-fitting hose whose
gay plaid in blue, yellow and red was repeated in the great
woollen scarf which crossed the battered cuirass and was
fastened at one shoulder by a heavy tooled silver brooch. A buff
leather doublet was attached to the cuirass and covered his
broad shoulders. His sword belt held a sword like a Roman
gladiator's, and a curious sack made of goat-skin. On entering
Catherine's room Kennedy laid his claymore in one corner – the
traditional two-handed sword whose name the Scots shouted in
battle as a rallying cry. In spite of its size and weight Kennedy
handled his claymore with alarming ease.

'Madame, I did not expect to have the honour of saluting
once again the most beautiful lady in France when I came here,
otherwise I should have made greater haste.'

He spoke rapid and fluent French which was almost without
a trace of accent. Doubtless he had long occupied himself with
the French peasantry! Catherine's lips curved in a smile which
did not reach her eyes.

'Thank you for the compliment, sire. Forgive me for not
having asked you to call on me before but my health ...'

'I know, madame. Do not apologize. I am grateful for the
privilege you have accorded me ... doubly happy since it
proves you are mending. This evening my men will sing a Te
Deum in your honour in the chapel.'

Catherine's hopes rose as he spoke. She had feared that she
might be faced with an implacable gaoler but the Scotsman's
behaviour suggested that he might not be so strict with her.
She pressed his fingers in a friendly manner and gestured to a
seat. Then ...

'I do not know what Count Bernard said to you when he sent
you here, messire, or what Messire de Montsalvy may have

said on your arrival, but I should like to know what my position here is – am I a prisoner?'

Kennedy's eyes went round as blue marbles beneath their
arched brows.

'A prisoner? How so, madame? Your husband, whom I have
known for many years, has entrusted me with this fortress and
yourself, telling me that he must be absent for many months. I
therefore have the honour of defending you, madame, and the
pleasure of watching over you.'

'Perfect!' Catherine said. 'Then you will be only too happy
to oblige me. I think I would like to make a short journey soon.
Will you see to my escort?'

She managed to smile charmingly as she spoke, but he did
not answer in the same vein. His cheerfulness vanished in a
twinkling; his face lengthened and a great furrow marked his
brow.

'Gracious lady,' he said, with an effort, 'this ... is alas the
one wish I may not grant you. You must not leave Carlat
under any pretext ... save perhaps to visit Montsalvy, in which
case I am to entrust you to the venerable father Abbot with
two trusty men to take care of you.'

Catherine's hands tightened on the carved arm-rests and her
eyes flashed.

'Do you realize what you are saying, messire, and to whom?'

'To the wife of a dear friend,' the Scot breathed. 'To one
who has been entrusted to my keeping, and is dearer to me
than my own kith and kin. Even if it brings down your
anger upon me I cannot forgo the duty Montsalvy laid upon
me or break my word. You see, your husband is my brother-
in-arms.'

Well! Catherine's nostrils flared indignantly. Was she always
to have her way barred by this unreasonable masculine solid-
arity? They clung together like the fingers of a hand and nothing, it seemed, could break the spell. Clearly she would have to
try a ruse ... or even brute force. The Scot was strong but what
man could prevail against her trusty Norman?

Catherine turned with exceeding grace and beckoned to Sara.

'Go and find Gauthier for me,' she said with unaccustomed
sweetness. 'There is something I want to say to him.'

'I am sorry, madame,' Sara replied. 'But Gauthier went hunting at dawn.'

'Hunting? And who gave him leave?'

The governor spoke: 'I did, gracious lady. On our arrival

the other evening my men killed a bear. The female is raging
the countryside maddened with anger and a man has already
been killed. Your servant ... an astonishing fellow, between
ourselves ... asked me to let him hunt it alone. It seems he
knows more than anyone about killing bears. And I must say I
can quite believe it.'

Catherine sighed. Gauthier's passion for hunting was no news
to her. The experienced forester could no more miss the spoor
of an animal in the woods than an old war horse fail to hear
the bugle call. She felt some amusement at the thought of her
giant who could find nothing better to do that roam the highways and byways now that his anxiety about her life had been
stilled.

'Indeed, messire, you were quite right. My squire is a woods-
man; he loves the wide open spaces above all others, and he is
a remarkable hunter. Let us hope he happens upon your
bear. . . .'

She held out a hand as a sign that the audience was over.
Kennedy took her hand and pressed it to his lips.

'Have you no favours to ask of me? Apart from letting you
wander the countryside unguarded there is nothing I would
not do for you and . . .'

He got no further. The door of the room burst open and
Gauthier appeared on the threshold carrying a strange burden
over his shoulder. He was indescribably filthy and scarlet from
his exertions. Catherine saw a greenish face framed by long
black hair hanging down over the giant's chest.

Gauthier paused a moment, looking from Kennedy to
Catherine so pale and upright in her chair. Then he loosened
the load he was carrying and before she could utter a word he
had laid the body of Marie de Comborn at her feet.

'I found this near the river,' he said without preamble. 'In a
thicket where one would have had to search for a long time
to find her. She would not have been found till full summer
when the stench of the corpse revealed its whereabouts.'

Catherine gazed in horror at the black coiling locks spread
out on the ground near her velvet slippers. Marie's eyes were
frozen by death in a look of horror and fury. She must have
died as she had lived, raging, cursing Heaven and earth. A great
brown stain had dried over her heart. Kennedy looked in
amazement from the corpse to Gauthier who stood beside it,
arms folded and legs straddled. His British sang-froid rose to the
occasion.

'Ugh!' he said, pointing at the body. 'This doesn't look much like a she-bear to me.'

'It was a witch,' the Norman spat out, 'whose damned soul has been taken by the infernal furies.'

But Catherine bent over for a closer look at her dead enemy, on whose face putrefaction had laid violet stains. The blue lips were drawn back from the gums. Death had made Marie de Comborn hideous, and Catherine shuddered and crossed herself. She looked at Gauthier.

'Who killed her? Have you any idea?'

In reply he took a long-bladed dagger from his leather tunic and threw it on to her lap. It was still covered with dry blood.

'That was in her breast, Dame Catherine. The man who struck that blow knew he had good reason for it.'

Catherine saw the knife, hardly tarnished by three nights in the damp woods, gleaming against her black gown. On it was carved the silver sparrow-hawk crest of the Montsalvys. The last time she had seen that weapon was in Arnaud's hands on the battlements ... he had been toying with it as he told her that he loved his cousin and wanted to go off with her. Now Marie was here, dead, and it was the Montsalvy dagger which had killed her.

'Arnaud!' she whispered. 'I must be dreaming. It couldn't have been him!'

'Yes,' Sara affirmed, drawing nearer. 'It was undoubtedly your husband who killed her!'

'But why ... he told me that he loved her?'

Sara shook her head. She took the bloody dagger for a moment and examined it.

'No,' she said gently, 'he never loved her! He wanted you to believe he did! But I've no doubt she was too evil for him to tolerate for long. He could not wait any longer, and so he killed her!'

Catherine leapt to her feet, snatched Sara by the shoulders and started to shake her.

'You are hiding something from me! What is it you know? Why were you so silent while I was dying of despair and anguish? How could you take part in this atrocious comedy? It is driving me mad! Speak! I must know the truth even if I have to drag the words from your throat, even if I have to ...'

But then, in spite of her anger, she stopped and felt ashamed of herself. Yes, she had been on the point of threatening Sara, her oldest, truest friend, with torture! There was such wild madness in her blood that the mere mention of Arnaud's name was enough to drive her to the limits of savagery. Sara bowed her head like a penitent.

'Do what you wish,' she murmured. 'I have not the right to speak ... I have sworn on the Madonna and on the salvation of my soul.'

'And you have kept your word, Sara ... thank you!'

At the sound of this new voice Catherine gave a cry and spun round. She grasped the arm of her chair to prevent herself falling. Arnaud de Montsalvy had just appeared on the threshold, pale and thin in his black doeskin clothes. The cry died in her throat. She believed she saw a ghost but this ghost was alive! He came slowly towards her, and all the love he had ever shown her was in his dark eyes. He had never looked at her with such despairing passion.

'You!' she whispered. 'It is you! God has heard my prayer. He has allowed me to see you once again!'

Now that he was there nothing else mattered to her, everything else had vanished: this room where she had lain dying of love, Gauthier, the Scot, even Sara, even the pathetic remains of her old foe. There was no one but he ... the man she loved above all else!

What did the rest matter?

She went towards him with outstretched arms, wild with happiness as she had been wild with grief. But once more he stopped her.

'No, my love ... don't come near me! You must not touch me, ever again! Gentlemen, will you please leave us now. Thank you for all you have done!'

Once more Kennedy's plume swept the floor. Gauthier bent one knee, fastening his sad, grey eyes on the man whom for the first time he now recognized as his lord.

'Messire Arnaud,' he said. 'You have done the right thing. Forgive me for ever having doubted you. Henceforth, I am your servant.'

'Thank you,' Montsalvy said sadly, 'but your service will be brief. And I regret, comrade, that this time I am unable to offer you my hand.'

Kennedy and Gauthier went out and Sara departed to fetch Michel who was with his grandmother. Catherine and Arnaud were left alone to face each other. She stood devouring her husband with her eyes.

'Why?' she faltered. 'Why do you say ... I must never touch

you? Why this abominable drama? Why did you make me believe you loved a woman you hated? Why have you made me suffer so?'

'I had to do it! I was determined to drive you away from me, at whatever cost. I no longer have the right to love you, Catherine ... and yet I have never loved you more.'

She closed her eyes the better to glory in the blessed music of those few words which she had never expected to hear again. Almighty God! God of all mercies! He still loved her! He still flamed with the passion she felt herself! But why these strange words? Why did he put her from him so obstinately? It seemed as if this mystery which had enveloped him for so long was at last to be solved, but now ... she was afraid! She trembled on the brink of the revelation as at the edge of a whirlpool.

'You have no longer the right to touch me?' she repeated uncomprehendingly. 'But who can stop you?'

'The sickness I carry in me, my love. The sickness I wanted to hide from your because I was so afraid that it would horrify you. But now I see I fear your hatred and scorn still more. I was afraid – so afraid you would go, return to that ... other! That ... knowing you were with him, imagining your body in his arms, your lips against his ... that would be hell! I could not endure it. Better to return ... better to tell you everything!'

'But what? For the love of God, for the love of our love, Arnaud, speak! I can put up with anything ... anything but losing you.'

'And yet you have already lost me, Catherine! I carry death within me – I am already half dead!'

'But what are you saying? Are you out of your senses? Are you mad? You dead?'

Abruptly he turned away as if he could no longer bear the anguish in her loving face.

'Better for me to be quite dead. God would have been merciful if he had allowed me to fall in the mud of Agincourt or below the wall of Orleans, like so many others. . . .'

Catherine, tense as a drawn bow-string, cried out:

'Speak ... for pity's sake!'

At last he spoke. Six words, six dreadful words which for months were to haunt Catherine's dreams, shock her to wakefulness bathed in a sweat of agony, filling the echoes of a deserted room.

'I am a leper! A leper!'

Then he turned to look at her and caught back a cry of grief. For never had he beheld a face so crucified. She had closed her eyes and great tears rolled slowly down her pale cheeks. Standing there with her hands up to her mouth, she seemed to balance by a miracle. She was so fragile, so defence-less ... instinctively he held out his arms only to let them fall to his sides again. Even this final solace, to weep together in each other's arms, was denied them. She panted softly, in little gasps, like a hunted doe. He heard her murmur:

'Oh, it cannot be! It cannot be!'

The call of a bird cutting the air on swift wings stirred the silence, bringing into the room the smell of the earth, the call of reality. Catherine opened her eyes, and Arnaud, who had been dreading the moment when that tender violet gaze would rest on him again, felt his heart contract. There was neither horror nor disgust in her shining depths ... only a love as limitless as the blue sky. Her lovely curving lips parted in a smile dazzling with tenderness.

'What does it matter?' she said gently. 'Death has been lying in wait for us, day after day, for years. What does the manner of its approach matter to us? Your sickness shall be mine. If you are a leper, I shall be a leper: wherever you go I shall go and whatever fate awaits us will be welcome if it finds us together. Together, Arnaud, you and I ... for ever! Outcasts, cut off from the world, reviled and accursed even, but together!'

Her beauty was so dazzling then, transfigured by the im-mensity of her love, that Arnaud closed his eyes in turn. He did not see her open her arms and run to him. It was not till she was leaning against him with her arms twined about his neck that he came back to earth and tried to push her away. But she clung to him and it was a delicious but terrible torture to have her sweet face and tremulous lips so near.

'My sweet love,' he murmured brokenly, 'it is not possible. If there were only you and I in the world I would hold out my arms to you and heed no call but that of my selfish love ... I would carry you off to a place so remote and deserted that no one would ever find us again. But there is our child ... Michel cannot live alone in the world.'

'He has his grandmother!'

'She is old and weak and she too is alone. She can do nothing for him but weep for his misfortunes. Catherine, you are now the last of the Montsalvys, our only hope. You are brave and strong. ... You will fight for our son, you will rebuild Montsalvy!'

'Without you? I could never do it! And you, what will become of you?'

'I?' He turned away and walked across to the window. He stood looking out for a moment at the sun-filled valley and held out his arms towards the south.

'Down there, midway between here and Montsalvy, the canons of Aurillac built a hospital long ago for all those who will henceforth be my brothers. Once there were many of them, but now there are but a few cared for by a Benedictine monk. I shall go there.'

A heavy pain filled Catherine's heart. 'You in a lazar-house? You, with your ...' She did not add: With your pride, your passion, your arrogance, you who are life itself, loving war and sword-play passionately, condemned to a slow death, the most horrible of deaths! But the grief in her voice was plain to hear and Arnaud understood and smiled tenderly at her.

'Yes, at least I shall breathe the same air as you there. I shall see from afar, till my dying breath, the mountains of my country, the same trees and sky which you see. I would willingly die for you, Catherine ... but perhaps you will still want to go away....'

'You cannot think that now....'

'No. I know you will remain here. Promise me to be both father and mother to Michel and to live for him as you would have lived for me. Tell me, do you promise?'

She was blinded by sudden tears. She hid her face in her hands to shut out that slender black silhouette in the window which already seemed to belong to another world. Sobs tore at her heart but she gathered up her strength.

'I love you,' she stammered. 'I love you ... Arnaud.'

'I love you, Catherine. When I am only a monster, a human wreck too hideous to encounter the gaze of other men, I shall still love you and the memory of our love and of its glory will help me. I wish I could have found death in a foreign land, with my sword in my hand, but if it is God's will, it is well that I should die here on this earth which belongs to me and to which I will some day return ...'

His voice was faint, and seemed to come from far away.

Catherine's hands fell to her sides, she opened her eyes and gave a piercing scream.

'Arnaud!'

But he was not there. He had silently left the room.

That night Sara had to lock herself up with Catherine in her room with Gauthier sleeping across the door. Forgetting her husband's pleas for resignation, Catherine wanted only to run after him, to be with him again. He had gone to seek refuge with the good curé of Carlat for by now the news had spread through the village and castle like a trail of gunpowder and everyone, from the rudest soldier to the humblest rustic, trembled now as they tried to recall what contact they had had with the afflicted man. An uproar could be heard from without the castle walls. Men cried out, demanding that the leper should be taken away to the leper-house that very hour. The old curé had to lose his temper with them and vow that he would die with Arnaud if anyone tried to harm him. The fear of the disease was so great that the terrified peasants were capable of setting fire to the house which received him. The presbytery alone, being holy ground, would be safe.

For the first time old Jean de Cabanes was presented to Catherine. He bowed respectfully before the young woman in mourning and told her that the next day the infected man would be taken, as the law demanded, to the leper-house at Calves. But first a last Mass would be said for him in the village church. He wanted to know whether Madame de Montsalvy wished to assist at this cruel rite.

'You cannot doubt it, I think,' Catherine had answered hardily. To see him again, to be with him if only for an instant, she would go to the gates of hell.

And now night had come. The people of Carlat had barricaded themselves in their rooms after chalking a yellow cross on the presbytery door. The sentries were shut up in the guard room, hardly daring to watch from the battlements for fear, perhaps, that the grisly shape of the red death would rise up from the shadows. Those few whom Kennedy's threats had obliged to stand guard shivered on the battlements. Catherine stood at her window with folded arms trying to make out in the darkness the house which had become Arnaud's last refuge. Her eyes were dry and her forehead burned. She kept a fierce silence.

Isabelle de Montsalvy, sitting in an armchair a little way off, maintained the same silence. The old lady's pale fingers told her beads. Catherine could pray no more. God was too exalted, too remote for the anguished prayers of mere mortals to reach. He had granted Catherine the wish she had cried out in her fever: to see her best-beloved once again, and touch his hand. But what price was she to pay for this favour?

Now she understood the inexplicable. Sara had told her how one night Arnaud had wakened her to show her the white, lumpy stain on his naked arm which she had stared at in horror. It was indeed, as he feared, the first sign of his malady, the cursed seal of the leper. She told how the young man had made her swear to keep silent. He was determined to estrange Catherine from him so that he could then go on to another life without regrets. But he had not reckoned with her desperate love, or his own passion. His generous plan had gone awry and now Catherine knew ... just as Isabelle had known, on another night, in the chapel!

When she turned to look at the old woman Catherine was surprised to see that her face was ravaged by a sorrow equal to her own. Could another woman suffer as she did? ... In the depths of the night a wolf howled. It was the time for love and it was calling its mate. Catherine shivered. For her the time of love was ended. ... There remained only her duty, austere and unyielding, the only occupation of a heart which tomorrow would be reduced to ashes. ...

She would become old, like that woman beside her weeping inwardly; alone, her whole life wrapped up in the child who would one day leave her too, till the time came at last for her to go to rest.

Suddenly a great pity filled her for the old woman who had climbed a terrible calvary step by step and had not yet reached the Cross. Her husband had died while she was still young. Then there had been Michel's atrocious death. Michel, tenderest and sweetest of her sons and her favourite. And now this abominable thing. Each one of her great sorrows was inscribed in the wrinkles furrowing her face. Could a woman's heart endure such grief without losing courage and breaking completely?

She went over to Isabelle and placed a timid hand upon her shoulder. The faded eyes, red with tears, lifted pitifully to hers. Catherine swallowed and made herself speak. Her voice was husky and, when it came, little more than a murmur.

'Michel remains with you ...' she began, 'and I ... if you want me. I do not know how to say these things, and I know that you have never loved me. However, I am ready to give you all the respect and tenderness I can no longer give to him. ...'

She had exhausted her strength and her sorrow burst its banks. Kneeling before the old lady she laid her head in her lap, clenching her fingers in the black gown. But already Isabelle de Montsalvy had taken her in her arms and clasped her to herself.

Catherine was surprised to feel warm, urgent tears splashing on to her forehead.

'My daughter,' the old lady faltered. 'You shall be my daughter!'

They stayed like that for a long while, united by their common grief as no life of shared glory or joy could have done. It was a long way from that night of Isabelle's disdain for the humble shop of Gaucher Legoix. The common sadness of mother and wife was a bond, so that they were no longer alone and heartbroken, and their mingled tears broke down all the barriers and cemented the foundations of a deep tenderness.

The wolf still howled in the depths of the wood. Isabelle's arms did not press her so tightly that she could not feel them trembling.

'Wolves!' Catherine said sorrowfully. 'Is it only wolves who have a right to love in this world?'

CHAPTER SIXTEEN

The Empty Road

Kennedy's Scots and the few soldiers in the garrison were ranged, in double file, facing each other, down the steep slope leading from the castle to the village. A light breeze lifted their bonnet plumes and barred plaids. The sun was high and it glinted on their breastplates and arms. It might all have been the setting for a festival, save that the still faces were grave and below in the grey granite bell-tower, the bells of Carlat tolled a knell.

As she came to the foot of the mound, with Arnaud's mother leaning on her arm, Catherine stiffened. She wanted to be brave for these last minutes she would see him. He should be proud of her as he left the world. She clenched her teeth and raised her little chin, staring hard at the rocky path. She took a step forward. Isabelle stumbled, at the end of her strength, but she held her with a firm encouraging hand.

'Courage, mother,' she whispered. 'You must be brave ... for his sake!'

The old lady made a heroic effort, clinging to Catherine's arm. The two black-clad figures stepped forward into the glorious morning sunshine which made the fields steam and the birds sing, unaware of the drama being played out.

Kennedy followed the two women, leaning on his great sword, and old Cabanes, supporting himself with a lance, and then Gauthier and Sara, their faces stony. There was not a sound to be heard, except the beating of their hearts between the dismal strokes of the bell. Only Fortunat was missing. The poor boy could not bear the idea of attending this dismal ceremony for his departing master. He had shut himself up in a cellar to weep.

As they drew near the church Catherine could make out the confused mass of peasants, standing fearfully, packed against each other at a safe distance from the holy house which for the time being was unclean. Afterwards it would be necessary to burn incense and sprinkle holy water to cleanse the place of the leper's presence. Everyone, men, women, children and

old people, knelt in the dust with bowed heads singing in
solemn voice the canticles of the dead, making a dismal, buzzing counterpoint to the ceaseless funereal bell.

'My God!' Isabelle murmured. 'My God, give me strength!'

Under the thick veil which covered poor Isabelle's face
Catherine sensed the tears about to spring, and she struggled
to keep back her own. She quickened her step to reach the
last few yards of the path encircling the church before leading
into the church porch. She had not a glance for the kneeling
peasants. They were repugnant to her in their terror, and
aroused her anger. She did not wish to see them, and they
peered out at her from under lowered lids, this woman re-
putedly so beautiful who seemed to carry all the sorrows of
the world on her slender black shoulders.

The church was not large, but to Catherine it seemed like a
long black tunnel with yellow light blazing at the far end.
Candles burned on the altar where the old curé stood waiting
in his black chasuble, with his back to the tabernacle. Before
him, at the foot of the steps, a man in black clothing knelt.
Catherine's heart missed a beat and then started to pound like
mad. She took Isabelle's hands in hers, clasping them so tightly
that the old lady winced. Slowly she led her to the high pew
and sat her down but she herself remained standing, forcing
herself to look at the kneeling man.

Was Arnaud conscious of her gaze bearing down upon him?
He turned slightly. Catherine caught a glimpse of his proud
profile. Would he turn to look at her? No ... his eyes went
back to the altar. No doubt he was refusing to allow his courage to weaken.

'My love!' Catherine stammered below her breath. 'My poor
love!'

The priest's cracked old voice could now be heard, frail and
compassionate. Then the sacristan, a wan peasant who placed
two lighted tapers clumsily on either side of Arnaud.

'Requiem aeternam dona eis, Domine, et lux perpetua luceat
eis ...'

As in a nightmare Catherine followed without seeing,
listened without hearing, to this Requiem Mass for a living
man. Soon Arnaud de Montsalvy would cease to exist as surely
as if the executioner's hand had struck off his head. He would
be no more than an unknown man, cloistered in a leper-house,
a being still alive but nameless, a lump of suffering flesh behind
doors which would never open again for him. And she ... she

would be a widow! A movement of revolt seized her, and she
felt a sudden desire to rush out in the middle of this Holy
Mass and snatch away the man she adored from these cringing
hands as she had once snatched away his brother Michel from
the Parisian populace. Yes, that was it ... to run to him, take
his hand and flee! But now there was no longer the happy
guile of Landry or solid good sense of Barnaby to help her. Who
would help her ... or understand ... Gauthier, perhaps? But
the giant had remained outside the church he refused to enter
and those peasants formed a solid mass. Arnaud and she would
never get through that living wall. Besides, would he ever
agree to follow her? He who had spent his whole life protecting her?

Consciousness of her own weakness beat down Catherine's
courage. Scalding tears rose to her eyes, and with a childlike
gesture she held out her hands helplessly as if reproaching them
for their own frailty. Those hands which had not been able
to hold her love, to divine in that beloved body the symptoms
of that terrible sickness which consumed him, a sickness no
doubt contracted in La Trémoille's infected jail. La Trémoille!
The thirst for vengeance rose in her as she thought of the fat
figure of the gross chamberlain. She did not know how long
she would suffer the pain of this love of hers, but this man
who had been the cause of all their misfortunes, who had pur-
ued her with implacable senseless hatred, must pay dearly so
that Montsalvy might rise again, so that a sunlit future might
open before Michel, and that she herself might at last die in
peace.

'I shall avenge you,' she muttered between clenched teeth.
I swear to avenge you ... as God hears me, I swear this to
you.'

Mass was over. The priest was saying the Absolution. Clouds
of incense swirled about the kneeling man, who already, for
many, had ceased to exist. Then the holy water fell on him,
and the final benediction. And suddenly Catherine's heart shuddered in agony. Arnaud's own voice soared up to the blackened vaults above. He sang, and it was his own requiem.

'Have mercy on me, O Lord, in Thy great goodness! In Thine
immense mercy wash out my crime. Wash me, wash me clean
of my iniquity, purify me of my sin, for I recognize my fault
and my sin: it is always before me! Turn Thy face from my
faults for they shatter the bones which Thou hast broken.'

She had never heard him sing before. His voice was grave and

deep and it had a poignant beauty which overwhelmed her
soul. This was the despairing farewell to life of the man who
loved her passionately. . . . A storm was roaring in Catherine's
ears. She thought she might faint and she clutched at the
wooden bench, so rough-hewn that a splinter drove into her
finger. The pain revived her. . . . Beside her, Arnaud's mother
sobbed unceasingly, rocking on her knees on the stone floor.

Catherine could not see the light now. Tears and her black
veil had hidden it completely. She sensed rather than saw
Arnaud's black form rising to his feet, still singing, and moving
off alone towards the exit. Then she snatched off her veil, offering her face uncovered and streaming with tears, as a last gift,
a mask of sorrow which no candlelight could soften. Only the
black arrow of the hennin crowned the pure, narrow oval.
Arnaud stopped, drawn against his will to gaze once more
upon those huge eyes of hers, and bared face. The song died
upon his lips. His eyes rested for the last time on those tear-
drenched violet pools, but he did not speak. He was so close
to her that Catherine could hear his breathing. . . . He stepped
forward, he was passing in front of her. Then she unwrapped
the tribute she had brought from the castle wrapped in her
veil. On to the poor, uneven flagstones of the church a flood
of living gold poured down and rolled silky and shining at
Arnaud's feet: Catherine's hair, the dazzling glory of which
she had been so proud, which a prince had honoured and
which her husband had loved so much. At dawn on this woeful
day she had cut it off without regrets, with the same dagger
which had killed Marie de Comborn.

Arnaud went pale and stumbled. A tear rolled down his
cheeks and was lost in his black doeskin mantle. He closed his
eyes and Catherine thought for a moment that he would fall.
But no . . . slowly he knelt and gathered up the mass of hair in
both hands and pressed it to his breast like a treasure. Then
he got up and walked towards the lighted arch of the door,
without turning around. When he came out the sun made the
harvest of love he carried glisten. The peasants recoiled, seized
by sudden terror, but he did not see them. As he walked on
smiling, with his eyes up-turned to the blue heavens, he did
not even see the monk in a brown habit waiting at the bend
in the road. He carried the red cape and grey robe and the
rattle which were to be all his equipment as a leper. No more
the shining swords and sumptuous clothes of a warrior and
nobleman, but this miserable livery and the rattle which gave

warning from afar of the approach of the outcast. The church bells once more took up the funeral knell. . . .

Forgetting Isabelle, Catherine dragged herself rather than walked as far as the porch and clung there . . . her legs trembled and she feared that they would give way, but a strong hand supported her.

'Hold hard, Dame Catherine,' Gauthier's hoarse voice implored her. 'Not in front of these folk!'

But she saw nothing, not even the black silhouette of the man walking away with his arms full of sunshine. A trumpet sounded on the ramparts echoing the sinister tolling bell and then all along the cliff top the bagpipes took up a slow, wild lament, a tragic sound in which there were yet martial stirrings of war. It was Kennedy's last farewell to his brother-in-arms.

Below, Arnaud had joined the monk. The bagpipes made him turn for the last time. He looked at the village and the castle on its proud crag, and then at the Benedictine's grey, pitiful face.

'Farewell, life,' he murmured. 'Farewell, love!'

'My son,' the monk murmured, 'you must place your hope in God.'

But for him God seemed far away. A desperate fury overtook Arnaud. His voice swelled, so loudly that the echoes rang from the four corners of the valley.

'Farewell, Catherine!' he cried.

That voice . . . it was the voice of her love! Could she let her lonely husband go unanswered? The same supreme revolt which had torn that great cry from Arnaud's throat now entered Catherine's soul. She tore herself from Gauthier's hands and ran wildly down the rocky road holding her arms outstretched towards the man whom the monk was even now leading away.

She stumbled on a stone and fell on her knees in the dust. But the monk and the leper had reached the bend in the road and the road was empty. . . .

A series of historical novels in the lusty, turbulent tradition of *Angélique*

JULIETTE BENZONI

One Love is Enough 5/-

Set in fifteenth-century France against the horrors of the Hundred Years War, the squalid Cour de Miracles in Paris, and the magnificent Burgundy Court, this novel tells of Catherine Legoix. She was a lovely and desirable woman, virgin wife of the Court Treasurer, unwilling mistress of a Duke, and in love with a man she could not hold ...

Catherine 6/-

In this turbulent sequel, Catherine follows her lover all over France, encountering adventure, brutality and the lust of greedy men.

PIERRE SABBAGH and ANTOINE GRAZIANI

Fanina 5/-

She was chosen to become a vestal virgin. Should she break her vows of chastity, she faced being buried alive. But when she met a blue-eyed young man from Gaul, she found her life and her values changing. Set in Ancient Rome during the reign of the wicked Emperor Tiberius, this book lays bare the corruption, cruelty and superstition of a bygone age.

Angélique

'The intrepid, passionate and always
enchanting heroine of the most
fantastically successful series of historical
romances ever written.'
DAILY HERALD

ANGELIQUE I: The Marquise of the Angels
ANGELIQUE II: The Road to Versailles
ANGELIQUE AND THE KING
ANGELIQUE AND THE SULTAN
ANGELIQUE IN REVOLT
ANGELIQUE IN LOVE

These novels by SERGEANNE GOLON
comprise a tremendous saga of
17th-century France, tracing Angélique's
career from childhood through a series of
strange marriages and amorous adventures,
perils and excitements, unequalled in the
field of historical fiction. Translated into
most European languages, a sensational
runaway success in France, Angélique is
one of the world's most fabulous best-sellers.

The most ravishing — and surely the most
ravished — heroine of all time.